ADVANCE PRAISE FOR *LADIES OF THE HOUSE*

"I was absolutely charmed by *Ladies of the House*, a modern retelling of *Sense and Sensibility*, and a delightful and insightful exploration into finding your own voice, discovering your best self and falling in love, in its many iterations. What a wonderful debut."

—**ALLISON WINN SCOTCH**, bestselling author of
Cleo McDougal Regrets Nothing

"A warm, witty, and whip-smart modern spin on *Sense and Sensibility*, *Ladies of the House* pulled me in on page one and didn't let me go until the last, satisfying scene. Edmondson's talent shines in her expertly crafted story of two sisters using their brains and hearts to break free of their father's legacy and voice their desires, despite the sexist double standards that would keep them quiet. A sensational debut."

—**AMY MASON DOAN**, author of
The Summer List and *Lady Sunshine*

"A fun and clever take on *Sense and Sensibility*, *Ladies of the House* is replete with witty banter and keen social commentary. Like any good modernization, it also stands alone as a stellar novel, one that celebrates sisterhood and the way women can step out of flawed men's shadows. I delighted in every page of this fast-paced, redemptive novel."

—**AMY MEYERSON**, bestselling author of
The Bookshop of Yesterdays and *The Imperfects*

LADIES of the HOUSE

A NOVEL

LAUREN EDMONDSON

GRAYDON
HOUSE

**GRAYDON
HOUSE®**

Recycling programs
for this product may
not exist in your area.

ISBN-13: 978-1-525-89596-8

Ladies of the House

This edition published by arrangement with Harlequin Books S.A.

Graydon House
22 Adelaide St. West, 40th Floor
Toronto, Ontario M5H 4E3, Canada
www.GraydonHouseBooks.com
www.BookClubbish.com

Printed in U.S.A.

For Jane and Jim Edmondson

LADIES
of the
HOUSE

"I wish, as well as everybody else, to be perfectly happy; but, like everybody else, it must be in my own way."

—*Sense and Sensibility*

January

One

The brick went through the window on P Street on what would've been my father's sixty-fifth birthday.

Cricket had scheduled his private memorial service for that morning. He'd been gone for three months already, but she had been insistent we wait. She thought it poetic, for my father was big on birthdays. To be more precise, he loved *his* birthday, while routinely forgetting those of his immediate family.

It was predictably freezing, the kind of January day that was too cold to even think about snowing. After we had our coffee, Cricket, sergeant-like, ushered Wallis and me into a black car bound for Georgetown Presbyterian, then staged us in the narthex, where she checked on our postures, our hair. There we stood, the women the great Senator Gregory Richardson left behind, ready to greet the guests, many of whom no doubt suspected the very belated memorial was a ploy to keep our names in the press. But if any of the invitees minded the photographers outside, capturing their exits from their black cars, they didn't reveal it. This was DC, after all, and being regarded as one of Gregory's closest friends had a definite cachet.

My boss was part of the first wave to arrive. Miles was skipping a hearing on financial literacy and retirement, but he said it was fine, nobody would miss him. He took Cricket's blue-veined hands in his own, looked into her eyes, and told her how sorry he was for our loss, before solemnly choosing a seat in the sanctuary next to the junior senator from Arizona.

Following Miles was the rest of the staff. L.K. complimented me on my dress; Bo said I cleaned up nicely. A handful of years ago, after I'd spent thirty minutes in a fast-fashion fitting room agonizing over the flashiness of a single blouse, I decided only to buy clothes that were white, black, gray, or cream. Little did I know I'd been meticulously preparing my closet for interments.

It wasn't until the secretary of defense and his wife showed ten minutes later—she standing mute as her husband gave Cricket a brief hug, pursed his lips, and squinted his eyes to assume the look of condolence—that the three of us dropped our formal facades.

"Asshole," Cricket whispered as he disappeared inside, though her smile remained broad. "Has some nerve showing up here, when he's been going all over town saying Gregory Richardson owed him money."

"Dad owed someone money?" Wallis asked.

I glanced at my mother as she reached for another close family friend. My parents had never wanted for anything in their adult lives, but rumors spread like the flu in this town, and I didn't want a bad germ to spoil her day. The friend, a governor, pecked her on the cheek, then did the same to me and Wallis.

"Of course he didn't," Cricket said, turning back to us. "Secretary of defense! Unbelievable. Couldn't find his own ass with a map, let alone lead the armed forces into battle. It's like he's spitting on your father's grave. And now I'll have to smile and serve him pound cake at this afternoon's reception."

Yes, the reception. I still had questions about the final guest count, what she'd arranged for parking. Had she given the caterers the check? They'd left me a voice mail that morning wondering when—

Wallis's abrupt squeal of joy interrupted my thoughts. "He made it!" she cried, and Cricket and I spun toward the narthex stairs in time to see Atlas taking them two at a time. My best friend, whom I hadn't seen in close to a year, was back stateside, and the sight of him in his favorite tailored, dark blue suit had me teetering close to the edge of grateful, sloppy tears. The months since my father had passed had been grueling, and I'd wished countless times that Atlas hadn't been three thousand miles away.

He reached Cricket's open arms first, bending from the knees to envelop her as she mumbled something about *delight* and my name, *Daisy*, into his narrow suit lapel. Then Wallis hugged him tightly and all but threw me into his arms.

"Hi, Daisy," he said softly, pulling me close and resting his cheek on my hair, his hand on the back of my head in the way that made me feel delicate.

"I can't believe your adventure getting here," I said when he released me. "What a debacle."

"One canceled flight, another delayed, and a couple of British Airways agents who would do well never to see me again. You should've been there when they called my name from the standby list," he said. "I shrieked like a little girl. I didn't know my voice could even reach that high."

"Sounds like a thrilling performance," I said. "Will you stage a reenactment for us at the reception?"

"Certainly," said Atlas. "I just need my own trailer to get into character."

Behind the altar, the organist began to play a dirge. I wanted Atlas to keep us laughing but, sensing his time was up, he squeezed my hand and left to take his pew.

Cricket and Wallis looked at each other and then at me.

"He came all the way from London," Cricket said, as though I didn't understand how travel works.

"He was moving back anyway, Cricket," I said quickly, anticipating where this conversation was headed, wanting to cut it off at the pass. "He didn't come here *just* for us."

"And is he back for good?" Cricket procured a vial of lip gloss from the pocket of her full, black skirt and aimed it at my face.

"Atlas is hard to pin down," I said, swatting her away, "when it comes to long-term plans. He gets restless. London is where he was born and raised. I can't imagine he'll stay away from it forever."

Another couple, Georgetown doctors both, hustled in, and Cricket was forced, reluctantly, to abandon her beautification efforts. The pair seemed to appreciate that the service was about to start; from the sanctuary doors they blew us kisses and mouthed *talk to you after.*

"People leave their hometowns *all the time*, Daisy," said Wallis, holding her smile and waving. "That's a thing that happens. And anyway, I think the timing is right for you and Atlas." She turned to me, then said bluntly: "Finally."

"He has a *girlfriend*," I reminded her as the last guests receded inside.

"In *London*," Cricket said.

"How long do you think that will last now that he's back in DC?" Wallis asked.

"Sorry to interrupt." Our soft-spoken pastor, out of nowhere, made Wallis jump. Thankfully, he was not there to judge our unchurchy topic of conversation, only to borrow Wallis; he wanted a few words about her eulogy.

As I watched them review her script and the funeral program, I had to note that my sister wasn't wrong. Long-distance relationships were tricky. But this was Atlas—steadfast, loyal, undaunted by things like time differences and the Atlantic Ocean. And I was just a friend. How far would he go for a lover?

While I still had Cricket beside me, I diligently tried to ask her about the caterers, the reception. But she wanted to talk about none of these things. Instead, she chatted easily about how well Atlas looked. How tall. "His shoulders look broader," she said. "He looks fit. Was his hair always that blond?" She liked that he seemed to be letting it grow. "It works," she said. She agreed with Wallis, that the timing for the two of us might now be perfect.

I considered walking away because it pained me to hear the hope in her voice. I'd been trying to fall out of love with the man for approximately fifteen years. But my father was gone, and she was my only parent left, so I stayed beside her, and listened, and tried to forget the feel of Atlas's fingertips in my hair.

Two

The heart attack was so strong that the paramedics didn't even have time to get him to the hospital. This was the first thing Cricket had said when she'd called me three months ago. I'd been cozy in my club chair by the small bay window in my Corcoran Street apartment, looking forward to reading all my usual Sunday stuff: romance novels, pages of legislation that would never pass, drafts of speeches for Miles. *They call this kind of attack a widow-maker,* Cricket had said. My father had been at the lake, in the cottage Grandduff had left him. *He was alone. He died alone.*

Wallis had recently finished her teaching contract in South Korea, but she'd been planning to travel through the fall; when we'd gotten ahold of her, it was via a hostel's landline somewhere south of Ho Chi Minh City. She landed at Dulles seventy-two hours later with barely enough time to splash water on her face and under her arms before we were off to Richmond to view our father lying in state, then back to DC, to the Capitol, where more mourners waited in line for hours to pay their respects to the distinguished yet down-to-earth senator who considered public service a higher calling, but never missed an opportunity to crack a disarming, cheesy joke or get on the dance floor with moves less embarrassing than one might expect. Even when you disagreed with him, the consensus around DC was you couldn't help but think of him as a friend.

A month had passed by the time we organized his public funeral at the Cathedral, a massive see-and-be-seen kind of affair, a competition of: Who was my father closest to? Who was the saddest? Who would miss him the most? People had networked in the pews. The Secret Service had been there, and so had the television cameras.

I'd already returned to work at that point—Cricket had considered it quick, my decision rash, but I had been determined to carry on my father's legacy—and the planning involved in his send-off had become like a second job. We had to do all the important rituals, and then some, to honor his life, mark our loss, and publicly acknowledge our shift from one type of family to another. In the flood of flowers and tributes and personal notes and *Did I wear this dress already?*, I'd barely had time to process his death. So when Cricket and Wallis wept through the eulogy, given by a senior statesmen, I was too numbed to produce a single tear. As booming as the eulogist's voice was, my father's voice, in my head, had been louder: *Jesus, Daisy*, he said. *You know how to cry on cue. I was the one to teach you. People will think you're glad that I'm gone.*

Now, two months later, in the middle of yet another church service in my father's honor, as I studied the brass chandeliers hanging from the ceiling so at least it would appear I was blinking back tears, it occurred to me that in many ways the whole mourning experience had been a performance. Even though this was the smaller, invitation-only memorial for family and close friends, I still felt their gazes on my back, couldn't avoid the stares coming from the pews on either side of us. And though there was nothing in their faces to signal anything but sincerity, I still thought of them as an audience with expectations for how Gregory's elder daughter—the daughter, as the story went, he'd been closest to, who had followed him into politics and once upon a time even worked for him—should grieve. Sad, but not overcome. Staid, but not emotionless. Appreciative of the time I had with my father, but not celebratory.

By the time the service reached the Lord's Prayer, I'd pretty much captured what I hoped was the right expression, the correct body language. But then the phones started.

First the small *ting*, coming from the back of the sanctuary, followed closely by more insistent buzzing from the row behind us. I was between my mother and sister and let them do the job of pointedly turning to shush, jaws set, eyes blazing.

Give us this day our daily bread…

More phones made music from purses and jacket pockets. I knew I shouldn't—we were supposed to be praying, for God's sake—but the suggestion I might be missing breaking news was too great. I shifted my folded hands ever so slowly and snuck a look at my own phone in my purse at my feet. The screen lit up with text after incoming text.

And forgive our debts, as we forgive those who debt against us…

"Let me just—" I whispered, bending to retrieve it. The sheer volume of notifications—whatever had just happened outside the church had to be very, very bad. Only anger and fear spread that quickly.

For thine is the kingdom...

"What is happening?" I heard Wallis ask, after someone a few rows back actually murmured, "Hello? Yes, I'm here..."

And the power, and the glory...

Seventeen missed calls, and a dozen texts from an editor I knew at the *Times*. "Shit," I said, clutching my phone tighter.

Forever and ever...

"What?" Wallis and Cricket asked at precisely the same time.

No longer caring about propriety, I held up the phone so they could see the latest *Times* news alert on my screen. Gasps, perhaps from them, or from others, echoed in the room, one after the next.

Amen.

Three

The last word of the minister's benediction was still hanging in the air when the exodus started in earnest. Even he, from the center aisle, was bewildered as folks made haste for the sanctuary doors. "Was my homily that awful?" he asked Cricket, who remained immobilized with shock next to me in our front pew.

"It's not you." I looked up from my phone for a second. "It's us."

"We apologize, Pastor," Cricket managed to say, collecting herself enough to pat his arm reassuringly. "There appears to be some new rumor about my husband that people are taking seriously. The timing couldn't be worse. I'll just squeeze by you and go out and tell our friends that everything is—"

I caught her elbow. "We can't be seen until we figure out how to respond to this. We don't need to churn the rumor mill."

"It's not a rumor!" exclaimed Wallis, flushed and flustered. "It's in the *Times!*"

"We don't know what it is yet," I hedged. She was right—this story, this *scandal*, hadn't been broken by some gossipy magazine. But my words were true. I hadn't even had a chance to read the whole article! "I'm getting calls," I said. "We need to deal with this now, preferably not in a house of worship, and ideally not around a crowd of people who are absolutely out there talking about Gregory, and about us. With that being said, Pastor—if we use that fire exit door there, will the alarm go off?"

"Oh, dear," he answered, feet shuffling nervously under his frock. "I don't know. We've never had to use it."

"We are not just sneaking out the back door," Wallis said. "I mean, that's ridiculous. We didn't do anything. We don't have anything to be ashamed of. Fuck that. Sorry, Pastor."

"Wallis, please call the black car and have him come around to this side of the parking lot," I said, ignoring her. She did as I asked, although her teeth were clenched. "Pastor, thank you, for everything. And I'm sorry, in advance, if we trip the alarm. Cricket, do you have your purse?"

"I have five dozen tea sandwiches at home," said Cricket. "I hired a bartender. There are people delivering glassware at any minute! What about the reception?"

"Believe me," I said, "people know it's canceled."

In the car, on the way back to Cricket's, the *Times* called. I recognized the number and chose to answer because they'd been the ones, only minutes earlier, to break the story that Senator Gregory Richardson had died with his twenty-seven-year-old girlfriend in his bed, and I had some things to say to them. Wallis did, too, and told me to put them on speaker.

"I couldn't get a heads-up?" I asked the reporter on the line.

"Heads up," he said flatly. The gentle sound of fingers on a keyboard infuriated me.

"We were at my father's memorial, *Todd*." I did not bother to keep the sharpness from my voice.

"Yikes." The typing paused. Then resumed. "Actually, I'm calling about another piece I'm working on about your father."

"What else do you possibly have to say? Are you going to report on whether they were in a queen or a king at time of death?" It was singularly humiliating that, of all the outlets in the world, I was talking about this to the *New York Times*, the distinguished Gray Lady. Beside me, Cricket dropped her head into her hands, and I immediately regretted my question.

"There is evidence," he said crisply, "that Senator Richardson used his office expense account to buy Andrea Pell a cell phone, a car, and plane tickets."

"Who?" I stalled, even though I recognized the name. Cricket was asking me for a tissue; her eyes were wet. I fished in my purse and handed her an old receipt. It was all I had.

"The lover, companion, whatever the correct nomenclature is these days," said the reporter. "She was—is—a photographer, and she's listed on Senator Richardson's most recent expense ledger as his employee."

My mind emptied, then swiftly filled with every swear word in every iteration I could imagine. He had the woman on his payroll?

Todd continued: "We even have a source who says your

father gave her money to buy a condo in Bethesda. Did you or your family know about this?"

"Who is this source?"

"You know I can't tell you that."

"We have no comment at this time," I said.

"I figured. Publication will probably be within the hour online and above the fold tomorrow morning." He ended the call.

I stared at my phone, which was still pinging with incoming texts. The letters shuddered and twitched on my screen. Or maybe that was just my shaking hands. Wallis asked me several questions in a row, none of which I could comprehend. Cricket went on dabbing her eyes with my receipt.

When we arrived at the house, the driver asked if we needed anything else from him, then told us, sunnily, to have a good rest of our day.

Once inside, we all appeared lost. We bobbed around the living room like flotsam in the ocean, Cricket running her fingers across the dessert plates and linen napkins she'd stacked on the sideboard the night before, having unceremoniously vetoed my idea of disposables. And Wallis, gazing at the upright piano and the silver-framed photos on its lid. She picked up the one of me, around age nine, cuddled into Gregory's side on a horse-drawn sleigh. We'd been on Prince Edward Island, a trip after Christmas, and I'd fancied myself Anne of Green Gables, minus the red hair and good spelling.

I dragged myself into the kitchen, where trays of croissants and pastry awaited, tucked under plastic wrap. Apple tart, too, and tiny muffins. Cricket had laid out small cans of soda and sparkling water; the ice bucket stood at one end of the counter, ready to be filled. I drew out a chair from the round wooden table, wishing that I could magic the stuff away.

The longer I sat, staring out the window at the winter trees, the more I thought of this kitchen, and my child-hood, and my father, who inhabited this house the way he inhabited the six syllables of his own name: boldly, fully, never lacking confidence. He'd take his place across from me, eating the sugary cereal Cricket rarely allowed for her children, telling us Norse god Loki stories, reading Anansi the Spider, or doing his perfect leprechaun voice. It was those moments, the glimpses of safety, predictability, when I understood what having a good father felt like. *This is what we do at breakfast. Here's how he looks at me. Here's what he says.* They made the other ones—the bad ones—bearable. I loved—love—my father, is what I'm saying, even though it was proving very risky to do so.

I pulled my necklace out from my black dress. For my seventeenth birthday, he had gifted me a sixpence. *Your mother wore this in her shoe,* he'd said, *when she walked down the aisle. May it bring you fortune.* Even then, there was no pretending he was a perfect father, what with his ungov-ernable moods and torch-hot temper. But I'd been touched by the gesture, thinking it a kind of peace offering, and had a jeweler mount it in a pendant frame before I left for col-lege. I'd worn it today as a tribute.

Cricket called for me as I rubbed the pendant between my fingers. Would she miss me if, instead, I just left, dashed south as quickly as my kitten heels could take me? Past M, over the canal, under the freeway, straight to the boardwalk, where I could hurl my father's lovely gift into the depths of the Potomac and allow the ancient currents to carry it away for good. An old clock clunked into the top of the hour, and

I stood, took a few steps toward the kitchen door. Then I stopped. Who was I kidding? I'd get about three blocks in these pointy, pinchy shoes.

I found Cricket in the parlor, resting in one of the cream armchairs by the fireplace. Wallis was curled on the sofa, gnawing at her cuticles, which she'd do until they bled. I sat at Cricket's feet, on the rug, hand loomed, no doubt. A gift from one of my father's trips abroad.

I didn't want to, but I turned to my phone, compelled, in a self-flagellating way, to check the most recent news alert. "She—there's apparently a recording of the 9-1-1 call Gregory made when he was—during the heart attack," I paraphrased. "You can hear her in the background. And her name is on the police report the *Times* found. She was there. She was with him." I looked up at my mother. "He didn't die alone, Cricket."

"I'm furious," she said, and I nodded. Her arms were crossed, her expression blazed. The discovery that she wasn't her husband's only—anger was more than expected. But then she continued: "He broke the rules. I told him no sleepovers. I told him she couldn't be in our houses."

This I didn't expect. "You knew about her?"

"Of course," she said, as though it should be that obvious. When we were silent, she shrugged. "We were going through a rough patch."

"Why," I asked, trying to be patient with her, "didn't you tell me?"

"It was private. Between your father and me."

"No," I replied. "It wasn't. *I* knew."

"How did *you* know?" asked Wallis. Her hands, with their inflamed fingers, dropped to her lap.

"Our father never went to the lake house alone," I said. "I figured he had to have been with another woman."

"But you didn't say anything," said Cricket, sitting forward in her chair, the popped collar of her starched white shirt almost reaching her earlobes, "when I told you he died alone."

"But I didn't *know* you were lying," I admitted. "I thought you truly didn't know about it."

"That's almost sweet." Cricket smoothed her skirt over her knees, turned to Wallis. "Wallis, I'm sorry you had to find out this way."

"I already knew, too." Wallis traced the brocade embroidering on the couch, following the petals and the stems, the intricate gold blossoms. "I've known for a while. When Dad visited me in Seoul last year, he left his email up on my laptop by mistake. He asked me not to tell you guys."

"So, we all knew," I said.

"But no one admitted to knowing," said Wallis.

"He was a great man," Cricket said. "We didn't want to ruin that for each other."

"He was a cheater." Wallis rose, began to pace. "And a liar. And now they are accusing him of being a thief."

"I don't know anything about that," Cricket said.

"If you do," I said, "please tell us, right now."

"I don't. He's an adulterer, but he wouldn't steal money from his own office. He's not a criminal. I wasn't married to a criminal."

From my spot, cross-legged on the carpet, I took hold of her hands, guided her body so she was facing me. "Cricket," I said. "What if you're wrong?"

A knock on the front door. "If that's the bartender, tell

him to stay," Wallis shouted as I got up and walked into the small foyer, or *foy-yay*, as Cricket pronounced it.

I answered the door, surprised to find Atlas on the stoop, his peacoat buttoned to the chin. "I don't want to impose," he said immediately. "Are you all right? I just wanted to check." He rubbed his gloveless hands together. "Sorry, Daisy. I should've called—"

I opened the door wider, relieved to see his face, to hear his voice. I rocked forward on my toes and smiled, trying to embrace the power of his calming presence. "You've been invited in, Dracula."

"Dracula, is it?" In the entry, he glanced in Cricket's small giltwood mirror topped with a nose-diving eagle. "I am pale enough."

"Look at me." I took quick stock of my own reflection. I swear I had put on makeup that morning, although there seemed to be no evidence of it now; my dark circles and fine worry lines had defiantly surfaced. "Better yet, don't."

"An impossible order," he said quietly. "Despite—everything, you look lovely, Daisy. Really."

"Atlas!" Wallis had found us. "You didn't bring vodka, did you?" she asked, hugging him.

"Afraid not," he replied. In the living room, Cricket kissed him twice on the cheeks and then wiped off her lipstick stains with her thumbs. "But I have tea."

"Perfect," said Cricket. "I'll set the kettle. And I hope you're hungry. I ordered enough finger sandwiches to feed this entire town." There was a pause as we all considered the emptiness of the room. Cricket had rented chairs, the nice bamboo sort, placed them carefully around the room to encourage flow and conversation. Unlit votive candles decorated nearly every surface alongside small vases of roses, white, classy, timeless. "You can have your pick," she pressed on, cheery. "Smoked salmon? Tuna? Watercress? Don't know why I ordered that last one, never liked watercress."

"I like watercress," said Atlas. "My father does, too. Watercress and—"

"Egg salad," I finished for him. "Your favorite. At The Savoy, right?"

He tapped my temple with his finger and smiled at me. "Memory like a steel trap, this one."

We gathered around the kitchen island, and Atlas inquired again how we all were. All of our answers included the word *okay*.

I'd been about to ask Atlas what would come next—if he might be able to predict how this story would play in the current news cycle—when the sudden sound of glass shattering made Wallis scream. I saw the alarm in Cricket's eyes before Atlas pulled me down with him behind the island. My back slammed against his broad chest as he curled—fell?—around me, his arm around my waist. For a moment I was completely encircled; he'd even placed a hand on the top of my head. But no debris fell, no sound, even, followed the initial crash.

"Are you all right?" he asked me. Then, louder, to everyone: "Are we all okay?"

"What the actual fuck," cried Wallis, her voice wavering.

Atlas's grip loosened, and he scooted around so he could see my face.

I nodded. "I'm all right," I told him, wanting to appear brave.

He pushed to his feet, and made for the front of the house, ignoring my pleas to be careful.

When I got my shaky legs under me, I circled the island and helped Cricket up.

"What on earth?" she said, breathless, as she got her bearings.

Wallis made a move for the kitchen door, but I yanked her back.

"It's okay!" Atlas announced from the living room. "It's just a brick."

Indeed, as we discovered when we joined him, the brick had torn through the bay window overlooking P Street, leaving a comet's tail of glass both inside and out. Georgetown bricks—old South bricks, Jeffersonian bricks—are the color of rust and amber and clay, but this brick was new, almost lipstick red. I wondered, as it taunted us from Cricket's rug, if someone had gone to a home improvement store and bought it. How much did one brick cost? The brick through the window, such an old-fashioned way of delivering hate.

"Did you see who did it?" Wallis asked Atlas.

"I'm going to find out." Atlas threw on his coat.

Cricket protested, as did Wallis, but I'd seen his face change, the slight reshuffling of his features, turning him from polite guest to man on a mission. He was a journalist. Here was a story.

"I'll call the police," I said.

It was thirty minutes before the officers arrived. Wavering between sympathetic and disinterested, they took our statements and scouted the room, nudging pieces of glass with their boots, explaining how difficult it would be to lift prints from a brick. Only then did Atlas return, with names and numbers of possible eyewitnesses, the addresses of security camera footage, and a dozen pictures of the scene. The officers weren't nearly as happy to receive this information as I would've hoped, but they dutifully jotted it down and departed, giving us absolutely no confidence that we'd ever find the culprit.

We spent the rest of the afternoon in an anxious kind of silence. Cricket gingerly trod through the broken shards back to the kitchen, returning with a dustpan and a mop. Wallis sat by the hole, a sentinel in stockinged feet, armed with a hammer from our late father's toolbox. Atlas kept the kettle hot, made sure we ate finger foods, bandaged Cricket's hand after she had a run-in with a stray piece of 150-year-old glass on her sofa.

I spent time dry heaving over the porcelain sink in the powder room, clammy, retching and feeling wretched, unable to catch my breath. This was my father, my blood. This was Senator Gregory Richardson.

My entire life, I'd taken this as fact: he was a complicated man but *brilliant* politician.

I'd suspected the affair, but never this.

Later, as the sun set on P Street, we patched the window with a cardboard box and duct tape.

Four

"I don't know anything about this," Cricket kept saying the next morning. Wallis and I sat on the couch in the parlor, embarrassed, as officials in blue windbreakers carted away papers and electronics. "You don't know my husband." Cricket swooped from one room to another, trailing the Feds, tidying what she could of the mess in their wake. "You don't know him."

After a few too many of these refrains from Cricket, Wallis pulled me into the kitchen. "The lady doth protest too much," she said. We could hear footsteps and floor creaks directly above us, strangers searching through our parents' bedroom.

"You think she knew," I asked, "about the stealing?"

"How could she not?" Wallis said. "She lived with the man."

I had wondered, in fact, about this very thing. No—*wondered* is the wrong word. One doesn't spend all night, as I had, *wondering* about things. *Wonder* didn't make me toss so violently that the corner of my fitted sheet had popped off and curled around my feet. *Wonder* didn't cause me to take a scalding shower at three in the morning, or to buy a multipurpose can and bottle opener from an infomercial at dawn. Only the agony of obsessive thinking could do that. Around breakfast, as I had been preparing to meet Cricket and the Feds at P Street, I'd come to this disquieting realization: I believed my mother. Toward the end, my parents hadn't even been speaking to each other. If I was coming by the house, I had to inform each of them separately. So it was plausible, *likely*, even, that Cricket hadn't seen or known. Yes, she *had* known about the adultery; she had *not* bothered to think about the money it required.

"He must've taken pains to hide things from Cricket," I said to my sister, not wanting to load her down with the ugly reality of our parents' estrangement. "Even if they'd fallen out of love, I think he would've wanted to protect her."

Wallis rolled her eyes. "Bullshit, Daisy. He didn't care. Clearly! All he cared about was the show. And how many hours have we spent performing for him, Dodo? How many years of our lives have we wasted?"

"Girls," Cricket said from the doorway. "I can't get ahold of Uncle Danny." She meant our father's former chief of staff, not our real uncle, just the kind of guy who liked to be called one. "He's not picking up my calls. I know he went to law school. Was he ever a lawyer, before working for your father? I can't remember. Maybe he can come over and help."

I turned to Wallis. "His office is right off Farragut Square. He told me before the memorial. The exact address is in my planner, which is in my purse, which is on the table with the fake flowers in the hall. Can you go get him?"

"Why do I have to go?" Wallis frowned. "I'm not the one who needs a lawyer. Dad is dead anyway. What are they going to do? Prosecute a corpse?"

"You're being a—"

"A what?" she asked, eyes narrowing.

"Wallis." I tried to stay calm, if only because someone had to be. "I need you to go downtown and convince Uncle Danny to brave the ridicule and come over here, so he can talk to the guys who are, as we speak, reading my old diary and opening the drawer where you hide your vibrator."

"How in the world are you so rational right now?" she asked me. "How are you not joining me in this freak-out?"

"Wallis," I repeated, taking a breath. "We don't have time for this."

"God, Daisy! Who even are you right now?" she said, and without a backward glance, she left—stormed, rather—out of the kitchen, smoke in her wake.

"She didn't mean that." My mother slumped against the doorframe. "She's just upset."

"We all are," I said, hands on my hips, wondering if we should offer the Feds the remains of yesterday's catering stuffed in the fridge. If only Miss Manners provided etiquette for raids! "She doesn't have to take her anger out on me."

"She's young," Cricket said. "She's still learning."

"She's twenty-five." Something crashed in the parlor, and I closed my eyes, hoping it was just a lamp, and not the urn that contained my grandfather. "She's not that young."

"Lord, Daisy, then what am I? A world heritage site? Might as well send a bus of tourists to snap some photos of me."

One of the Feds—he'd introduced himself earlier, Finkle,

Fickle, Fickett, something like that—cleared his throat from behind my mother. "Ladies," he said, "I'm sorry to trouble you. Can you point me to the bathroom my guys can use?"

"My husband, when he was drunk, sometimes relieved himself in the ficus by the piano," Cricket said, waving her arm in that direction. "That should be fine for you and your henchmen."

"The powder room is right under the stairs," I said quickly. "Let us know if you need more toilet paper."

"Obliged," Ficus said.

"Uncle Danny will come." I turned back to Cricket. "He'll have some good advice."

"Daisy," she said. "I—"

She was interrupted by two men who came into the kitchen and asked me to please step aside as they unplugged Cricket's answering machine from the wall with an efficiency that suggested they'd done this task many times before.

"I'm worried," she continued, lower. "This house is still mortgaged, Daisy. Your father's salary is gone. We've long since blown through his book income."

"You've got money from his life insurance," I said, bidding a silent goodbye to the ancient answering machine. Maybe now Cricket would move into the twenty-first century and give up her landline.

"There was none," she said, stillness in her voice.

"What?" I smiled with the cheerful intensity of one clinging to their last threads of optimism. "That can't be true," I insisted, though her face conveyed that this was not a joke.

I started for my father's study in the back of the house, but found it jammed with people. "Excuse me." I tried to push through to his filing cabinet.

Cricket followed. "I met with our old financial adviser last month. I've always hated him, you know. He always showed up to meetings in a golf shirt and blazer, totally unprofessional. But he reminded me that Gregory's life insurance policy had already been cashed out five years ago."

"Why would he cash out his life insurance?" I said, giving up on my efforts and pivoting back to face her.

Cricket avoided my eyes. "He—we—were having some liquidity problems at the time."

"At the time? Cricket, it sounds like you're having liquidity problems *now*."

"That's what I'm trying to tell you!" She said this as though I hadn't been listening, when in fact each word she'd said rang furiously in my ears.

"If things were this bad, why did you pay my rent for so long? I could've lived with you here."

"You didn't like it here. And anyway, I just wanted things to be as normal as possible for you and Wallis."

We scrunched ourselves against the wall of the hallway as more agents on a mission brushed past with fistfuls of evidence. Somewhere in this house, there was a warrant. Cricket had said they'd presented it when they knocked on the door early this morning, but she couldn't remember where she'd put it.

"Where's your money, Cricket?" I asked. "There has to be some left."

"Sure there is." Cricket's eyes touched on her hardwood floors, the painted balustrade of the upstairs landing, her custom window treatments. Then she looked back at me. "You're standing in it."

Five

"Honey," I said to Wallis. She was in her bedroom, pulling on a pair of boots. Twenty-four hours after the Feds had ransacked Cricket's house, the address had been doxed. It was now widely available to anyone with an internet connection. "The photographers are still out there. If you're going to go out, let me come with you."

"Fine," she replied. "But I refuse to hibernate anymore. I've been inside for a full day. I'm going to get a coffee, and then I'm coming back. I need to remind myself what fresh air smells like."

Cricket called my name from downstairs. All morning she'd been showing me the latest news: leaked emails between my father and his girlfriend. They were filthy, as we should've expected. She'd learned, after almost forty years of marriage, that her husband had a foot fetish and seemingly loved to describe acts involving breasts, toes, and butts that were, by all accounts, physically impossible.

"Can you wear a hat?" I asked Wallis, ignoring my mother. "Or go out the back and climb over the fence?"

Cricket yelled for me again, louder this time.

"Mom!" Wallis exclaimed. "We'll be right there. Christ!" Then to me, she said, "Cricket is driving me nuts. At least you have your apartment to escape to. I'm ready to check into a hotel."

"We don't have the—" I began, but Cricket, apparently tired of waiting, showed up at Wallis's door.

"'You're slime,'" she read from a letter in her hand. "'Die already.'" She scoffed. "Modern day Tennyson."

I took the envelope from Cricket, and when our hands touched, I realized, despite the flippancy, hers trembled. "Is there a return address?" I sounded hoarse.

"Not even a stamp."

Wallis snatched the paper from me. "'You're slime,'" she read. "*You're*—Y.O.U.R. This person is garbage. He probably isn't smart enough to blow his own nose."

"Wallis," I said. "They were here, they hand delivered it to our mailbox. I think we need to call the police."

"Fine," Wallis said, throwing the letter on her bed. "Although they were zero help last time. I'll call, but after I get some damn coffee." I reached for her arm, but she tugged it away. "Let me go, Daisy! I need to get out. Do you hear me?" We sure did. She was all but shouting. "I have to get out of here because I'm starting to believe all the things people are saying about us. I'm starting to believe that we are slime."

"It's not safe," Cricket pleaded.

Wallis pointed to her open laptop. "It's not safe in there, either." Determined, she left the room.

"Grab that letter, please," I said to Cricket, "and put it

somewhere safe. Worst case the police might be able to fin-gerprint it." I hurried downstairs and tried to remember where I put my coat. There—over the back of the couch. I shrugged it on, set to chase after my sister.

"Let me get my shoes." Cricket had followed me. "Hold on! Just let me find my shoes. I'll come with you."

I prepared to go out the back, but suspected Wallis had not exercised such caution. "I'll meet you outside," I told Cricket.

My assumption proved correct when I pushed open the front door and saw her on the sidewalk below, along with a man in an oversize jacket and yellow T-shirt stretched tight across his belly. He was indignant, accusing, standing in Wallis's way and slapping the back of one hand into the palm of his other.

"You're all liars," he insisted. His face was bloated like a tick. "Where's the money?"

"Leave us alone." I rushed down the stairs and stepped between my sister and this stranger. "Get back."

He talked over me like I wasn't there. "Shame," he con-tinued. "Shame on you." *Slap.* "Shame…" *Slap.* "…on you."

"Go away," I pleaded, voice shaking.

"I've called the cops!" Cricket, now, behind us too. She held her cell phone up and waved it as though it were a flag on the Fourth of July. "Aren't you men going to help?" Two paparazzi had appeared and were filming us with their shoulder-mounted cameras from farther down the side-walk. There was no indication they heard her or cared; the one wearing a flat-brimmed baseball hat darted around the shouting man, looking for close-ups, good angles.

"Take a picture of him, Cricket!" Wallis ordered. "I want to compare it to his future mug shot."

He sneered. "You all should be the ones in prison."

The three of us had formed a wall, one right next to the other. "Get gone," Cricket said. "Sad, sorry worm of a man."

He spat at the ground, then with some crude hand gestures and mutterings about bitches and losers, shuffled away, down the sidewalk and around the corner.

"Are you okay?" I asked Wallis when he was out of sight. I was touching her face and she was touching mine. We both seemed to be checking for wounds.

"Holy shit," she said, her brown eyes catching mine. "Holy shit, are *you* okay?"

"Do you want to go back inside?" I asked. "I can go and get you coffee."

"No," said Wallis. "I'm okay. Just stay close to me."

"We're fine," Cricket shouted at the paparazzi, who'd chased the man partway down the street. "In case any of you scallywags were wondering!"

Wallis and I couldn't help it; Cricket's words immediately had us clutching each other, laughing until tears leaked from our eyes. Wallis kept repeating Cricket's insult: *scallywag!*

"I'm getting something chocolate," Cricket said when we recovered, and we set off down the block. "Something with whipped cream. Something with a million calories. After that encounter, I think I deserve it. Jesus, my heart is still racing. Who was that man? And why do I feel like he's going to come back around the corner with an army behind him?"

⁓

He was one, but there were many more who followed.

I left my apartment and temporarily roomed with Wallis and Cricket on P; though I was glad we were together, I'd severely underestimated the number of people who were interested in shouting directly in our faces. They were there, the angry, the indignant, the betrayed, the taxpayers of this country, the only honest ones left in this town, on the sidewalk almost constantly, staring, taking pictures, leaving posters and nasty handwritten memos all over the front door and the stoop. We huddled inside, nervous, jumpy, wondering when the next brick would crash through.

I called Miles. I hated to do it, but I had to take some time away from the office. I'd return as many emails as I could, I told him, be on all possible conference calls. But Cricket and Wallis needed me.

But even indoors, the glorious world revealed new fears to me: the sound of my phone ringing, the flat, hard voice of the IRS, again, on the other end, the stack of Cricket's folded bank statements, the parade of congresspeople going to the Senate floor to denounce my father on live TV, the chime of a news alert on my phone—a more courageous person, I believe, would have put the phone on silent and kept it there. But I had to check; I had to know what they were saying. Otherwise, how could we begin to defend ourselves?

That, it turned out, was the wrong question to be asking in the face of unbridled vitriol. The question was, should we even *bother*? The masses had already reached their verdict: we were canceled. What was the use in mounting an appeal?

In the week after, we managed to get the charming lake house in Virginia on the market. We priced low and received an offer, seemingly within moments. We'd spent so many Augusts there, along an old trade route that someone forgot to pave, the pulse of the water lapping at the dock as Wallis floated in her favorite pink inner tube, the smell of pine trees and earth. The night after the contract was accepted, I dreamed about the bunk room under the cottage's sloping tin roof, where I read whatever I wanted, listened to owls and crickets and frogs. It was there I felt like I didn't have to *try* so hard.

The proceeds from the sale would help pay the retainer for our litigator for Gregory's estate and a meager percentage of billable hours. But I knew it wouldn't be enough.

The house on P, after more than half a century as the Richardsons', would have to pass from our hands to strangers.

February

Six

The apartment on the floor above mine had recently been vacated by some graduate students, so soon after we resolved to let go of P, I made arrangements and my mother and Wallis signed a lease. Although first Cricket had to take issue with the building's charmless architecture, the thin, greige carpet on the stairs, the narrow and gloomy hallways…

It wasn't as terrible as all that. Since it was on the top floor, the ceilings were higher than in my unit below, and the rooms flowed in an open and comfortable way. The main room, which Cricket immediately took to calling the living room, was bright and square and cozily sat six. The two bedrooms both had windows with generous views south over the ginkgo trees and slate turrets of stately Victorians, toward the leaf-shaded center of Logan Circle.

Before the estate-sale people came through P, we had to do the deciding: here, the pile to donate. There, the pile to sell. *No, Cricket, the new apartment won't fit your mother's old sewing machine desk.*

Wallis, still pallid in yoga pants and an old rugby shirt, was no help. I tried to get her through her bedroom the first afternoon, but she'd find an item in the corner of her closet and call me up from Gregory's study to reminisce. Dolls, lunch boxes, school T-shirts, a big green mason jar filled with pennies and dimes. All had to be touched, all had to be discussed. *Remember...?* she'd begin.

My childhood bedroom I saved for last. Most of my former possessions—into a single pile. Trash. Best to throw it out. Best not to dwell.

When I was done, I joined Cricket in the kitchen, sunny yellow with butcher block counters. I sat on a counter stool and watched her sort silverware.

"Your father was born upstairs in this house," Cricket said, "too impatient to wait for Grandmomma to get to the hospital. Did you know that, Daisy?"

"You've told me," I said. About a hundred times, including twice in the last week.

"The Limoges," Cricket said. Spoons. Spoons. More spoons. All on the counter. "You should take it. Wallis wouldn't want it now, I don't think. Maybe someday. But now it's yours."

"Which set is the Limoges?"

She pointed to the stack of white porcelain with petite purple flowers.

I thought about how often I chipped my sturdy white cereal bowls as they came out of the dishwasher. The Limoges would be wasted on me. If I were the kind of person who wanted to own and display fine china, I'd know that by now. "There are one hundred pieces of china in that set. Isn't most of it in a barrel in the attic? Where would I keep it?"

"Use the barrel as a side table," Cricket said, "next to your couch. I was in that shop on M we love the other day—"

"You can't shop, Cricket." I tried not to sound like a scold. I really did.

Cricket's hands paused in her work. Then she cleared her throat. "I was just looking," she replied. "Anyway, the girl was trying to sell me an old soda pop crate for seventy-five bucks. Can you imagine?"

"I can't take the china, Cricket," I said, hoping this would nudge her toward the inevitable. The china she'd have to sell; we had Gregory's debts to pay, and our lawyer cost six hundred dollars an hour.

"You mean you *won't* take it." Knives now. Butter knives, so many butter knives. *"This. Is. Our. Home,"* she said, and I knew she meant more than this house. All over George-town, there were plaques that bore our name, on the church, the park, the university hospital. As a tween, she had walked me around the neighborhood and pointed them out, giving me, in her words, *an education.*

Two decades later, those plaques remained. For now.

"It's just plates, Mom. It's just stuff."

Cricket stopped sorting. She walked around the island and wrapped her arms around me. I tensed, feeling trapped, wishing Wallis would come down. Cricket had put on per-fume, bless her. "This is yours, though, Daisy. This stuff," she said, voice cracking, "it's really the only stuff you'll get, in the end."

"Please don't cry." I gripped her forearms, not knowing if I should push her away or draw her closer.

"I was a good mother, wasn't I?" she asked. "Did I not

teach you civility, dignity? Enroll you in the best schools? Give you priceless experiences? Those pink curtains in your bedroom, with the pom-poms? I *made* those."

"Breathe, Cricket," I pleaded.

"I still have Grandmomma's scrapbook, of all the news clippings that mention the Richardsons," she whispered. Then, seeing me at once moved but unpliable, she tried one last tact. "We can't go because there is no way I can leave."

My Aristotelian mother, felled by circular reasoning.

"I'll take the Limoges, Cricket," I said, ceding the point that was easiest. "The barrel will make a nice side table."

Her cell phone rang and she pulled out of my arms, looking sheepish, patting her tears away with her fingers. She answered, cautiously, wondering, as I was, who was next to collect, to rubberneck, to exploit. I doubted it was Uncle Danny, who'd been of no help; when Wallis had gone to fetch him, his assistant had in effect used her body to dead bolt his office door. Certainly not a relative, many of whom had stopped returning our phone calls, including Cricket's own brother. Friends, too, had declined to text or, worse, sent vague, pandering emojis.

"Mac!" Cricket's face relaxed against the telephone. "It's Mac," she explained to me. "Dear Mac." Her attention was back to her old friend on the other end of the line. "Thanks for calling. Yes, we're okay. Thanks for checking in. Yes, it's been miserable. But we're so looking forward to your wedding. It will be nice to see everyone, get our minds off everything for a bit." I was about to leave, but her next words stopped me. "Yes, of course we're coming. Did you not get our RSVP card? I know I sent it in." Cricket cocked her head, clearly confused. She didn't see the wave, not even when it was right on top of her. "We're coming,

Mac," she said. "What is this—you don't want us there?"
She turned away from me, but not before I saw the crash.
"Well, thank you for your concern about my feelings, but
we still plan on attending." Her voice, quieter now. "I'm
sorry if you feel like our presence will be an embarrassment... No, that's what it sounds like, Mac. Truly... Okay,
then, fine. You're fine with it. And so are we. We will see
you in three weeks. Goodbye." She hung up and faced me.
"That was Mac," she said, matter-of-fact.

"I got that."

"Confirming the wedding," she said.

"Maybe we should consider skipping it?" I asked, hopeful.

"And let him, and that twenty-eight-year-old cocktail
waitress he's marrying, win?"

"She's not a cocktail waitress. She was his paralegal."

"He divorced Louise for that bimbo."

"That 'bimbo' went to Yale."

"So there aren't any bimbos at Yale?"

"If we skipped the wedding, it wouldn't be because they
won. It would be because we're going through a lot right
now, and it may be best for us to lay low."

"We're going." Cricket continued to stack silver. "Do
you have a dress? Does Atlas have a tux? He's still your
plus-one?"

"We're going to get looks," I said.

"Then we better look good," she said. Utensils forgotten, she drifted out of the room, muttering about dresses,
about a Carolina Herrera she may or may not have already
consigned.

I, too, left the kitchen and made for the dining room, cat-
aloging what still needed to be done. The polished, three-
leafed table—where my grandfather had built his business

inspecting land plats, making deals with pawnshop owners and small-time hustlers, prospecting where people had still sold peaches and apples from farm stands, collecting titles from dairy farmers—would have to be sold, hopefully for a solid sum. Cricket had cared for it; there was not a single scratch. Mahogany chairs, old books, rugs, most everything would have to find new homes.

That thought, and the realization that this would be my last night sleeping in my childhood bedroom, made me shiver. This house hadn't just shaped my youth, but my adulthood, too. After college graduation, when Cricket had to pry me away from the tiny apartment in Charlottesville I shared with two beloved friends and their gray parrot, I'd moved back to P Street. I'd meant only to stay a few months, maybe a year. A master's degree, I thought. Education, maybe. It had been a brief, bright window when I could've escaped my father, the scale that measures concentrations of power, the running list that tells us who is up and who is down. But Wallis had been there, in the room next to mine, my baby sister, a young girl on the cusp of womanhood, needing my advice on outfits, on boys, on which brand of tampon to buy, and this house, this town, my family, all of it had turned my bubbly plans into sludge.

The evening shadows crept up on me. I turned on the chandelier, then the hall light, then the sconces along the stairs. I paused and listened for signs of life—or at least the sounds of packing tape—from upstairs, but it was silent.

No surprise, then, that I found Wallis sprawled on her back on her twin-size, scrolling through her phone. When she noticed me, she scooted over, and I crawled in beside her, turning on my side and tucking my hand underneath my cheek.

"If your life was a book," she said, our noses inches apart, "what is the title?"

It didn't take me very long to answer. We'd been playing this game, when times were rough, for years. I sometimes played it by myself when we were apart. *"Everything Is Delightful."*

Wallis giggled. "Book of essays, I assume?"

"Clearly. And yours?"

Wallis considered this for a minute. *"Remeasuring the Moon,* or *When Everything You're Sure of..."* She stopped and rolled back to face the ceiling. "I don't know. I used to be good at this game. Now I'm getting tangled in subtitles."

"The first part is good," I said.

When she left for college, Wallis had asked Cricket not to alter her room, as she had with mine, swapping out my double for a beautiful canopied daybed. Wallis felt the idea of coming home to one's childhood bedroom left untouched by time was poignant and meaningful. But I now recognized the dolls and lunch boxes and the faded floral wallpaper were making it harder to say goodbye.

"You know who I haven't heard from?" Wallis asked me.

"If I start guessing, I'll never stop," I said, flopping onto my back.

"And your tone tells me that we shouldn't bother."

I shrugged. "People do what they need to do. And, mostly, they need to judge."

"But it's one thing to judge Dad," Wallis said. "It's another thing to stop responding to my texts. To just completely ice me out."

"Who's cutting you out?" I meant, who *now*?

"My newsletter people," Wallis said, sitting up and reclining into her pillows. "I think they must've started a new group text without me. And I'm off the LISTSERV. I mean, this is a volunteer task force. I literally want to give my time away to destroy the patriarchy, and they're like, *nah*."

"I know there are good people in that group." I also sat up, tucked a knee under my chin. "Maybe some even disagree with you being left out. They just must've been thinking about the optics."

"They were pretty quick to kick me out. And without giving me a chance to defend myself? That's hard to swallow. I anticipated some hostility. I just didn't see it coming from my own friends."

Speaking of friends. "Mac just called Cricket," I said. "He doesn't want us to attend the wedding."

"He's uninviting us?"

"Not exactly. He was trying to guilt Cricket into dropping out. She didn't fall for it."

"God, people are vile."

Although I didn't like it, I understood Mac's position. We weren't the most desirable of guests. But this subject would not exactly cheer my sister, so I gave her the best advice I could summon. "Remember how Cricket always used to adjust our shoulder blades? She wanted us so badly to have fine, upright posture, with our chins high and boobs out. Well, for the next few months we're going to do the opposite. We're going to hunch our shoulders and assume the posture of a turtle retreating into its shell, okay?" This made Wallis smile. "This will pass." She nodded like she believed me. Good. At least one of us had faith.

"I want to talk about something else," Wallis said. "Let's talk about Atlas. I'm so looking forward to seeing him at this miserable fucking wedding. How is he?"

"He's good," I answered, as honestly as I dared. "I mean,

he's happy with his work, and generally still the good person he's always been."

"It's a shame he's still traveling so much. It's a shame all he does is work, period."

"A shame?" I asked. "Why would he not devote his life to his work? It's important and he loves it."

"I didn't mean it like that, Dodo. And anyway, it doesn't matter what I think. It matters what *you* think. What you *feel*, I should say."

"I think he's honest. He's an amazing journalist. Always compassionate, even when people are yelling obscenities at him. Levelheaded in situations that would send me running for a cliff." I chose my next words carefully. "I admire him so much. I respect what he's doing for journalism and this country."

"You respect him?" Wallis threw her hands over her face. "You admire him? Oh my God, Daisy, you're killing me."

"I can't do anything more than admire him," I said. "Don't encourage me to do more."

"You've done it!" Wallis cried, all drama. "I'm dead."

"He has a girlfriend," I reminded her, again. "He always seems to have a girlfriend. This one is especially gorgeous. I've seen her picture. Besides, if he liked me that way, he would've done something about it by now."

"But—" Wallis began, serious once more.

I shook my head. "There are no buts. At least, not about this."

Wallis took a piece of my hair between her fingers and twirled it as she spoke. "I think you're wrong. And I'm really trying not to pry, you know. And I'm *well* aware you don't want me hoping that you two get together."

"Your hope sometimes transforms into expectation."

"Yes, but I can't help but marvel at how good you two fit. You carry yourselves similarly, you know? You aren't the kind of people who say stuff just to say stuff. Not like me, anyway. You don't mind the quiet."

"You seem to know me very well, despite claiming the other day that you had no idea who I was."

Wallis stopped playing with my hair. She held my hands and wouldn't let go. "I'm sorry I was so mean to you, Dodo. I've been super on edge and moody." Then she laughed, bitter. "What I mean is, I feel like I am channeling the ghost of Dad."

She seemed desperate, and I could sense she needed reassuring words about how she shouldn't worry. About how she wasn't like Gregory at all. But the day had been long, and I was tired, and I wasn't sure it would come out the way it should.

"Don't do anything else tonight." I pulled away from her, silently begging forgiveness. "Get some sleep. We'll have the day tomorrow to pack up the rest of this room."

She told me she loved me, and I just managed to say it back before I slumped outside her door, exhausted and terrified that I might go back in there and tell her the truth. Our childhood home was up for sale because of what passion did to Gregory Richardson. Entitlement, power, and hunger can't be untangled. I wonder, then, why it caught us all by surprise. We should have known. The only thing uglier than politics is love.

Seven

Atlas entered my apartment messenger bag first. It took a minute to unburden himself of his gear, umbrella, sodden coat, and Converse, then we were sitting on the couch and I was watching him run his fingers through his soft hair. It was Saturday, a week after Cricket and Wallis had moved upstairs. He'd been on an assignment in New York all week and promised to swing by once he'd returned. Cricket and Wallis were right, of course. He did look wonderful. Smelled it, too—like vanilla and spring water. If sliding into a bed with cool, fresh linens had a scent, it would be his. He'd been living in London the past two years, but when he sat close to me, he appeared absolutely the same, which was both nice and painful.

I was glad to have him back in DC, but to want to not want something is a peculiar kind of torture. Like a student furiously erasing a wrong answer from an exam, I've been hovering for the past decade and then some, trying to scrub off any stray mark that would hint at my wrong-headed love. It's not lost on me that while I was working, harder than ever, to fall out of love with my best friend, my father had been, by all accounts, falling into bed with a woman who was not his wife.

I'd first met Atlas in Virginia coal country, where Gregory Richardson thought I, his college-aged daughter, could help reinforce his threadbare support. I spent many nights counting the bumps on the popcorn ceilings of motel rooms, dreading another morning of runny eggs and talking points, of being a prop for my father. (Only later would I fully recognize the good he was doing, bringing dentists and doctors to underserved communities, repaving crumbling roads, introducing broadband internet. It would be several years more before I realized I wanted to get into politics to do the same.) I would've despised the assignment entirely if it hadn't been for Atlas. He wasn't necessarily supposed to befriend the daughter of the guy he was writing about, but the campaign trail is narrow, and the loneliness makes it claustrophobic.

My Atlas—because I was already thinking of him as *my* friend, *my* person—and I stole moments to talk everywhere: in elementary school gymnasiums, buses that smelled of hand sanitizer and french fries, dim veterans' halls, back roads bars filled with journalists with moderate alcohol issues and campaign staff with major ones. Atlas had spent his childhood off Marylebone High Street, in a dusty flat that implied inherited wealth, mostly gone, walls coated with lacquered paint and rooms filled with furniture not meant for children. His mother: American, a struggling actress. His father: Welsh, a mediocre barrister and part-time writer of mystery novels. They never married, and she left when Atlas was fourteen. When he told me this, he admitted that other people often found him reserved. He wondered if I thought his description of his childhood, as an example, was terse. No, I'd insisted. The way he recounted these details suggested a writer's mind, always capturing the pertinent details and finding a concise way to convey them. It suggested someone who thought before he spoke. Sometimes Atlas sounded English; other times his accent was barely detectable. His face was slightly asymmetrical, his nose had a bump from when he fell off his bike freshman year at Stanford, but I often caught myself staring. I was nineteen and in love for the first time—with his deadpan manner, his way of sitting that made his rickety chair look comfortable, his big tips to tired waitresses.

My Atlas. In fifteen years he never made one move.

While he'd been overseas, I could forget, partially, how badly I wanted him to. Now I feared this desire would be plastered over my face.

"So," I said, leaning across the couch to give his arm a gentle punch, "how's your girlfriend?" The second this question left my mouth, I flinched, realizing just how jumpy and awkward I was being. Asking him something so personal before I'd even offered him a drink! And some light boxing thrown in for good measure? Cricket would be horrified. "I'm so sorry I haven't asked about Ariel in a while," I said, reclining again, trying to be casual, trying to recover.

"It's...complicated," he said, and my heart jolted. "She's not leaving London anytime soon, and I'm feeling like I need to be in DC for a while. I'm not sure if we're going to do long-distance. We're still figuring it out."

"I've been a lousy friend." Was I glad he was single? Yes.

Did I want to see him go through a breakup? No. This was a strange spot to rest. "Do you want to talk about it?"

"No." His eyes met mine. He was smiling, but it wasn't all there. "I want to talk about you."

I'd put on jeans, a real sweater, which I, in fact, now regretted, as I'd started to sweat and wool wasn't breathable. I had to look away from his tidal basin eyes to collect myself. "Those websites that have our pictures," I said, "never publish the flattering ones. Wallis is always beautiful, but they always seem to catch me with a double chin. It's not fair. Still accurate enough to be recognized, though."

"This may sound odd," Atlas said. "But I'm glad Wallis is here with you. I think this all would've been harder for you had she still been in South Korea."

"I wanted her first months home to be nice. I made reservations. I got tickets. She's been away three years and she comes home to this?"

"Three years away?" Atlas said. "I thought it was two."

"Three," I said, recalling the slow minutes of her years on the other side of the world. "She left shortly after her college graduation."

"I'm really quite a failure at keeping track of time."

"That pocket planner I got you," I said, "like, five Christmases ago. Tell me the truth. Did you ever use it?"

"No, but not because I didn't love it," he said quickly. "Really, I did try to be that kind of a person. The scheduled person. Like you! With your day planner. It just didn't stick."

"So I'm also a failure then," I said, "at giving good gifts."

"Hopelessly deficient," Atlas said, teasing.

"Trade me in for a new model," I said, and chuckled to myself. "My father always used to say that."

"So, how are you then?" Atlas asked. "Really. Tell me."

The way he said this did not sound like an order, but an offering. "We sold P Street," I began.

"So, it's gone then?" Atlas asked. "Officially?"

"The closing is later this month, but the terms are agreed on and the contract is signed." Cricket had had reservations about the listing price, but the agent with the pencil skirt and trendy glasses said that if we wanted to move fast, as with the lake house, we had to tender a bargain. "The money is gone, my father is, too. What's done is done. But I can't help feeling like I should've done something to stop my parents' marriage from unraveling. Maybe then he wouldn't have gone off and had the affair. He'd still be dead, but at least he'd have his dignity."

"I mean this in the kindest way," Atlas said, "but it's really unreasonable to find fault in yourself."

"Of course it is. It's completely illogical." That didn't mean I couldn't still blame myself.

"Well." He looked at me fondly. I hoped, at least, it was fondness and not pity. "Then I guess you've settled it."

I could've used a pet just then, a cat, maybe, to leap between us. To give me something to caress thoughtfully as I was processing hard things. Instead, all I had to clutch was my knobby old couch blanket.

"What's your plan?" he asked. "In the short term, that is?"

When I worked for him, my father, when bored, would sometimes come into my office and tell me stories about his childhood with Grandduff. *Look, Daisy*, he had said once, maybe a year into my tenure with him. *I'll give you the same advice your grandfather gave me. Want to be a success? Don't be an idiot. Get to the center of photos. Give as many attaboys as you get. When you find yourself at the right place at the right time, you'd better not blink.*

And, I'd said, *do some good.*

Yeah, Gregory had said, *that, too.*

"I'm going back to work," I told Atlas. "I'll try to recalibrate, undo my father's damage. Do some good and redeem myself."

"Redeem yourself after a crime you didn't commit?"

"Exactly!" I said, remembering the snarl of the man who had shown up at P. "Have you met America?"

"I'm so sorry," Atlas said, "I don't have any more words except those."

"Coming from you," I said, "those words are plenty."

He draped his long arm over the back of the couch. "I want to talk to you more about this, but before we go on, I do have to tell you something," he said, fiddling with a piece of thread unraveling from the upholstery.

You're marrying your girlfriend. She's pregnant. Your children will be beautiful and brainy and charming. You're moving away and I'll never see you again. I've had something in my teeth this entire time. "What is it?" I asked.

"The *Post Magazine* commissioned a long-form feature on your father. His rise. His…crash. The cover-up. The editor thinks this kind of story is in my wheelhouse."

"The editor assigned this to you?" I'd expected this kind of coverage of my father after his death—the excavation of his past, the turning over of all the stones—I just didn't imagine my best friend would be the one to write it.

"I'm still a freelancer, so if I don't want the story, I could turn it down."

"You *could*?"

"I could."

I frowned. "It also sounds like you don't want to."

Atlas blew out a breath. "It's a big assignment. An important one."

"But, you know me. I mean, we're...close. Isn't that a conflict of interest?"

"My editor actually likes that I know you, that I originally met you covering your father all those years ago. Makes it gonzo. Reporters are becoming part of the story again, especially when it comes to true crime. Not that your father is a criminal—"

"He is."

"I'm not explaining this correctly."

His explanation, actually, was fine. It was me that was a mess. I stood, walked into my tiny galley kitchen. "I'm so sorry that I didn't offer you anything to drink. I have water. And red wine. Oh, there's a can of soda in the back of my fridge. You can have it, if you want."

"You're upset." He peered at me from his spot on the sofa.

"No." I looked around my kitchen. There was nothing I wanted. "I'm just conflicted."

"I understand." He rose. "I'm also conflicted. It's a good assignment. But I— You're my friend. I don't want you to be upset with me."

That *word*—"friend." How I wanted to ring that word's neck. "I don't want your career to suffer just because a giant scandal has ripped through my family, leaving death and destruction in its wake."

"Then I won't do it."

"Stop." I opened a cabinet and then immediately forgot what for. "You have to."

"Daisy," he said, "are you trying to talk me out of this or into this?"

What *was* I trying to do? I certainly didn't want to take away a good career opportunity from Atlas. But would I really be comfortable with someone so close to me writing about my father, possibly my mother, and maybe even— *Oh*.

This was a scary thought.

Slowly I closed the cabinet door and met his eyes across the room. "Will I be part of the story?" I asked.

"I want to do this story right, Daisy. I think I'll be able to. I'll be able to be fair. If you want to be interviewed, have your side on the record..."

"Atlas, you know I can't go on record." Cardinal rule: children of politicians *cannot* air their family's dirty laundry. Not even when they're dead. Not even when they're guilty. Especially not when they're guilty.

"But you *knew* your father," he said.

"I didn't, obviously. And we just can't handle the scrutiny right now. It's bad enough what Gregory did. But he's gone, and I'm still getting the finger from strangers on the daily." I plucked the last can of soda from my fridge, popped it open. Flat. Atlas was right. In so many ways I was organized. Yet I couldn't manage to get to the grocery store before *soda* went bad. "And isn't it true that reporters end up hating their subjects?"

"You're thinking of biographers. Will you come out of the kitchen now?" He cocked his head. "I feel like you're hiding from me in there."

He was right. Reporter or not, this was Atlas. "Yes, I will. But once I do, we will not talk about my father, or your story, for the rest of the afternoon."

"You called it my story." He smiled, slightly at first, then wider. Even with the distance, I could see the laugh lines deepening around his eyes. "Come on, then. Let's shake on it."

For better or worse, DC has a short memory. People seem more willing, here, to soon forget a scandal. In the meantime, Atlas had moved back. Wallis was home. Cricket was managing. I still had a job. Things could be worse.

I left my bad soda on the counter and stepped out of the kitchen, walking as slowly as a bride down the aisle. He stood by my couch, waiting, watching, and I thought of grooms and altars and all those other lovely dreams before I shook myself awake.

When I reached him, he held out his hand for me.

"I will think about the interview," I said, taking it.

"Good," he said with a nod as we shook.

I took in his familiar, comforting face. The way his hair settled just over his ears, the way he made words into cozy blankets—he was near, and this article he was talking about, and my father, for that matter, seemed very far. I wanted to keep it that way. "But no more work-talk for the rest of the day."

"A gentleman's agreement," he said. "Although I am no gentleman."

I was still grasping his hand. The broad palm. The long fingers.

Jesus. If I wasn't careful, he'd surely see how I felt. And how does a friendship come back from that? I gently broke off contact, wondering whether he might try to resist, to keep us close. But he let me go.

I cleared my throat. "You know what I need?"

"A vacation?" he joked. "A time machine?"

"A big bowl of beautiful, spicy umami ramen."

This made him laugh, an accomplishment that always

filled me with pride and pleasure. "With a nice little egg on top?"

"Yes, please," I said, trying to compose myself back to normalcy, or whatever semblance of it was still possible.

"What should we do while we wait?" he asked after we'd put in our perfect order.

"I got a new game." I pointed to my console. "It's basically a joust tournament. You want to be the last woman standing."

"Turn it on." He settled back on my couch, right at home. "Although it's the definition of stupidity to keep playing you at this stuff. You always beat me."

"You're English." I handed him a controller, turned on the system. "Jousting should be in your blood."

Atlas looked me square in the eye and smiled again. "I'm glad to be back, Daisy. We have much to catch up on, yeah?"

"We do," I said. "Including this wedding in a few weeks. Wait until you hear what the groom said to Cricket. But I know you're really busy, so whenever you need to go, just let me know. I don't want you to feel like you have to keep me company all day."

"I'm good," he said.

And, yes, here he was: a man I could still believe.

Eight

After a month of personal leave to help Cricket and Wallis with triage, it was time to return to work. I donned makeup and real pants, the latter of which felt strange after so much time in loose denim and black spandex. On the Red Line, I practiced the several dozen talking points I'd prepared:

Yes, this is truly unfortunate…

I was just as shocked as you…

I appreciate your concern, and hope you understand why my family requests privacy during this…

I prefer to keep my father's life separate from my own…

That last one was probably my weakest. Who would believe me? My father had given me my first real paying job in politics, after all, though nepotism had only gotten me so far; he'd hired me as a legislative correspondent, one rung above an intern. *Don't say I never did anything for you,* he told me on my first day.

His last gift: this mess. I was furious with him. But I also wished he was here. He would know, with certainty, the quickest way to mop it up.

"Your dad is a dick," I heard someone say.

Looking up from my notes app, I discovered the young woman in the seat directly across the aisle staring at me. She had inky-blue eyes and a short, chic haircut.

"He is a complete asshole," she said again, loud, making sure I heard over the rumbling whine of the train.

Is. Present tense. She held my gaze, which I read not so much as a threat, but a dare to respond, to defend. I thought I might simply remind her that my father was dead, but as we pulled into the station, she rose abruptly and stood by the door. I didn't notice it was also my stop until it was too late.

———

Sara was behind her high desk when I arrived at reception. Tardy, thanks to my Metro detour. When she saw me, she smiled her slow smile and asked after my mother and sister. She'd known us all for ages, and had actually worked for my father before I'd lured her away three years ago. She liked to grumble often that I'd delayed her retirement.

"What do I need to deal with?" I asked. I was more than ready to be back in the office, with its familiar if mundane sounds and smells. "Tell me what I missed."

"I'm so sorry." She reached for my hand. "What a shock. What a nightmare."

"Yes." Already one of my prepared statements making itself useful. "It is really unfortunate."

"I'll let you get settled," she said. "No need to dive into anything straightaway."

"Sara." I withdrew my hand, grabbed my day planner from my bag, and held it up for her. "You know I've got this."

"Understood." She folded her fingers under her chin. "The copy machine upstairs is broken, and everyone has been using mine. We need you to do that magic thing you did last time that fixed it."

"Noted."

"People are overusing reply all."

"Got it."

"I've been telling them not to, but people just keep putting papers on your desk. I know how much you hate that."

I did, though trying to stop paper falling into my lap often felt like a Sisyphean task, and therefore a complete waste of energy. "They'll hear about it, believe me."

"And there's a new intern."

"Name?"

"Does it matter?"

This was all so blissfully easy. "No," I said happily.

"We missed you," she said. "Miles is upstairs."

I found him sitting in the little room by the staircase that housed the signature machine, jacket off, cuffs rolled, positioning a piece of paper under the autopen. When Miles wants to be alone with his thoughts, he signs his own letters with a contraption that is supposed to forge his signature. The whir of the machine, he says, the tedium of it, helps him relax. I tried once myself, but it didn't work.

Today he was signing copies of his recent book. Part memoir of growing up mixed-race and gay, part argument for mental health reform, it had been published when I'd been on leave. Instant bestseller. There was talk of a movie. I waited for him to turn, noticing some gray in his barely there buzz where I could've sworn there hadn't been at my father's memorial service. Miles doesn't rattle easily, not like the rest of us do, but there it was—the reminder of how stress manifests itself outwardly, even when we do our best to hide it.

"Daisy," Miles said, the machine still whirring, "is that you?"

"I'm back," I said, and I meant, *Here I am, set to go.*

"Good. It's been hard out here without my chief of staff. First, will you look at a statement Bo wrote for me yesterday? Please convince him to quit using the phrase 'commonsense solutions.'"

"It's not a bad line," I said.

"Thank you, Daisy." Robert Smalls Reed himself, speak of the deputy, was suddenly beside me in the doorway. Bo, as everyone knew him, had left the Low Country when he'd enlisted in the army a dozen years ago. He still had the basic training haircut, still wore unfussy clothes in colors that could be found in camouflage, still could sneak up on you without unsettling the dust. "You've been gone, and nothing has been right," he said. "Miles talks shit about everyone and everything. For the past forty-eight hours, he's been on a rampage about some bro from K Street who won't take *no meeting* for an answer."

"What else do you need me to do?" I asked Miles, because here it was: the first opportunity to disentangle myself from my father. "Besides helping you fend off the bottom-feeders?"

"What I need"—Miles finally swiveled on his stool to face me—"is for you to be at full throttle. Are you ready?"

I've been up, and I've been down, my father used to say. *Up is better.* "Yes." I smiled brightly. "I'm ready to go yell at lobbyists for you."

He didn't laugh often, but when he did, like now, he

showed teeth. "Daisy Richardson, yelling? A month out of the office and you come back roaring."

"That might be my stomach you're hearing, boss," Bo said. "L.K. texted and said she's bringing food."

"I'm here," Lorelei Kaufmann, who much preferred to be called by her initials, rounded the corner with her briefcase and a plastic grocery bag. "I got bagels. Oh—Daisy! You're back! Are you—I mean—how are guys doing?"

"Did you bring the good salted butter?" Bo took the bag out of her hand, inspected the contents.

"We're fine," I said, smiling, chipper, and L.K.'s face relaxed into relief. "Are there any sesames?"

"You can have mine," L.K. said. A Midwesterner with a healthy distrust of government, but a firm belief in the goodness of people, she was by far the nicest of us all. "I don't need a second breakfast anyway."

"Daisy can have my bagel. I haven't been to yoga in two weeks. I could barely button my pants this morning." Miles rose, tapped his trim waistline. "Consequently, I'm going to send L.K. back out for a green juice."

"Do you mind opening that butter?" L.K. said to Bo. "I'm going to just dip my carb in it, then run out again. Daisy, Bo, juice?"

I shook my head. Nine dollars for a cold-pressed? Better not.

"Also, Daisy," Miles said. "I know you have a voice mail from *Politico* asking if I am going to do a walk-back on that tweet yesterday."

"The answer is, of course, no," I replied.

"Just what I wanted to hear. Thanks. And did you see the email from the guy at…"

"The guy at the OMB? Taken care of."

Miles nodded, approving. "Thank God you're back." And then, as he passed us on his way down to his office with the double height windows and the desk full of long, exacting memos and directives, he stopped, pivoted. "I heard you sold your family's house in Georgetown," he said. "I'm sorry to say it, but I agree it's a smart move. Let people see you're being punished."

"It's good optics," added Bo. He'd eaten half his bagel in one bite and was eyeing a second.

"It's good money," I said. "And we need it."

"It's really no fair to you guys," said L.K., who had been following Miles out.

"We didn't know," I said, "about my father. You—you all believe me, I hope."

"Look where you are," Miles said, patting my shoulder. "You're in the office, talking to me. Isn't that proof enough?"

Fair point, though I wasn't convinced. As a gay man of color in politics, he couldn't afford to make mistakes. And neither could his staff. "I feel like there is a *but* coming," I said.

Miles paused, scratched his temple. "I've already had two calls this morning." I'd seen them on his schedule, the pollster and the strategist. I didn't suspect this would be good for me. "*But*," he delivered, as expected, "you've got to be careful. We've got folks making speeches about how your father fucked up. Anyone who even shared an elevator with your father has issued a press release saying they didn't know him well. People are calling him a stain on the country. Melinda Darley was on the floor last week calling him a traitor."

Miles's tone was gentle, but I felt defensive, all of a sudden, about my father. "I mean, Senator Darley," I said. "Everyone knows she's full of shit."

"You're right," Miles said. "But your last name is in the sound bite. You get what I mean? Folks are out for blood. Since they can't have Gregory Richardson's, they'll settle for yours. If you aren't careful."

Atlas popped into my mind. *You called it my story.*

Still, I nodded at my boss, anxious to prove myself. Which I planned on doing, just after I retreated to the quiet of my office, closed my door, and screamed out my frustration into my lumbar pillow. When Miles was gone, Bo and L.K. sandwiched me in a group hug I didn't ask for, but also didn't hate.

Nine

The trendy thing to do in DC is name restaurants after fruits or flowers. A new establishment in Shaw had decided, apparently in all seriousness, to call itself Fruits & Flowers. It was the kind of place that didn't have a phone, didn't take reservations, and didn't blink an eye when diners wanted accommodation based on their ideological dietary choices. *Washingtonian* raved, the *Post* guy declared it mandatory eating, and so it was inevitable that Wallis wanted to meet me there midweek. Fortunately, it was cheap eats, so I agreed.

"Pomegranate hummus," she said when I found her shivering in line outside. "I'm so hungry I might eat the entire bowl myself."

"Wallis, my God, your hair," I said. Her natural caramel brown was now highlighted with strokes of gold and—wait for it—pastel princess pink.

"I got the urge to do something. So I did. I did a thing."

The guy behind us asked if we were in line. Wallis rolled her eyes and we shuffled closer to the unmarked door.

"I wanted to make a statement, especially at Mac's stupid wedding. They might be able to ignore us, but they won't be able to ignore this new look. Oh, you're gaping at me like you hate it. No, Daisy. Seriously, if you tell me you hate it, I will cry."

Pivot around the question, I always reminded Miles, *when the truth would hurt.* "You are very trendy and beautiful."

"She said sarcastically." Wallis ran her hands down the arms of her coat.

"I'm not being sarcastic," I said. My hair—dark brown, one-note, in need of a root touch-up—was pin straight and shoulder length, usually parted in the middle. Hairstylists were always suggesting a change, but I'd take this cut to my coffin. "I don't think you're capable of doing anything I truly hate."

A petite lady with a clipboard came out of the restaurant and asked for our name. "Richardson," I answered, without thinking. There was a moment when she looked between Wallis and me, blinking slowly, and I thought she might turn us away; she certainly seemed to be considering it. In the end, she just muttered something that sounded like *ew*, wrote us on her list, and moved down the line.

I contemplated whether Atlas's article would make this open hostility from strangers increase or decrease. Since he had asked me to go on record last week, I had toggled between wanting to know nothing about the piece and wanting to dictate every last punctuation mark. I didn't think my family could take any more scrutiny, but I was still a politician's daughter at heart, and couldn't help but consider all angles. Would my participation tip the scale of public opinion one way or the other? I felt cold and cynical thinking this way, but that was the game I was being forced to play. One of calculated risk. An interview with a writer I trusted to be fair could be an opportunity to pivot our family's narrative into more sympathetic territory, remind readers of all the positive change Gregory had affected.

"I guess we need fake ID's now," Wallis said, grouchy now.

"A good pseudonym, at least." I stomped my feet, trying to warm my toes inside my flats.

"How long do you think this is going to take?"

"For us be to anonymous in public again?" I didn't have an answer to that question.

"For us to get inside this damn restaurant."

"Hold our spot." I walked around the line to peer inside the front windows. It was just a shoebox of a place, no more than forty people, no table holding more than six. And there, seated at the four-top in front of my nose, were my father's former chief of staff, his former communications director, and his former executive assistant. Through holidays and graduation parties, Wallis and I had regarded these men as part of our extended family. As a child I'd had nicknames for them, been a flower girl in one of their weddings; one even taught me how to bowl. Yet none of them had reached out since the news broke. We made eye contact through the window. The expressions on their faces went through shock, appraisal, mild embarrassment, then dismissal, and it became clear to me that our relationship had been decidedly severed.

I rejoined Wallis. "We can't eat here," I announced.

"The food looks bad?" she asked, glancing up from her phone.

"There's an entire table of Gregory's former staffers.

Uncle Danny is in there, Goldie, too. And I just can't handle the awkwardness. Please, let's go somewhere safe."

"God, those dicks. You think they'd at least pretend to care. Cricket said she hasn't heard one peep from them."

This didn't surprise me. Not anymore, at least. "Their years with our father are now nothing but a huge blemish on their résumés. It's not entirely their fault they don't want to be seen with us."

"Let me ask you a question, Daisy. If Miles had a boyfriend—"

"He claims he's in a relationship with his job."

"Fine. If he was even casually sleeping with someone, would you know?"

"Yes," I said.

"Right. So, they knew about Dad's affair. Maybe even the money he spent on her. They should be out here, on their knees, begging for *our* forgiveness."

"All right," I said, waving toward the door. "Go in there and tell them that."

"Maybe I should. Sometimes I think making a scene would help me feel better. The only thing that's stopping me is that I would really like to come back to this restaurant one day. God! Let's just go to La Vic. I need to drown my emotions in a giant bowl of French onion soup."

"Are you going to tell clipboard lady that we're leaving?" I asked.

"I'm over clipboard lady," said Wallis as we began walking. "Just like the man in there formerly known as Uncle Danny."

Our old faithful—La Victoire—the corner brasserie equally beloved by tourists and Washingtonians, was relatively quiet, and we were able to get two seats at the bar without divulging our names. As promised, Wallis did feel better after enjoying her soup, and we spent a long time talking, feet entangled in each other's bar stools, sipping on the cheapest wine from the menu. For a minute, I even forgot about Uncle Danny, our father, Agent Finkle and his warrant, the vandal with the brick, who'd managed to stay anonymous despite Atlas's pursuit and the police's half-hearted efforts. I was just with my sister, reminiscing, giggling about her series of college boyfriends, several of whom I'd met when I'd traveled to Williamstown for Wallis's championship soccer games. For someone who had spent most of high school in cleats, she sure had a knack for choosing indoor boys. We laughed about the one who quoted David Foster Wallace in bed. The one who claimed never to watch television. The one who loved his a cappella group like it was his own child.

By the time we'd paid the bill, the bar was jammed, and bodies packed around our seats. We'd no sooner slipped off our stools than two young women, anxious, like we'd been, for wine and food, filled them again. We worked our way toward the exit, but at the hostess stand I realized Wallis wasn't by my side anymore. On tiptoes, I searched the room and found her still close to the bar, waylaid by an older man, his face vaguely familiar, lumpy red nose, disheveled hair, his arm snaked around her waist.

"Yes," I heard her say loudly, defensively, as I pushed back through the crowd. "I'm Wallis Richardson. Who are *you*?"

He looked at his companions, who had formed themselves in a half-circle around Wallis, and said, "This girl must really be stupid," then went on to explain how he was a famous publicist—yes, that was how I knew him—and how it would be good to get our side of the story out into the press, how it would be such a *savvy* move for our family. How he would be *so* happy to help.

"Sir." My heart was in my throat as I grabbed for Wallis's hand. "We need to go. Please, let my sister go."

He whirled his face toward me, and I had the feeling that a dinner plate was being tossed in my direction. "Relax, ladies," he said with the confidence of a man extensively practiced in dismissing women. Again, he turned to his companions, who laughed like this was a skit. "I'm just trying to be your friend."

"I prefer to be strangers." Wallis twisted her body away from his arm.

"Same," I agreed, though rather weakly.

"You should be really careful about who you're telling to fuck off in this town." He was still laughing as he said this. "You should be grateful that I would even entertain the idea of taking on your family as clients. Everyone knows what you all were into. Come on, you worked for your father." This last comment was directed toward me.

"You don't scare me." Wallis moved toward him and stuck her finger up at his chin. "You don't know anything about us. You certainly don't know shit about my sister. So back up, buddy."

"I don't want to be your buddy." He brushed her finger away. "You're too much of a bitch."

Other people were noticing. The bartender, even, was staring, swirling a towel around the same glass over and over. There were many eyes on us and not many of them friendly.

"Wallis," I said, shriveling, "let's go. Enough. It's not worth it."

"As soon as he moves," said Wallis, "out of my fucking way."

"Bro." A man, youngish, square-jawed, was now at my shoulder. "You're not being cool. Come on. You don't look like you're this guy. You don't have to be this guy."

"I didn't start this." The publicist raised both hands, as though to prove his harmlessness.

"Bro, it doesn't matter. Step aside and give them some room."

Lumpy stepped back, and the air suddenly felt less turbulent. Amazing what a baritone and a set of biceps can do in a situation like this. The patriarchy is alive; don't let anyone tell you different.

But Wallis, evidently, wasn't satisfied. "I still have more to say to this walking bucket of fried chicken!" she said, making some bystanders laugh, including our new friend at my side. Even I had to suppress a smile.

I don't know what would've happened next if a woman identifying herself as the manager hadn't charged in, asking *what was going on here.*

Wallis looked like she might explain exactly what was going on, but our defender got there first. "My man here was just backing up. Right dude? He's good. Yup, just like that. Going to let these girls have a good rest of their night." Like a bodyguard, he escorted us past the human chicken thigh, who managed one last scowl, through the crowd to the revolving door, and out onto the street, where Wallis let out a stream of curses into the cold air.

"It's okay." These words were mostly for myself. "It's done."

"No," said Wallis. "I left my fucking coat in the coat check." More curses.

"I'll get it." He asked for her ticket, and Wallis gave it to him without hesitation.

"Who is that guy?" Wallis huddled close to me when he'd gone.

"Someone seizing his white knight moment." In the bar, I'd noticed his accent—Southern, not too twangy or noticeable, just a softening of consonants here and there. The voice, as the outdated trope went, of a gentleman. Could anyone argue, though, that he hadn't been chivalrous? I imagined how the situation might've appeared to him: Wallis, aggrieved, foulmouthed, surrounded, a young woman (and it helped that she was beautiful) intimidated by a bigger, much older man.

He returned clutching Wallis's jacket, and I got my first good look at him. Our boy was handsome, no question, and was wearing a gingham shirt tucked neatly into slim khakis. He had dark hair that flipped out behind his ears and a smile that went higher on one side than it did on the other. You could tell this was the kind of man who had been devilishly cute in boyhood and figured out how to manscape his way into sex appeal as an adult. His features, independent of each other, were so dashing that it took a second to really see what was in front of me. When he came into focus, I swallowed hard, finally recognizing him.

"Well, thanks," Wallis said. "God, that was wild in there. I didn't catch your name."

"Blake." His drawl wasn't especially pronounced, but the *a* in his name still stole the show.

"Darley," I said. "As in, Melinda Darley." As in the woman who'd been on television not two weeks ago calling our father an abomination.

"The senator?" Wallis didn't seem concerned, only curious.

"You got me." Blake smiled and extended his hand. He

shook mine warmly, though I sensed his attention drifting back to my sister.

"Daisy," I said, pointing a bit foolishly to my chest. "And Wallis. Richardson." I declared this with the expectation that if he didn't know who we were already, he'd soon put it together, wish us a pleasant night, and take himself back into the bar.

"We've never formally met, I don't think," he said, turning back to me. "But I know who you are. The brilliant Daisy Richardson, deliverer of election night upsets, securer of plum committee assignments, chief of staff extraordinaire. A pleasure to meet you."

It was truly surreal, feeling flattered by a man whose mother thought abstinence was the only proper form of birth control.

Wallis: "You were pretty good in there, Blake. I'm impressed by your de-escalation tactics."

"When you come from a family of politicians, you come from a family of arguers," said Blake, taking a mock bow. "As you guys probably know. Still, sorry about all that *bro* and *dude* stuff. That was lame. But men like that have to be sweet-talked into submission."

"He was gross," said Wallis, though she didn't seem worried about it anymore.

"You guys are cold." He observed my sister shivering. "Do you want to—no pressure at all—but there's another little place down the street with great cocktails. Quiet. And they have a strict no-douchebag policy."

"And they still have customers?" smiled Wallis. "In this town?"

"I did say it was quiet," he responded, eyes only for my sister.

"Daisy?" Wallis asked. "What do you think?"

Perhaps he saw my hesitation, because he said he was going to make a quick call, and stepped down the sidewalk and out of earshot.

"I want to go," Wallis whispered.

"He does seem very nice," I said, trying to be discreet. "And very pretty. But…" This last word I stretched, hoping she might finish my thought for me. For as worldly as my sister was, sometimes she forgot how things worked in DC.

"You don't want me to go?"

"Well, I can't go with him."

"Why not?"

"I can't be seen hanging with the son of one of Miles's biggest adversaries." In my quest to be inconspicuous these past weeks, I'd dodged reporters and photographers, avoided predatory PR agents, deleted my weight in hate mail and blocked mean tweets. And now the laughing, pernicious universe had sent me a Darley. Fine, perfect, I'd shake him, too.

"But who was the creepiest guy in that bar?" Wallis said. "It sure wasn't Blake. I for one am not going to be one of those people who categorically dismisses the other side."

"Like me." I folded my arms.

"I didn't say that, Dodo. But you have to know that when you heap scorn on someone for long enough, the more likely they are to double down on their beliefs. Who knows? Minds can change."

"He has to be in his midthirties, right? I'd venture to guess his beliefs have long since crystalized."

"So no one has ever had an epiphany over the age of twenty-nine?"

I sighed. I knew she would steamroll me, and, really, it was only *one* drink. "He does have a cute accent. But if he starts talking to you about pheasant hunting or naming your kids after Confederate generals, then run."

She clasped my frozen hand. "I can take care of myself, Dodo."

I prayed that this bar was indeed quiet and they wouldn't be seen. "Try not to let anyone record you, or take a photo of you." She gave me a look. "For me," I pressed. "And you better text me after."

"Text you?" Wallis grinned. "I can knock on your door if it isn't too late."

"That's right." I cheered a bit that she was close again, after years of being overseas. There was safety in that.

Blake meandered back, asked solicitously what we'd decided. "I have an early morning tomorrow," I begged off, "but Wallis…"

"I'm coming," she said with the authority and confidence of someone entirely sure of what she was doing. I watched them stroll down the block and disappear around the corner. Then I zipped my coat and took myself home.

Back at my apartment, I watched bad television about women who were cruel to each other. Another dessert was needed—gummy worms straight from the bag. I fell asleep with the lights on, expecting to hear Wallis at the door.

The next morning I woke up and fumbled for my phone, only to find a single text from my sister: he's lovely, she'd written at half past midnight. And possibly perfect.

Ten

The most quintessential of DC weddings. At the Hay-Adams—where else? The ceremony for my parents' old friend Mac and his new bride—the previously accused bimbo—was in a large, stately wood-paneled room that reminded me of my father's study on P. Cricket, Wallis, and I were running a bit late, the flurry of nerves, I think, had gotten to all of us, and by the time we'd arrived most chairs were occupied. I pushed Wallis and Cricket to sit together and squeezed down a back aisle to a pair of seats between a pleasant group of elderly out-of-towners and a power couple who used their phones to politely ignore me. I didn't like that we were split up, but I knew once Atlas got there I'd feel less on edge at this event to which we had been all but disinvited.

The groom, tuxed, sweaty, stood before a makeshift altar draped in cascading roses, looking very much like a sixty-eight-year-old doing his best to look fifty. He ran a dino-

saur of a law firm and had a reputation that had just as many
black smudges as you'd expect from a formidable lawyer in
this town. His daughter and I happened to play tennis together in high school, and our parents spent countless hours
on the bleachers dissecting our backhands. When the bride
walked down the aisle in a strapless gown I swore I'd seen
at a wedding last summer, I thought of Mac's ex-wife, and
how lovely she'd always been to me. There'd been a game,
long ago, when I'd double-faulted match point. I'd been
furious with myself, ready to quit the sport entirely, but
Louise had come to my side with kind eyes and tissues and
a chocolate chip cookie about the size of my racket head. I
hadn't thought about this in a long time. At weddings, like
at funerals, where there is such emphasis on tradition, where
old friends gather, where families make nice, the current of
my thoughts always seems to flow backward, into the past.

During the first scripture reading, Atlas dropped down
in the chair beside me and apologized. "Work," he whispered. "You look great. What did I miss?"

I beckoned him closer. "The groom is as old as my father and the bride is as young as Wallis. Neither of them
wanted us here. Also, no one in attendance has made eye
contact with me, except this nice couple to your left, who
are from Grand Rapids, Michigan. When I introduced myself, they asked if I was named after the sour cream brand."

"Don't tell Cricket," Atlas said dryly. "She'd be so sad to
hear people are associating her daughter with a condiment."

"Is sour cream a condiment?"

"I think so," Atlas said. "Like mayonnaise."

"Then, no, we will not tell Cricket. I love your bow tie,
by the way."

He lifted his chin proudly, showing off the very bright

Union Jack pattern around his collar. "Black tie *optional*, they said. I prefer other options."

We were shushed by the nice people next to us, and I made it about two minutes before starting up again. This couldn't wait. I tilted my head toward him. "Have you heard who Wallis is dating?"

"Who?" Atlas asked.

I shared the name. Atlas's eyes widened. "Well," he said thoughtfully, "fuck me."

This earned us another shush, and a few stern looks. I lowered my voice. "Exactly my reaction. And I'm sure the reaction of most everyone at the Hay-Adams tonight. He's here, too."

"No," Atlas said, dubious.

"Yes. They've only been dating two weeks. But Wallis prepared herself for this like it was prom." Meanwhile, I'd worn my plainest little black dress, hoping to just melt into the background. Shifting to more amusing subjects, I gestured toward the altar, where the groom was presently looking between his bride's vertiginous veil, the waterfall of flowers behind the officiant, and the packed rows of guests, as though he couldn't quite believe the pageantry. "I went to college with one of those bridesmaids," I told him, sighing exaggeratedly, pretending to be sorry for myself. "I doubt *she'll* invite me into the photo booth later."

"I'll go in the booth with you," he said. "I hope there are props. I love a big, fake mustache."

He made a mustache with his finger, while I pretended to adjust a top hat. "Do you think Uncle Mac will notice I bought the cheapest thing off his registry?" I asked.

"Salad tongs?"

"Cheese knives."

Atlas smothered his laugh in his suit sleeve. "Miss Sour Cream Richardson," he eventually whispered, "I am so happy I get to be here for this."

———

I've mastered the art of getting in and out of parties within fifty-five minutes, an appropriate amount of time to make the rounds and not appear rude. It's relatively straightforward: you nibble on a cube of something, take a few sips, remember names of children and—this is important—use their social media to inform questions without revealing your source. For example: *Traveled anywhere recently?* You know they have. They know you know they have. Yet, it is part of the social contract that neither of you admits to knowing.

At a wedding, from the ceremony to cocktails to speeches and dinner, you're ensnared for at least four hours, so my only method for surviving, especially this particular one, was to not draw any attention to myself. I hoped to be seated at a high-numbered table, the closer to the bar and the farther away from the dance floor the better. I intended not to slide, shuffle, or otherwise engage in choreographed dancing. I would eat whatever the waiter put in front of me without fuss, even when they inevitably forgot I ordered the vegetarian plate. No hard liquor, thank you.

With this plan in place, it was distressing when Wallis, having found Atlas and me after the ceremony, stood up on my recently vacated chair and waved across the room to Blake Darley, who was on the bride's side of the aisle, waiting his turn to exit his row.

"Wallis." I tugged at the hem of her dress. It was the color of lemons, and with her pink hair and natural tan, she looked like a piece of candy. "You'll see him at cock-tail hour."

But he was already maneuvering his way through the crush to get to our row. They kissed, she stepped down from the chair, they kissed again, his hand alarmingly close to her butt.

Atlas cleared his throat, and Wallis linked her arm through Blake's and turned to us, beaming. "You remember Daisy," she said.

"Of course." Blake kissed me quickly on the cheek. "Who showed great bravery during the battle of La Vic."

"Hardly." Now seeing him in daylight, I noticed Blake had the appearance of someone you should know, a movie star or a news anchor. There was an effortlessness about him that made me want to check that my bra straps weren't showing. "Have you met my friend Atlas Braidy-Lowes? He's a journalist. Most recently published in *GQ* and *The New Yorker* and—what else? Atlas, remind us."

"That's the gist of it." Atlas was the only person less comfortable with flattery than I. "Nice to meet you."

"You're also a bow tie man," Blake observed, returning Atlas's handshake. He then pointed to his own bow tie, which, if I wasn't mistaken, looked to be monogrammed with his initials.

Atlas and I exchanged a small smile as we moved slowly down the aisle, trusting the herd to take us in the direction of much-needed cocktails and dinner, to be held on the top floor of the hotel.

"How unique to hear First Corinthians at a wedding," Blake said with mock seriousness. "I thought it was an inspired choice."

"And should we hyperventilate over these flowers?" Wallis added, skimming her palm over a bouquet attached by a white ribbon to an aisle chair. "Can you believe it? Red roses? In February?"

"Did everyone see the groomsman on the end?" Blake grinned back at me, and it was winning. "He looked like he had jammed himself into a tux made before the internet."

"Can you even call them groomsmen?" Wallis laughed. "I think we should call them groom's geezers."

We found Cricket waiting for us by the elevator bank. Again, Wallis made introductions. Blake hugged my mother like she was his own. When the next car arrived, she, Wallis, and Blake fitted themselves inside with other black-tie guests, a few of whom, I noticed, whispered shiftily. Who could guess what about? I signaled to Cricket that Atlas and I would take the next one, and her expression before the doors closed was tense. Elevators made her claustrophobic. She also wasn't fond of heights. This wedding was off to a great start.

While we waited, Atlas asked me what I thought of Blake.

"He has no worries, obviously, about showing his feelings for Wallis in a room full of people who will gossip about it later."

"Did you expect him to be stiff?"

"I don't know what I thought. Maybe a little hesitation. A little more discretion."

"For one," he said, "I expected him to be taller."

That made me smile. I hadn't considered Blake short. He and I were about eye level, but like so many men confident in themselves because the world had given them no reason not to be, he carried himself like a celebrity. Another elevator arrived, and we boarded along with another group of guests, this one less openly contemptuous than the previous. "One more thing." I kept my voice low as we ascended. Now that we'd be sitting down for dinner with Wallis and Cricket, there was something else I needed to tell him. "I haven't said anything to my family about your Gregory story. Yet. I'm waiting till you have a run date, then I can come to them with all the facts."

The elevator dinged at the top floor, and he nodded in understanding. His fingers zipped his lips.

When we made it through the doors to the reception, we were confronted with towering vases of roses and greenery that emerged from the tables like mushroom clouds. The tables themselves, draped in gold linen, were chockablock with glasses, plates, silver, and tapered candles, and I had a brief, ludicrous flare of worry that someone might set a napkin, or themselves, on fire. I just hoped it wasn't me.

"What a spectacle," Cricket stated when Atlas and I located her, partially hidden by a curtain on the back wall, as far as possible from the doors to the balcony. She was working on a glass of something I suspected was gin. "There's going to be a lot of dark money on this dance floor."

"And schmoozing," I said, and Atlas chuckled. "So much schmoozing. But how are you? Are you okay?"

"I go back and forth," Cricket said. "For the time being, I choose to believe Mac's side of the story. That he didn't start up with this woman until after he and Louise separated. That's the way I can stomach it."

"I meant how are you dealing with being on the outs? Like with the people, right over there, giving us the stink eye?" Right on cue, those people—people Cricket once knew, former bridge partners and bunco socialites—having finished sizing us up and down, gave us the pleasure of viewing their glamorous backs.

"Oh, them," she said, fluttering a hand. "They'll get over it once the band provides them with other entertainment."

"As my mum would say, *They're just jealous*," Atlas said. "You look spectacular, Cricket."

He was correct; my mother had chosen a halter-neck beaded gown that brought out the green in her eyes. Following in Wallis's footsteps, as she often did, she'd changed her hair, made it a shade lighter, as though she'd been basking in the sunshine rather than in meetings with lawyers and bankers and boxes of tissues. Her nails were red and she'd bronzed her neckline. It was quite the reentrance.

"Have you seen Wallis and Blake?" Cricket asked.

"Have we ever," I said.

"That's a tone."

"He's…beautiful, as Wallis said. He resembles his mother. It makes me queasy."

"Careful there." Cricket spotted Wallis and Blake at a high-top table near the bar, and they waved us over. Like a tree grows away from a power line, so the crowd arched away from us as we crossed the room. "You haven't been too fond of people comparing you to your father. Give him a chance."

I let her and Atlas go to the new couple and proceeded to wait uncommonly long for two glasses of champagne.

"How are you so important that you're at table seven and we're exiled to table twenty-one?" Wallis was asking Blake when I joined the group. Outside, the sun was setting, painting the sky behind the White House shades of orange and purple. "What sorority did I have to pledge to get in with the bride?"

"Kappa kappa blonde," he said. "Will you miss me?"

Wallis pouted and he kissed her above her ear. "If they

have more than two courses, I am going to be very angry. Can I switch the place cards?"

"No, Wallis." I was sharp.

Her head snapped my way. "Why not? I'd be stealthy."

"Do you want to get us kicked out of here?" I raised my eyebrows.

"God, Daisy," she said. "What is this, a club? Where's the bouncer?"

"She's in a big white dress, about five feet nine inches tall, one hundred and twenty pounds, currently standing by the shrimp tower and scowling at us. Can't miss her."

Wallis accompanied the bride in giving me a distasteful expression. Blake must have noticed. He tugged at her hand and said, "I can't let either of you be grumpy. It's not allowed. The Richardsons are out and about and are not going to let any shade ruin the fun. Right?" He looked at us for confirmation, and we nodded like good soldiers. "Good. Wallis, dance with me until we have to sit for dinner?" And with that, her frown vanished.

⌒

All through the first course, Wallis picked at her bread and barely touched her mesclun. She fidgeted through the best man's speech, which, in her defense, was long and unfocused, and by the time the filets and flounder arrived, she was texting under the table. I tried to engage her with Atlas, mostly because he was working on a story about pot legalization, and I thought it might be of interest to Wallis, who enjoyed an edible every so often. But only one thing was on her mind, no matter how many times I encouraged her to put her phone away.

Just as the main course was being cleared from our table and the band members—all fifteen of them—came back onto the stage, Blake reappeared, commandeering an empty chair from another table and sliding between Wallis and me. When the cake, thick with buttercream, arrived soon thereafter, Cricket and I ate our individual pieces, then split Wallis's, too busy, as she was, discussing every topic under the sun with Blake to notice: films, television, sports, preferred pets (would it amaze anyone to learn that growing up, Blake had a series of pedigreed retrievers underfoot?), best breakfast foods (Wallis, waffles, he, eggs Benedict with smoked salmon), correct and incorrect footwear for men, the current state of pop music, the legacy of boy bands, and, of course, literature.

"If you're anything like your sister, you must have a full bookshelf, Daisy." Blake turned to me as Cricket and I were fighting over the last glob of buttercream. "Any recommendations? What are you reading?"

I figured he wouldn't be interested in any of the paperbacks in my bedside table drawer, so I went with a book that seemed more in his wheelhouse. "Have you read the new one about the presidency in the Gilded Age?"

He shook his head. "I want to. Can I borrow it after you're done?"

Atlas laughed. "Sorry. I've claimed that one next. You'll have to get in line."

"You're a big reader, too, then?" Blake asked Atlas.

"I read whatever Daisy recommends," he said, patting my shoulder. "She's never steered me wrong."

"Maybe Daisy and I should just start our own book club," said Wallis. "I don't think we'll be invited into any now."

"I despise book clubs," Atlas said. "I've been obliged to join a few, and I have made a promise never to return."

"Why do you hate them so much?" Wallis asked him.

"The conversation isn't conversation at all. It's one-upmanship. Before it devolves into people talking solely about themselves and their lives."

"I was invited to join one, once, by a girl who worked in the office," I remarked. "She didn't call it *book club*. She called it her Sunday Salons."

"The pretension of DC knows no bounds," said Cricket cheerlessly before excusing herself to the restroom.

"Sunday *salon*," Atlas said, his French accent not too terrible.

"Sal-*LAH*," I said, high Parisian.

"Atlas." Blake pointed at my plus-one. "Now I remember. You wrote that story about my mother and her friendship with my godfather. You remember? Melinda Darley and Frank 'Fracking' McGill?"

"I do remember." Atlas glanced at me. "Was a few years ago now."

"It was so fucking unflattering," Blake said, straightforward. Wallis mussed with his hair. A warning to back off, maybe?

"Was it unflattering?" Atlas took a sip of his tea and shrugged genially. "Or is your godfather just a prick?"

Wallis's hand paused in Blake's hair. My glass of wine stopped midway to my mouth. But Blake just threw back his head and laughed. "You're right," he said. "He's a paranoid, self-serving asshole who, I swear, gave me soap in the shape of coal every birthday. In high school, I was Jean Valjean in *Les Mis*, and he told me—to my face—I couldn't sing for shit."

"I love *Les Mis*," said Wallis.

"I'm sure he wouldn't like you hanging around with us,"

I said. "Disgraced daughters of a crooked senator and a bona fide member of the dishonest press."

He kissed my sister's cheek and smiled. "I'm not too worried about appearances."

The brass section of the band was having a moment, and further talking became impossible. Atlas scanned his phone unhappily and, when he caught my gaze, mouthed *I need to take this*. He got up, phone to ear, just as Wallis put her drink aside and pulled Blake to the dance floor. I waved goodbye, then felt awkward about it when they didn't see.

I sat alone at the large table with only my coffee, which I take black.

—

"You should slow down," I said to Wallis a while later in the ladies' room. She was fiddling with her bobby pins and smiling goofily in the mirror. She'd taken off her strappy shoes and was now wearing a pair of cheap flip-flops that had been in baskets by the dance floor. She and Blake were having fun, that was clear, but I needed to remind her what was at stake before they got serious. If it wasn't already too late. "You're running through conversation topics so quickly that you won't have anything left, and there will be nothing to do except fall into bed."

She adjusted the waist of her dress and said casually, "We've already slept together. And it was amazing."

"Quiet, Wallis." I hoped no one was lurking in the bathroom stalls.

She laughed. "Stop clutching your pearls. No one is here." In the mirror, she narrowed her eyes coyly. "You don't want to hear at least one salacious detail?"

I crouched to check for feet, then, confident we didn't have company, I stepped closer to her.

She turned to face me, hands to her heart. "Oh, my God. It was amazing. Daisy, he did this thing with my hair. He kind of—"

I think she was about to reenact, but the door to the bathroom opened, and a few women came in, laughing, talking over each other about the band, the friends who couldn't attend, the unflattering cut of the bride's dress.

I straightened, realizing that I'd gotten sidetracked. "Blake worked for his mother," I said, keeping my voice soft, though the other bathroom occupants were so loud and consumed with their own conversation, I doubted they were paying attention. "He ran her reelection campaign."

"So?" She crossed her arms, inflexible as an ax. "You've never come to the aid of your family?"

"What is he doing now?" I asked, trying to ignore the sting of her question. "Is he still working for her?"

"As a matter of fact, no. He wants to start his own media strategy company. Consulting, coaching, that sort of thing." She looked at me lazily, as if my line of inquiry was about to put her to sleep.

"This isn't just about his mother, you know. His late father started the organization that—"

"I know."

"And his uncle is a lawyer, and defended that person who—"

"Daisy, I know how to type words into a search engine. But Blake isn't like the rest of his family. He's been sleep-walking—his word. The ideology of his mother isn't his. The passion of his mother, and the rest of his family, for that matter, isn't his." Wallis inched toward me. "You're going to have to trust me on this, okay? I love you. Let's not argue. Let's go get more wine instead."

"You go," I said. I'd already stayed much longer than I'd planned. "I'm going to leave soon, I think."

"Don't you dare," she said. "Atlas is here looking as cute as can be, and he deserves a dance. Dodo, don't look at me like that. You dragged him to this thing. You can at least press your boobs against his chest during a three-minute slow song."

Eleven

The song turned out to be a raspy, soulful one about evening shadows, stars, and storms. The female vocalist embraced the poetry of it, and she wasn't half bad. She closed her eyes when she got to the chorus, and so did I.

Atlas and I were barely swaying, more like shuffling in a tight circle. No matter. I was comforted by his hums near my ear, charmingly out of tune.

Wallis and Blake were on the floor too, somewhere. Earlier I'd caught them staring into each other's eyes with an intensity that would be hard for anyone in the immediate vicinity to miss. But people seemed to be minding their own business; perhaps the initial jolt of our presence had passed.

Maybe it was this small victory—and the fact that I hadn't received one repugnant look from a stranger in over twenty minutes!—that had me exhaling gratefully into Atlas's tuxedo. I even felt confident enough to let the tips of my fingers graze the short strands of hair resting against his collar.

"Blake is a good dancer," Atlas murmured. "He's giving Wallis dips and twirls. And here I am just taking you around in a circle like a dog spins before a nap."

"I'm happy to take it easy. Remember what happened to us at that bar in Hampton Roads?"

He laughed. "I still can't drink Jägermeister. And my little toe healed crooked. I'm very self-conscious now in flip-flops, thanks to you."

"Poor baby." I gave him a squeeze. "What a burden."

"Don't look now," he whispered into my ear, giving me chills. "But just over your right shoulder, your sister is kissing Blake Darley on the dance floor like the apocalypse is upon us."

I groaned. "With tongue?"

"Loads of it."

"We were supposed to be flying under the radar," I grumbled. "I really don't want to have to tell Miles that my sister is involved with a Darley."

"You got her to resist switching place cards," Atlas said. "That's something."

I watched my sister across the floor. Admittedly, there was something brave about the way she was clinging to Blake; to trust that you could grasp that hard and that the other person would grasp you back with the same furiousness was a feat for which I envied her.

"You know, no boy was ever good enough for her, before now," I said. "Her standards pleased my father immensely. He called her discerning. Meanwhile, he scolded me for kissing my boyfriend on our front stoop after prom."

Atlas gasped dramatically. "A kiss! I'm scandalized."

"Well"—I fluttered my lashes—"there might've also been a little bit of awkward groping, too."

Atlas chuckled, then grew serious. "Your father was quite awful when he felt like it. Do you miss him?"

"His voice doesn't leave me. I find myself having conversations with him some days. These days, they happen to be angry ones."

Atlas brought our intertwined hands up to his face, used mine to scratch his cheek. "Why was he so hard on you?"

I began to answer. My therapist and I had our theories about this, after all, but we were dancing, and he was saying such nice things, and it made me wonder— "Is this you asking as my friend, or as a journalist?"

The band switched melodies. The lead singer, no longer in soul mode, brought out a tambourine and ordered us to put our hands together for, horror upon horror, the YMCA.

Atlas let his arms drop from around me. "No, Daisy. Do you think I would be that smarmy?"

"Sorry. My father told me to always assume I was on the record." Couples and groups gyrated around us. *YOUNG MAN.* I had to raise my voice. "He said there were always people listening, ready to get you."

"That piece of advice was singularly cynical. You think I would put you on record without saying so?" He talked quickly, irritated. "Or that—worse—I'd trick you into saying something about your father, after you told me you weren't sure you wanted to be interviewed?"

He was right; being at this wedding had caused my lingering feelings of paranoia to swell, and it really wasn't a good look. "I didn't mean to question your character," I said. "I'm sorry, Atlas. Look, I'll prove it." When the chorus came, I did the letters, and really sold it, pretending I had pom-poms, even marched in place with gusto. It was cheesy and embarrassing, but it made Atlas crack a smile, and had me thankful for the song for the first time in my life.

His phone vibrated in his suit jacket, interrupting whatever moment we were having. "Sorry, again." He looked at the screen, eyes not quite meeting mine. "I have to answer."

I needed a break from the trumpets and twisting bodies on the dance floor, so I followed him as he weaved between tables and out onto the terrace. I stood beneath a space heater and tried not to stare as he paced, sounding at times placating, at others annoyed. I could've given him more privacy, I suppose. But tonight, emboldened by surviving the public exposure, by the champagne bubbles in my head, I felt possessive, and even one room's distance between us was too much.

He hung up and rubbed his hands through his hair like he was trying to shake something out of it, then spotted me and drew near. "Hi," he said.

"Hi." The heater was pulsing out warmth, but I gathered my pashmina tighter around me, feeling suddenly nervous. "Is everything all right?"

It was dim on the balcony, but in the glow from the party and the lights below on Lafayette Square, I could see his troubled eyes as he peered at me. "You know, you said you were okay with me writing about your father, but are you really?"

If I were honest, after what had happened at La Vic, being at an event like this, even with people we'd once called friends, made me want to sink below everyone's eye level, army crawling if I had to, and give Atlas a resounding no.

"If something is on your mind, tell me," he said. Behind him was the bright expanse of our city at night. Removed from the traffic and the pavement, I could take the time to appreciate its beauty and grandeur.

"I'm fine," I said, shifting away. "It's nothing."

"It's something." He was nearer now and looking ready to demand answers. "I'm not scared of you or your feelings, Daisy. I can handle it."

"Yes, okay, fine, I *am* worried about you writing about Gregory."

"Getting closer."

If I reached out, I could grab his jacket. All evening I'd been so keen to run the fabric between my fingers, to feel the skin underneath. He cared, that much was true. But would readers? I wasn't convinced. "You can't possibly argue that people would be interested in what I have to say."

His expression was one of disbelief. "Absolute rubbish."

"No, Atlas." My vehemence startled both of us. "Look at me. I'm the daughter of a liar and a thief. For years I stood by his side, working and living with him, and I didn't see it. People will say I'm not worthy of consideration. And they'd be *absolutely* right."

"Daisy," he said, relaxing into a relieved smile. "This is an easy one." He took my face between his hands. "You're more than worthy of consideration."

I felt such love for him then, I almost staggered under the weight of it. All the promises and bargains I'd made with myself crumbled at my feet.

I moved toward him and put my lips to his. It had been so long since I'd kissed someone; I let my fingers drift into his hair, feeling acutely the pressure and warmth of his mouth. My kiss wasn't teasing, or coy, it wasn't even particularly skillful, but it was honest. So, when I removed my lips from his, I was hoping for something other than the incredulity in his eyes. His gaze focused, and it was then I noticed his arms were not around me, but on my shoulders, as a coach might give a player a pep talk.

The noise of the band and the party were gone; I heard only our breathing. Finally he lifted a hand and ran his thumb across my chin. He seemed to be wrestling with what I had just done. I didn't move for fear of spooking him. I clenched my teeth, knowing that if I opened my mouth I'd resort to begging and pleading that he stop thinking and kiss me back. There was a moment when I thought he might. His nose grazed mine, but, no, nothing. His silence stretched, and my hope contracted, until I felt very, very small. I braved another glance at his face—his expression could only be described as a wince—and drew back, giving him the space he clearly wanted.

"Oh, Daisy," he whispered, "I don't mean—"

I cut him off, waving my hand with enough force that I stumbled into the high balcony railing. "I'm drunk," I said, although I wasn't really. "I am—please don't—I mean, please forget what I just did."

"I'm trying to sort this out," he managed.

"I'm really sorry about this," I said. "I'm sure that was so confusing, and sudden, and it is something you don't have to waste any emotional energy untangling."

"Will you just stop? Oh, wow, sorry. That came out harsher than I meant it to. Here's what I mean—" He reached for me, but I stepped away, miserable, and he let his hands drop. "You did surprise me, okay? And I'm trying to get my thoughts in order. I'm reckoning with the fact that I am, technically, still seeing someone. That was her—Ari—on the phone earlier. She has been calling—well, actually, she is a little upset I'm at this wedding with you."

A pause, once he saw my expression. "Perhaps I shouldn't have told you that."

"It's fine." I attempted to collect myself, but the task was hard. My heart had shattered into so many oddly shaped pieces. "I didn't know you were still seeing her. I mean, I did…" *But I wanted you to forget, and you didn't.* "I must have black holes in my brain."

"Daisy, I wish you wouldn't feel the need to—"

"You need to hear me," I interrupted. "You know I would never do anything to break up your relationship." *But please tell me it's over.*

"I know?" This sounded like it might have a question mark at the end.

I waited for him to say more. I waited for him to tell me that he didn't believe that I was sorry. To tell me that I was a liar, and he loved me more than Ari. That I—that my insecurities, fears, and now my family, the clouded legacy of my father—wasn't ever going to be too much for him. But I was afraid I'd be waiting forever, so I started apologizing again. I blamed myself, my therapist, stress, lack of sleep, the internet, media, Congress. The list was long, and I hoped some of it was coherent.

Atlas occasionally offered an understanding phrase until I petered out, still rigid with pain, but unable to conjure any more excuses. He threaded his fingers together under his chin. I gnawed on my lips and waited for him to speak again.

"Guys!" Wallis's voice, from the terrace door, detonated our sad bubble, and made us both flinch. "She's about to throw the bouquet. Daisy, get in here and watch me catch it!"

Blake peeked out behind her. "Daisy needs a try, too," he announced. "Atlas may be in more of a rush than I am."

"They are so cute, aren't they?" Wallis declared.

"They're so adorable," said Blake. "I could cry."

I wanted to skittle like a cockroach down the stairs and out of the hotel and through a pothole that led to anywhere else. "Be right there," I croaked, and they disappeared. I turned back to Atlas. "I'm going to leave," I said. "It's been fun."

Atlas caught my arm. "So, what was *this*?" By *this* he meant me, him, the moment there was no space between us.

I wasn't sure how to answer. I wasn't even sure how I'd make it back to our table to collect my purse; my legs were deadweight. Maybe I'd just leave it. Come back tomorrow in the light of day. "You're important to me," I told him. "And I'm sorry I kissed you. It was a mistake." I grasped his arm somewhere around the elbow, desperate for him to forgive me, to forget what I'd done, to lay his hand over mine and tell me it would all be okay.

He looked down at my hand on his arm, then back at me, distant. From the other room we heard cheers. Someone had caught the bouquet.

Twelve

The morning after the wedding, there was too much to do to dwell on the previous night's horror show. A stack of papers from the lawyers needed my eyes. Cricket had responded to a phishing email with her credit card number, and someone had managed to spend a thousand dollars at a home improvement store within an hour. My bathroom sink pipe was leaking and maintenance wouldn't return my calls. Miles needed to comment on a tricky news story.

A year ago, I'd set up a nice little desk overlooking the patch of scraggly garden below my window. I'd bought a banker's lamp and a paperweight that looked like a gemstone, fancy filing folders, and a cup for my pens. All very pretty. All underused.

Instead, I dragged my laptop and papers into my bed and propped myself up on pillows, which was definitely not good for my back. I was making progress on my tasks and avoiding all thoughts of Atlas when Blake and Wallis,

having spent the night together, showed up on my door-
step, intent on coaxing me out of the apartment before
Sunday dinner.

"The weather is divine," Wallis declared in my doorway.
"Unseasonably warm. Put down your work for a few hours.
Leave your phone. Blake will drive us to Georgetown and
we'll take the water taxi to Southwest."

Going outside was low on my priority list. I had no plans
to leave. "But Miles—" I said.

"Miles doesn't need a chief of staff with a vitamin D de-
ficiency," said Blake.

"Where's Cricket?" I grasped for excuses, wishing I'd been
quicker. I already sensed Wallis anticipating the next obstacle
I'd throw down. Her whole body was poised like a hurdler.
I saw it in her elbows, her knees. "Shouldn't we invite her?"

"I have no idea where she is. She dashed off this morning with her laptop and reading glasses. Didn't even have
time for coffee. She's quite the busy bee these days. Come
on, we don't need her."

"Let me text her," I said.

"Call," Wallis ordered.

I've heard people use their children as pretexts to get out
of things. *She has to nap. Bedtime, you understand.* Though
I was ambivalent about becoming a mother—what baby
wanted to exist mainly as an escape hatch for introverts?—I
did envy the parents who always had this ready justification.

I managed to get ahold of Cricket on my second try; she
sounded frazzled, but promised to meet us at the water taxi.
My brain, dulled by a morning of paperwork and frozen
pancakes, could think of no easy way out, except to admit
that I was sad, and wanted nothing more than to continue
drowning my feelings in PDF documents. But I could not

find the words to tell Wallis and her beaming bright side of a boyfriend.

"Let me change," I said. Wallis clapped and grinned. So did Blake. "But if there are typos and errors in Miles's briefing binder tomorrow, I'm blaming you both."

This is how our small family found ourselves on an impromptu outing to the Southwest Waterfront, a part of town on the Potomac that, as recently as three years ago, had been home to the nation's longest-running fish market and not much else. On the boat, I gave everyone a brief history of the land and the development—or, at least I tried. Cricket already knew everything, she claimed, and Wallis and Blake were preoccupied with snuggling and taking photos of each other. No matter; some nice out-of-towners were interested in my lecture, so when the attention of my family drifted, I still had an audience.

We disembarked, walked along the cobblestone promenade. Blake ducked into one of the massive glass-and-steel apartment buildings. "To grab a brochure," he said when he returned. In we went to a bookshop, then an art gallery. Cricket considered an oil painting, fallen petals and lemons and a hyacinth in a chinoiserie vase. It was lovely. The price—impossible. It was gone, her old life, and I saw in her eyes she was still adjusting to her new one.

I wrapped my arm around my mother's shoulders as we made our way past restaurants full of young people drinking cocktails, and the luxury hotel, to wooden steps near the water.

As we sat, my phone chimed with an incoming message. Atlas. My pulse skipped. If this text was about the kiss, I think I'd throw myself off this beautiful dock into the harbor. His pity would be worse than his rejection. I read with trepidation:

Hi. My editor has scheduled the story about your dad to run on April 15. If you'd like to go on record, we can speak any time before then. No pressure. Lots of fun last night. Thank you for inviting me.

Okay. That wasn't so bad.

Why, then, did my heart still feel like lead?

Confusion must've shown on my face, because Cricket asked if I was all right. "Work," I told her. She accepted this lie.

I hoped the right response to Atlas's text might materialize as I listened to Blake and Wallis describe their night previous over the bag of gourmet nonpareils he'd bought from a chocolate shop the size of a stamp. "We were celebrating—oh, God, Daisy." Wallis raised her hand to her head. "I completely forgot. I got a job."

This was wonderful, yet overdue, news. Maybe Wallis's pay would be good. Private-sector good. Principles withstanding, a defense contractor salary would be very useful right now. Glad to have one problem in my life solved, I rallied, clapped my hands like she and Blake had earlier in my apartment. Now she could help contribute to her rent. "Where?" I asked.

"Women First."

"A remarkable organization!" Cricket pronounced.

Cricket was right. Wallis would be helping to safeguard women's breasts and uteruses, though I couldn't overlook the fact that nonprofits in this town pay almost nothing. Less-than-federal-government nothing, and that's saying something.

"You're going to kill it," Blake said, displaying no concern at all that his girlfriend was going to work at a place his mother fought every year to defund.

"I'm so happy for you." And I was. Our family had been accused of many things, but selling out would not be one of them. "Are you happy?" Wallis nodded. "That's great, then. I know you've been looking for a while. I was almost going to suggest you come work for me."

"No offense, Dodo," said my sister, smiling sweetly, "but who would want to work in Congress?"

"I remember when my mom announced she was running," Blake said, "we all tried to talk her out of it. It's a thankless thing. You're blamed when things go badly and you're forgotten about when things go well."

"We do acts of good every day," was my response. "Incremental change, while not always sexy or newsworthy, is still a reason not to lose all faith."

"I remember reading something a while ago," Cricket said. "Gosh, let me see if I can remember it. The writer was saying, *there used to be artistry in politics, and now we've found ourselves in a music class for toddlers.*"

"That was Atlas," I said, recalling with a pang the exact article. I read them all. He'd been talking about Parliament, but might as well have been writing about us. "Atlas wrote that."

"That's right," said Cricket. "Gosh, he's a good writer."

"What is Atlas up to today?" Wallis asked. "I didn't see him after you two left last night."

Blake whistled. "You guys left together? I called it, didn't I, Wallis?"

"We didn't," I said shortly.

"We should text him," said Wallis, pulling out her phone. "See what he's up to."

"Don't." I was terse, and everyone looked at me curiously. I deliberately softened my face. "I mean, let's not bother him."

"Why are you being weird?" said Wallis.

"I'm not being weird." If anyone has discovered a way of saying this without sounding profoundly weird, please do let me know. "He did me a favor and came to Mac's wedding. Today, I'm just giving him a little bit of space. Space is sometimes a good thing. Sometimes people need space."

"Say space one more time and I'm committing you," said Wallis.

"Space," I said.

"Why do you need space from Atlas?" asked Cricket.

"Fine, okay." I settled my breath. The truth—or at least part of it—would get them off my back. "He's writing an article about Gregory."

Cricket and Wallis gaped at me.

"And we're okay with him writing this?" Blake asked diplomatically.

"He'll do a good job," I said. In truth the kiss had made me wary of the whole undertaking, but that was not a topic we would be discussing today. "And it will be a fair treatment, I believe, of Gregory. Of his best parts and his bad ones."

"I don't know how I feel about this," said Wallis.

"When is this coming out?" Cricket asked.

I checked my phone's calendar. The article would be published in less than two months. The clock was officially ticking. "Middle of April," I said. "It's long-form, and I know he's doing a lot of research, some interviews."

"I wonder if we should get out of town when it drops," said Wallis. She was thinking about the renewed attention, the looks we were still receiving, even at that moment on the Wharf, the second glances, the *is that…?* squinty-eyed stares.

I turned away from the gawkers. There: I could *almost* pretend everything was back to normal. Though how I would ever face Atlas again was still to be determined.

"Atlas is a great journalist," said Blake. "He's curious and smart. I like reading everything he writes, even when he is writing about my own family." He smiled kindly, and I realized he was offering these words for my sake, too. He was trying to make inroads, and I couldn't fault him for it. In fact, I appreciated it.

"I hear you," replied Wallis. "But I still think wistfully about moving somewhere else, like San Diego, or LA. I feel like I'd be so much healthier there. I'd be away from the drama."

"Yeah, right!" said Blake. "Wallis, you say one of your favorite things in the world is the crunch of autumn leaves. You'd be bored of the sunshine within a year."

"And you would never leave us," said Cricket.

"You could always come with me."

"Perfect." I laughed, glad to be done with the topic of Atlas. "Let's dream of moving to a place where housing prices are even more absurd."

"When I imagine you," Blake said, "you're always in DC. It suits you."

"You imagine me in a town filled with gossip and gridlock, literally and figuratively?" asked Wallis.

Blake shook his head and turned his face to the water. Just then, the sun reemerged from the clouds, illuminating his skin, which was fair but flawless. "This town is giving you a hard time," Blake said. "But for all its faults, it is really beautiful. It is small enough to feel manageable, but it has a sprawling history. It adapts to the times—they're *still* building monuments here. This is a town of colleges, of intellectual debates. The Metro tells you how many minutes until the next train. Baristas learn your name. This is a place of marble palaces but also of the tiny toy store on H Street that has been owned by the same family for sixty years. People move in and out of here, the tide sweeps in and retreats with every election, but there is something dependable about DC. It doesn't try to be quaint, unlike Charleston, which is overrun by carriages pulling tourists down the Battery."

"Someone call the mayor," Wallis said, raising her hand. "DC has a new spokesman."

"I had no idea I could like this place as much as I do." He pulled Wallis close; she rested her head on his shoulder. "I'd been coming back and forth for some time, and never fully engaged with it. I didn't even really ever unpack. But I've been happier here than I have anywhere else. Even when I am supposed to be in South Carolina, I'm here. Maybe if every city had a Wallis, I would be as comfortable as I am now."

Wallis looked at Blake with an expression that suggested she felt exactly the same. "You've talked me out of it," she said. "California dreams will remain just that, wisps of fantasy that fade once I awake."

Blake grinned broadly and kissed her on the mouth. "Can she also promise that she won't trade me in for someone else?"

Wallis laughed. "Who in the world would I trade you for?"

Although Blake was still smiling—he was always smiling—I could see he was serious. His eyes flicked to me, and I wondered if he was thinking not so much about who Wallis would otherwise prefer, but who *I* would choose for her. He wanted my approval.

True, a man from the Darley family would, even a month

ago, never have been my first choice. But Blake was real, their relationship was happening, and I realized with a start that it didn't worry me so much, after all. I wouldn't get my love, but my sister would—had, actually—and he was here, and good, and kind, and the type to share his snacks and jacket and say nothing of it. Here was a man who was with us on a Sunday. Here was a man who was talking about giving up his hometown, his former life, his roots, his mother's expectations, to be with us.

I'd think of this day often, later. Whether Blake was lying, I still don't know. Perhaps he wasn't deceitful; maybe he just changed his mind. In the end, of course, one doesn't know how they'll react to power until they're offered it.

~

We stayed at the Wharf until the sun set, then went back to Cricket's. Wallis made us one of Blake's favorites, pimento cheese and crackers and dirty rice, and after dinner we borrowed blankets from bedrooms and started a new show. Cricket promptly fell asleep. Wallis, too, as Blake rubbed her back. I, curled on the floor, leaning against the couch near Cricket's feet, pulled up Atlas's text from earlier on my phone. I wondered if he'd seen on his screen those three gray typing dots pop up, over and over, throughout the afternoon. I must've begun and ended at least a dozen drafts.

By the time I finally composed a reply, even Blake had dozed off. Thanks for coming yesterday, I wrote. Agreed, lots of fun. I was overserved. Too much champagne! Thanks for article info. Still mulling. Talk soon. I ended with a happy face emoji, figuring it was more appropriate than a red heart and a knife.

March

Thirteen

Bo and I had the Senate gallery to ourselves. It was a Friday morning, and generally quiet on the Hill; most members of Congress were already back in their home districts for the weekend.

Minutes earlier in the hall, we had run into my dearest friend Todd from the *Times*. "Hey there, you," he had said, his tone so simpering it made me want to choke him with his press lanyard. I could only bring myself to nod curtly before he went on his merry way.

As Miles readied himself to speak down on the floor, I had to marvel at how easily Todd was able to stroll from one story to the next, while I was stuck up to the neck in my father's. Although the hate mail I was still receiving outnumbered the lawyer's bills by about fifty-to-one, I couldn't decide which I dreaded more. And there was the matter of Atlas. In the two weeks since the wedding, we'd texted. Friendly stuff. Fluff, really. He'd offered to meet me for lunch at Old Ebbitt, coffee at Blue Bottle, a drink at CityCenter.

I was always busy. Even when I wasn't.

"Mr. President." From behind our side's wooden podium, Miles addressed the freshman senator from Georgia, who was, for the morning, acting president pro tempore. I couldn't help but notice that this man sat in his elevated chair with the posture of one scanning his phone under the desk. "The bill will fund a five-year Department of Education study, screening public elementary-school students for learning disabilities and mental illness." Miles's voice carried. "Catching these issues early will almost certainly offset future special needs and remedial education expenditures. It will touch every aspect of school retention, including lowering the number of suspensions and expulsions, not to mention dropout rates."

"He's not punching the opening hard enough." I leaned back in the gallery's auditorium-like seat, aggravated, though I kept my voice low. "I told him not to hold back. I knew he wasn't listening to me."

This bill was a good idea, maybe even a great one. For months we'd worked on it, consulting every expert that would take our calls, attending meeting after meeting with the suits in the Office of the Legislative Counsel. And it was personal. For Miles, who hated school, flipped trays in the cafeteria and cursed his bus driver, who got suspended more than once before he was diagnosed with dyslexia at seventeen. For me, who spent my entire sophomore year eating lunch alone in the girls' bathroom, whose anxiety went undiagnosed until I was eighteen.

"I envy the way the British do it," Bo said, sinking into his seat and crossing one khakied leg over the other. "Speeches over there are given to full houses. You look your detractors and skeptics in the eyes as you dismantle their arguments. There are cheers and applause when you get it right."

"What are we doing here," I asked, "except screaming into the wind?"

"Hoping someone will hear us," Bo said. In the army, he'd worked with computers. He never elaborated on his particular duties, but often I caught him staring at people as though deciphering lines of code. Now I was the target of such a gaze. "You all right over there? You seem to care about this one speech a lot."

"I always care," I said, defensive.

Bo nodded. "I know you do. But—I say this with all due respect—why are you here? Both of us didn't need to come."

He was right. I'd been micromanaging. "I want to be sure," I said, "that we're making some progress, somewhere. After my father...you know." I lifted a shoulder. "I feel that I need to—"

"Prove yourself?" Bo finished for me.

"Is that lame?"

Bo shook his head. "I get it."

"You're not going to tell me to back off?" I asked.

"If I did, would you listen?" Bo smiled.

"Probably not."

I scooted up to the edge of my seat, willing Miles to amplify his performance: "This bill is especially important for LGBTQ youth," he continued, "who are disproportionately affected by our country's uneven distribution of mental health services. Yet the distinguished senator from South Carolina, Chairwoman Melinda Darley, has chosen to *continually* block this bill in Committee."

"I should have told Wallis," I said, mostly to myself, "that we're punching up at her future mother-in-law today."

From Bo, an abrupt turn of the head. "What? Wallis is engaged?"

During Miles's campaign, Wallis had still been in college, but she'd pitched in on breaks. She and Bo had been buddies. There had been talk of them starting a politics podcast—he, the play-by-play, she, the color commentary. There had been picnics on conference room floors. With her humor and love of impromptu dance parties, she'd lessened the tension of those brutal summer months before the election. She was a little sister to us both, is what I mean.

"No," I said, my eyes still on Miles. "No, it was just a joke. Wallis is—God, I can't believe I'm about to say this—dating Blake Darley."

It was hard to shock Bo. He'd held weapons, he'd gone without nights of sleep, he'd take state secrets to his grave. But I'd managed it. "Not *Darley* Darley."

"The same."

Bo was quiet for a moment. "I know Blake Darley. From around Charleston."

I poked his shoulder and badgered him for details. At the Wharf, I'd come to accept Blake and Wallis's relationship, but here was Bo, reminding me that there was still so much to learn about the man who'd managed, in only a few short weeks, to steal into our lives. *What? How? When? Did he still know him?* Instead of answering my questions, Bo asked one of me. "He and Wallis, they're serious?"

"Here's what I know for sure—Wallis likes him," I said, checking my phone and starting to scroll through the latest barrage of emails. "She might think she loves him. Is it enough to survive all the flak? I don't know."

Bo remained very still. "She loves him. Okay."

"I know," I said. Miles. The delicacy—impossibility?—of dating across the aisle. "I'm going to have to tell him. But I'm waiting to see how the next month goes. Wallis insists that Blake isn't concerned with his mother's politics. And I've made it clear that I won't be pulling any punches for her sake—or his. Now, tell me what you know of Blake."

But Bo didn't have much. "I've met him a time or two," he said. "All that matters is that Wallis is happy and he's treating her well."

"He is," I admitted.

"Then why does it look like you're about to throw your phone off this balcony?"

It was true. The way I was glaring at my phone, you'd think it was spewing personal insults. I relaxed my grip. "It's not about Wallis." I said. "I'm just doing some light cyberstalking."

I'd drifted from my email folder into Google, to a page left up from last night.

"Who are we vetting?"

"See for yourself." I handed Bo the evidence.

The McFarland Group, Who We Are:
Ariel Greer
The world's most innovative companies turn to the McFarland Group because our team members know how they work, and how to make government work for them. Ari is an integral part of our commitment to deliver for our clients, having experience both inside and outside government in America and abroad.

"She's attractive," Bo said.

He wasn't wrong. In her headshot, Ariel's face was bright, perky, but in an intelligent, animated way. She looked at the camera like taking a picture this gorgeous was easy. This was a girl who knew her best side. She knew where to part her hair.

"She's dating my friend," I said. "Tell me what you think."

"After consulting on the environment, her latest job was with a multinational energy corporation."

"Did you get to the part where she calls herself 'A citizen of the world'?" I asked.

"I imagine this is the kind of woman who owns an American flag bikini and calls herself patriotic." Bo handed back my phone.

"I shouldn't judge her. People in government leave for K Street all the time."

"You don't have to tell me why people become mercenaries in Armani," Bo said. "They want to feel what it's like to accomplish something. Unlike you and me, who can't even move the needle. Which friend is she dating?"

"My friend Atlas. You've met him before."

"Yes, I remember. The English guy," Bo said, pensive. "Huh."

"Why, *huh*?" I asked.

Bo hummed. "I got the impression that he was into someone else." He stood, adjusting his shirtsleeves.

Below, Miles was winding down. I rose, feeling confident that this job, at least, I could do. It was clear in a way other parts of my life certainly were not. "It is with optimism in the wisdom of my fellow senators," Miles concluded, "that I yield the floor."

Fourteen

My door opened, and I heard the sound of paws and collar tags jangling. "I'm back here," I called to Wallis. "Don't let that dog into my bedroom."

Too late. Crabtree bounded in and began sniffing in corners, in half-open drawers. I closed my computer and groaned. "This dog is a menace," I said, rising from my bed to snatch a bra out of his mouth as Wallis appeared in my doorway, her hair up, athleisure on.

Wallis had an uncanny way of keeping her life entwined with Blake's, even when he was gone. This meant doing him a favor and watching his friend's wild-eyed labradoodle for the weekend. Crabtree had already shredded the corner of one of Cricket's armchairs, and marked his territory on most of the rugs, but I had agreed to a walk through the congressional cemetery by the Anacostia. I wanted to see Wallis, and if it required a canine third wheel, then so be it. In the weeks since the wedding, Wallis had either been with Blake, going to see Blake, or at work. She sent me pictures from all the places he took her—the symphony, the Anthem, the rooftop bar where Atlas and I once, years ago, had pretended to be fancy, ordering pitchers of expensive cocktails and waving at people we didn't know to confuse them.

Despite the regular texts, I missed her. It was a particular kind of loneliness to feel far from someone who lived so physically close.

"How are we getting to the cemetery?" I asked, sitting on the edge of my bed to pull on my socks. "Taxi?"

"I have Blake's car." I glanced up and noticed her nosing through the bowl of stud earrings on my dresser. "We practically share it now."

"That's generous," I said, back to minding the busybody Crabtree.

I'd spent the first decade of my life begging Cricket for a sibling. The odds had not been good; Cricket really liked being slender and subsisting mostly on diet soda, fruit salad, and coffee-flavored yogurt. So when she met me at the door after school and without preamble announced I had gotten my way, I ran straight to my room and decided which of my stuffed animals I could share with the baby.

Wallis came and she was perfect—a curly brown-haired cherub who I claimed as mine. There was a nurse and a nanny in the early days, but I stole her away as often as possible. I bathed her so much her skin peeled and I was admonished. She preferred to be held, to be in laps and slung over shoulders, and even when she learned to walk she was still a cuddler. She slept in my bed once she could toddle herself there, and I never kicked her out, which irritated Cricket, who had ideas about independence and grit.

Blake had replaced me as her favorite person in the world. I wasn't angry about this. May we all be so lucky in love.

"I brought a note," she said abruptly, my pair of pearls now in her ears as she revealed a card from her jacket pocket. "For Dad."

"I see," I said, not knowing what else to say. I'd been to our father's grave, once, soon after he'd been laid to rest. It was in the south corner, with a view of the river, and I'd brought a small Christmas wreath with white roses and a red bow. I'd considered him differently then. I thought I'd known him.

Wallis waited, assuming, it seemed, that I would have my own offering. But I ducked away from her eyes and instead lunged for my sneaker before it ended up in the dog's mouth.

"Aren't you going to ask me what my message says?" she asked.

"It's yours," I said, wanting this day to be about us, not my father. "You don't want it to stay private?"

"From you? Why? It's a letter of forgiveness. I'm in a good place. I have a good relationship, a good job. I'm ready to release the resentment. Love and light, you know?"

I'd thought time would be a positive force, moving me further and further away from the pain of what Gregory had done. But I was finding the opposite was true.

For Wallis's sake, I kept this to myself. "Love and light," I echoed.

⌒

We parked Blake's Audi near the cemetery, in an adorable part of town with two-story row houses and tree-lined streets. Wallis would have been happy to walk slowly, enjoying the neighborhood that reminded her in many ways of her beloved Georgetown, but Crabtree had other ideas.

He dragged us to the iron gates of the cemetery and, once inside and off-leash, took to the muddy grass with a woof that sounded almost human in its joy.

We trailed behind, trusting him to lead us through the cobbled paths and worn routes between headstones. It was the time of year when our jackets became too heavy, after the gray skies and ice storms of winter, and we both regretted bringing them. With the dog occupied, Wallis turned her attention to me, asked me what was new.

"Nothing much," I said. "What's new with you?" I thought she might bring up what happened last weekend, when she and Blake had been caught by a camera together at DC's annual march for science and, more broadly, logic and facts. Wallis had been carrying a sign that said, *The oceans are rising…and so are we*, and appeared to be shouting, or cheering. Blake had a smile on his face. They'd been holding hands. The picture had made a brief splash on social media, enough to reenergize the worst of the trolls.

"Nothing much." Wallis twirled the leash in her hands and grinned. If she was concerned by the picture, and the reaction to it, she certainly didn't show it. "What's new with you?"

I laughed as I nudged a rock with my toe. "You go first."

"Nose game."

She beat me, as usual, as Crabtree returned, threading through our legs and looking for praise for getting mud up to his belly. Wallis bent and stroked his neck affectionately, and he was off again.

"Really, I just want to hear about you," I insisted as we continued walking. "You have this amazing job. You're rubbing elbows with television stars and famous comedians at all the cool parties. You're in love. Your skin has never looked better. How do you do it?"

"You're deflecting," she said, amused. "You know, I texted you the other day—how are you, what's new, what are you up to? And when you responded *hours* later, you sent me a GIF of Elmo shrugging. What does that even mean?"

I had only a moment to process this question before Wallis cursed. "Crabtree!" she yelled, "you stupid dog. Get back here!" He had charged through a copse of cherry trees just on the verge of budding and then disappeared, and as we followed in his direction, we saw, a few rows away, what seemed to be a press conference around a modest headstone. A woman in a magenta pantsuit was being interviewed, a video camera on a tripod recording it. Circled around were various staff, presumably, and a few other members of the press corps, credentials on lanyards, thick-lens cameras. "Damn. Damn," said Wallis. "Where did that dog go?"

A minute later we spotted him, scampering about, perilously close, in fact, to the media event. Birds glided above, occasionally diving toward him as he stood on his hind legs, reaching, jaws snapping.

"The dog is going to be on camera soon if he's not careful," I said as we jogged toward him.

We managed to wrangle him when he was distracted by a particularly pesky bird. While Wallis clipped his leash on, I knelt in the grass, holding his torso. From this closer position, I was now able to fully observe the scene.

"Wallis," I stammered with the wisps of breath that were still left in my lungs. "That's Atlas." He was listening intently and taking notes, his stance that of someone engaged but not overly eager.

Wallis looked up, and the color was gone from her face

in an instant. Because standing right there with him was Melinda Darley. "What do we do?" she whispered as we studied them from our crouched positions among the marble angels.

Melinda Darley was holding forth, her shoulder-length blond hair flipped out at the ends like a sixties housewife. She wore trendy sneakers and gold drop earrings. I thought of her recent words about Miles after he'd criticized her on the Senate floor—he and his office were unfit to run a *moral* democracy, she'd said. That word—*moral*—I'd felt sure was aimed directly at me. The unfairness of it, less than two weeks later, still smarted.

Crabtree, ever the clever dog, must have sensed our shock and took the opportunity to lurch forward, his leash flying out of Wallis's hands, and head straight at the scrum like a ball to pins.

We watched in horror as Melinda Darley paused; the reporters lowered their pencils. The dog vanished, *again*, along with the echoes of his jangling collar tags, and all eyes turned to us, cowering above the remains of a Civil War soldier.

"Daisy?" said Atlas.

I stood, brushed off my knees, as he approached, clearly confused. "Hi," I said, like this was all perfectly normal. I'd hoped my aforementioned *space* from Atlas would have given my feelings of mortification post-kiss time to diminish. I'd been wrong.

"Hello," he replied. He seemed happy to see me, in spite of my recent history of dodging him. "Was that a dog I just saw, or a heat-seeking missile?"

Wallis's eyes were on Melinda Darley. "I don't know what

to do," she said quietly, chewing her lip, and I wasn't sure if she meant about the dog or the senator.

A pair of sunglasses was hanging from the top button of Atlas's shirt, and I saw myself in their reflection. Inside I was shaking, but at least outwardly I looked calm. This image gave me confidence, and I did a decent job explaining to Atlas why we were there. When I asked the same of him, he gestured toward Melinda, who was now partially blocked by the crowd. "I'm profiling that gang in the Senate that calls itself 'the outlaws.' It's a fast turnaround, unlike some other work." He glanced at me, and I realized he meant the story about my father. "But it will make me some good money. I do have a mouth to feed." Then, as though I didn't get the joke, he added, "Mine. *My* mouth. I mean, me."

"She's letting you profile her?" asked Wallis, still in a daze. "Can you…introduce me?"

"Well, she's not giving me any special access," Atlas said. "But she can't prevent me from following her around, can she?" He shrugged. "It's not so bad. I'm not so much interested in writing stories about heroes. Frankly, they're never that interesting."

I thought of the wedding, of Atlas's breath, my name on his lips: *Daisy.* I had hoped this word, in his mouth, would've sounded like homecoming. Instead, it had sounded like an ending. "I know you prefer villains," I said quietly, unable to stop myself. "Isn't that why you're writing about our father, too?"

He had no answer for this. Wallis suddenly grabbed my hand. "I'm doing it," she said. "I'm saying hello."

She strode off into the crowd around Blake's mother, leaving me and Atlas by ourselves. Godspeed.

"Daisy," Atlas said. "I've been— You've— It's been a while, I mean. We keep missing each other."

I'd made a mistake at the wedding, kissing him. I did a trust fall, betting he'd catch me. I wouldn't make the same assumption again. Vulnerability would do me no favors. "Work," I said, watching Wallis approach her target, "has been nuts." I heard her ask, "Excuse me?" But then a man with steak-house waistline and an imbecile's half grin—I figured a member of her staff—hid her from my view.

"Right." Atlas sounded unsure. "How are you?"

My eyes were still on Melinda Darley as her "bodyguard" stepped aside, and she and Wallis were—hugging. Whatever I expected, it was not that. I had to consciously return my jaw to its normal position.

Atlas had to ask his question again. "I've been good. Busy."

"Yes," he said. "You said that."

"Sorry. I know." I focused on him. "I'm pulled in a thousand directions. Including now. I know I owe you an answer about the interview."

"Yes, I—" He stopped, noticing, as I had, Wallis beckoning me over.

"Excuse me." I had no desire to talk to Melinda Darley, but I was also itching to escape this conversation. "If you see that dog, just yell."

I made my way around a few stones, and then Melinda Darley was before me, diminutive but commanding, sipping from a takeaway coffee cup; burgundy lipstick stained the lid. I extended my hand.

"Absolutely not," said the senator in her unmistakable palmetto drawl. "Come give me a hug." I did as I was told. She smelled of rosy perfume and copper pennies. "I was just telling your sister," she continued, "that we're honoring the first anniversary of the death of that young doctor. Do you remember? He was in his car and swerved to avoid a bicyclist who ran a stop sign. Happened right on Capitol Hill. No? I see you don't recall. It was really unfortunate. He was from Spartanburg, originally, and was working at Walter Reed." She shook her head sadly. "Cities are setting up too many bike lanes. And don't even get me started on these scooters. There's a war on cars, girls."

This statement was so abjectly outrageous, it made me briefly forget the prior discomfort with Atlas. In fact, I almost smiled. But the impulse was snuffed out a mere second later, when Crabtree returned, seemingly out of nowhere, and reared up, placing two muddy paws on the front of Melinda Darley's fine jacket.

Wallis cried out. I think I might've cursed. Melinda Darley definitely did, and all appearances of civility dropped from her face like an anvil in a cartoon. Crabtree, with all the intelligence of one of the birds he so desired, jerked free of Wallis's grasp and made for the hills. "I'm sorry!" Wallis exclaimed as she gave chase, Atlas close behind her. "I'm so, so sorry!"

One of Melinda Darley's staff had procured a wet wipe, and she was rubbing the stains irritably.

"He's not our dog," I pointlessly explained. "I just—we're sorry. Excuse me, I better go help my sister."

"Daisy." Before I could make my getaway, she laid a hand on my forearm.

"Ma'am?" I said.

She quit work on the stain, gave the trash to her staff. Then she was leaning in, encouraging me closer. I noticed the blond fuzz on her cheek, the wool of her suit jacket, which she wore as easily as someone might wear pajamas.

"Your father," she said, "I didn't know him well, but he told funny jokes. His punch lines, I mean, they were really good."

This—from a woman who'd publicly accused my father of being a traitor and me and my boss of being morally unfit. Had I been unfair? I was caught off guard. "Thank you," I said, as sincerely as I could.

"You're a smart woman, right?" she asked, a finger tapping the corner of her mouth.

It took me a beat to pivot. "I'd like to think so."

She pressed her lips together, hummed. "Surely, you've already calculated cost/benefit of your sister's relationship with my son."

"They're very happy together," was the only response I could muster.

"That sounds like a shrug off." Again, with the lip press and the hum. "It isn't good," she said softly, "for either of us. You see that, right?"

Yes, I did see that. On paper, their relationship wasn't sensible, but I'd made the effort to get to know Blake, and the kind of person he was outside of his family. "My sister is a good person."

"So is Blake." She surveilled me, managing to look down her nose even though I was taller.

"Well, in that way, they are a good match." It felt odd to be defending a couple I had been so wary of a month ago, but the evidence of their love was everywhere, and all of us, even Melinda Darley, would have to heed it.

Wallis reappeared from behind the trees, lunged for the leash and missed. Then she was out of sight again. I should have run off to assist, but I had to hear, as unreasonable as it was, what came next.

"They aren't a good match," she said. "Of course you know that." Her lackey came forward, whispered something into her ear. "I must go," she said, then touched me lightly on my shoulder. "Good seeing you. Hello to Miles." She strolled away, sure-footed, her hands clasped behind her back. The crowd of reporters and staff closed around her like a pair of jaws.

Wallis and Atlas returned with Crabtree, all out of breath. "What were you guys talking about?" she demanded. "God, this dog. Never again. Were you talking about me?"

"I—no," I said, because I couldn't say the truth aloud, for then it would be real, and I would have to live with it, and sleep with it, and my bed was full of enough worry already. "Just...the defense authorization bill. Aircraft carriers, nuclear weapons."

"I didn't make a great impression. God, I made no impression at all. What did I even say to her? I was in some kind of fugue state... Shit." Wallis put her hand to her head. "We forgot about Dad."

"Another day," I said. I couldn't spend one more minute there.

Atlas, still breathing shallowly, managed, "Lunch this week, Daisy? I—I'd like to catch up."

"I'll let you know," I said, noncommittal, trying to keep a neutral expression as we said our awkward goodbyes.

I turned Wallis toward the cemetery exit and we began our procession out. Of course, now that I was desperate to leave, Crabtree moved at a snail's pace, probably exhausted from the most eventful walk of his short life. Atlas and I hadn't embraced, and I felt the drought of it on my skin as we made our way through the rows of graves and pine needles and first daffodils of spring.

"You're sure Blake is worth all that?" I broke the silence when Wallis and I were at last through the gates. "You're going to have to fight for him. Harder than you think."

But Wallis simply smiled to herself and said, "She hugged me tightly. I'm optimistic." Then she gave all her attention to Crabtree, leaving me alone with thoughts filled, unlike hers, with worst-case scenarios.

⸺

The pictures were leaked less than twenty-four hours later. Miles was the one who alerted me, texting me about a dozen screenshots in a row, then about thirty-seven question marks, also in a row.

The camera had caught Melinda Darley, Wallis, and me candidly. The smiles, the hugs. We all looked like friends. From the angle of the pictures, it seemed like they were taken by an enterprising photographer, one who'd undoubtedly received more money for these photos than from any related to Melinda Darley's graveside presser.

I knew I should resist, but I followed the links to the comments, then to the hashtags, and became lost in the consternation and scorn of the social media universe, in which mercy and measure were absent.

That night I did not go upstairs to see Cricket. Wallis called me. She knocked on my door. But she couldn't find me because I was outside, crouched on the curb outside our building, my face all but in the gutter. Because where else do you go if your phone won't stop ringing all day? Where else do you run when you are sure the floor will collapse under your feet, when you are positive your home will turn to rubble around you?

Wallis discovered me, eventually. She shook my shoulders. She told me to breathe.

"I'm fucked," I gasped. "I'm finished."

She knelt in front of me in the gutter, in the runoff and the leaves. "No, you're not," she said, wrapping her arms around my shoulders. "Daisy. No. You're. Not."

The force of her, the certainty behind her words, momentarily consoled me. I met her eyes, and she waited, silently imploring me to say *All right, yes, I believe you.*

The night stretched before us. Our breath came out in frosty clouds. Sirens, the sounds of go-go music a block over.

I couldn't give her what she wanted.

Yet still she waited.

Fifteen

The Monday after what I'd come to think of as The After-noon I Dug My Own Grave, Miles called a staff meeting. All eyes naturally turned to him, sitting at the head of the conference table, his sleeves rolled to the biceps, impatient to get started. He had been in rural Western Maryland when he saw the photo, parading down the main street of a charming small town celebrating its sesquicentennial, wav-ing flags and shaking hands, holding babies. I'd answered his texts, which ranged from irate to disappointed, from my bed, trying my best to apologize and explain, then ate dinner, lukewarm noodles washed down with a big glass of dread, and finally fell asleep around three in the morn-ing, fitful, my dreams full of nothing.

"We've been off to a slow start this year," Miles began. "As a result, we're not getting visibility on the right things." His eyes flicked to me. "What are we doing to get back on our feet? I want ideas. And if someone tells me to rename a post office, I'm going to lose my mind."

Tariffs, someone said. That domestic violence act, said someone else. A good plan to get on board with the marijuana decriminalization act. That one is popular. Student loan forgiveness. Honeybees.

"Daisy," Miles said. "What have you got?"

"Could ask DOT for more money to get high-speed rail running," I said. "Northeast corridor runs right through Maryland."

Miles narrowed his eyes in concentration, clicked the button on his pen. "High-speed rail?" *Click, click. Click, click.* "Wasn't that one of Gregory Richardson's pet projects? I remember he was an early evangelizer. And investor, no?"

There was a knot in my sternum, right below my neck. Miles was right. What was I thinking? Those investments were long gone, but still, it could very well look to the average observer that I was trying to line my own pockets. I closed my notebook gently and wondered if I might have to excuse myself to throw up. "Student loan forgiveness," I said.

"Already been said." Miles quit his clicking, placed the pen in the crease of his notebook, and shut it. It didn't make a noise, but I winced nonetheless. "Everyone out, please, except for Daisy and Bo."

They followed his order and left the room. You'd think I was radioactive, the way they avoided my chair as they filed toward the door. Only Bo had mercy and inched his seat closer to mine.

"I'm disappointed, Daisy." Miles spoke as though these words tasted awful. "This isn't good work."

"I hear you," I said. "You're saying that I'm not on top of my game."

"This isn't therapy; I don't want you to just repeat my words back to me. Furthermore—" This was the type of man Miles was. He spoke with transitions. His sentences had semicolons. I felt outgunned. "If you had heard me, on your very first day back in the office, when I told you to lay low, be careful, we wouldn't be staring at pictures of you smiling with Melinda Darley all over my socials."

"If you look at them, though"—Bo wore glasses for reading; today, as he studied the aforementioned pictures on his phone, I noticed they needed a cleaning—"we can tell it was Daisy's campaign trail smile, not her real one." He braved a glance at our boss, gauging his reaction, as did I.

"Stay in your lane." Miles raised his finger at Bo, and my friend's valiant stand was over before it started.

"The optics aren't great," I conceded. Above us, one of the fluorescent light tubes in the drop ceiling hummed and flickered; I *really* hoped its death rattle wasn't an omen.

"I was forgiving after all this shit with your father. Because that was him. That wasn't you. However, now your sister is dating a Darley and you're both caught hanging out with his mother." Miles's finger focused on me now. "I can't be linked to that woman, Daisy. I can't be near enough to smell her perfume."

"I get that." If only I had a picture of my eyes that morning, red-rimmed, dark purple half-moons underneath, maybe I could prove to him that, yes, I *get* it.

He closed his eyes for a moment, inhaled with his full body. "Obviously you don't. And it concerns me, because we have things to do, and battles to wage, and you don't seem like you're here. You seem like you're somewhere else, flouncing around in a world where my reelection doesn't matter, and love conquers all."

"To be fair," I said, trying to diffuse some tension, hoping this new approach might help my case, "I've never flounced anywhere in my life."

Out of the corner of my eye, I saw Bo hide a smile behind his fist. Miles didn't laugh, but one side of his mouth did inch upward, which I counted as a victory. Still, he went on: "You're making mistakes, Daisy. You're fumbling on easy plays. It makes me think—" He stopped and recalibrated. "I think your father's death and the news of his royal fuckup has affected you more than you realize. Maybe you came back to work too soon," he said.

"No." My reaction was quick, vehement. Without work, then what? This job was the only thing in my life that was making sense.

"The shit with your father, that you couldn't control," Miles said, softer now. "But this you could've. Take some more time off, okay? I'll call you in two weeks. Deal with your family. Be there for each other. I know things have been difficult, and it's clearly getting to you. Bo, you're acting COS."

Miles stood, adjusted his cuffs, and left the room. Outside, the sounds of business—phones, footsteps, shuffling paper. Someone had turned on the television in the press office, and it was too loud. Commercials for diabetes medicine blared. Catheters would come next. Then, life insurance for the over-fifty.

"That was tough." Bo studied me in his typical way. That is, it felt as though he was doing some back-of-the-envelope calculations about my mood and what he could say that wouldn't hasten my spiral.

"An understatement." I stared at my phone. I needed to look busy so I didn't look ashamed. I'd helped Miles get elected; now he felt I was deadweight. "But that's business."

"He's angry about the picture," Bo said. "Once the news cycle changes, he'll get over it. They'll all get over it." His hand squeezed where my shoulder muscle should have been. Instead, what did he feel? Flesh, padding, softness—no real definition at all.

My phone I placed facedown on the table. Its protective, rubberized cover used to be bright white before time and everyday use and the occasional mishap soiled it into a beigey gray. "Miles is right," I admitted. "I'm off. I'm not performing like you all need me to."

"You make yourself sound like an internet router," said Bo.

"Unplug me," I said. "And plug me back in… You know what gets me?" I spun my chair so we were facing and, carefully, removed Bo's glasses. It was stuff like this that made people confuse us, early on, for a couple. There had been a night on the trail, with red wine and long conversation, hotel room, barefoot possibilities, when I briefly considered him. He was wholesome and unfussy and kind and *there*. But he wasn't Atlas. And, despite the copious amount of wine we'd consumed, I could tell he wasn't thinking of me when he spoke about wanting love in spite of—because of?—our eighty-hour workweeks. "There are so many single men in this town." I used the edge of my cardigan to wipe the smudges from his lenses. Satisfied with my work, I handed them back to him. "And Wallis finds herself Blake *Darley*. I can't fathom the odds."

He adjusted his newly clean glasses on his nose. "It's so..." he said, gaze drifting to the awful popcorn ceiling.

"Inconvenient!" I finished for him, laughing, because it was either that or cry.

Bo folded his hands neatly on the conference table, frowned at them. "For me, too."

He was right. He'd be doing my job—and his—for the next two weeks, without an increase in pay. This was not just an inconvenience. It was an imposition. "I'll be back in fourteen days," I promised, nudging him with my shoulder. "I just have to figure out what in the world I am going to do in the meantime."

"I think I have an idea. Well, I'll borrow an idea from Wilde." Then he straightened, and recited one of his favorites:

"'Nay, let us walk from fire unto fire,
From passionate pain to deadlier delight,—
I am too young to live without desire,
Too young art thou to waste this summer night...'"

When he finished, I gave him a little applause, and he bowed in his swivel chair. "Are you suggesting that I go snag myself a boyfriend?"

He chuckled. "Wilde is reminding you to have some fun. In other words, he and I both think you need to get out of DC."

"I almost was fired a minute ago. And you're asking me to plan a vacation?"

"Fair enough." Bo sighed. "I can't believe I'm saying this, but I'm considering a visit back to Charleston."

"When was the last time you were home?" I asked.

"About four years," Bo said, "give or take. The family's come and visited me in DC, just how I like it. Going home feels harder, somehow, than them coming here. It feels like I'm on their turf. When I go to Charleston, that's when the wheels fall off. I always come back needing twice as much therapy per month." Bo had skipped college, and his mother, seemingly the only one who cared or remembered, liked to remind him of it often.

"Then why are you going back?"

"My twin sister is having an engagement party. Attendance is mandatory, according to my mother." Bo stood; so did I. I had an office to shut, a walk of shame to complete. "Think about it, Daisy. Take a break from DC. Some good might come of Miles kicking you out of here. Even if you leave just for a night."

Bo's advice was tempting—to sail away for a minute, to move out of range from the faces who knew us, from the cameras that found us, even in graveyards. The alternative was to stay here, in DC, inventing busywork, crossing off days on a calendar.

My phone rang. It was Cricket. Her computer mouse had stopped working, and she really couldn't use the track pad, and could I come by during my lunch break to help?

"Lucky for you, Cricket," I said. "I actually have the afternoon free."

Sixteen

The door to my mother's apartment was unlocked, so I let myself in after dumping my work bag in my apartment on my way up. No need to carry it around everywhere anymore.

"I like your sweater," I said, catching a glimpse of Cricket puttering in the kitchen. Her top looked familiar, a form-fitting crew neck with a swirl of sapphire sequins on the front. She had worn it to one of Gregory's holiday parties a few years ago. "It's very sparkly."

"I had a lunch," she said as I sank into her sofa. "Wine?"

"It's three o'clock."

"And?" She walked out of the kitchen holding the bottle, giving it a little shake side to side. "I feel like celebrating."

"Okay. Fuck it." I cursed so rarely, this really shocked her.

She said *Daisy!* in a way that made me seem like a teenager in need of stronger boundaries. And I said *Oh, Mom*, in a way that made it seem like I was bored of her over-reactions. Then we both chuckled and she poured me a glass of wine. If she recognized my laughter as forced, she didn't show it.

"Who did you lunch with?" I asked once she situated herself comfortably next to me.

"Whom." Her feet were covered in nude-colored stockings—always stockings when it was cold, or slacks. This was a woman who thought a pair of ironed jeans was loungewear. She pointed her toes out in front of her; they were painted the usual pale pink. "A friend."

"Do I know this friend?"

"I think not," Cricket said, taking a slow sip.

"Is it a boy?" Wouldn't that be fun? Cricket's love life accelerates while mine reverses off a cliff. I'd been drinking too fast, and my wineglass was already half empty, which was a shame, as I really could've used more.

"Jesus, Daisy," my mother said, swatting my leg. "Don't joke."

"I'm not joking. Why else would you be cagey about who you had lunch with?"

"Whom."

"For God's sake."

"It's for a job. Okay? Will that make you feel better? I saw my old friend, one of the few who still keeps in touch. She works at the Smithsonian, and gave me the name and email of the volunteer coordinator there."

Cricket's philanthropic inclinations were back, and the timing couldn't be worse. "Just volunteering?" I asked, gifting myself another gulp. "You have a master's degree."

"I know." She was curt. "We need money. I heard you the first one hundred times."

I stared down into the remains of my wine. What leg did

I have to stand on? None. Thanks to a series of unfortunate events, it had just been lopped off at the knee.

Now, it seemed, I'd arrived at the unavoidable. I'd have to share the events of the day. Because how long could I keep my job situation from her, from Wallis, even, when I lived beneath them? When the debt of one became a debt for all? Not a viable option. So, I went with the truth. "Today… well…" I started. "Miles told me to take time off. And since I used up all my PTO and vacation in January, I'll be on unpaid leave for two weeks. And we just got a bill from the lawyer. And my rent is due." I started strong, kept it together, kept steady. But my voice wobbled near the end, rising in pitch, unable to conceal my anxiety.

"Darling," she said, calm, but not before I saw her widened eyes. She took my glass and placed it on the coffee table alongside hers, then wrapped her arm around my back. "You see so much that needs to be done in the world," she said. "You see so much that needs to be done for this family. It's a wonderful thing." She looked at me like I was her baby, like she would gather me into her lap if she could. "I know that's what drives you. But it is all right to rest, Daisy. It's okay to take some time. You don't have to do everything."

"I'm not good enough to—" I cut myself off because the list of what I was failing at felt so long I didn't know where to begin.

But Cricket smiled, one of a coconspirator, and leaned close. "You're not qualified to do everything. There's a difference. I'm not qualified to change the oil in my car—or, I should say, the car I used to own—but that doesn't mean I'm no good as a human being. It just means I needed to hire a certified mechanic."

"I wouldn't know how to change oil, either," I said, unconvinced by her words. "And Grandduff owned car dealerships."

"Yes, and you helped me write the jingle! Remember? *If you're talkin' about savin', you're talkin' 'bout gettin'…*" she prompted me.

"*Rich…*" I sang, obliging but unenthused.

She belted out the grand finale, still able to hit the high note after all these years: "*…ardson's!*"

I clapped limply and Cricket patted me on the back. "No oil," she said, "but she can write a dynamite hook, ladies and gentlemen."

"I should put that on my résumé," I said, resting my head on her shoulder. "Maybe it's time I update it."

"Nonsense," said Cricket. "Miles won't even make it a week before he begs you to come back. Mark my words. In the meantime, enjoy your time off. You've barely had a break in months. Even when you took the time in January, you were still working to get us on our feet. Take it one day at a time. One thing at a time, even."

I breathed deeply. Two weeks. It was manageable. I could do this. "One thing at a time," I said to Cricket, picking myself up from the couch, giving myself a mental brush off. "Starting with your broken mouse."

"And then a nap."

The mouse was not so much broken as unplugged from the monitor. Although it took me all of ten seconds of labor, Cricket was pleased.

She had nothing else for me to do. No documents to review, calls to make, ice maker to fix, nothing. Believe me when I say I asked. I considered for a minute organizing Wallis's jammed closet, but I decided against it. Knowing Wallis, within the mess there would be a system, and I would just disrupt it. I was on my way out the door when Cricket summoned me to her bedroom, where she still had a few unpacked boxes stacked in a corner.

"The last of them," she said, ripping off the packing tape. "Your and Wallis's stuff from P, I think. Once you go through them, I'll be able to move my computer desk to that corner. Maybe I'll get one of those chairs that's really an exercise ball. Work on my abs."

"I knew you were thinking about boys," I said, smirking.

"My new abs will not be for men," she said before she slipped from the room with a wink, her laptop tucked under an arm. "They will be for me."

Cricket had been only marginally accurate. The boxes did contain some of my old history and poli-sci textbooks, but mostly they housed my father's yellowed photographs from college and early adulthood, some Princeton yearbooks, and seemingly the entire cannon of Shakespeare's tragedies, all in soft paperbacks printed before 1970. Gregory Richardson had written his name in pencil on the inside covers of many of them, as well as the address of his eating club, where he could be found if the book were lost. Underneath his name, he'd written, *President, Undergrad Student Assoc.*

I wasn't sure what to do with these relics, so I called Cricket back. She crouched next to me. "He took a class with a famous professor about Shakespeare," she said. "It was the semester I met him."

"He never seemed like a Shakespeare fan," I said.

"I think he wanted to believe he'd be good at it." Cricket put her wineglass down on the old parquet floor and leafed through a copy of *Richard II*. "No notes in the margins." She smiled weakly. "Not surprising one bit. He wasn't so interested in subjects that didn't come easy for him. I wonder why he kept them. Maybe he had plans to read them, eventually. He had so many plans, I couldn't keep track."

Before she went back to the living room and her laptop, I asked what I should do with the books. Over her shoulder, she said, "You might ask Wallis. She loves The Bard."

I turned back to the boxes, all the stuff from a part of my father's life when he'd demonstrably done good. He whipped the votes to allow women as members of his eating club, mobilized antiwar protests, marched for civil rights. Over the decades, he'd worn these actions like a cape, and they'd made him appear noble to most of the public. To me. But the rot from the last years of Gregory's life had spread, and I was finding it hard to keep the good he did from being spoiled.

Perhaps Atlas's article could help with the containment. *But*, even if I were interested in excavating the past, I'd just been placed on leave because of *one* photo. Miles's strident reaction hadn't come as a complete surprise. After all, he'd been generous to keep me on after my father's scandal; less confident, less loyal politicians would have made a different call. But his political pragmatism also ran deep, and I could now predict with some certainty how he would react if I sat down with a journalist to discuss in-depth my father's legitimate crimes. There would be no leave of absence next time, and my window to redeem myself in the wake of Gregory's scandal would slam shut.

Atlas's article was scheduled to run in a couple weeks. I hadn't seen him since the graveyard, and I knew he was still waiting for my answer. It was time to deliver it.

It took only one ring for him to pick up. "One second," he said quietly, and I heard the sound of a door shutting. "Sorry, just had to step out of a meeting."

"I interrupted you." My voice was timid, already regretful of letting him down.

"Blessedly." He chuckled. "What's up?"

Though I knew what I needed to say, the words were all of a sudden gone. I shifted the phone from one ear to the other. "Well," I began. Then I groaned. "This is hard."

"I think I know what you're going to say," he said, patient. "It's about going on record, isn't it?"

"I can't," I said. Now that he'd given me the opening, I found it easier to explain. Briefly, I summarized. Miles, the picture, the fire and the fury. "You understand?" I asked when I was done.

"God, Daisy. Miles is a fool for casting you out because of one fluke run-in with the enemy."

"He's not." Quickly, so as not to think too hard about what I was doing, I stuffed the majority of Gregory's old things back into the smallest box. "If I were Miles, I would've done the same thing."

"Really?" Atlas wasn't convinced.

"Miles had to protect his office. I could distract the public, his Senate colleagues, from his goals, impede on his ability to get things done, hurt his credibility." I held the phone between my shoulder and ear and took the box out of Cricket's apartment and to the trash room on the other side of the hall. "Cricket just gave me a lovely little pep talk. Part of moving forward means finding a way to protect myself, too. The Melinda Darley thing made that more than clear." Into the chute went the box, thudding on the way down—the sound, I imagined, of my father spinning in his grave. "So, first, I'm going to rest. Then, I'm going to try my hardest not to say the name Gregory for a few days, or maybe ever again. My family needs me employed. I need myself employed. Forgive me?"

"Nothing to forgive," he said. "You think this is the right thing, Daisy, and I believe you."

"Okay," I said, not knowing what else there was to say.

"Okay," he said. And the silence between us, usually comfortable, grew awkward.

Once I was back in the hall, I gave conversation another try, hoping our friendship could resume as normal without this decision hanging over our heads. "Well, I guess—"

But just then he spoke, too. "I'll let you—"

We both said *oops*, and Atlas laughed, but it was tinny and weird, and once again things ground to a halt.

"I was going to say, if you'd like, you can read the piece before it runs."

"Thank you. I'd like that," I said, simultaneously appreciating the gesture and dreading it.

He said something like, *I'll let you go*. And I said *okay* for what felt like the hundredth time. Then we hung up.

In the end, I saved a picture of Gregory in a suit—probably a class photo—and his yearbook from 1973. I also kept *Richard II*. I stored them in a plastic grocery bag in the back of my closet, imagining that one day, far in the future, I might draw Wallis's children around and say:

Here, you see? Witness the artifacts of a man who treated politics as an art until it became a business. Notice how it began. Remember how it ended.

April

Seventeen

A gloomy Sunday afternoon; winter was back, annoyingly, and DC was complaining that we had already suffered enough. There was talk of frozen cherry trees and frost on the Mall.

Thirteen days out of the office, and I was running out of things to keep me occupied. Out of habit, I still wrote tasks in my day planner. I didn't like seeing it empty of meetings, panels, commitments.

I'd made some decent progress on my to-be-read pile of books. I'd cleaned out my meager pantry, throwing away old pancake mix and bread crumbs. I'd organized my bag of bags, separating plastic and paper. I'd taken very old, empty shoeboxes from the back of my closet to the recycling room. I'd watched online videos and fixed my leaking bathroom pipe, and it took only three trips to the corner hardware store. When thoughts of Atlas's face or Miles's disappointment arose, I did not beat them back, but instead tried to look at them as objectively as possible, as though gazing at a passing cloud. My therapist was rah-rah about this way of framing problems, and I did have to concede that 50 percent of the time, it worked.

The other 50 percent, though, my fingers reached for my briefing binder before I remembered it wasn't in my bag. I scrolled compulsively, through my news feeds, through my work email, searching for tidbits I could use, new ideas, opportunities I might leverage with Miles. My two weeks were up tomorrow, and when he called I wanted to sound fresh, rested. I was decontaminated, ready to get back to making the world better. All this I'd have to prove over the phone; Miles was traveling for a summit. I knew it because I'd booked the trip. I was supposed to be going with him—to Paris, of all places. On the other hand, it might be to my benefit that he was overseas when Atlas's story was published tomorrow. Just in case it brought renewed attention to our family.

We hadn't spoken much since our previous conversation, but Atlas had phoned earlier and asked if he could pop by that evening to discuss the story. I'd agreed, hoping there would be no surprises, no twists. A courtesy call. That's what it had to be, what it needed to be. In the meantime, Cricket and I would be spending the afternoon at the National Gallery of Art. She'd proposed the outing in part, I think, because she was worried about me. The day before yesterday, she'd used my key to enter my apartment, and upon seeing me splayed out on the couch, unable to even pull my yoga pants up to cover my underwear completely, she'd tenderly suggested I get my hormones checked. She recommended yoga. I'd been half dressed for it already. She went out to the twenty-four-hour pharmacy to get me probiotics. *Tired*, I had said. *That's all*. I hadn't fooled her. So today I took care to put on real clothes with buttons and zippers, even put on a touch of makeup. I didn't want her to think I'd gone off the rails completely.

At the gallery, I was reminded that Cricket was my ideal museum buddy; my father never had any patience for them, and while Wallis was always appreciative, she zoomed through at her own pace, never bothering to read more than one or two descriptions. My mother and I, on the other hand, meandered the airy rooms, marveling at the bold hand of Calder, the deft, lacy brushstrokes of Monet's cathedral, following the sun as it dappled the marble floors. We stood for a long time in front of Titian's voluptuous Venus and Rembrandt's unflinching self-portrait. Cricket and I both observed the same feature in the painting of Emperor Napoleon: his infuriating smirk. Afterward, we got large coffees and wandered through the sculpture garden beside the Mall, watching children in Velcro sneakers run circles around massive bronzes. We sat for a while on a stone bench under a budding elm tree, huddled in our jackets, and read news on our phones. Every so often Cricket would show me a headline, shake her head, and cluck her tongue.

On our return to the apartment, I recognized Blake's car parked in the space directly in front of our building. I pointed this out to Cricket, and when we made it inside the vestibule, we paused wondering if we should call Wallis before barging into the apartment. As we debated, Blake himself came hurrying down the stairs. It may have been his hastiness or something on his face, but I felt no small amount of wariness as he approached us.

Cricket asked if he was all right.

"I am," Blake said, contorting his mouth into a smile

that was supposed to fool us into believing what he said was true. "I mean… I am physically fine." There were red splotches around his eyes, and his clothes, normally so neat, were hanging off his frame.

"Come back upstairs," Cricket said, concerned, motherly, patting his upper arm. "Something has clearly happened to have you so rattled."

"I wish I could." He swallowed hard and continued, "But I am actually on my way back to the airport. I have to be back in Charleston tonight. My mother has recently lost her reelection campaign manager. She's called for me to fill in while a replacement is found."

"But you just got here! Wallis said you only landed this morning." Cricket turned to me, as though I could change his mind.

"When will you be back?" I asked. Hurried footsteps on the stairs, and I thought it might be Wallis, coming after him. No, I soon saw—it was just the nice couple from 2B, who squeezed by us in the narrow hall with a friendly, *Hi, guys.*

"Not for a while, I'm sorry to say," Blake said after they'd gone out the front door. "I have to stay in Charleston through the summer at least."

"Through the summer!" Cricket exclaimed. "I don't believe it. You absolutely can find excuses to come back up here, surely. We'd miss you entirely too much."

"My mother has been flexible with me up until now," Blake replied, halting, awkward. It was strange behavior for a man usually so confident. "But she's pulled rank, so to speak. I have to commit myself to the work in South Carolina."

"I suppose Wallis will join you down there soon enough," said Cricket. "We can spare her some weekends, I suppose."

Blake's eyes fixed over Cricket's shoulder, at the neat rows of metal mailboxes on the wall. When he didn't respond, Cricket looked at me with amazement.

"The Charleston office must really need you," I said softly, wondering at my desire to console him. "I know you wouldn't be leaving so suddenly without good reason. We understand, right, Cricket? We—" I almost said *We trust you*, but I stopped myself when he shook his head.

"I don't really want to keep doing this," he said, pained. "The conversation I had with Wallis was hard enough. I have to go. Can you let me through? Sorry, but I just have to go."

We could do nothing but move aside, and he brushed past us without a backward glance, pushing open the door with enough force that it crashed into the railing outside. Cricket and I, from the doorway, watched him fumble for his car keys at the curb. Within moments, with a squeal of tires one doesn't often hear in the city, he was gone.

"What in the world was that about?" Cricket asked, letting the door shut before moving swiftly toward the stairs.

"They must've had a fight," I said, close behind her. We had made it to the second-floor landing and were trucking it toward the third. A lovers' spat was the sensible explanation, but my mind revolted. I couldn't picture an argument between two people so determined to be in perfect love.

Cricket and I entered their apartment, looking for signs of Wallis. She wasn't in the main room, so Cricket knocked gently on her closed bedroom door. "Wallis?" Cricket's palm rested on the door. "We just saw Blake downstairs. Are you all right?"

"No," Wallis cried.

"Ask her what's wrong," I whispered to Cricket. "Ask her if we can come in."

"Stop muttering about me," Wallis ordered. "You're making it worse."

"We just want to talk to you," Cricket said.

"Then just come in already."

Cricket charged in first; I followed. Wallis was curled on her side on the bed, and when she removed her hands from her face, I could tell she'd been crying. My throat tightened.

"What's going *on*?" asked Cricket, emphasis on the final word.

"Blake told his mother how serious we are last week. It did not go well." Wallis sniffed, wiped her nose with the sleeve of her sweater. "And, I don't know if this is a coincidence or not, but his mother's chief of staff in the Charleston office quit, and she wants Blake to fill in while a replacement is found. It's going to be, like, weeks." I noted here this word—*weeks*. Minutes ago, Blake had said it would be *months*.

"Wallis, my love." I moved past my mother, sat down next to Wallis on the bed, rubbed her arm. "I'm so sorry."

Wallis, embittered, laughed. Or maybe it was a groan. "I had convinced myself his mother's approval wouldn't matter to him."

"I would expect for this to be hard for him. I know his family is important to him, even if he doesn't agree with them a lot of the time."

She looked at me with swollen eyes. "I don't need an explanation, Dodo."

Cricket handed Wallis a tissue from the box on her side table. Wallis took it, blew, and commenced staring at her phone.

"I'm sorry," I offered. I turned on her floor lamp—it was the best I could do—and withdrew silently to the living room with Cricket.

———

Wallis usually cooked for us on Sunday evenings. She'd been into ancient grains recently, and fish prepared a dozen different ways, including shrimp and okra stew that had made Blake euphoric. I doubted Wallis would be in the mood tonight. I ordered pizza. When I'd hung up, Cricket busied herself getting comfortable next to me on the couch.

"I've thought it through," she announced. "This Blake thing."

I couldn't help laughing dryly, as it had been less than twenty minutes since he'd sped off like he'd just robbed us blind.

Cricket continued, "It seems clear as day to me. Melinda Darley's hoping, no doubt, that distance will dull Blake's love for Wallis, and that the whole relationship will suffer because of it. It is deliberate sabotage. There you have it. It makes sense, no?" I didn't challenge this; she'd summed it up remarkably well. Cricket nodded to herself. "Think, Daisy, about how he acted. He was haggard. Did you see how he was? Just awful. I have to believe this is a guy who was not acting on his own free will."

Here, though, I had to step in. "Cricket," I answered, "this is a grown man you are talking about. Even if what you're saying is true, Blake is a person who is capable of living a life independent from his mother's wishes. There are other jobs. He could've made it clear to his mother that Wallis was a nonnegotiable. In your theory, the fact that he *did not* choose Wallis over himself is suspicious and, I'd argue, very telling." He'd hurt my sister, and the more I thought about it, the angrier with him I became. He had been a part of this family for the past couple of months, so how could I not have begun to think of him like a brother? I didn't want to believe anything could tear him away from Wallis. But he was gone, and what mattered to Wallis was his absence, not the reasons behind it.

"But, Daisy, you've seen them together. You know how much he loves her."

"I know what he's shown us." Cricket looked like she was ready to object, and loudly, so I put a finger to her lips and pointed to Wallis's closed door. This was turning into a conversation that I didn't want Wallis, as upset as she already was, to overhear.

"Can you honestly say you haven't had doubts? Not about how much he loves Wallis, but about his own—I don't know—resolve? To have a relationship like theirs takes a certain amount of steadfastness. It isn't an easy task for anyone, not even for someone who is in love." I recalled Melinda Darley's face in the graveyard when she'd said those proprietary words—*my* son—like a child guarding her toys.

"He loves her," Cricket maintained. "That we can all be sure of." She was seated on the edge of the couch now, ankles crossed. Her gaze seemed designed to disarm any further argument I might volunteer.

"Fine," I conceded, though I was far from satisfied. "But let's focus on protecting Wallis's feelings, and not defending Blake at the expense of them."

Before Cricket could answer, there was a knock at the door.

A second later Wallis burst out of her room. "Who is that? Is it Blake?"

"It's probably just the pizza," I said, but she lunged to open the door.

We were both wrong. It was Atlas. I couldn't believe I'd forgotten him. For weeks, I couldn't get him out of my head, but the minute I do, he turns up. I watched for Wallis's reaction, wondering if I should tell him to go, but Atlas was probably the only person in the world she could forgive for not being Blake Darley. She hugged him, drew him inside. I stood, feeling unprepared, and shaky, and—oh, God, he looked so nice and I hadn't washed my hair since Thursday morning.

"I knocked on Daisy's door downstairs," Atlas said, obeying Cricket's command and taking a seat in one of the wing chairs. "But then I thought since it was Sunday evening, you might all be up here."

"Sorry," I said. "I—we—" I checked Wallis, who shook her head. This stuff with Blake, it seemed, she wanted to keep quiet. "It's been a day."

The door buzzer sounded, and Cricket said something about how popular we were. This time, it was the pizza, and she made business of going downstairs to retrieve it.

"How are you? We haven't seen you since—" Wallis stopped. I thought she was remembering, like I was, the events in the graveyard two weeks prior. "Well, it's been a minute. Where have you been?"

I cast my eyes toward Atlas. I couldn't resist. I thoroughly wanted to know what he would say. What had he been doing? Who was he with? Did he love me yet?

"Here and there," he said unhelpfully.

"Not here," Wallis said. "Unless Daisy has been hiding you."

"He's been in my closet the whole time." I laughed, but it was high-pitched and graceless.

"You're right." He laughed too, just as stilted. "I'm the boogeyman. Reporting is just my cover."

"Is this some inside joke?" asked Wallis. "I don't get it."

"I'm just kidding." I was making the awkwardness worse, wasn't I? "Boogeymen don't live in closets anyway. They live in mirrors." Yes, much worse.

"You're thinking of Bloody Mary," said Atlas.

"You're right!" Someone needed to stop me. "And Candyman." I made my hand into a hook and sliced it through the air.

"Oh, *my* God." Wallis looked at me as though I'd jumped the shark, as though I was pirouetting over the shark. Or as though I was the shark. "I think we've exhausted this topic of conversation."

Thankfully, Cricket returned, arms stacked with pizza, and beckoned us into the kitchen. I could barely get a box onto the counter before she was offering its contents to Atlas and encouraging him to have first pickings. We squeezed ourselves around the table that Cricket had placed in the part of the kitchen she referred to as the breakfast nook, using plates and silverware that were too fancy for pineapple and ham. I tried to make something that resembled normal human dialogue. Cricket, Atlas, and I discussed the weekend, the weather, the new restaurant a few blocks over with the amazing pho. Wallis's eyes glazed over. She picked at pepperoni, peeled her cheese off her slice, poking, never really ingesting.

"Daisy told us about the piece you're writing," Cricket said to Atlas. "How's it going?"

Atlas folded his napkin into a miniature square. "It's going," he said, not sounding at all like himself. "We're... well, part of the reason I wanted to see Daisy tonight is that my editor and I have decided to push the publication date."

So, the article wouldn't drop just as I was returning to work. This felt like a blessing.

"My editor," added Atlas, "wants me to follow up on a couple things."

"What things?" My relief vanished.

But Cricket interrupted whatever answer Atlas was preparing. "Since you have more time, Atlas, you should interview Daisy! She worked with Gregory, and she would be a wealth of knowledge."

"Great idea," said Wallis, rousing. "Daisy should do it."

"I...have asked," said Atlas.

My mother and sister spun toward me.

"Definitely not," I said. *Folks are out for blood,* Miles had told me not so long ago, *and they'll settle for yours.* When they looked disapproving, I sighed. "I'm not really in the market for notoriety right now." I meant to come off light, breezy, in spite of the circumstances, but Atlas didn't smile. He turned his eyes back to what was left of his napkin.

"All right, so." My sister, suddenly galvanized, dabbed the corners of her mouth in a move that struck me as preposterously formal. "You don't want fame. What are you in the market for?"

"Peace of mind. Happiness." The stuff, in other words, that was eluding me now. "I suppose the rest of the world feels much the same way."

"And fame has nothing to do with happiness?" Wallis said.

"Fame, no." I thought of the photo of me smiling at Melinda Darley. "Maybe fortune." I thought of the little cottage on the lake that was no longer ours, and my old bedroom on the top floor, and the childhood summers spent under the slanting gable, with its painted floors and iron bed and stacks of books I devoured when I was supposed to be sleeping. I'd caught a trout in that lake once, after just four hours and six failed reels. Gregory, uncharacteristically patient throughout, had celebrated like I'd won an Oscar. We'd been happier at the lake; my father, too, was less of his politician character, less thin-skinned and more—Dad.

"Oh, Dodo," Wallis said, pushing her plate aside. "I think you're just saying that because we've lost all ours. I don't need a fortune to be happy. Just enough to be comfortable."

"I think," I said, "that your definition of comfort is my definition of luxury."

"We should all start buying scratch-off tickets!" Cricket piped in.

"I can image exactly what I'd do with my share of the winnings," Wallis said.

"I can guess," Atlas said. "You'd buy back the house on P Street." A beat or two of silence followed before he cleared his throat. "I'm sorry. That was the wrong thing to say."

"Not at all," Wallis said. "I don't mind thinking about our years in that house. I know it holds painful memories for Mom and Daisy, but I was always happy there. You're right. With my imaginary fortune I'd almost certainly have to go back to that house."

"Our riches, for now, remain imaginary," I said.

Wallis had no response to this, except to shrug. "We're not rich in anything. Not money, not credibility. But I still think Daisy should do the interview."

She soon excused herself with little attempt at civility, and retreated to her room. In her absence, Atlas seemed to withdraw into himself, leaving Cricket and me to clean the table wordlessly. I was rinsing dried red sauce in the sink when I heard him push back from his chair.

"There is something truly awful about cold Sunday nights," he said, coming up behind me.

"The Sunday scaries." I focused on the sponge.

"I always liked to have a full house on Sundays." Cricket sipped from a mug of tea and gazed out the window at the sidewalk in front of our building, the wiry, shapeless bushes that always seemed to be on the verge of death. She'd threatened, a week or so ago, to pull them out and plant some new rhododendrons herself. "Made things better. Your father always liked to either be out on Sundays, or have big dinners in. Do you remember, Daisy?"

"I do," I said, scrubbing a plate that didn't need it.

"Stay for coffee, Atlas, will you?" Cricket asked.

"I don't want to go back to my charmless apartment," Atlas said, "but I must."

Cricket soon left the room, with a look that suggested she thought she was doing me a favor. The dishwasher loaded, I dried my hands.

"I really meant to catch you alone tonight," Atlas said. "But then Cricket waltzed in with food, like she could sense I was starving." He paused, smiling slightly, hoping I might say something.

So, I did. "I'm glad to see you." I leaned my hip against the counter and hoped I appeared relaxed.

"Me, too." He ran his hand across his face. "I'm sorry I wasn't there for you like I should've been after Miles put you on leave. I've just been traveling so much." He crossed his arms, his fingers drummed against the short sleeve of his T-shirt. "It's a flimsy excuse, but—well, I've been in Arizona, actually."

"What's in Arizona?" He dropped his eyes. "Oh," I said

quietly, getting it. Gregory Richardson's lover. "Is she nice?" I asked. "Is everyone going to feel sorry for her?"

"Polite, yes. Overly so. She is determined to charm me." He smiled reassuringly. "I won't be swayed, don't worry."

"And the things she's saying about my father… Will people end up hating him more than they already do?" I didn't want that. Although I knew he probably deserved it. These competing thoughts I held simultaneously.

Atlas chewed his lip. Then: "I've— In the course of following this story, I've stumbled into something. And I'm not sure. I need to dig further. I still have at least a dozen more sources I want to talk to, more research."

"More?" I asked dimly. "Is this why you're pushing the pub. date?"

He stepped near enough to see my hands trembling, as they tend to do right before bad news comes down like a guillotine. I think he saw it, because he continued gently, "Daisy, your father had been stealing from his office expense account for much longer than originally reported."

All my affect, all I had constructed to appear calm and cool in front of Atlas, was completely swept off its foundation. Unable to move, I cast about for alternate explanations, for reasons this might not be true. "How much longer?"

"Off and on, at least a decade. Maybe more."

"Decade." It was barely a word. More like an exhale.

I looked over Atlas's shoulder, into Cricket's living room, and back, further, into the past. And I saw my father, standing before a crowd, glass of wine in hand, ready to toast. He had placed himself by the fireplace in our sitting room in P, taller than most, his smile broad, appearing less tipsy than he actually was. *Go,* Cricket told Wallis and me. *Go, get up there.* Wallis must've been in high school; she clasped my hand as we joined our father. *I'm going to be brief*, he said, wrapping his arm around Wallis's shoulder, drawing her into his side and away from mine. She was delighted and leaned into him as I stood there, awkwardly, inspected, without a shield. *I just want to say how terrific it is to have the gang all here for our annual farewell to summer party. I'm preaching to the choir here, but we are going to have quite the fall. I find myself up for election, again. It seems like just yesterday I was asking you all for donations.*

Probably because it was yesterday! someone shouted. Laughter.

I see some of you are already pulling out your checkbooks, and that tells me I can wrap it up. My talented daughter Wallis will play the piano for us next. And Daisy will go around with the basket for the alms. Just kidding! Look at Daisy's face. Oh, I scared her. Anyway, cheers—to all of you, my dear friends. Drink, eat, and give generously.

Gregory had spent his career asking people for money. But he'd really been stealing it, even then.

My friend—my Atlas—watched as I slid down the cabinets to Cricket's cold kitchen floor, pulled my knees to my chest, and laid down my cheek. "We won't ever be free of my father, will we?" If this news came out, any hope for normalcy would be extinguished, blown out by the roar of the crowd.

"I'll kill the article," he said, taking a seat across from me on the floor, back against the stove, maneuvering his long legs so one was on each side of me. "I'll put the entire thing in the ground if you want me to."

"No." It wasn't an answer, more like a denial, because I couldn't believe my ears. This would be more than a kind gesture. It would be an enormous sacrifice. "I can't ask you to do that. You've done so much work. You paid for all that travel." And this, which was too painful to say aloud: *How can I ask you to give up the truth?*

"Just say the word." He was resolute. "The work isn't more important than you."

He could've offered this begrudgingly, hinted that I would be a coward to accept his offer. I studied his eyes, fair skies blue, the arch of his brows, and saw that he was sincere. And in spite of the pain of yet another of Gregory's betrayals, for once I felt I was not entirely on my own.

From the bedroom, we heard Wallis's music raised, then from Cricket's a request to *lower the volume, please.*

For my family, then. For Wallis, who was recovering from a breakup. For Cricket, whose life had already been upended once. For me, too, my career.

I uncurled my body, straightened my shoulders, and rose from the floor. Did it feel icky? Undoubtedly. But everyone already knew Gregory was a crook. Revealing this information wouldn't change that. Right? And keeping it to myself would protect our precarious new life from imploding further.

I waited for Atlas to stand too, then readied myself to do what was required. "Kill it," I said.

Without hesitation: "Done."

"Thank you." I jammed my hands into my pockets, not sure what came next with us. "Thank you."

He nodded. "I can't promise, though, that this will never come out. Miss Pell talked to me. She might talk to others."

"Yes." This had occurred to me. "But you've bought us time. The longer it's been, the less likely anyone will be interested." We would cross that bridge, in other words, when we got there. But I didn't even want to imagine it, somewhere in the distance. All I could see was what was right in front of my nose. *One day at a time*, as Cricket had said.

"Of course," he said. I couldn't tell if he believed this, but he smiled like he did, turned and collected his blazer from the back of his chair. "I've overstayed my welcome. We'll talk tomorrow, yeah?"

"Yes." Tomorrow. I liked this promise.

"And sometime, preferably sooner rather than later, you, me, ramen, video games."

"Yes." This one, more enthusiastic than the previous.

After he left, I regretted not hugging him closer. Maybe I should've said—*wait, Atlas, don't go?* Maybe I should've checked to see if he gave me one last glance before he showed himself out. Maybe then I would've let myself fall into his arms. There was a good chance, I thought, that he would've caught me.

━

I went to find Wallis. In the space of a few steps, I added, I subtracted, I tried to do some knotty calculations. Did I need to tell Cricket and Wallis? When was the right time to lay this at their feet?

Wallis was on her bed, slender feet tangled in the duvet, absorbed in her phone. I gripped her doorframe. "What can I get you?" I asked. "You barely ate anything at dinner."

She removed her headphones. She'd been listening to a Bon Iver song that seemed specifically designed to amplify melancholy. I repeated my question, but she declined my suggestions of ice cream, chocolate, whiskey.

Still, I lingered. I thought I should tell her what Atlas had found, not least because she deserved to know, but also because I was curious if she could've suspected. "I just—I think—" Despite my stumbling, Wallis was patient. She raised her eyebrows. "Did you—did you know that Gregory…?" Her phone rang, an interruption that managed to be both frustrating and welcome. She grabbed for it eagerly, then emitted a choked groan when she saw it was not Blake on the ID. Whoever was calling must've been really deficient, because she silenced the call and threw her wrist across her face.

"Let me be, Dodo," she said softly. "I'm sure Blake and I will figure out a way to see each other soon. And I'm going to be better then. All right?"

How could I detonate this hope of happiness? *It doesn't have to be today*, I told myself. *I can sleep on it.*

I washed up in Cricket's bathroom, amazed at her ongoing love affair with impractically tiny hand towels, and returned to the hallway. Cricket had taken my position in the doorway to Wallis's room. They must not have heard me emerge, because they were talking about Atlas, and their tones, although hushed, still carried.

"Here's what needs to happen," Wallis was saying. "One of them needs to act just the *slightest* bit in love, and the other will admit that they, too, have been in love the entire time. But Atlas is not cooperating with my plan. He talks to us both like we're his sisters. I'm annoyed with him."

"And Daisy, too," Cricket said. "She barely gives him any encouragement."

With their judgment, as well-meaning as it might've been, whatever optimism was leftover from Atlas's visit drained from my body. "I'm going." I decided I should alert them to my presence. Cricket turned, and had the decency to at least look mildly abashed. It was, I had to admit, a fitting way to end the evening.

Eighteen

I'd been away from work for twenty-one days, and with every passing hour my inner alarm howled louder. All week, I'd been unsuccessful getting Miles on the phone. Bo had tried, but Miles always had a ready excuse. *He says he's just walking into a meeting. He's just about to hop on the phone. He's getting ready for dinner.* Each morning, I thought, *today. Today he'll call and tell me to come back.*

Phone never leaving my hand, I spent my nights up very late on my couch, watching PBS documentaries, including one the previous night about NASA. I had tuned in just as an off-screen producer asked a former astronaut, *If you hadn't worked for NASA, what would you have done?* The man who'd floated near stars stated—and I'm paraphrasing here—that this question was dumb. He was an astronaut. There was no plan B. Still, the interviewer pressed, *If you had to choose another job...*

"Leave the poor spaceman alone!" I yelled at my television. See what happens when I don't have meaningful work? "He had no backup plan! That is fine and normal!"

His answer was succinct: *My choice would not be a person. I'd choose to be a satellite in gentle orbit, living usefully and long, unperturbed by earthly disturbances.*

Of course he would feel that way; he'd orbited earth, witnessed the sun rise over its curvature, had an unbroken view of our world as a whole. Maybe I'd be able to think of removing myself from the fray, too, after I'd actually accomplished something, years in the future. Something to look forward to! Until then, I had to work. We—meaning, our lawyers and bill collectors, the American taxpayer we were paying back—needed the money.

And the pressure to carry this out had only increased after what Atlas had uncovered. I hadn't told anyone about it yet. I'd simply informed Cricket and Wallis the morning his article was supposed to run that he'd opted not to publish after all, brushing off their questions, which hadn't been particularly pointed. Both had seemed preoccupied with other matters. Wallis, continually hollow-eyed and grumpy, delivered only one-word answers if she had anything to say to me at all. Cricket was always running to one thing or another; she'd begun work on a journal, she said, and spent hours at the petite desk in her room, one set of glasses on her nose and one on her head. Every time I considered bullying them onto the couch and forcing them to listen, I pictured Miles, in France, eating croissants and running through the itinerary I'd prepared for him, who'd never have me back if this news got out.

Fortunately, sensing my rising desperation, Bo had given me a tip: Miles would be attending tonight's book launch party for Wallis's boss—the perfect opportunity to *oh so casually* run into him and beg for my job. All I needed to figure out was the proper wardrobe for groveling.

——

After great deliberation, I selected a serious black pants suit and white blouse and made my way with Cricket to the Willard Hotel at the prescribed 7:00 p.m.

"It's great you came," Cricket said once we'd found an unpopulated corner of the ballroom, near the bar, where we could give side-eye to the familiar faces in the crush. Wallis's boss had written a memoir about fighting zealots, loons, and men who didn't know a uterus from a hole in the ground, so of course half of DC and a sliver of Los Angeles had packed into the Willard for the free drinks and food.

"That's about the fifth time you've said so," I said. "I came to a book party, Cricket. You're acting like I'm walking on the moon."

"Need I remind you," asked Cricket, waving off, to my chagrin, a waiter with small spring rolls, "what you were doing when I came down to check on you the other night?"

"No," I said, sipping from a glass of wine, not keen on reliving a low point.

But Cricket pressed on, "You were in bed, eating old pasta and chocolate pudding."

"The pasta was new," I said, snagging a crispy shrimp before Cricket could send that tray away, too. "And the pudding was vanilla."

"Daisy, I know you're upset about this Miles thing, but you have *got* to pull yourself together. A class, a hobby, anything."

"You think I'm living a meaningless life," I said. A baby-faced reporter eagerly roaming the ballroom with both a digital and video camera headed over to us, but now it was my turn to say, *No, thank you.* Our presence, still tinged with scandal, did not need to be cataloged.

"I don't want you to be lonely," Cricket replied.

She sounded more troubled than necessary, so I attempted to pivot. "I'm finding stuff to do," I said. "I went for a run the other day."

This cheered her. She'd always believed in the transformative power of aerobic exercise. "And how did that go?"

I hadn't been jogging in years. I had grand plans to run the trails in Rock Creek Park, but had barely made it out of Adams Morgan. I must've appeared to others like a machine on the fritz; occasionally my legs and arms worked like they were supposed to, but mostly I moved in fits and starts, and sometimes not at all. I returned home, red-faced, sweaty, and mortified. "It went well. I did three miles."

"Good work," said Cricket. "Now we just have to make you some money." She grinned. "Well, look at that. Your financial worries have finally rubbed off on me."

"Any day," I said, "I'll be back at work." Just then I spotted Bo by the door. "Guys!" I tried to temper my wave, but it was still entirely overeager. "L.K.! Mom, it's Bo and L.K. They just walked in. And Miles is here!" I think I actually said the word *yay*, but I'd like not to dwell.

Bless them, the gang did head our way. I got friendly squeezes from everyone, even Miles, who afterward greeted my mother with a firm handshake and a smile. "Mrs. Richardson," he said. "How are you?"

"Just fine, Senator, thank you. This is a very nice party, and I'm glad Wallis included me. I don't get invited to many things anymore."

Miles nodded. "I know this town has been very hard on you and your daughters. It is really unfortunate." I felt myself leaning forward, hopeful, so desperate for him to say *And I've been hard on Daisy, too.* Instead: "I'm only going to be able to stay for a few minutes. I have a caucus meeting in an hour."

"This late?" I asked.

"Breaking news," he said. "Sec Health has been asked to resign."

"Live by the sword," said Bo, "die by the sword."

"I'm sure you're going to get calls for appearances," I said. "We should try to book you on the Sunday morning shows." Around the circle, there was the kind of silence that comes when everyone holds their breath. All Miles needed to do was nod, or say, *Yes, Daisy, get on it.* When he did neither, I felt myself scrambling. "Sorry," I said. "I meant Bo should book you on the shows."

"Just keep holding fast," Miles said to me. "Everything will work out."

This platitude provided no comfort. I pulled at the sleeves of my suit jacket. "I'll keep my ears to the ground about nominations," I said. "If I hear anything—" But I had to stop, because one of Miles's colleagues, the senior senator from Florida, cut in with all the grace and delicacy of a yacht crashing into a dock. "Miles!" Senator Hopkins roared, grasping Miles's hand. "I thought there'd be a line to get to you. They didn't let any of your fans in, I see."

"I don't know what you mean," Miles said, extracting his hand.

"Don't be bashful," Hopkins said. His tie featured whales wearing sunglasses. "I've seen the way these college kids mob you. Hell, you got most of the Senate pages following you around wanting to pick up your trash." He then looked at me like I should back him up. "Your chief of staff is back, I see. Howdy, Miss Richardson. I guess Miles didn't fire you, after all."

"I'm not fired." My voice was an octave too high to make this statement truly believable.

"Right," Hopkins said, winking at me. "Well, once Miles decides to cut you loose, you can come work for me. My office in Tallahassee needs someone with half a brain. All I got down there is a former dentist who lost his license and a bunch of frat boys who are as useful as tits on a bull."

"Charming," I heard Cricket mutter.

"That's…an offer," was my reply. Just when I thought I couldn't fall any further, another floor collapsed from underneath me. At the very bottom, the Florida Panhandle.

"You won't steal Daisy from me without a fight," said Miles.

"Pistols or swords?" asked Hopkins.

"Fists," said Miles, droll, and I could've hugged him.

Another burst of laughter from Hopkins that could likely be heard across the ballroom. "Just think about it," he said to me, then clapped Miles on the back. My humiliation complete, Hopkins guided the conversation between proposed regulatory changes and his recent colonoscopy. "The doctor told me I was full of shit!" he said to only polite, perfunctory laughter. Miles met the eyes of L.K. and Bo, then excused himself to make the rounds. Miles gone, Hopkins also departed, and we shuffled closer to each other.

"The balls on that guy," L.K. said. "You're not working for him, Daisy."

"I'm working for Miles," I said reflexively.

"I mean—if," she replied.

That word—*if*—crash-landed in the center of our group.

I gawped at it. We all seemed to. My wine was warm and fruitless, but I finished it anyway. "I need another drink."

"Do they have your brand of chardonnay at this bar?" asked L.K.

I turned to her. "You know my brand?"

"Babe, we know your brand of tampons," L.K. said, threading her arm through mine. "Of course we know your drink of choice."

"I miss you guys," I said as I tracked Miles across the room, wondering if I'd get another chance to speak with him.

Bo nodded. "We miss you, too," he said.

"Before you all arrived," Cricket said gaily, encouraging us to shake off our somber faces, "I was about to encourage Daisy to mix and mingle."

"I'm happy to help," Bo said. "As the resident cool kid of the group, I can give Daisy some pointers. I take payment in the form of bourbon, which I need about a gallon of to make it through this party."

"Cool kid? You recently sent an email to everyone about the Oxford comma," L.K. said.

"The Oxford comma is what separates us from the un-civilized masses. I stand by that email."

"When I'm back, I'm going to leave an extra space after all my periods," I said. "Just to tick you off."

"I see Wallis," L.K. said, craning her neck to the right. "God, she looks so pretty. I wish I had that rack. Sorry, Miss Cricket."

"Jesus, L.K.," said Bo. Talking about tampons was fine, but apparently he drew the line at my sister's breasts. I think I saw him blush.

"No apology necessary," said Cricket.

"I'm just saying," said L.K. "Whenever the trolls start mouthing off about ugly feminists, let's just jangle Wallis around, like keys in front of a baby. That will shut them up for about two seconds."

"What's the latest with Wallis and Blake Darley?" Bo asked, sipping slowly. His eyes had located my sister across the ballroom, chatting easily with a group of suits.

"It's a long story," I said. I didn't want to talk about the Darleys here, not thirty feet away from Miles, but L.K. poked, both literally and figuratively, until I caved. "Fine," I said, slapping her hands away. "They are together, but Blake has been called back to South Carolina by his mother."

"She's on a mission to break them up," added Cricket.

"Judging from Wallis's mood the past few weeks," I conceded, "if that was indeed Melinda Darley's plan, it seems to be working."

"I believe it," L.K. said, and Cricket nodded approvingly. "Melinda Darley would sooner raise taxes than let Blake date Wallis without a fight."

"What does Wallis have to say about all of this?" asked Bo.

"Not much." I said. Fried shrimp guy was back, and we all helped ourselves, even Cricket. "I mean—she is in so much pain, we try not to bring it up."

"What!" L.K. cried, gesturing with her shrimp. "That would never happen in my family. My sister would jab until I gave up and spilled."

"In my family we let each other keep secrets," Bo said. "My mother still says"—he paused, affected the drawl—"'*Darlin', it's a beautiful day to leave me alone.*'"

"She does not say that." I suppressed a grin.

"I'm fixin' to take y'all to meet her," Bo said. Then his

face brightened, struck by a thought. "Daisy, now that you have the time off, why don't you come to Charleston next weekend?"

"Sure," I laughed, wiping my fingers with my napkin. "Why not?"

But Bo was serious. "Don't you think it's a good idea, Miss Cricket?" he asked. "My sister is having an engagement party. Plenty of eligible bachelors for Daisy. L.K., you come, too."

"I wish I could," L.K. said sadly. "I have a wedding in Vermont. And it's not even in the cute part. I'd much prefer Charleston."

"Charleston is simply fabulous!" Cricket clapped. "It's a perfect place to get Daisy out of her funk."

"Where would we stay?" I asked, hoping this might reveal an out. Did they not remember I had no income?

"With my parents," answered Bo. "They've got enough bedrooms in that house. It's huge. Interesting people always coming in and out. It's also the place where I was the loneliest as a kid. Go figure. Am I selling you on this yet?"

"I couldn't possibly impose on your mother in that way." I looked at Cricket. She, of manners and propriety, would certainly say something here. But, no. She still seemed enthused. "And during your sister's engagement party of all times!" I added for good measure.

"Now, Daisy," Bo said, clearly enjoying this, "here's what I think—you need to *impose* more."

Out of the crowd, Wallis appeared in a black cotton dress. *My* dress, I might add. She must've been in my closet recently. "Hide the gin," L.K. said, kissing her on the cheek.

"Wallflower has arrived." Bo's nickname for Wallis made us all smile.

"I'm so glad you all came," Wallis said. "I see Miles over there, too. Did you have a nibble? I made sure to order eel sushi. I know that's Daisy's favorite." The delicate gold bangles she always wore stood out against the dress.

Glasses clinked, the staff paused their canapé distribution, and the author of the hour gave a short reading of her memoir. When it was over, the room applauded politely.

Wallis took hold of my wine and helped herself. "What have you guys been talking about?" she asked. "Anything good?"

"I have put forward a proposition," said Bo, crafty, "that your sister should come with me to Charleston on Friday. As a matter of fact, you should come too, Wallis."

"No," Wallis said, wide-eyed, glass frozen to her lip. "Stop."

"True story," Bo said. "And since you're the type of girl who would enjoy wearing preppy clothes under Spanish moss, I think you'd like—"

"Say no more," Wallis cut in. "I think we should absolutely go."

"I agree," said Cricket.

I thought of Blake and his family, and their ancestral home in Charleston, probably some mansion with columns and a room just for the hunting dogs that Wallis was itching to see. "Let's just hold on—"

"We should leave them to discuss," Bo said to L.K. "I need another drink anyway."

"I'm looking forward to dismantling all your excuses, Dodo." Wallis crossed her arms over her chest. "So, please, do begin."

"I'm just not sure," I said after Bo and L.K. were gone.

"Cricket and I have a meeting with the IRS and the law-yers next week."

"And?" asked Wallis. "Bo invited us for a weekend. You'll be back in plenty of time for the meeting."

"How would you feel, Cricket, if Wallis and I just jetted out of town?" I said, turning to my mother.

"I'm a woman, Daisy, not a goldfish," she said. "I can feed and care for myself."

Next: "The airfare must be expensive this last minute…"

"I don't want to hear one word about the expense of it." Cricket was on top of that one, too. "I think I have some frequent flier miles tucked away somewhere."

"But work—"

"You and Miles are on a break." Wallis eyed me with such glee I forgot to be sad about the fact that this was true. "We have to go shopping. And you, especially, Dodo. All your clothes are terrible."

My darling sister. "Even the dress you're wearing?" I asked.

"Bring hats, too," said Bo, back from the bar, sliding in beside us. "If you have them."

"For the party?" Wallis asked.

"No." He grinned. "For church."

"I need another drink." I had the urge to stick my tongue out at all of them as I walked away. "Cricket, want to join me?"

"Am I in trouble?" Cricket said as we headed toward the booze.

"You shouldn't have encouraged this trip," I said. "Blake might be in Charleston. Wallis is going to go hunt him down."

"So?" Cricket said. We scooted past a group that included

a reality television star obliging people with selfies. "Why shouldn't she?"

I halted, stared at my mother, astonished.

Cricket saw my expression, shrugged, and kept threading through the crowd. "Maybe he's come to his senses," she said.

"And what if he hasn't?" I said, following again in her wake.

"Well, then, Daisy, maybe she'll get some closure."

"At what cost?" I asked, dodging a guest gesturing vigorously with a glass of red wine. "I've never known exposure to even more pain and possible humiliation to bring closure."

"Perhaps that is because you've never been in love."

An accusation, delivered so frankly, it took me a moment to really hear it. "That's not true."

Cricket grinned, lifted a finger as though she'd caught me and gave me a push toward the drinks line. "Get me another club soda, will you? I'm going back to your sister."

The wine was absolute crap, and I hadn't been planning on a refill, but this was what the night was doing to me. As I waited my turn, I stared at my phone, searching for a good reason for me—and Wallis—to avoid Charleston.

"You'd think they'd have another bar," said someone behind me. I was in the middle of a nice little headline skim, but glanced up briefly, murmuring my agreement and catching sight of a pair of gorgeous, private-sector-paycheck shoes the color of rattlesnake skin. I focused back on my phone, hoping I might be spared the inhumanity of long queue chitchat. "Daisy Richardson," the voice said, with just the slightest hint of bossiness, "you're ruining my big surprise."

I looked up in confusion, which swiftly became shock,

as she opened her arms for an embrace. Without full com-
prehension of what I was doing, I hugged her, smelling the
perfume of her hair, noticing her shoulder blades under her
jacket, feeling awkward and big-boned in her arms.

"I've done it, then," she said, pulling back and smiling.

I was incapable of words. When I spoke, I forced myself to do so cautiously. Calmly. "Ari," I said, wondering,
doubting, despairing. "What are you doing in DC?"

She smiled, her teeth uncommonly white, her canines
just the slightest bit wolfish. "Atlas," she said. "Why else?"

Nineteen

"Are you surprised to see me?" she asked again.

Ariel had been just a picture on my internet browser, a headshot I could inspect, but now here she was standing before me. The memory of Atlas's mouth on mine fluttered inside me, soft but persistent. Somehow, I stammered, "Yes. I am thoroughly shocked."

"I just landed last week," she said, clearly pleased. "And this is really my first night out on the town. And here you are. It's fate." The line toward the bar inched forward. "I have been asking Atlas for your phone number. I was hoping he could set us up on a friend date. After three years away, I don't have many friends left in the city."

"So," I said, trying to get my wits about me, "you're back to visit?"

"I've moved back for good," she said, blunt, smiling.

"Right," I said. "Totally." I looked for a lifeline. Around me were only the faces of strangers.

"Long-distance relationships are impossible. And trans-atlantic long distance for that matter. But this job appeared, and so I called him and asked if he was really committed to making us work. I mean, if he had met someone in the meantime here in DC, that would've affected my decision to move. I think I would've stayed in England."

My breath shortened and my fingers had started to tin-gle, but I didn't feel in immediate danger of a panic attack. I considered running away, changing my number. Any-thing to survive being stuck with her for the remainder of this line. "That's perfect."

"It is!" she said. Her lips curled upward. "As soon as I began the conversation about the possibility of me moving back, it was like the floodgates opened for him. He con-fessed that he was really lonely here. He even said that he'd been jealous thinking of me being single in London. Is it bad that I loved hearing that?"

In the wake of this question, for which I had no answer, I wondered if Atlas had confessed to my kiss. Ari's face was still perfectly composed, but I had to suspect that this was the type of statement meant to quash any claims I might have over him. "Atlas is"—I spoke like a child, reading a sentence aloud for the first time—"great."

Would the bartender judge me if I ordered a tequila sun-rise? I remember it tasting pretty decent in college.

Ari cocked her head, evaluated me. "What do you want?" she asked.

What did I want? Hmm. For my life to have meaning? For my sister and my mother to be happy and settled? For the air inside my lungs to feel like it was air, again, instead of salt water? And if I'm really being greedy, Atlas.

Ari continued to look at me expectantly, and I realized

we had made it to the front of the line. She'd been asking what I wanted to drink. The bartender, who must've been about sixteen, wore an oversize black vest and appeared very eager to serve us. "Wine," I said, gathering myself, remembering where I was and who I was supposed to be. "White." After she ordered her whiskey, she tipped, and so I felt compelled to dig through my wallet. I had a twenty and a one. The former was out of the question, so I guilt-ily stuffed the dollar bill in the tip bowl.

Drinks and fresh cocktail napkins in hand, we moved out of the way of the guests behind us. Ari took a sip of her two-finger pour, grimaced, then told me an overly long story about doing a blind taste test of cheap and ex-pensive whiskeys one night after a client dinner that had turned into drinks at a Central London speakeasy. She was the only person who could differentiate the top shelf stuff from the swill, she claimed. "Girl power," she said, finish-ing her tale and cheersing her glass with mine.

You beat the men at a whiskey tasting. Good for you! That is pre-cisely what the third wave feminists fought for. "You mentioned a new job," I said instead. "Atlas told me you were lobbying?"

Ari wrinkled her nose. "You can call it *legally bribing*, Daisy. I know you want to."

Legally bribing. I hadn't heard that one before. Bo and L.K. would love it. "I wouldn't presume."

"My firm had an opening for a principal here in DC, and I went for it. I may just make enough money to live here."

"The market has accelerated since you've been gone. There was an NPR story the other day—" I stopped my-self, wishing I'd ordered the tequila.

"Did Atlas tell you his rent is going up ten percent this year? His lease is up in two months, and I'm considering asking him to move in with me… Daisy," Ari said, "how old are you?"

"Thirty-four," I answered, mechanical, before I could absorb what she'd just revealed.

"Baby!" she exclaimed. "I am thirty damn eight. You still have some good eggs left in there. Mine are shriveled like capers. I have plans, and I don't have much time."

A waiter carrying a tray of tiny toasts and caviar stopped before us. Ari partook; I did not, unable to bring myself to eat roe in the middle of this particular conversation.

"I know I just met you," I said as the waiter moved on, "but I have the feeling your eggs will do as you command." I didn't mean this as a compliment, I felt too petty and rattled for that, but she flipped her hair behind her shoulder in a way that suggested she was flattered.

My phone rang; finally, someone who could get me out of there. One of the lawyers. A telemarketer. Someone informing me I'd just won a cruise. I'd take any of them.

But no—it was Atlas. "Speak of the devil." I showed her my screen.

"Please don't tell him," Ari said, covering my phone with her hand. "When I ask him to move in, I want it to be a surprise."

I pressed decline. She could have her secret. But also: Atlas could have my silence. He hadn't told me that Ari was coming to DC. Our friendship, I could only assume, wasn't as mended as I'd thought.

"I know you and I haven't known each other that long," Ari said, earnest, "although it feels like it's been years. Atlas talks about how close you are. He trusts you, so I trust you."

But he hadn't trusted me with this. And by this I meant her, her plans for a shared apartment, her agenda for her eggs.

"This is where I'm leasing," she told me, pulling up a page on her phone. "Do you think he'll like it? Or is the building too generic for him?" She had chosen a modern high-rise along the H Street corridor, once a thriving commercial part of town before succumbing to urban decay. People were saying now that it was "back," which I understood to mean there were new vegan restaurants and apartment buildings with rooftop pools and cabanas. I scrolled through pictures of a marbled lobby complete with coffee shop and zoomed-in shots of cabinets and light fixtures. "Will Atlas like it?"

"As long as it gets Premier League on the television, he'll be happy," I said, stepping back onto the heel of someone behind me, needing some distance but finding none. As I corrected my position, I somehow wound up even closer to her. The truth: he'd hate the apartment. No cozy corners or exposed brick. He despised open floor plans. Why pay DC prices to live in a glass tower that could be anywhere? We were in complete agreement on the subject. At least, we used to be.

"I just wish he didn't have to travel so much," she said sadly. "I just got here, and he's already going away. I'm rooting for him to get out of journalism." Ari smiled, if you could call it that. Then the edges of her mouth dripped back down. "He'll get paid a little," she continued. "No retirement. No benefits. And the owner of the paper he's freelancing for is a billionaire. I mean, come on."

"Atlas is great at what he does." I didn't like the fact Atlas had, by omission, allowed her to ambush me. But the way she was talking about his work—flippant, eye-rolly—I *really* didn't like. "We need more people like him."

Ari made a sound of agreement, then waved across the

room at a person she recognized. "He is trying, I guess, to convince people that the first amendment matters to democracy. If I were Atlas, I would've said a long time ago, 'You know what, I've done my part. You all go live in the small-minded world you've made for yourself.'"

"What would you have Atlas do?" I asked, miffed at her open cynicism. "Tend to a garden somewhere?"

"You've read Voltaire," she said. She wore a turquoise ring on her middle finger, and when she gestured, it clinked her glass.

"This is DC," I said. "Find me one bookshelf without *Candide*."

"I so admire people like you," Ari said. "You've got a sense of the world that is so unique. It's old-fashioned, isn't it? I'm so glad we're friends." Ari took the final sip of her whiskey and declared pleasantly that it was so great to see me. Before I could escape, she handed me a business card. "I do have to discuss with you something related to worky-work." She sung this last bit, as though it were part of a nursery rhyme. "With Miles on HELP Committee—well, we have to talk about the short list for new HHS secretary."

"As soon as we start to hear names, I'll be happy to have a conversation," I said, relieved that this was over and that she didn't know I was on leave.

"I'll give you a name." Ari tipped her head toward mine. "POTUS wants a *yes* man. Or should I say, yes *woman*. Word is she'll tap the Senate's own Melinda Darley."

I looked over Ari's silk-draped shoulder, searching for Bo. This could be an important bit of gossip, one that might help me get back in the fold. I said something to Ari about being in touch, then crossed the room, handing my half-drunk glass to a cheerful waiter with a tray full of crumpled napkins and shrimp skewers.

Bo was by the exit, putting on his coat, turning up his collar. "Melinda Darley," I said, catching him. "On the short list. We've got to tell Miles."

From his unchanging expression, I could tell this was already old news. "Miles already knows this, doesn't he? Why am I two steps behind everybody? I didn't used to be this way."

"I just found out five minutes ago, so, you're not two steps behind," he said, reassuring. "Only like half a step. Maybe even a third of one."

Around the room, everyone else was happy. Everyone else was socializing gracefully. Everyone else was publishing books and renting new apartments and doing great at their jobs.

Bo laid a supportive hand on my shoulder. "Let me know about Charleston, will you?" Then he left, taking Miles with him.

I considered returning to the party, finding Cricket and Wallis, stuffing some cheese straws into my pockets and making a mad dash for the exit. But Ari was still in there, and the thought of having to see her beautiful face again, hear more about the wonderful life she was building for herself and Atlas, destroyed my appetite. Coming here, to this party filled with accomplished people, people not under investigation by the IRS, people without crooked fathers, people who'd found love and kept it, had been a mistake. Knowing Cricket would absolutely chastise me later, I left without saying goodbye.

Twenty

My psychologist, Patricia, works out of a garden-level suite in an old brick house in Georgetown. The irony isn't lost on me that I seek refuge so close to the house on P. But she understands me, I like her voice, and she does not have a waiting room, which I appreciate. If you aren't sad and lonely already, a therapist's waiting room filled with other haunted souls and back issues of *The New Yorker* will make you so.

I was telling Patricia the very uplifting story of how, after the book party, I went home to my apartment and sat in my closet for about an hour. This will come as absolutely no surprise to anyone who's been in therapy, but before long I was talking about my childhood. "When I was young," I said, glad to have her willing ear and comfortable, feathery pillows to lean against, "I built forts in my closet on P Street. It's funny, how it happened, but around the time I grew breasts that closet fort became a fortress."

She told me that made sense. She reminded me that children often seek out quiet, dark spaces.

Patricia sits serenely in her leather club chair and is usually always wearing cashmere. She favors blue blazers and takes notes in a black jotter. She is always drinking cold sparkling water. She has one teenage son. That's the extent of my knowledge of Patricia. Although I hadn't seen her since my father's death for reasons that included lack of time and money, I knew I could count on her professional distance and impartiality, even though it had become nearly impossible to find someone in this town who hadn't already made up their mind about me.

"That childhood closet," I said, "was my sacred space. Until my father tore the door off its brackets one night I refused to come down for dinner."

She asked me how old I was when this happened.

"Fourteen. It was a cheap bifold that never ran smoothly on its tracks. He ordered me to come downstairs, so I yelled that I hated him and wouldn't eat with him even if he paid me."

I must've been scared, she observed.

Patricia had a small water feature, a fountain that gurgled over smooth rocks. I stared at it long enough that my heart rate slowed to normal. The truth—and I'd really never dwelled on it—was that yes, I had been scared. I'd been terrified. But my father eventually apologized. And it seemed like one of those things that should be forgiven. My father, powerful, under constant pressure, was a person, and people make mistakes. *What doesn't kill you makes you stronger.* My tennis coach had that on a bumper sticker. It sounded, at the time, wise and true. Now it sounded wildly off the mark.

Patricia redirected my attention to the particular closet I found myself in last night.

It was dark, I was sad, and there, among the skirts that

no longer fit and the special occasion dresses I no longer wore, even the dust bunnies around my shoes looked vicious. "The closet in my current apartment has a curtain. I sat in there and pulled it shut."

And what was I thinking about?

"My life not being where I want it, or where I expected it to be." I paused, reflected on the images from last night. "With work, especially. Miles unilaterally decided that I shouldn't be at the office. Which is really hard, because I want to be there. I need to be there."

For the money?

"Yes, but no. My father, he did good, but he also screwed things up so monumentally. Work was my only way of righting the scales. With time, perhaps I might've been able to do enough good to balance his bad. And now that chance is slipping away."

Patricia was curious. She asked what my mother said the night my father tore my closet door off its hinges.

I'd wanted Cricket spitting mad; I'd felt it a requirement of motherhood that she defend me. But it wasn't in her nature, and when she didn't, I understood. My closet door was evidence of what happened when one took a stand against Gregory Richardson. "She said I should've come down for dinner. And the next day, a stranger came and took the broken door out of my room. Cricket never replaced it, and we never spoke of it again. Maybe Cricket didn't want to replace it, probably because then she'd have to reckon with this awful thing my father did. Or maybe she left it off because she wanted to remind me."

Of what?

I glanced at the mantel clock, placed discreetly on the bookshelf behind her; I couldn't forget that I was paying for her to listen. Without a salary, it might be another four months before I saw her again. But we were over time, and I didn't want her next client to be delayed. "It reminded me," I said, "of how little power I actually had."

"Or, maybe," said Patricia, "your mother just didn't want you sitting in the dark."

"That's where I am, though. Despite her best efforts. I'm sitting in a dark room, scared, trying not to make any sudden movements. And I'm still getting clobbered."

"So," said Patricia, closing her notebook, "this seems like a simple solution. Switch rooms."

"How?"

"You mentioned earlier your friend had invited you to Charleston. Why don't you go?"

I protested. Blake was there. What if the cameras caught us again? All it would take was one uploaded video of uneven quality and bad sound, and any hope of getting back into Miles's good graces would be squashed, understandably. I would have to hold myself to the same exacting standard that the political world held him.

"Fine," Patricia said. "Stay here. Because it's working out so well for you." She looked at me, smiling, knowing she'd just dropped the mic.

Touché, Patricia.

I gave her a quick thank you. I did the whole graceless *goodbye, see you soon, maybe, depending on this little job thing.* "No problem," she said, understanding, yet firm. Patricia was nice, but she wasn't a charity. It went unsaid that if I wanted to return, it would once again be one hundred and twenty-five dollars for an hour. "Be well," she said. "Take the trip." Then I was out into the world again.

My route back to the bus stop took me a stone's throw from P. On a whim, I walked over. There was a dumpster on the curb, and a portable toilet partially hidden behind

Cricket's beloved Japanese maple. In the window—the same I'd paid to replace after the brick—construction permits. It was true, as Wallis had said to Atlas, and I had just discussed with Patricia, this house wasn't entirely filled with happy memories. But it had still been my home, and I felt uneasy witnessing its evolution into someone else's.

Curious, I started to climb the front stairs with the intention of peeking inside. It was a Saturday, and there didn't seem to be any activity. I thought it would be safe. I'd only made it to the stoop before I heard a voice call out. "Excuse me! Can I help you?" I whirled, feeling like an intruder caught in the act. On the sidewalk below, a man, toolbelt, hard hat, the whole ensemble, stared at me, arms crossed. "This is a closed construction site."

"Sorry!" I said. Then, hoping it might assuage his suspicions: "I used to live here."

His unfriendly expression didn't change. "Well, lady," he said, "you don't anymore."

I felt a throb of anger in my throat not only at his tone but because he was right. I apologized again, then scurried down the steps and across the street.

As I made my way back toward the bus stop on Wisconsin, I acknowledged that Patricia had been right; I was worried about Wallis and the scene she'd make if reunited with Blake, but I did need to change views. The touchstones of my old DC life were no longer recognizable. P Street, my job, even Wallis and Atlas were transforming, and all the while, what was I doing? Eating fried rice and doing laundry and playing *Minecraft* and burying the truth about my father. That is to say, nothing worthwhile.

I pulled out my phone. Pack your bags, I texted Wallis. We're going to Charleston.

Twenty-One

"That's a nice dress," Wallis said. We were on the jet bridge, bags wheeling behind us. Mine had a crack in its shell, Wallis's a bright green ribbon around its handle. These details encapsulated our different states of mind pretty well, I'd say. "Is it new?"

The dress was cream with ruffles around the shoulders. I'd bought it yesterday at the last minute upon realizing that Wallis was right; my wardrobe was mostly workwear. Inside I was tense, but at least outwardly I could try to mask it with some frill.

"The clearance racks are always full of size twelves," I said, as we shuffled forward. "I got a few new things."

"Wow," Wallis said, tucking the label into the back of my dress.

"Why are you surprised? You said to go shopping. I listened."

For about the hundredth time since we'd arrived at the

airport, she drew her phone from her jean jacket pocket and checked her texts. "I say so many things." There didn't seem to be anything that required her attention, so back the phone went. I could sense her gazing at me, wanting me to respond, perhaps to ask: How's Blake? Or is Blake excited you're coming? But when I couldn't, she said, "Okay, what's wrong?"

"Nothing," I said, staring at the back of the blue-suited business traveler in front of us. "Why would something be wrong?"

"You seem, like, *blah*," Wallis said. "I know you were on the fence about this trip, but I'd hoped you might have come around by now. This weekend will be so fun."

Her words reminded me that a text from Atlas awaited my response. He'd messaged me that morning, asking about my weekend plans, what I was up to that night. But in the frantic pre-airport hours filled with last-minute packing and a ride share that canceled last second, I'd forgotten about it. I fished through the contents of my overpacked purse, found my phone and his text, and a more recent one, too. Keen to catch up, he'd written just an hour ago, an addendum to all the ones from earlier.

He'd been sending quite a few of these texts over the last couple days, ever since I'd ignored his call at the book party. I suspected the reason he wanted to see me—to tell me that Ari was back—and I couldn't dream of a conversation I needed less. I didn't know why he was so desperate to inform me of their relationship status. He was with her. I *got* it. I was all set. I had been running out of excuses for why I was busy, but now I finally had a real one.

"So?" Wallis nudged me for my answer to her question. "Can you just tell me what's up with you?"

"There's been a lot going on, Wallis," I said as I began my text to Atlas. "A lot to manage."

"If you're trying to manage me, you can take that off your plate." Wallis stood on her toes to see over heads. The line to board, already at a crawl, had stopped moving entirely.

"Manage you?" I asked.

I'm about to board a flight to Charleston for the weekend.

"I see it, sometimes," Wallis said. "Don't you?" At this question, I looked up from my phone. "You're like someone from the bomb unit in your protective padding. Fiddling with my wires. Or at least putting a protective box over me. I want to give you a break from that."

His response came immediately: Charleston? For anything specific?

"Wallis, honey," I said. Bo has invited us down for a party. "It's adorable you'd think I'd even attempt to manage you."

We were able to start walking again, which was positive, as Wallis seemed about ready to bulldoze through the line. "It's adorable," she said, "that you think you aren't doing it."

I figured it might have something to do with Blake Darley. He's in Charleston, right?

The flight attendant gave our boarding passes a cursory glance, and to the second-to-last row we went, me to the window and Wallis to the aisle. I didn't mind sitting in the back of the plane; I'd heard somewhere that was the safest place to be in the event of a crash-landing.

Bo had wanted us to travel together, but there had been less expensive flights available, and he couldn't argue against that. We'd land a few hours behind him, taxi to his family's home, try not to make a fuss upon arrival.

"Fine," Wallis said, once we'd found our assigned pair of seats and I still had not answered her. "You say nothing's wrong, and I am going to choose to believe you. Besides, I don't think your mood will last long in Charleston anyway. How can one drink sweet tea and be pissy at the same time? Doesn't seem possible."

"I'm not so sure," I said, packing our suitcases into the overhead compartment as an impatient passenger tried to jam herself by me. "Sugar can conceal a lot."

"I know you're secretly happy, even if you're acting like a grump now," Wallis said from her seat. She took a tangled pair of earphones from her purse, unfurled them with more pleasure than the task deserved. I could tell she was trying to fuel her own excitement with the possibility of my own. I could practically feel her anticipation. She seemed to levitate.

Let me rephrase. Wallis is going for Blake. I'm going for Bo.

I see. Sorry we're missing each other.

I'm the worst, I wrote to Atlas, not sure if I meant it or not. Then, sliding in past Wallis and taking my seat: "I won't dampen your spirits anymore. Heaven forbid I carry with me a stench of grumpiness."

"Daisy," Wallis said, sparing me only a glance, "I'm just kidding."

The cockpit announcements came, along with the reminders of everything we'd heard dozens of times before. Wallis was instructed to put her phone on airplane mode. I, on the other hand, wore my seat belt tight on my hips and had already made sure my window shade was up. The flight attendants never had any commands for me.

"Will Blake be in Charleston this weekend?" I asked once Wallis had complied. "Have you made plans to see him?" This was something, in case our plane went down, that I wanted to know. I wanted to know what my sister was dying for.

"Have to figure that out," she said. "We've been dealing with his busy schedule. He's pretty sure he'll be in town. We've been texting. We email. Why are you looking at me like that?"

"I wasn't aware," I said carefully, "that you've been in touch to *such* an extent." I understood that it wasn't really over between them, but I'd thought the status was more tenuous.

She shrugged. "You haven't asked."

"You told me when he left that you didn't *want* to talk about it!" I said. "I was respecting your wishes."

"I'm talking about it now, aren't I? I'm happy. I'm positive. I think he and I can get back on track. With his mother on her way out of the Senate..." She trailed off and lifted her body slightly to see past me and out the plane's window.

Ari had been right, after all. POTUS had released a statement last week nominating Melinda Darley for health secretary. On-air anchors and pundits chewed over the nomination all day long and into the predawn hours, when I, red-eyed, dreading another day filled with empty hours, didn't have the will to change the channel.

"Things seem possible, now," continued Wallis, back in proper flying position and evidently satisfied with her view, "in the way they didn't before. He won't need to run her office. When she's confirmed to the cabinet, she won't be up for reelection. That is potentially life-changing." Wallis rubbed her hands together. "It's the maneuverings of the universe."

"Bo has been so generous to invite us to his parents' house," I cautioned. I wanted to temper her expectations; I hadn't forgotten Melinda Darley's proprietary words in the graveyard weeks ago. "Bo's mother, by the way, is a former Freedom Rider, lawyer, and current judge on the Fourth Circuit Court of Appeals. His father was the first African American to chair the State Board of Education and is currently a professor at The Citadel."

"Bo is such a gem, I'm not surprised his parents are also amazing," said Wallis, before putting the buds of her headphones in her ears. "I just downloaded the album of this great Charleston band. Blake told me about them. They're, like, Southern and rock and soul."

I wanted to remove the wires from her grasp, the way a parent pries sharp scissors out of a child's hand, to make sure she heard me. "We have to be on our *best* behavior."

"Always." This, and a smile, was all she gave me.

We had an on-time departure, maybe a little early. There was a hard shudder after takeoff, but I fixed my eyes on the scenery below, begging the plane to right itself, the pill I had taken to work. We flew over the low buildings of Old Town Alexandria, the Wilson Bridge and its tangle of off-ramps, the cherry-red roof of Mount Vernon, and into the clouds. The flight attendant made the rounds at cruising altitude. Would we like to buy a sandwich or a drink? My last paycheck had come last week. It was meager, just covering the few days in the cycle before Miles had put me on leave. Until I was back at work, I would get nothing, which meant no special snacks. "No, thank you," I told the flight attendant. "But I will take those free pretzels."

I practiced deep breathing and affirmation mantras. *You're safe. You're safe.* I used Wallis's jacket as a blanket, and watched the clouds below. Maybe it was the pill, the hum of the plane, or the sounds of pressurized air, but I sank into that place between sleep and wakefulness. I thought— dreamed?—of Atlas in Cricket's kitchen, his hair beautiful and mussed, his voice deep and assuring, his eyes, blue, fixed on me. Had there been signs of what he'd been hiding about Ari's return?

I believed if I stared at him long enough, I might be able to articulate the truth of how he made me feel—safe, frustrated, lonely, loved. I had the words, almost, but then Ari appeared next to him. In her eyes, I saw her plans and her orders, her agnostic views of us all. She was beautiful, and she would take him.

My head jolted and I became fully alert. The pilot announced that we were beginning our descent into Charleston, and I had to blink several times to get my bearings. Wallis looked at me and grinned.

When we touched ground, and I turned my phone back on, there was another text from Atlas: Please call me when you can.

—

Leaving the airport, we drove through the late-spring drizzle to the appointed address on Rutledge Street. By the time Bo met us at the gate, the clouds had moved on, the sun returned.

"Shorts!" Wallis exclaimed after jumping out of the taxi and giving him a hug. "I've never seen you in shorts. And they're pink. We are really letting loose this weekend, aren't we?"

In DC, Bo was rarely out of solid-color button-downs, overlarge khaki pants, and square-toed black shoes. But here he stood before us, head to knee in pastel, stylish loafers without socks. "I've already had two Bloodys," Bo said. For all his talk of his complicated relationship with his parents and his hometown, he did seem very relaxed. Maybe it was the vodka, or the smell of jasmine, or the weather that allowed for summer clothes that elevated his mood. "Put me in shorts, and I'm a different man."

We dragged our bags up the pea gravel drive toward the house, which was three stories with front facing piazzas on the bottom two. Brown brick and black shutters, porch ceilings painted haint blue.

"Tell us about the house," Wallis said. "You grew up here?"

"We had a smaller place on the East side of Charleston when I was little, but we moved over here once my sister and I were old enough to start school. This is Judge Collette Reed's labor of love. Mind you fawn over it. That will score you some points."

A truck, looked like catering, came in the gate behind us, and we stepped aside to a wisteria-draped stone wall along the driveway to give it room.

"What is the plan for the day?" I asked after we resumed our walk to the house, our suitcases making tracks in the gravel. "Just tell us where we need to be."

"My parents are hosting an intimate dinner for thirty tonight. Cocktails and appetizers at quarter past five. My father likes punctuality."

"Thank you," I said, already fretting about what to wear. Which of my new clothes would be appropriate? "We'll gladly take any and all instruction."

"Daisy likes to know the rules for social situations," Wallis teased.

"I don't want to screw up," I said.

"You won't. And the big party, the *official* engagement party," Bo said, using air quotes, "is tomorrow night. We're going south of Broad for that one. My mother's best friend is putting up a tent in her garden."

"How lovely," I said, thinking of my mother, back at home, and wishing she were here. She loved garden parties.

"My mother couldn't turn her down, although she wanted to. The stakes are higher, now, for the actual wedding. We can't be upstaged by an engagement party!" He said this with mock horror as we took the porch steps, painted a glossy gray.

"Can we get your mother something?" I asked. "For hosting us this weekend?"

"Tulips," Bo said in front of the door. "Orange. Now, she's put you on the top floor, so we have some steps. You'll have to share a room, but it comes with a bathroom. Here, give me your bags. And come on in."

We entered to find Collette Reed in the flesh, holding court in the foyer. Behind a pair of robust black glasses, her eyes—Bo's eyes—turned to appraise us, then went back to the young woman standing before her with a notepad and a stressed expression. An assistant, I guessed. She had that posture, and when Judge Reed dismissed her, she scuttled away, her ill-fitting flats hitting her heels.

"The Washington set," Judge Reed said, extending her hand in a way that made me wish I'd had a chance to wash mine.

"Thank you so much for having us," I said. And I meant it. There was a gorgeous array of fresh flowers on the console table, hydrangeas the size of pom-poms, pink-and-orange ranunculus blooms, fragrant greenery. Off to one side of the hall, I got a glimpse of a library, rows of bookshelves, and two matching green velvet chaises. Maybe Bo and Wallis would let me sneak off to read. I could just shut the pocket doors, which appeared to be original to the house, curl in one of those fluffy blankets, pluck a Jane Austen from the shelf, and dream the afternoon away. There was something so calming about being a welcomed guest in a well-kept home. I mentally thanked Patricia for her advice.

The assistant returned with water. "Your home is stunning," I said to the Judge as I accepted a chilled bottle. "We are so grateful to be included in this special weekend."

"I assume you're Daisy, and this is Wallis over here?" replied Judge Reed, pointing.

"Yes, sorry. I'm Daisy. My sister——"

"Ma'am. I'm Wallis," my sister said. There was a moment I thought she might go in for a hug, but she refrained, and I counted my blessings.

"You're both so young," Judge Reed said. "From the way Robert talked about you, Daisy, I'd assumed you were older."

"Ah, well," I said, at a loss for how to respond. I looked at Bo, who had closed his eyes and was shaking his head. "I'm not *that* young," I offered.

"You've many years ahead of you to consider just how wrong that statement is," Judge Reed said.

I was not offended by the Judge's ruling that I was incorrect. She spoke with such authority and grace, I suspected she could tell me the sun was green and I would still believe her.

"You'll show them upstairs?" Judge Reed addressed her son. "Robert is also bunking up there this weekend."

"In the *servants'* quarters," said Bo, enunciating.

She waved a hand. "He's just salty because I kicked him out of his old room."

"You've been picking up some lingo from your clerks, I see," Bo said.

The assistant was back with a coffee mug, and Judge Reed took a sip, eyes on her son over the rim. "Shouldn't you all be working? What are you doing here with things the way they are in DC anyway?"

"You told me to come down here," said Bo. "I thought I should at least try to achieve some work-life balance."

"When you're older you can start talking about work-life balance. Now, aren't you hungry?"

Bo looked warily at his mother. "For lunch or for work?"

"What do you think?" She laughed. I figured I better get laughing too, even if at Bo's expense. Mine, too, I remembered. "Boy, you've gotten soft, and not just around the middle. At least when you were in the army you had some muscle."

Bo inhaled through his nose. His smile was one of tested patience. "Only reason I enlisted," he said. "For the six-pack."

Wallis laughed, but quieted when she saw Judge Reed's expression, which suggested we should not be laughing about Bo's decision to enlist rather than major in prelaw.

"All right, now," said the Judge. "You'll take the girls out for the afternoon? You'd only be in the way here."

"Yes, ma'am."

"What are you planning to do?"

"I was going to walk them down to the Battery."

"If you walk by Market Street, that's where Aunt Jane is staying. In that hotel I told her to avoid. You might call her and see where she is. See if she's ready to hear my *I told you so* yet."

"Excuse me, is there Wi-Fi in the house?" Wallis interjected.

"Wallis," I said, embarrassed.

"I'll give you the code," Bo said.

"I hope you enjoy your stay," Judge Reed said, and out she went. In her wake, I feared what she thought of us. Entitled millennial? DC types, singularly worried about Wi-Fi? Me, surely, the idiot who couldn't remember to introduce herself.

"The Judge is wearing her leopard print scarf today," Bo said as we began our trek up the regal, curved staircase. He carried both our suitcases, one in each hand. "That usually signals a mood that is more, let's say, feisty than usual."

"I think she looks like an artist," Wallis said. "Is this the part where you tell us that underneath her stern demeanor is a heart of mush? Please tell us she has a soft spot for romantic comedies."

"Alas," Bo said, laughing after the first flight. "What you see is what you get."

"How old did you tell her I was?" I asked Bo.

"I don't think I said anything that would suggest you were a geriatric. Maybe because I always talk about *my boss* this and *my boss* that. Anyway," he said. "This is the family's floor. My parents' room is at the end of the hall. Mine is just to the right of it, with the dark green walls. Originally, I was up a level, but when I was in high school, my mother moved me down here. Wanted to keep an eye on me."

"Because you were a huge party boy," I said, grinning.

"Exactly," said Bo. "Partying with my model train set."

Wallis squealed. "I forgot you were such a nerd!"

Bo gazed toward his childhood bedroom. I'd never known

him to be ashamed of his admittedly dorky adolescence before, but there was something in his face that seemed regretful. Whatever it was, he heaved up our suitcases and continued the climb. "Okay, one more flight to go."

"I'm dying for a tour," Wallis said, gawping at the Judge's art along the staircase, which ranged from modern, geometric circles to classic oil still lifes. "Do you think you can sneak me through later?"

"Yes," said Bo, somehow charging up the stairs much faster than we were. "We'll start with the cellar first. That's where the good wine is."

"And the Wi-Fi code," Wallis said.

"Wallflower," Bo said as we caught our breaths on the final landing, "I got you. Hand me your phone." A few seconds later: "There now. Happy? Yes, Daisy, look at Wallis's face. It's the face of someone who can now scroll and 'like' the day away."

"Daisy is always after me about my data usage," Wallis said.

"Right," he said, gesturing to a room on his left. "You're here."

Ever the gentleman, he held the door open for us as we filed in. Our room was sloped-ceilinged, and had a sleigh bed made of dark wood. The walls were painted valentine's red. Two dormer windows overlooked the drive; below us, the catering crew unloaded linens. Someone—maybe Bo or the Judge's assistant—had placed a smaller arrangement of the entry hall flowers on the bedside table. It was cozy and charming, this room, and I loved it.

Wallis toed off her shoes and flopped on the bed. "Feather pillows," she said. "Bo, you won't be able to get rid of me."

"Do you need a rest?" Bo said, watching from the doorway. "We can do our house tour and walk later."

Wallis launched herself off the bed about as quickly as she fell onto it. "Absolutely not. We just need to wash our hands and I need to change quickly."

Wallis had noticed the pillows; I, the rolltop desk in the corner. I had tasks to accomplish before I could relax. "I need to send some emails," I said. "The lawyers."

We agreed to meet downstairs in half an hour, though Wallis would have liked it to be less. She changed her outfit and sat in the rocking chair by the window. Her phone, she picked up, put down, picked up again. I kept telling her, one more minute. Just one last thing. "We're wasting our time, Daisy," she complained as I slowly attended to my inbox. "We're wasting our youth."

Twenty-Two

That evening, Wallis stood over her suitcase, considering which dress to wear for the Reeds' dinner party. She had hot rollers in her hair and a toothbrush in her mouth.

"I think you should wear the pink," I said. Wallis had been right earlier; the pillows on the bed, feathered, deep, were so comfortable I wondered how I'd ever bring myself to leave them.

"Eh," Wallis hedged, then took herself into the bathroom to spit and rinse. "I was thinking the green."

I joined her in the bathroom, finding a perch on the lip of the claw-foot tub. I was in awe of the Judge, that a woman could have a remarkable career and a fabulous house filled with items of taste, chosen with care. Cricket would describe her as a *maximalist*. Her home was decorated in layers. Plates adorned the walls of the kitchen. There was wallpaper on nearly every ceiling. There was a magnifying glass in the downstairs powder room and needlepoint pillows with witticisms like *If I agreed with you, we'd both be wrong*. Surfaces were covered in candles. She had a fondness for jars. Pencils in jars. Cotton balls in jars. *Keep your eyes peeled for the jar in the jar,* Wallis had said to me earlier, after the grand tour. The way the Judge arranged pictures and pieces of art and artifacts, mixed fabrics and styles of furniture, made me want to go home and redecorate my entire apartment so it wasn't so ruthlessly curated. Read: empty. Cricket's style was more traditional—dark woods, creams and taupe—but like the Judge, she'd made sure the house looked *lived in*, warm. Despite the less-than-perfect memories, when we sold P, we'd lost much more than a house. It felt good to be back in one. "How long do you think it takes to dust this place?" I asked.

"Judge Reed just commands the dust not to fall," Wallis said.

"Bo seems somewhat afraid of her," I said.

"You think?" Wallis examined an eyebrow in the mirror, then began to pluck.

"He's different when he's here. Have you noticed?"

"He's in his childhood home," Wallis said. "We're all different at home. Including me." She laid her tweezers on the sink. In the mirror, she met my eyes. "DC has felt so awful recently. Like I'm living in a snow globe that someone just keeps shaking. But I feel good here. I like Charleston. Our walk downtown was charming. I like a city that comes to a point. I like homes with porches." She smiled and looked toward the ceiling. "I think something good is going to happen this weekend. I just feel it."

"What's the latest with Blake?" I asked, fiddling with the hem of my dress. I was in black, a high-collared number, sleeveless, floor-length.

Wallis shrugged. "He's busy. He'll get back to me. To-morrow, he said." She glanced at her phone resting on the edge of the sink. The screen was dark.

Though I was skeptical that any meeting with Blake would be productive, I envied her optimism. I coveted it. But it also made me resentful. Why did she get to have hope when I was floundering? I had a thought, briefly, of tossing a brick through her window, unloading on her the whole truth about Atlas, the kiss, Ari, why his article was canceled. My mouth opened, but the words gummed in my throat. She was my sister, and I loved her, and I could not. Anyway, this trip was supposed to be about celebrating with Bo and his family, champagne, good sleep and warm air, jaunts through narrow, colonial alleyways adorned with bougainvillea. *Too young art thou to waste this summer night*, right, Daisy?

Wallis studied her reflection and continued her work. Eyebrows done, and on to the powder, the concealer, the bronzer. It took her barely any time; her moves were prac-ticed and perfunctory, her mind elsewhere. Tonight, how could a little buffing up hurt? When she was done, I asked to borrow her mascara. She passed it to me like a baton.

A gentle rap at the door—Bo, collecting us for the party. He waited while I zipped up Wallis. Naturally she'd cho-sen the green.

Turned out *I'd* badly miscalculated. Downstairs, I was the only one in black. All others were in the colors of spring, except the bride-to-be, Bo's fraternal twin, Jessica, who was in white and pearls, radiant, petite, happy. The star of the party, she welcomed us, graciously.

And so the night went, Wallis and I sometimes together, sometimes apart. I mingled more easily than usual. The Reeds' friends and family were delightful, many had interesting anecdotes from long, distinguished careers, as well as hilarious stories of Bo and Jessica as babies and young children. When it was time for dinner, the head waiter rang a brass handbell with a wooden handle. *My grandmother's*, said Bo, as we moved to the next stage of the evening. In the large dining room, the walls of which were wrapped with a bucolic mural, we were seated on either side of Bo. During the meal, there was a toast or two—tears in the handsome groom's eyes but he spoke too hastily, fumbled lines, certainly not a natural orator. Is he good enough for Jessica? This question was a little uncharitable, admittedly. Did I really expect all men to dazzle? If so, my sister was rubbing off on me.

I checked on Wallis then, and throughout dinner, evaluating her mood, hoping she was having as enjoyable a time as I was. I could not fault her performance. It was convincing. But only I knew her well enough to see her moments of distraction, to notice the occasions when her eyes unfocused, when she activated her automaton—*uh-huh, yes, totally, right*. Her hands, always occupied with either a drink or her phone.

———

It was well after midnight when I woke up, cold, hungry, next to a gently snoring Wallis, who'd stolen all the covers. I had fallen asleep in my dress and mascara, my phone on my chest.

I changed into my pajamas in the bathroom. I'd brought my nicest ones, thinking, I don't know, of impressions? It seemed ridiculous now as I turned off my bedside lamp and crept out. The hallway sconces were still on, so getting downstairs was not a problem. Toward the kitchen, also illuminated, I heard footsteps and the sound of plates being stacked. A roadblock, then, between me and the remaining slices of cheese and salami from the charcuterie board.

I was standing in the dining room, gazing at the mahogany table strewn with used linen, considering my options—should I go back upstairs or brave the awkward chitchat that surely awaited me in the kitchen?—when Aunt Jane fell upon me. "Collette!" she called. "You have another poor soul who wants some leftovers." She, Bo's aunt, the one who deigned to stay at the wrong hotel on Market Street, was still in her party dress. She'd startled me, and she must have noticed, for she put a hand on my shoulder. It steadied me, and I saw that it steadied her, too. She wore glasses like her sister, though not as trendy, and behind them were wide, untroubled eyes. The eyes of a woman happy to be a little tipsy. "Bo was just in here, looking for a leg of something." Aunt Jane laughed, and almost singing, declared, "It's that time of night!" She bounced back toward the kitchen. I followed.

Judge Reed straightened when she saw me in the doorway. "Join us," she said from her rush-seated counter stool. In her voice, I searched for any hints that I shouldn't. I was interrupting a woman in her own kitchen, late at night. A conversation between sisters. I begrudged the fact that I was so hungry. But she nodded toward the island—and its cheeseboard, crackers, open tub of hummus.

"Join *us*?" Aunt Jane said. "I've been telling you for the last hour I'm going back to the hotel."

"It's early yet," Judge Reed said.

"It's one o'clock in the damn morning." Aunt Jane laughed again.

"Oh, you've got other plans?" She slid a basket of sliced baguette down the counter to Aunt Jane.

"You have a sister, don't you, Daisy?" Aunt Jane asked, selecting a slice of bread.

"Yes," I said, enjoying their banter and analyzing how best to scoop some hummus without making a mess. I pulled out the stool next to the Judge, careful not to drag the legs across the floor. "She's here with me. Did you get introduced to Wallis?"

"Y'all are sisters? Well, now, that makes sense. I saw her pushing a drink into your hand earlier tonight. I thought that looked familiar." Aunt Jane turned to her own sister. "You might as well hand me that bottle, then. But this is my last one, mark my words."

"Yeah, yeah," Judge Reed said, passing the Pimm's. "Pour Daisy some, too. Her hands are too empty for late-night chatting."

From a nearby cabinet the color of a latte, Aunt Jane found a short tumbler, a delicate one, glass, decorated with intricate bubbles and threads.

"You like Pimm's?" Judge Reed asked as Aunt Jane filled my cup with ice from the massive freezer.

"I've only had it once," I said, "when I was in New Orleans some time ago, on a trip with my boss."

"New *Orl*eeuhns," Judge Reed said, correcting, "is where our mother's family comes from. Some Tremé and other Uptown folk will be here tomorrow."

"My father always loved that city," I said.

"Sure he did," Judge Reed said. "He was a crook, and crooks *love* New Orleans."

A grandfather clock ticked baritones in the hall. The Judge sat on her counter stool in duchess satin, spinning her glass between her palms, looking at me, studious, expectant. A test, I thought.

"Very true," I said, because of course she was right. Aunt Jane handed me the glass.

"Cheers," Judge Reed said. We clinked, and with the first taste of the Pimm's, sweet and bitter, herbs and citrus, I remembered that I'd liked it. "Tell me, Daisy, is Robert good at his job?"

"Yes," I said. "So good he's been doing mine, too." I wasn't usually in the habit of admitting such things to virtual strangers, but dimly lit, late-night kitchens contain their own type of magic, don't they? Aunt Jane passed the baguette slices my way; I chose one, and a slice of cheese that turned out to be Brie with truffles. Heaven.

"You're not working?" Judge Reed narrowed her eyes.

"I've been—relieved of my duties. Temporarily, I hope. I've been in the wrong places at the wrong times." My thoughts flickered to the graveyard, the shadows of cherry trees and mausoleums, the lens of the camera that caught me. "It is what it is." It wasn't, but how could I really call it unfair when I was Gregory Richardson's daughter? I was supposed to be well versed in the partisan playbook.

"Politics is an obnoxious business," said Judge Reed. She cut us chunks from a block of cheddar with a cheese knife, the mother-of-pearl handle steady in her grip. "When Robert was little, I thought maybe he'd be a preacher. He had that presence. A litigator, maybe. But he had no interest in school." She closed her eyes and slipped into a memory. "He had potential in the military, but then he chose politics. Still can't fathom it."

"I'm beginning to forget, too," I said, "why I chose this profession." Constant concern for optics, appearance, could be extraordinarily exhausting and tedious. Even far away from DC, despite the pleasantness of the evening, I'd been unable to fully break myself of this habit of monitoring Wallis.

"I like your guy," said Aunt Jane. "Miles, I mean. He seems like one of the good ones."

"Always seemed a little cocky to me," said Judge Reed. "Like he thinks the sun rises just to hear him crow."

This cracked us up, and when we surfaced, I wiped tears from my eyes. We were quiet for a moment, until Aunt Jane had another question for me. "Speaking of cocky," she said. "Is it true that your sister is in a relationship with Charleston's own Blake Darley?"

Not sure how they felt about the Darleys and our former chumminess with one of them, I tried to chart a neutral course. "The relationship is somewhere between is and was."

Judge Reed paused, sipped. Even the way she drank was elegant. "There's rumors, you know, Daisy," she said. "Rumors about Melinda Darley's Senate seat. The successor she's handpicked…"

At this I turned my body on my stool to face her directly, bracing. "No, you can't mean… Blake?" I looked between the Judge and Aunt Jane, waited for them to break, for signs of mischief. Nothing. *How?* Blake had spent large amounts of time talking about how he *never* wanted to follow in his mother's footsteps.

"Money is passed through generations," said the Judge. "So is power. Are you really so surprised Melinda Darley would want to turn the seat over to her son?"

She was right; it shouldn't be so surprising, yet here I was, my mind blank with shock, my thoughts scattered off the page. "Oh," was all I could say.

"*Oh* is right," Judge Reed said. "Blake—well, let me tell you a story. So, for a while when they were in high school, Blake had a thing for my Jessica."

"They dated?" I gathered myself. This was more than Bo had ever let on.

"They did. Went to senior prom together, too. Hers was a different high school than Robert's. Jessica was dying to transfer, so when she was a sophomore, we let her. She knew people there, but we didn't."

"You were doing what was right for her at the time," Aunt Jane said. "It was different then, wasn't it, Collette? Between them and us. Between those type of people and us, I mean."

"I'll tell you this," said Judge Reed. "When Jess and Blake started dating, Melinda Darley was pleased as punch that her son had a Black girlfriend. I'm telling you, that woman took a picture with me every chance she got. She threw the whole damn prom dinner in her house! James and I suspected it was so she could control the photography." She lifted her hands to her face. *Click*, she mimed. *Click, click.* "Now, there they were at Melinda Darley's house, for prom dinner, at one long table, Jess told me later. And her friend, Rebecca, beautiful girl, by the way, I'm still friendly with her mother, she apparently starts putting some butter on her dinner roll. Blake's best friend—I mean, this guy, right out of the plantation house—Scottie Ellis, his partner in crime, makes a crack about her being Jewish and hogging all the butter."

"These damn people..." Aunt Jane said.

Yes, I thought. *These damn people.* Earlier that evening, I'd caught Wallis standing alone in a corner, next to a drop-leaf table with tortoiseshell inlay, topped with a crystal vase of tulips and a saucer of mints. Engrossed in her phone with *these damn people*, this Blake Darley—potential *senator*—with whom she'd rather have been spending her night.

"Melinda Darley was right there," continued Judge Reed.

"Right there peering over the tables making sure everyone got the right salad, God only knows. And do you know what Blake did? What he said to this nasty, anti–Semitic Scottie boy?"

Now this I could see coming. "Nothing," I said.

"He laughed!" She slapped her palm against the marble of the island. "He laughed and didn't say a damn thing. But then again, neither did Jessica." She took a sip of her Pimm's. "So many years James and I preached the importance of speaking truth to power. One fancy dinner in some old-money Charleston house and those lessons were all but forgotten." Another sip, this time sucked through her teeth. "Ah, but maybe I'm being too hard on Jess. God, she felt guilty afterward. Wrote this long letter to her friend apologizing."

"And what happened later, to Jessica and Blake?" I asked.

Judge Reed lifted a shoulder. "Blake went to some college around here with the rest of his shaggy-haired friends, looking to get some 'gentleman's Cs,' like they call it. Jessica went to Harvard."

My Pimm's was finished. Judge Reed topped me up, and I was grateful.

"I never told you this?" Judge Reed asked her sister. Aunt Jane shook her head. "Well, maybe I was embarrassed."

"You did great with Jessica," Aunt Jane said. "Bo, too."

"Both of them, spoiled down to the tips of their toes." Judge Reed looked toward the kitchen door, as though expecting one of her children to appear. I wondered if Cricket did the same when she talked about us. "God love 'em. You see, Daisy, even when Robert and I weren't as close as we are now…" She flinched—the pinch of a painful memory, it seemed—but it was soon replaced by a peal of laughter. She pushed her glass away. "Enough with this drinking.

Let's turn on some music, right, Janie?" the Judge said, but
she made no move to rise. "Daisy, what do you think?"

But my mind wasn't on music. It was on Blake. Like the
news about his upcoming bid for office, the Judge's anecdote about him and his friend wasn't shocking, really. I suspected I'd known the truth about him all along, though in
the face of Wallis's happiness, I hadn't wanted to believe it.
Wallis would be crushed. But something else was bothering me more. "It was Jessica who apologized to her friend,"
I said. Judge Reed tilted her head, quizzical. "And I'd bet
my inheritance—if I still had it—on the fact that not one of
those other boys apologized. You might get an apology from
Blake if someone calls him on it now that he's running…"

"That's just the way it is." Aunt Jane was more alert now,
her voice that of a woman who'd gotten her second wind.
"Men misbehave and the women apologize for it."

"Or women try to make excuses for them," said the
Judge. "I've spent enough years on the bench to have seen
plenty of that."

I took a sip—all right, a gulp—of my drink. I needed it.
"Here's what it is," I said. "Here's what gets me about this.
Blake doesn't even want it. The seat, I mean. I know him
well enough to know that with perfect, crystal clear certainty.
He might want it in the way I want that bowl of pretzel thins
there. He only wants it because it's in front of him."

"It's easier for men to take things, isn't it?" Judge Reed
asked, observing me as she might a novice lawyer pleading her case.

"Take things," I said, thinking of my father. Then, thinking again of Blake: "And be *handed* things."

Judge Reed was quiet. Then a grin, wide and disarming.
"Girl," she announced. "*You* should run for office."

Twenty-Three

Wallis was up early, with the sun, which blazed into our room gradually, then all at once, for neither of us had remembered to shut the curtains the night before. I kept my eyes closed, drowsy, thirsty, headachy, everything I didn't want to be. Wallis padded around, in and out of the bathroom, back in bed and out of it. Suitcases were opened. Zippers and snaps were fiddled with. After some time, when the possibility of more sleep was well and truly spent, I flopped onto my back, stared at the ceiling and said, "Wallis, sit and read or sit and stare at your phone, but just sit, be still, please. It's too early for rummaging."

"Should I shower?" Wallis asked. "I wonder if I should shower now or later, before the engagement party? Maybe twice. That wouldn't be such a bad thing, right? Can one overshower?"

"Shower," I said, rolling over and grasping my phone from the bedside table so I could forage online for any intel that might verify the rumor Judge Reed had relayed. I couldn't say anything to Wallis without confirmation. "Or don't. Bo is going to take us to see a very old house with some old furniture. He wants to have lunch at one of these trendy places uptown where you can order brisket or a banh mi. It's going to be casual. You don't have to wash your hair." Blake Darley, on the ticket. The thought of it made me ill.

Across the room, Wallis declared that she was not going to shower. Then she changed her mind. Her waffling, about a shower, of all things, annoyed me. I put down my phone and scooted up on the pillows. I could feel my hair plastered to my scalp. If anyone needed a shower, it was me. "Why the torment over a shower?" I asked, searching Blake's name on my browser.

She didn't answer; instead, she resumed the task of taking each item of clothing out of her suitcase and laying it over the arms and back of the rocking chair.

The bathroom free, for the time being, I gave up my search and dragged myself to the mirror over the sink to inspect my damage. It was just as bad as expected. I was stealing some of Wallis's makeup remover pads when the chime of an incoming text sounded.

"Where did I put my phone?" I heard Wallis ask, slightly panicked.

"I think that was my phone," I called.

"Yes," she said after a moment. "It was yours. A text from Atlas."

She leaned against the bathroom door and held out my phone. "Or should I say, about a million texts from Atlas."

Last night's borrowed mascara only half-removed, I took my phone, put it on silent. "Thanks," I said. "I'll get back to him in a minute."

"Just answer the texts, Daisy. Jesus. Quit playing these

games with him." She marched to the shower, yanked back the curtain, turned on the water.

"You're showering?" A question with an obvious answer, but—I don't know—a second ago it seemed like she was about to pick a fight with me and here she'd abandoned it so quickly. I'd been ready to try to understand, to draw out the real reason for her frustration with me.

"Yes. I'm expecting a text from Blake. We're going to meet later."

Speaking of *games*. I hesitated, hoping that she might expound, but she just undressed and stepped in the spray. "I see," I said.

The bathroom filled with steam, I gave up on my makeup removal and turned to my phone, Atlas's texts. She'd been right; there were already many of them, and more kept coming. I skimmed, anticipating Ari's name splashed everywhere. Instead:

I know you told me to kill the article...and I have...

...But I wanted to keep following the money, just to give you peace of mind, nothing else...

I think you should know...

Then these words, which had me clutching the edge of the sink:

...Stealing seems to have started with your college tuition... then escalated... Wallis's, too.

I put my screen to sleep and flipped my phone over. But it wasn't enough. I picked it up again and, from the bathroom doorway, tossed it onto the bed, watched as it bounced off the comforter and landed on the floor. Then I closed the bathroom door. I couldn't even look at it.

"You still there?" Wallis's voice, over the running water, sounded like she was keeping back tears.

I nodded, then realized she couldn't see me. "Yes," I said. But, no. No, I was not there. I was falling, down through the past, flailing for a hold, trying to find something to clasp, something my father hadn't broken. I'd thought we'd be safe in Charleston, but reality had tracked me down.

"Sorry I snapped at you," she said. "I'm tired and stressed."

With the side of my hand, I wiped off the steam from the bathroom mirror. "It's okay," I told her. I'd been born with Cricket's nose—a dainty one, turned up at the end. Somewhere along the way, though, it had inflated both at the bridge and the tip, a coup of my father's genes. My father, the hijacker, clear as the nose on my face.

"They've got good shampoo here," Wallis said. "It's making me feel better. It smells really nice."

"It does." I took up again the makeup remover and scrubbed. Soon the mascara was gone, but I kept going. "Everything here is so, so nice."

Twenty-Four

For our first activity of the day, Bo brought us down to Charleston's seawall and to the former home of a man named, naturally, Beauregard. On the walk there, I let Bo and Wallis stroll ahead so I could take many deep breaths and get straight what had to be the most convincing happy face of my life. This was difficult as I kept being sucked back to the same disquieting question: How could my father have done this? After Atlas's texts, I'd considered canceling the touristy plans we'd made for the day, but to what end? So I could panic alone in Judge Reed's third-floor guest bedroom surrounded by jars of potpourri and monogrammed pillow shams?

By the time we'd arrived at our destination—as Bo put it, it was *a well-preserved museum of atrocities*—I'd found no answers, but I did land on what I hoped was a working approximation of Daisy In A Good Mood.

We had about thirty-five hours left in Charleston.

Telling Wallis about our tuition and her ex—current?—boyfriend maybe running for Senate would take a wrecking ball to her weekend and fell whatever hopes Bo had for an enjoyable time at his sister's party with family he didn't see often. I wouldn't do that to him. I agreed to keep everything to myself until we got back to DC. A day and a half was nothing. I'd held the secret of my kiss with Atlas for much longer than that.

When we returned to the Reed manor for a rest after our day out, I was relieved. With Wallis leaking her sour mood all over our lunch of pork nachos and beer, and checking her phone every six seconds, it had taken infinitely more effort for me to pretend all was well.

This trip was *supposed* to have been a way for me to escape DC and all its machinations. I hadn't been that fortunate. But the day was almost over, and while I would never admit this to Wallis, it thankfully appeared she wouldn't see Blake this weekend after all.

Wallis, though, was now showing signs of hope once again. She showered for the second time that day, curled her hair, and put on a black dress, long sleeved and short skirted, low neckline displaying the ridges of her clavicle. If only my unrequited love burned calories, I thought, I wouldn't have to wear compression underwear.

The engagement party was less than a half mile south of the Reeds', below Broad Street. In the walled garden of the grand antebellum house, flagstone paths looped around formal boxwoods shaped like globes and cones. There was a small tent at one end where waiters in white and black served pisco sours and bourbon. There was champagne, too, the fancy type, and Bo was kind enough to fetch us glasses. In the meantime, we introduced ourselves to the hosts, who were standing by the reflecting pool. They were gracious, but only to a point; going inside the main house was not allowed, they told us with a smile. The bathroom for guests, they said, was inside the carriage house. *They're come-heya folks*, Bo said, rolling his eyes.

As a jazz trio took up on the porch, Bo led us around, introducing us to family and friends we hadn't met the night before. I did my best to follow the small talk, to ask all the right questions, to maintain the look of polite interest, but my mind kept slipping back to what Atlas had texted me that morning. It didn't help that the unfolding celebration reminded me so much of the showers, anniversary fetes, fundraisers my parents once threw at P. Cricket used to joke that my father would pop champagne when someone finished a crossword puzzle.

Look, there's the tray of shrimp canapés. There's the French macaron tower. Here's the cocktail napkin with the host's monogram. Observe: the same string café lights that Cricket used to have. And the guests, in attendance—people of influence, puffed, confident, assured that whatever they were talking about was of the utmost importance. I'd never been here before, of course, yet I felt eerily trapped within distorted memories of my father, my *life*, both of which, it turned out, were just as strange to me as this house.

When it was time for dinner, I trailed Bo passively through the buffet line. I tonged mixed greens onto my plate, not really seeing what I was collecting. I overdid it on the chicken and, for some reason, decided to pour Thousand Island dressing, which I hated, over everything. I was too focused on this question: Why was it *my tuition* that launched this whole disaster? I couldn't help but feel deeply, newly culpable.

Bo and I ate our plates of chicken and greens on the steps of the main house, and watched as Wallis, paying no attention to the party around her, lingered near the bar, restless, phone in hand, eyes on her nude pumps.

"Wallis is preoccupied," Bo observed, wiping his fingers on his napkin. Then: "So are you."

Bo was one of the most perceptive people I knew, and I wasn't that good of an actor. "I know." I set my plate down beside me and ran my hand over my face. "Sorry."

Bo's smile was wan. "I think I understand why." I recoiled, immediately wondering, irrational as it was, if he knew. But: "It's Darley, isn't it? You're both—what? Hoping he's here? That you'll see him?"

"Wallis wants to," I said, thankful that Bo, to the best of my knowledge, was still without psychic powers. The Blake news I could handle. "But he isn't being responsive."

Bo appeared to be looking for the right words. "I don't get it," he muttered.

"I have a theory about Blake Darley," I said. "I was up with your mother and Aunt Jane last night, by the way."

"Did they spill family secrets?" Bo asked, offering me his last slice of corn bread. "Judging from your expression, this isn't about Cousin Marcus, who claims to cure cancer with homemade vitamins."

"Your mother has heard a rumor that Blake will run for his mother's seat." I split the corn bread in half so we could both enjoy it. "After she's confirmed and sworn in." It felt good to get this burden, at least, off my shoulders.

Bo's eyes widened. "I'll send around a few texts," he said. Like me, he seemed concerned for her. Unlike me, he was noticeably calm. "By the end of the day we might have some answers."

I agreed this was a good idea, then we were interrupted by a clinking of a knife against a glass. There was a short performance by the groom's friends, a skit full of jokes not meant for outsiders, which we could barely hear, but that was universally regarded as hilarious. A toast, too, from the hosts, who were full of congratulations and wistfulness. Grandparents were applauded. Dessert—chocolate cake with yellow buttercream frosting—was passed. Soon enough, the tea light candles burned out, and guests began to leave.

Bo and I regrouped with Wallis and discussed where to go next. The Judge and her future son-in-law announced they were leading a contingent to a bar uptown. Mr. Reed was taking a group back to their house for nightcaps and cigars. I thought surely Wallis would want to return to the comfort of bed and quiet. I certainly did. But instead we fell in with the good-time crowd, through the snare of Broad Street traffic to upper King, into a bar that was once a bank.

"A tab has been opened," Bo told us, once we were able to get past the bouncer and near the marble-topped bar. "Don't ask by whom. Just order what you want."

Wallis went off to get us drinks, and Bo, too, was whisked away by an old friend to catch up. Alone, I shrugged off my light jacket, draped it over my arm. I took in the scene— the high-coffered ceiling, the wines by the glass chalked on a board behind the bar, the crowd decked out mostly in bright colors and Southern florals, and there, just a dozen feet straight ahead, was Blake Darley. I blinked again, daring my eyes to lie. But it was him, with a posse of similarly aged men, one of whom I recognized as Melinda Darley's chief of staff, as portly and smug as in the graveyard last month. They must've felt my gaze, because both he and Blake turned their heads and caught my eye.

I felt Wallis come up beside me. "He's here," she said, clutching my arm. Her hands were empty. I guess she hadn't had a chance to order before spotting him. "Jesus, he's here."

"I see that," I said. Meaning, yes, I see him. And he saw me. And you, Wallis. But, still, there he stands, with his friends, having made no move to excuse himself. He didn't even *wave*.

"Then, come on." She pulled me forward.

"Wait, Wallis," I said. Useless. Useless. Useless. She was already there, behind him, then beside him. The others in his group shuffled to make room. The music—bubblegum pop from my childhood—was terrible and unrelenting, and Wallis had to raise her voice to be heard. She said his name. Then she was forced to say it again.

"Hi, guys," he said, staring past us to a distant point. "How's it going?"

"Where have you been?" Wallis asked, still slightly tipsy, I realized, from the engagement-party champagne. "I've been here all weekend. Where have you been, Blake?"

As he drank amber liquid from a tumbler, his hand shook, though it might have been my imagination. "Didn't I text you, yesterday?"

I felt a finger on my shoulder and turned, expecting Bo—I don't know why—but the touch was soft, a woman. "Excuse me," she said. A brunette. Maybe a dirty blonde. The light wasn't great. "So sorry—can I just?" It was a demand, cloaked as a question, and I was scrunched aside. "Hello," she said. To Blake, to the men, not to me, as she reclaimed her space.

"You said that things were busy," Wallis went on, interrogating Blake. "But this?" She held both her hands out, palms up. "This doesn't seem so busy."

Melinda Darley's chief of staff dropped his chin to his chest and chuckled. If I didn't despise him before, I did now. Sweat dampened the back of my dress.

I studied Blake. He did not seem tired, he did not look like one tossed and turned by the waves of seasonal politics. His shirt was pressed. He wore a snappy belt, embroidered with mallards. He was clean-shaven.

Wallis scooped his unoccupied hand into hers. He stared at their intertwined fingers, started to speak, then stopped, composed himself, and began again. "Do you know Drew Porter?" He removed his hand from my sister's and gestured to the man across from him. "Drew is my mom's chief of staff. And this is Chris over here." Blake cleared his throat. "Daisy, have you met Chris? He's field director for my mom's Low Country office. Keeping things locked up down here. Am I right, Chris? He used to work for Goode, when he was still in office. You might've met on the Hill then. No? But we can't forget about Katie here. She's head of philanthropy for our family foundation. Do you know Katie?"

"I haven't had the pleasure of meeting Katie," I managed. She looked at me like this was my fault—not knowing her.

"Didn't you get any of my texts today?" Wallis sounded wild, desperate. "Seriously, what is going on? We were supposed to see each other. You promised me we'd talk. You promised that you'd make these past weeks up to me!"

Blake gave her no reply. He finished his drink and placed it carefully on a high-top table behind him, then motioned to his friends, who did the same. Finally, to us, he said, "We're going to head out. But it was great running into you both."

"Wait," Wallis said. "Wait." She slapped a hand square on his chest, seized a fold of his shirt's fabric. "Just *wait*, okay?"

"Wallis," I said, fearing any second I would be forced to physically drag her off him.

"Daisy," Wallis pleaded. She was pale and shaking. "Daisy, help me. He can't just leave."

"He has to go, Wallis," I said, my voice ringing in my ears.

"Daisy," she cried again, as Blake stood frozen in her grasp. "He promised me. He made a promise." The eyes of those standing nearby turned to us. We were becoming a spectacle. Across from me, I saw a bystander draw out a phone.

"Blake," I said firmly. The coward's face was flushed, his eyes darting. "Just go."

It seemed that was the permission he needed. Tugging himself free of my sister, he slipped away, following the rest of his group as they cleared a path through the center of the room.

Bo came to my side just a moment before Wallis collapsed into me. Had he seen all that? I strained to hold her weight and felt a seam rip, somewhere under my armpit. Bo supported her left side, I her right.

"Where do we take her?" I asked. There was more attention now, from his family, the groom-to-be. "We're okay," I chanted. "We're okay. We're okay."

Awkwardly, gently, Bo helped me maneuver Wallis through the crowd to a vacant bar stool. Collette Reed appeared. "What's wrong here?" she asked.

"She's heartbroken," explained Bo, uncharacteristically frayed.

Wallis's face was white and her shoulders heaved. She gripped the seat of the bar stool, and I worried she might wobble off it. "Why did you tell him to go, Daisy? Why did you tell him to go?" she cried. "You have to go after him. Go, get him."

"He's gone, sweetie." She turned away from me and fell heavily against Bo's shoulder. He held her, whispered what sounded like her name.

"Bless this child's heart," the Judge said.

"Let's get Wallis some water," said Bo.

"You better not." The Judge's mouth was as straight as a ruler. "You're doing her no good keeping her here in front of all these eyes. How much have you had to drink?" she asked me. When I replied that it had been very little, she nodded and handed me her car keys. "It's the white Lexus parked just two blocks up on the far side of the street. I'll take a taxi or hitch a ride."

I babbled my thanks even as my insides were being shredded like tissue paper. Bo was already helping Wallis off her stool. Somehow, we made it out of the bar and on to the street. Wallis's gait suggested physical pain, and she clung to Bo and me as we passed Saturday night revelers. Some were more sure-footed than others, and at one point a young man in a backward cap knocked into Bo and didn't apologize. But we pushed on, determined to carry the weight of Wallis and her misery.

The car, at last, materialized. Wallis sank into the back seat and immediately lay down.

Bo directed me home; other than that, we didn't speak. The gate to the Reed driveway was open when we arrived. In the house, lights, music; the rocking chairs on the lower level piazza were occupied. I'd barely put the car in Park and Wallis was up and out, headed for the front door.

"I'm sorry," I said to Bo, dazed. "I'm so sorry for what just happened."

Bo rolled down his window, and I turned off the engine. Outside was the kind of soggy, fecund air loved by bugs;

it smelled of early summer, of perfume and brine, and of what Bo had called earlier that day *pluff mud*. Bo passed his phone back and forth between his hands, quiet.

"This weekend," I said. In the house, the music stopped, and a new song came on, a popular one, apparently, as indicated by the cheers of the guests. "This was supposed to be about your family. It became about Blake Darley, and about Wallis. I suspected something like this would happen. I'm sorry, Bo."

"You can't control Wallis, or whom she falls in love with. But I can't help—" He paused. "Seeing Blake tonight, with all those other dudes, his bros, brought back some not so great feelings about how boys like that treated me. Continue to treat me. Wallis is…" He exhaled. "I can't *believe* she'd love a man like that. But also, I know *exactly* why she'd love a guy like that."

"He wasn't that way, initially," I said. "Or at least he just hid it well."

"We fall in love with the wrong people all the time."

Yes, I agreed silently, thinking of my love for a man who didn't love me back.

I became conscious of just how much I didn't want to get out of the car. I wasn't usually fond of conversations in vehicles—too enclosed, too difficult to find the right point to end it and open the door, never an opportunity to say, simply, *okay, then, talk to you later*. But here, in this car, I wanted to loop time around my finger to keep it from going anywhere. To leave would be to reckon with what had happened in the bar, and back, to when my sister had fallen in love with a Darley who claimed, just as my father had, to be honest, to be a different kind of man. And even further, to the impromptu party my father had thrown when I got my college acceptance letter—had he known, then, when we were eating cake with our hands, dancing in the kitchen, how he would be paying for it? Had *I*, in some unknown, entitled way, pressured him into this choice?

"What are you going to do?" Bo asked, straightening.

"I'll make sure to go to your mother tomorrow and beg forgiveness," I said, watching a firefly float past my window. "She can do with me what she will."

"Cleaning up your wreckage on the way to becoming a better woman."

"Following along," I said, "in the grand tradition of being a white feminist in this great country."

"Preach," he said with a chuckle.

I leaned my head against the back of the seat. "And I'm going to take Wallis home earlier."

"What do you mean? Switch flights?" He groaned. "Daisy, you don't have to. That's burning money."

"I do. And it's just money." And I would have my income back soon. I had to.

"You know," Bo said, "when I asked you what you were going to do, I meant right now. About Wallis."

"What if I go up there and she tells me she's still in love with him?" This possibility made me even more reluctant to leave the car.

Bo nodded. "One of my old friends texted me when we were at the bar. He said that my mother was right. Blake Darley *is* beginning to tell people that he's running. Apparently he got the approval a few days ago."

"The balls on this guy," I said, shaking my head. "Confirmation hearings for his mother haven't even been scheduled yet. Now I'll have to tell Wallis before it's fully public."

Though maybe it would make her feel better, to know why he left. To know the truth about who he was.

Bo's eyes, and mine, flicked toward the house and up to the illuminated window of our guest room. "What did she mean in the bar when she was talking about how Blake *promised* her? What did he promise her?"

"I have no idea."

"Here's what I want to know," Bo began. He placed his hands behind his head and closed his eyes. "I want to know if he asked her to ride with him. I want to know—did he even *ask* if she'd give up your family name? Did he even *ask* if she'd delete all her old tweets and burn the bumper stickers? Did he even *offer* her a ring in exchange for her vote?"

"He knew her well enough. He knew that if he asked for any of those things, she'd refuse."

"Did you see her tonight?" Bo murmured, his eyes fluttering open. "I'm not so sure you're right."

⁓

Wallis lay on the bed, choking with sobs. She didn't tell me to go away, so I stretched my body next to hers, my cheek on her hair. We spent a long time this way. I knew the world was full of traitorous, cruel people, but I suppose the disappointment that came with trusting one still hurt. So I cried, too.

My tears stopped, after a while, but Wallis's continued. Eventually, she pulled me closer, and I hugged her back. My arm numbed and my shoulder cramped, and when her breathing slowed, I thought she might've fallen asleep. But she soon turned her face into the pillow and wailed again. I was familiar with this pain; there was nothing to do but let it be spent.

After a half hour of this cycle, she was able to speak.

"Who was that person in the bar?" she asked, her voice cracking. "I didn't know him. That couldn't have been Blake. Was it? Was it really?"

"Yes," I said, wanting her to feel angry instead of sad. "It was every inch Blake Darley."

But this only caused a new batch of tears to pour onto the pillow sham. Once she had collected herself, and some tissues from the box on the nightstand, she continued. "He said that once his mother's campaign was over that we could talk. He said now that she was looking at cabinet, there wouldn't be a campaign to run. He said..." Her eyelids drooped. "He'd asked me to wait for him. I can show you the emails, Daisy. I'm not making this up."

"I believe you," I said softly, stroking her hair.

"He said he still thought about me all the time. That he hadn't gotten over me, not even close. He used the word *love*."

"I think," I said, knowing now was the time, "that I can explain why he went from saying all of that to how he acted in the bar." I shifted up and rested my head on my hand. "I just found out maybe an hour ago. There had been rumors, but I didn't want to tell you until we knew for sure." I took a breath. "When Melinda Darley is confirmed, Blake will run for her open seat."

Wallis scoffed, and drew her arms to her chest. "Not possible," she said.

I summarized for her what Bo had learned, and from whom. She went very still. "I'm so sorry, Wallis," I said.

She did not speak again, even when I informed her that I would move our flight earlier. She left the bed to put on her pajamas and run water over her face, moving with a calmness born of desperation. When she asked me for a sleeping pill, I obliged.

Our room that night was full of echoes. Wallis's plaintive cry: *You promised me!* It chased me, from side to side, from ear to ear, no matter how I tossed and turned. It took long, too long, for the sleeping pill to find me. Echoing in my last thoughts, before I succumbed, was the sound of a ruptured promise. To Wallis, perhaps it had seemed, there in the bar, like the earth's crust was cracking, its plates grinding apart. For me, the sound had been quieter, the subtle tear of thread, the fracture exposing the unflattering flesh beneath the seam.

———

The alarm on my phone woke me. The light through the curtains was gray; the room was overly warm. I sat up, searching for Wallis, feeling the remnants of nighttime sweat on the back of my neck and between my breasts. She was sitting at the rolltop desk, typing intently on her phone.

"Are you okay?" I asked, feeling the utter pointlessness of such a question.

"No," Wallis answered. "What time is our flight?" I told her I'd have to call the airline. "You do that," she said. "I have to go talk to Bo."

"He might not be awake yet," I said.

"He is," Wallis said. "I've been texting him. I have to thank him for last night, and apologize."

"That's good of you," I said, rubbing my eyes, trying to ready myself to face the day, which meant dealing with what happened—*all* of what happened—yesterday.

"It's required," Wallis said. "Although I don't know how I'm going to look him in the eye."

"We also should prostrate ourselves before Collette Reed," I said, stretching my arms above my head.

"Add it to the list," she said. "Wallis Richardson's Tour of Apology. Let's make T-shirts." She tore off her pajamas and threw them toward her suitcase. When she missed, I thought she might start screaming. Instead: "You never have to do this, Daisy. You never make an ass of yourself in public."

This was so absurd I almost laughed. I rose from the bed, stood before her, my hands on her shoulders. "That's objectively false," I said, recalling Atlas, the way I'd lunged toward him with a passion that was entirely unreciprocated.

Wallis made a sound like she disagreed, then pulled away to half-heartedly rummage through her suitcase. After she'd tugged on a short-sleeve blouse and frayed jean shorts, she left to find Bo. Meanwhile, I got myself through the airline's automated system to an actual human, who switched us to a noon flight for the minor fee of a couple hundred dollars. Onto my credit card. A full savings account was officially a distant dream.

In the hallway, there were shuffles. Floorboards creaked. The house was waking up.

Wallis came back with word that Bo had accepted her apology, but that Collette Reed was not yet awake to receive ours. We would have to send flowers and a card. As Wallis ordered the car, I calculated how many orange tulips it would take to mop up our mess.

Twenty-Five

"Family meeting," I said from my sister's doorway, though I wasn't sure this could be considered such, as Wallis was prone in her bed, Cricket beside her, caressing her hand. "What are we going to do about this?"

"About what?" Wallis's back was to me, her pillow muffling her voice. "Blake's gone. Nothing left to do."

"I meant about you," I said. On the plane, I'd reiterated to myself the importance of keeping the tuition news to myself. Wallis, and now Cricket, too, had enough to deal with. I also wasn't ready to talk about it, wasn't even sure how. In the taxi, I proposed ways to keep us both occupied and distracted: an activity, a movie, a hike along Rock Creek, even the mediocre open mic night at the bar down the street. But Wallis had found fault in all my suggestions, and stubbornly remained despondent, her eyes lonely and blank. "We've got to figure out a way to piece you back together."

"It's not some switch I can flip," she argued. "If it were so easy to *get it together* don't you think I would've done it by now?"

I was tired, scruffy, in need of a shower. I'd eaten a dense, flavorless muffin in the airport before we'd boarded, hours ago. It had been the opposite of nourishment. Still, I couldn't let up. "It's excruciating for me to see you in this pain. Please," I begged, circling to the other side of the bed. "Remember, my God, there is a silver lining here. And I know you may not want to acknowledge it," I said as she burrowed deeper in her pillow. I raised my voice. "But think of what might've happened if he'd kept you strung along for months and months, through the campaign. Or worse! Think of if you'd gone through this election with him, only to discover who he really is after you'd given up everything."

"I've already given up so much," she said.

"What are you talking about?" I asked, dropping to my knees, reaching out to tuck back hair that had fallen over her eyes. "What have you given up?"

"My *heart*, Daisy. My time. You know, he told me to wait for him until after his mother got reelected. Then he just wanted us to wait until after the confirmation hearings. And so I waited because I *believed* him. I believed in us."

"Cricket?" I looked up at my mother, pleading. "Ideas?"

She stared at me blankly, then returned to Wallis. "I wish I could take away some of your pain, darling," she said. "I know how much you love him."

"That's not helpful, Cricket," I said.

Cricket released Wallis's hand and, without preamble, got up and escorted me from the bedroom by the elbow. Once we were out of earshot, she wheeled on me. "You can't snap at her like that, Daisy. She needs to wallow. She also needs you to allow it."

Frustrated, I threw up my arms. "I can't just sit here—"

Cricket stopped me. "No one is asking you to. But Wallis isn't like you. She can't just keep busy and forget about it."

If only I *could* forget: about Atlas's text, entrenched in my phone: *Stealing seems to have started with your college tuition.* There was not enough busywork in the bureaucracy to make me forget those words. They had set up camp in my brain. The tent was pitched, the fire lit. For more than a day it had been blazing, and I still couldn't figure out how to respond to this news, and to Atlas himself, who was waiting on my response. Cricket sensed me spiraling, I think, because though she still held my elbow, she'd softened her grip.

"I'm not busy, Cricket. Not anymore. So how am *I* supposed to deal with everything now?" I closed my eyes. My mother chanted my name. *Daisy. Daisy. Daisy.* Then we were on the couch, and she was telling me to breathe deeply. I obeyed, but the task was harder than it should've been. I had to consciously remind myself that panic was impractical. When I felt more stable, I opened my eyes. Across from us were my father's same old wing chairs. But the walls—no longer psych ward white. "Cricket," I said. "The walls are blue."

"Delicious color, isn't it?" She admired the room. "I got the paint at the resale shop. Took a gallon and most of the day. And I only ruined one pair of shoes."

"You did this?"

"Yes, Daisy, I painted a few walls. They say, change your wall color, change your life. Right?"

"Change your hair," I said, smiling at the idea of Cricket acclimating to this apartment. "Change your life."

"Well, I like my hair currently," she said, tossing it back. "So, walls it was."

"I like it," I said.

"That's a relief. Now, Daisy, you and I both know that Wallis will be fine. But if you *tell* her she will, she will insist she won't. This is one of the earliest lessons I learned as a mother."

"Reverse psychology?"

"No," Cricket said, bemused. "Just backing the hell up."

I appreciated her confidence, but she still hadn't solved the problem of what we should do in the meantime. I searched the room, landing on the television. An idea came to me. "When we were little, when Wallis or I felt lousy, you would pour us a giant bowl of cereal with half-and-half and let us watch soap operas or episodes of *ER*."

Cricket looked confused. "That cheered you up?" she asked. "That was me being lazy."

"That was you being wonderful." There'd been a day, around sixth grade, when a cool girl had made fun of my saddle pants. In retrospect, she'd been right; those pants (violet, stretchy) had been heinous, but she'd been cruel, and I'd been *so* down about it. Until, that is, Cricket had introduced me to Dr. Ross.

Cricket gestured toward her refrigerator. "I have some light cream for coffee. Would that work?"

"Yes. Cereal?" She shook her head no. "I'll go around the corner to the store. I'll get some beauty supplies, too. She can wallow in a mud mask."

"When you're back, you can set up the Netflix."

I placed my hand on her shoulder. "Cricket, you can set

it up yourself. You still have the paper with the instructions I wrote for you? Good. I believe in you."

She puffed up her chest, which made me grin. I didn't actually expect her to succeed; this was a task that required remote control mastery and an understanding of the difference between HDMI 1 and 2 on the outdated television we'd saved from P. Nevertheless, when I returned with bags of feel-better supplies, she stood in the living room, triumphant, a show already queued. Wallis was curled on the couch under a heavy blanket, chewing her cuticles. I knelt before her and wordlessly lined up my drugstore offerings on the coffee table: nail polish, ice cream, fruity loops, fuzzy socks with rainbows, gummy worms.

"Which one first?" I asked.

Wallis only hesitated a moment. "All," she said, not even glancing down at the array of selections.

Cricket procured spoons. And for a few hours, we practiced the delicate art of forgetting.

May

Twenty-Six

After the night of indulgence with Cricket and Wallis, I turned to a blank page in the back of my day planner and began to formulate a list.

The first bullet point: my job. I needed it back, now more than ever.

My guilty conscience was thumping from beneath the floorboards. In a way, I envied the person I'd been before, the version of me who had sat through classes and lectures, enjoyed meals with friends and office hours with professors, delighted in books and readings, blithely unaware of how my father had paid for it all. I even looked wistfully on the Daisy of a week ago, who recognized the disgraceful side of her father, but didn't yet understand how it had benefited her directly. But now I knew, and I couldn't unknow, and measures needed to be taken to make up for it.

My father was gone, and so the entirety of restitution rolled forward, onto me. Fine. I was a part of this; I needed urgently to make amends—through work, doing some good. Miles still hadn't called, but I wouldn't let a small thing like that derail me.

As motivation, in case I lost momentum or hope, I jotted down what the Judge had said in Charleston: *It is easier for men to take things.*

To get my job, I'd have to take it.

That's how I ended up at Union Market on the Thursday after Charleston for lattes with Ari. The workday lunch crowd was there, as was the stroller set. I, in a coat too heavy for the weather, waited for her in the appointed place—an espresso stall selling designer coffee. Naturally, I was blotchy and breathless from the ten-minute power walk from the Red Line. If only I had the courage to dab my cleavage with a napkin, to shrug off my jacket and reveal sweat stains to the neatly aproned baristas and their clientele.

Ari had texted me midweek. Atlas had informed her I was on leave, and she asked if we could grab dinner, she might have something that could help. I had no desire to get to know her better, but I couldn't turn down the offer of assistance.

There was also this issue of loneliness. I'd been out of the office for almost a month, and other than the trip to Charleston, I hadn't had a lot of variety in my personal life. Cricket was often gone during the day, and Wallis, as despondent as ever, was still dragging herself to work. There was only so much pleasure one could get by making small talk with grocery cashiers and other strangers forced to interact with you. I couldn't suffer through a whole meal with Ari, but a coffee seemed reasonable and, at this point, preferable to sending a Hey, long time! text to one of my former friends who'd distanced themselves after—everything.

I could combat my love for Atlas another day, in private. In public, at least, I could pretend that Ari's presence didn't bother me. I envisioned bringing up the subject of Atlas myself, as though to say, *Oh, I see your superior claims on him, and raise you one tone of nonchalance.*

I'd reread his texts many times since Charleston, though I wasn't sure why. I knew the lines by heart but still had no answer for him.

It was possible that Atlas had told her about his discovery; they were sharing a bed, after all. I didn't know what they talked about on their pillows, but if it were about me, I would be mortified.

"I love this place," Ari said when she arrived at the stall's counter. She wore a beautiful cream coat that tied in the front like a bathrobe. She hugged me—squeezed me, rather—with an enthusiasm I wasn't ready for. The perfect swoop of her ponytail reminded me of cursive letters, of signatures. "I haven't been here since I left DC. It makes me think of Borough Market."

Union Market was as trendy now as it had been when it opened a handful of years ago. The neighborhood had formerly been known only for its industrial warehouses, but was now dense with cranes and newer structures that advertised themselves as "mixed use." If you build it, they will come. They weren't wrong. From the outside, Union Market's once scruffy exterior had been buffed, so it looked less like a run-down terminal and more like a big, modern food hall. Inside, it was full of colorful stalls selling microgreens, oysters, and tea towels. The butcher would let you taste the difference between soppressata and chorizo before buying. One could purchase a cactus in a pot. Sepia-toned pictures of the original purveyors hung on the interior walls.

In the summer, there were beer festivals and crawfish boils. You can easily imagine the lines for the smoked fish counter during the holidays.

"This is so nice, Daisy," Ari said after we'd located an unoccupied table next to the glass garage doors that would be raised soon when the weather was warm enough. "I'm so happy we could get together and catch up." We clinked takeaway cups of chai. "It's incredibly painful trying to make new friends as an adult."

I cleared my throat, preparing to do what was needed to land on her good side. "Yes. And, you know, I feel a little weird about when I ran into you the other week. I was so shocked to see you. I feel like I might've come across as cold. I didn't mean to be."

In her response, she managed to both call me ridiculous and a sweetheart, but I let it go. We did the business of stirring, of sipping, of comparing lists of people we knew. Then I let her do most of the talking. Ari spoke like many slender women do—animatedly, with shoulders hunched slightly forward, elbows extended out, creating even more definition in their biceps. She was naturally clever, and had a filthy mouth with a natural instinct for just the right place to use the word *fuck* for maximum impact.

It took me by greater surprise how little she did to conceal her opportunism. This was actually pretty rare in Washington—not the ambition, of course, but the acknowledgment of it. Usually these types at minimum attempt to cloak their ferocious ladder-climbing with some humility. DC *loves* a mythmaker. How often have we heard: *My grandfather worked in a factory,* or *My mother drove a school bus,* or *I was so poor I didn't have two nickels to rub together*? My father didn't let a speech go by without informing the crowd he was the son of a car salesman. Not this from Ari. "My lips," she whispered to me, "were once thinner, before the injections." That was her harshest criticism of herself, for which I had to give her credit.

What could I tell her that she didn't already know? She knew everything, everyone. She'd been living in England for the past three years, had only just moved back, but there she was, insisting she had the best manicurist, the best suite at the baseball park, the best tarot card reader, if I happened to be so inclined. Did I want to try cryotherapy?

Instead of revealing my ignorance about what in God's name that was, I changed the subject. "Do you miss London?" Maybe she'd delight me and say yes. Then she'd go back. And though Atlas still wouldn't love me, at least I wouldn't be ambushed by visions of them together.

The night before, Ari had added me as a friend on social media and I became one of two thousand followers. I scrolled for hours. Not one picture was dingy, not one suggested a life less than ideal. There were some photos of Atlas, though never when he was looking straight at the camera, and still more of her, by lakes, in forests, holding wine, holding cupcakes, holding other things she certainly did not end up eating.

"Not really," she said. "I mean—I miss some parts. The feeling of living in a city of little villages. The ability to fly anywhere else in Europe pretty easily. The fact that you could buy bags of potato chips in pubs. The shopping and fashion."

"I suppose DC doesn't compare to the London fashion scene," I said hopefully.

Ari's lips curled. "No," she said. "Have you thought of living abroad?"

I had the sense, muted but insistent, that we were circling each other. "No," I said. "I went to Charleston last week and that was enough travel for a while."

"Atlas told me you were there." Of course he did. Lovers told each other things. My jealousy at their intimacy flashed so bright I had to blink it away. How lovely it would be if I could say his name like she could, dropped so casually, like ice into a glass. She continued, "With the Darleys all over the news, there must've been a lot of talk of them down there. How is Miles preparing for the confirmation hearings next week?"

"Don't know," I said. "I've been—"

"Out, yes." She sat upright in her dainty chair as though it were a throne. "You're taking some time off. There's nothing wrong with that."

"The rumors suggest otherwise. People are saying I've been fired. And have you heard the one about my nervous breakdown?" This last one I hated the most for its callousness and objective sexism.

She smiled. "Yes, that one's been floated. But don't worry, Daisy, I've been defending you to everyone. Atlas, too."

She sounded sincere, looked it, too, so I couldn't help but lower my defenses and admit, "Miles is having a hard time trusting me. It's a bit of a problem."

She tapped her lips with a manicured finger. "Miles is going to want to dent Melinda Darley's fender in the confirmation hearings, I assume?"

"Dent? More like total."

She nodded. "I may have some gossip you can bring to him. It may help."

I perked up, glad she had brought up the reason for this meeting, finally. "Source?"

"We have a client who is—shall we say—deathly afraid of Melinda Darley's nomination."

"Big Hospital doesn't want to lose their Medicare funding," I said.

"Of course not," she said. "More funding, extra cash, big raises for CEOs."

The market was getting busier; I moved my chair to the side so people could more easily pass around me. "When you said 'deathly' afraid, you're talking about the *very* real fear of having to sell your personal helicopter, I assume?"

"Correct. Okay. So. Hold on to your panties."

"Holding." The sun had shifted in the time since we'd sat, and now a bright beam was almost directly in my eyes. But I didn't want to take even the spare second to pull my sunglasses from my purse, I was so desperate to hear what she was about to say.

"When Blake was at College of Charleston, he was part of a fraternity."

I felt my pulse accelerate. "This is about Blake?"

"About mother and son, yes. So, Blake is a senior, and as part of the frat's hazing rituals, he stuffed five freshmen into a port-a-potty and pushed it down a hill."

"Shit."

"Exactly. It crashed into the side of a building and cost a few thousand in damages. A pledge also broke his leg. The pledge happened to be a prized basketball recruit. The coach was not thrilled."

"And Blake was suspended?" This was turning into a story of a college kid doing dumb things, and while it was entertaining, I wasn't sure how it would be useful.

Ari scoffed. "Maybe if the pledge had broken his neck. But for a leg? No. That was only a violation. But something happened after that, like Blake was trying to get himself expelled. His entire senior fall semester was spent jumping on land mines as if he liked to hear the boom. The pièce de résistance was when he was caught in the doggy door of his English professor's home with a sword in hand."

"A sword?" I asked, struck by this bizarre detail.

"Ceremonial? From the frat. What makes it even better is that he'd cut himself up pretty badly with it. And that he was found drunk, asleep, stuck in this door the professor had built for his pug."

"He did have a few scars on the palms of his hands," I said, remembering the time Wallis had asked about them. "He had this heroic story about breaking into a car window in a parking lot to rescue an overheating dog."

Ari rested her cheek in her hand, amused. "If you classify heroism as drunken, bumbling ineptitude, yes. We could call him a hero."

"Breaking into a professor's house with a weapon is no joke," I said, though I, like her, was now on the verge of giggles.

"That seemed to be it for the administration," Ari said. "They put him on disciplinary suspension, but here comes your girl, Melinda Darley. She couldn't even let him take the hit on the chin like a man. Word is she bribed at least one dean, and made a pledge to the college president for an addition to the library. Blake graduated as planned, and the college library now has a coffee shop. Meanwhile, that same semester, a professor of Women's Studies was fired for having less than an ounce of marijuana on her at a family barbecue."

"A bribe?" *Melinda Darley*—widow of the minister, squarest of the square, proselytizer of family values—bribed someone? "What hard evidence is there?"

"Might be some emails." She blinked coyly. "Might be able to get them for you."

So she had proof. Good. I would need it. I checked the calendar on my phone. "Confirmation hearings start next week," I said. "If Miles is going to use this stuff, I should get it to him soon."

"What do you mean *if*?" Ari asked. "Of course he'll use it! People hate Melinda Darley. They'll be sending you fan mail for this."

"And for you?" There was no time to be delicate. "What are you looking for in exchange?"

Ari shook her head; it felt like she had anticipated this question. "No angles. Like I said, I have a few clients who'd like to see her jammed up. But otherwise this info is yours, free. Do what you'd like with it."

"Thank you," I said, and I meant it.

"I hope this helps bring you in from the cold," she said. "I'll be in touch. And of course, I'll tell Atlas you said hello."

Then she was gone with a hug that I couldn't quite make it out of my seat to reciprocate. I sat at our table, phone in hand, trying Bo again and again until he answered. Miles was currently in Annapolis, Bo said, with the Chesapeake Bay people, oyster and watermen, the nonprofit folks, representatives from the Corps of Engineers. The meeting was getting heated; best not to disturb. But Miles would be back in the office tomorrow. At last, a time was set to see me.

After she was done with work, Wallis met Cricket and me on the corner of Connecticut and Q. "An evening with my girls," she said, hugging us both, more buoyant than I'd seen her in days. "This is just what I needed." The perfume she wore to the office was light, touches of lily and citrus.

"What a treat," agreed Cricket, who'd been more than willing to join.

"I thought we could all use it," I said, happy to be out, together, in the spring. As we walked together north, away from the traffic swirling around Dupont Circle, I took a moment to enjoy the daffodils and hyacinth sprouting in planters along the sidewalks, and the budding canopy of green leaves and delicate white flowers. "The restaurant is just up here." I'd read the reviews. Five stars. Try the crispy brussels sprouts and handmade rigatoni, people said. A splurge, but I'd assured myself a paycheck was forthcoming.

Tomorrow I would be getting my job back. *I feel it in my bones*, my father used to say. This is how optimistic people carried themselves all the time—what a wonder! I was light on my toes. Feeling celebratory, I'd even curled my hair. The big ringlets had unraveled almost immediately, but still! It had bounce!

When we arrived at our destination, a converted Georgian townhome, Wallis stopped short. "This?" she said, calm, one hand extended toward the restaurant. "This is the place you picked for dinner?"

"Yes," I said cautiously, smile tight. "Is it bad?"

"Are all these people waiting for a table?" Cricket crossed her arms as she eyed the patrons sitting on the townhome's stoop and wrought-iron benches. "You know I don't like eating past eight."

"Blake and I ate here. It ended up being the last night we were together before—"

Good *grief*. Leave it to Blake Darley to sneeze over everything fun in this town.

"I'm so sorry," I said, wanting to assure her that I would never deliberately whip up those old memories. "I didn't know." I turned aimlessly in a circle, scanning the block for another place we might eat that didn't have a wait of hours.

"It's all right, Daisy. It's…not as painful as I thought it would be."

"We'll go somewhere else," said Cricket.

"Just give me a second." Wallis looked at the sidewalk and then at Cricket. The sun was setting down R Street, and from behind, she was illuminated. "I loved him," she said. "That's what I've been thinking about the last few days. I loved him. I wish I knew if he ever loved me, or if I was just deluding myself the entire time. Don't worry, I'm not about to forgive him, or excuse what he's done. I just had this idea that I could change his heart. That I could draw him out of his family. I was stupid to think I could."

"It's never stupid to hope," said Cricket.

Atlas came to mind, his long fingers as he once slipped a piece of printer paper under an industrious spider in my living room, placed it so gently over a glass cup, took it down three flights of stairs and released it, safe, in the mulch. Was it silly to hope that this careful, compassionate man would ever be mine? Or, like Wallis, was it time to up my dosage of reality?

"Blake and I were both so naive," replied Wallis, gazing at the sky. "Even if his mother could tolerate me, what would our future have looked like? He would've always been part of that family. And what could I have done with that? Don't you think we both would've started resenting the hell out of each other?"

The host, in a vest and tie, came out on the stoop and announced to a nearby party that their table was ready. *Maybe another night,* I thought, *and that will be our name he calls.* We wouldn't get our nice dinner, not there, but I'd have this: proof that my sister's pain was ebbing.

And I had one more thing that might help speed her recovery. I beckoned the two of them close. I'd planned to wait until dinner, but now, on the sidewalk, was as good of a time as any. We huddled together against the iron fencing, and they listened to Ari's story about the Darleys until the sun was well and truly set, replaced by the glow of the streetlamps and the lights planted under the trees. Wallis wanted every detail. Every word. I summarized as best I could, but I did not mention my source. I couldn't bring myself to explain about Ari.

After I'd gone through it twice, we walked north on New Hampshire toward home. Cricket ordered curry takeout from her phone, and Wallis had me narrate the story yet again. When I was finished, she said sadly, "I should've been able to see the writing on the wall."

Cricket complained of tight shoes and aching feet, so we hailed a cab. I had one final thought for my sister before we got in. "His behavior isn't reflective of you, Wallis. You don't owe anyone an explanation."

She gave me a grateful look and squeezed my hand. But in the back of my mind were thoughts of my father, and the checks he wrote, and the secret I still couldn't bear to tell.

—

After Cricket had disposed of the take-out containers, she and Wallis both retired to bed. I was still on their couch with a handful of Thin Mints and the local news on mute, not sleepy in the slightest, not ready to go down to my empty apartment, to give up the night that was supposed to be about a better future. *It's never stupid to hope*, Cricket had said. I knew exactly who I wanted to talk to. The phone rang only once before he picked up.

"Hi, there," Atlas said.

I tucked a knee beneath my chin. "Hi," I said.

"What are you doing?" he asked at the same moment I said, "Are you busy?"

We laughed. "I was trying to write," he said.

"What are you working on?"

"I'm supposed to be writing this piece on very public social media mistakes by government employees," he said, "but I fell down a YouTube rabbit hole. I started on White House dot gov and then all of a sudden I was watching videos of people singing show tunes in cow suits."

"You *know* that's my guilty pleasure, Atlas. Send that link over right now." He laughed, and I could imagine it was like old times. Just him and me and a late-night phone call. And the elephant. Best address it, so we all could move forward. "I'm sorry I haven't responded to your texts. I've been...missing."

"I knew where you were," he replied after a second. "You weren't AWOL. You were just angry with me."

"With you?" That I didn't expect. "No, not with you."

"No?" He sounded relieved. "Your silence—I thought you were furious I'd told you about—"

"Atlas," I said, stopping him. "I'm glad you told me. If I *had* to know, I mean, I'm happy I heard it from you." It

was true. And it did feel good to have someone supportive with whom I could discuss it. Keeping it to myself was
quickly becoming exhausting.

"I see." Then he was quiet. So was I. But eventually:
"That's actually why I went back to Arizona. I couldn't just
leave you with that uncertainty. Especially since I was the one
to cause you that headache to begin with. I wasn't being a
responsible friend last month when I came to you with hear-
say. *Maybe he did this, maybe he did that*—no. God, I cringe
at myself. I was wrong to have brought that to you without
all the facts. I hope you'll forgive me for continuing to track
this down, even when you told me to stop. I just, I thought
that you should know in case—"

"In case someone else discovers it," I finished for him. I'd
been aware of this truth for less than a week, but it hadn't
escaped my mind that if Atlas knew, other journalists might,
too. "I understand."

"All right," he said. "Then you don't feel like you were
hung out to dry?"

It would've been unfair, to say the least, to hold Atlas,
the messenger, accountable for how he delivered the news
of my father. But Ari's voice, materializing out of the ether
at the book party, still echoed in my ears. "About my father, no. But, seriously, Atlas, you could've told me about
Ari moving back."

From Atlas, a very deep breath. "Can we FaceTime?"
he asked.

I agreed, and soon enough we were looking at each other.
He wore a simple white T-shirt—his pajamas, maybe?—and
his hair appeared as though he'd been running his fingers

through it. I hoped he didn't notice the dark circles under my eyes like I noticed the ones under his.

"You felt I was hiding something from you?" he asked, earnest.

"Yes." Honesty, as necessary as it was, still made me uncomfortable. I pulled at my ponytail, cleared my throat. "And it made me feel—"

"Bad."

"Yes. Bad. But I'm sure you had your reasons—"

"Daisy." He put his hand out, mock stern. "Don't you let me off the hook."

"Fine." I smiled. "Keep groveling."

"I'm sorry I didn't tell you." He was back to seriousness. "I'll do better in the future."

I've had men in my past apologize to me like they are taking out the trash, like it's a chore. Another couldn't stop apologizing for his wrongdoing, a failure to call when he said he would. I had the sense he wanted to bury me in an avalanche of *sorry*s until I gave up and suffocated. Defensive ones. Lazy ones. And from my father, none at all. This one from Atlas was sincere, and though it was painful to bring up Ari, I was glad I had. At least now I didn't have to sit with the lingering resentment of her ambush.

Anyway, there were bigger concerns. And Ari—who wasn't so terrible, actually—had helped me. I could live with her in his future. "Forgiven," I said. "Best friends forever?"

"Besties," replied Atlas in that very drawn-out, high-falutin voice that always made me laugh.

Twenty-Seven

I was Miles's first meeting of the day. I'd come in, shoulders squared, ready to take back my office, my title, and the one part of my life in which I was usually successful.

"A bribe?" he asked once we sat down, scanning the emails from Ari on my phone. Every so often he'd pause, squint, pinch his fingers on the screen to zoom, take a bite of his organic apple. "Because her son got stuck in a doggy door? This can't be true."

I had wondered the same, but the facts were the facts, and I was ready to wield them. "The emails look to be authentic. The addresses check out, time line matches up. Have you gotten to the one where she says, *I don't want to do anything illegal, but...?*"

When he shook his head, I grabbed the phone and scrolled forward.

"Is this illegal, though?" Bo asked, getting up to stand over Miles's shoulder. "If we bring it up in the hearings, she'll spin it as a simple charitable contribution to the school. She'll claim she was planning on making the donation anyway."

Miles, incredulous, tossed my phone so it spun on its belly across his shiny wood desk. Outside the tall office windows behind him, rain. A soggy beginning to May, overall, and despite the nice weather when Wallis, Cricket, and I'd had our almost-evening out yesterday, this one suggested that summer would be delayed.

"You're disappointed?" I deflated back into my chair.

"You're not? Daisy, Jesus, this woman has championed voter ID laws, bathroom bills, creationism in textbooks. And the best we can do is strongly imply that she got her son out of a college disciplinary hearing?"

"It's something." This was falling apart, fast.

"Not once did she hook up with some younger guy in her office?" Bo said, only partially ashamed to ask. "There've been no shady dealings with au pairs?"

"This would be easier if she were a straight man," I admitted.

Miles leaned back in his chair, cradled the back of his head with his free hand, and chewed thoughtfully. Bo crossed back over and sat next to me again. They didn't say anything, just stared at each other, deliberating.

"Confirmation hearings," prompted Bo, "start next week."

"I can't use this," Miles said. He tilted forward in his chair. "No way would it derail her confirmation."

"If the situations were reversed," Bo advised, "she'd use anything she had against you. She'd bring up your father's service record, your mother's pay stubs, your bad ex-boyfriends. She'd get your dental records and hold your cavities against you."

"But we don't have to use this in the *hearings*," I interjected. I had thought this through all night after Atlas and I hung up. "We'll go to her, backdoor, say we want our highest priorities fast-tracked once she's in cabinet. Or else this embarrassing little anecdote might slip through our fingers, potentially complicating her nomination."

"Blackmail?" asked Bo.

"Not blackmail." My plan was not quite upstanding, but it certainly wasn't unheard-of on the Hill to *press* in this way. "Just a kind suggestion. A helpful hint, if you will. She does something for us. We do—or don't do—something for her."

Miles measured me. "Bo told me what happened in Charleston," he said matter-of-factly.

"I figured he would." I kept a straight face.

Miles continued to look at me, steady. "I understand now why you want to win this battle against the Darleys."

"This isn't a personal vendetta," I said truthfully. "Melinda Darley is all but formally confirmed. Blake will run and probably win. I'm concerned for us, for our objectives. That's the battle I want to fight. And I'm showing up, with every weapon I have, standing behind you."

With Miles, I knew when to speak, I knew when to wait. Now was the time for the latter. In his cheek, the evidence of his jaw clenching, unclenching. "Do it," he told me. "Call Darley's office. Arrange a meeting. And hope to God this works."

As he rose from his chair, I closed my eyes, just for a moment, and begged for favorable winds, for sunny skies, for a universe that was fair and just. I dared myself to believe that this might succeed. "Your vacation is over," said Miles, dropping the remains of the apple core in the wastebasket on his way out. "Hope you enjoyed it."

Twenty-Eight

No one over the age of five would confuse this for professional baseball. Some players on the field were graying. Many were testing the tensile strength of their uniforms. The pitcher for each team didn't actually throw from the mound. But the trappings were there. Big lights. Scoreboard. The mascots—Tom, Abe, George, and Teddy—ran around the edge of right field at the bottom of the fourth inning, shoving and tripping each other.

It was the annual Congressional Baseball Game for Charity. Bo, Wallis, Cricket, and I cracked peanuts and sipped light beer from our seats a dozen rows behind home plate. Next week we would be meeting with Melinda Darley, and I was gathering a certain amount of amusement watching the soon-to-be secretary strike out so hard she spun a full circle in the batter's box.

For many years, Gregory had participated in this event. Shortstop. Cricket, Wallis, and I had attended as a family, posing for pictures, playing the game that was more important than the one on the field—humanizing Gregory, the senator. Unlike the majority of our required outings, I'd actually enjoyed this one. I could eat cups of ice cream and run around with other children. I didn't have to wear tights or a dress.

Cricket had liked this tradition, too, especially as she became one of the veteran wives, leading the welcome committee for new families. She held court, kissed babies, and made friendly overtures to women on the opposite side of the aisle. And it didn't hurt that Gregory always managed to make some pretty dramatic plays.

In the third inning, Miles tripled to left field on the first pitch, and we all stood and hollered like it was our job. And so maybe it was. Cricket, inscrutable behind her giant round sunglasses, took this as an opportunity to excuse herself for a bathroom break and another round of beers. As the crowd died down and the next batter came to the plate, I spotted just the person I'd been looking for a few rows below: Claire, the chief of staff for Senator Armstrong, Miles's counterpart from Maryland. I knew she would make an ideal partner for a new initiative involving both our offices.

Since I had learned the source of my college tuition funding, I had been thinking of actionable, immediate ways to compensate for it. National Literacy Week was coming up, and I figured the two senators could jointly canvas Maryland, establishing Little Free Libraries at schools and community centers, inaugurating read-to-service-dog programs, promoting the 1000 Books Before Kindergarten campaign. All ways to remind elementary and middle school students and their families of the connection between reading and mental health before they left for summer break. Big impact, little money.

I grabbed the shoulder of Bo, who had been laughing with Wallis about the rep from Maine currently running the bases with his laces untied. He obliged me and hollered for Claire; we waved her over and she filled Cricket's empty seat.

"You had me at service dogs," Claire said, clapping me on the back when I finished laying out my plan. I'd always respected her unique combination of diligence and good humor. "Armmie will love this."

Bo agreed. "We could end at the governor's office. Make a resolution proclaiming May as Maryland's reading month."

By the end of the inning, we had a preliminary strategy in place and delegated the obvious first step duties. It was when Claire returned to her own seat that I realized Cricket wasn't back. I guessed she'd been waiting elsewhere, having observed that her place was occupied, then got sidetracked socializing with an old friend.

But when she was still missing at the end of the fourth, I worried something might be wrong, and went to find her. Maybe she'd gotten a phone call from our lawyer. I couldn't imagine she'd break her own cardinal rule and leave without saying goodbye.

I made it up the many steps, ignoring the rows of spectators on either side of me, to the concessions area, and noticed her sitting at a table by the ice-cream cart. "Cricket!" I called as I strode over.

She looked up, forlorn. "Daisy?" she said. "I can't go back in there, Daisy."

"Okay," I said, nodding, trying to mute the warning siren blaring in my head.

"Everyone knows I was married to a criminal. They probably think I abetted him. That's what they all think. I have zero credibility."

She hadn't ever talked about Gregory, or herself, in these terms. I pulled out the chair across from her and gingerly sat.

"I lost him, then I lost everything," she whispered, clinging to her watch, twisting it around her wrist. She'd removed her sunglasses, and her eyes darted nervously. "So what good am I, now?"

I noted our surroundings, still too stunned to formulate words. At a table nearby, an older couple gobbled soft-serve cones that were all but melting down their arms. By the entrance, a father struggled to calm a tantruming toddler. While on the field, powerful congresspeople were flaunting their lack of hand-eye coordination. And *Cricket* didn't feel good enough? I gave my best attempt. "Cricket, I don't think—"

"They're all judging me!" she said, and pointed to the park. "I can feel it."

Our presence at the game had certainly registered, but there hadn't been any stares I would classify as mean or gawky. Especially compared to what we'd faced all winter. I had thought this would be a fun diversion, but maybe the memories of past years, the contrast of where she was now and where she'd been, had gotten to her.

"Do you want to go home?" I asked, leaning in with my elbows on the table.

"No," she snapped, and I drew back, not sure what to make of the unfamiliar woman before me. "What would that say? That I fled? That I wasn't strong enough? That I should be ashamed?"

Inside the park a ball cracked into a bat, and I tried to

tune out the sound of the crowd. "Cricket," I said again. "You don't want to go back in. You don't want to go home. What do you want to do?"

"What am I supposed to do, Daisy?" she asked gravely. Then: "No—forget I asked that. You're my daughter. I'm supposed to be taking care of *you*. I'm not going to make you solve this problem."

Bo materialized in my line of vision at the entrance to the stands, probably sent by Wallis to check on us. I gave him the universal sign for *I need a minute*.

"You know," she continued, as I turned back to her, "it wasn't simple before, my life, but it was straightforward. I knew the rules, at least. I hate what he did to us, but I miss him, so much. I miss him. And I know I'm not supposed to admit that to you."

I'd been spending so much time on my own pain, I'd failed to truly comprehend hers. And she deserved her time to grieve, the same way Wallis and I had. Perhaps it had been easier to accept that Gregory was just cheating on her. The awfulness, in a way, was contained, centrally located in that house, in that beautiful parlor on P with the cream sofa and brass andirons. Though it hadn't seemed like it, these last months had been just as much a strain on her as on us.

"That chapter of your life, in there," I said, angling my head toward the field, the congresspeople on it, "is done. Yes, you're not the senator's wife anymore. But you have opportunity you didn't before. You have freedom."

She made a guttural sound. "I had freedom *before*. Thirty-seven years we were married. And most of the time I did what I pleased. Truly, I did. You know, Daisy, for such a progressive woman you have a really regressive view of me. I chose my own path, and I'm sorry that path doesn't suit you, but it is what it is. The bargain we made with each other wasn't terrible. Please don't blame me for it."

"I don't blame you," I said. I'd always known that Cricket was well-suited to be a politician's wife; I just hadn't understood how much she'd relished the duties of the role. I'd only seen what we'd had to give up as the family of a senator—namely, our privacy—and I'd failed to see what she had gained. "You kept our family together for as long as you could. I will never hold that against you." She still appeared doubtful, so I looked into her troubled eyes. "I promise."

She exhaled and shimmied her shoulders, as if shaking off a chill.

I tugged at the sleeve of her blouse. "Come sit with us. It's a beautiful day. We're right behind home plate. And I heard for the last inning they're going to let that cute congressman from Texas pitch."

"I'm a sight," she said, patting the top of her hair even though there wasn't a strand out of place. "I can't go back in."

"Do you think we care?"

"I just don't want to embarrass you and Wallis."

"You're our mother," I said. "You'll *always* be slightly embarrassing to us."

We had a little laugh, then she linked her arm through mine and we returned to our seats. Wallis and Bo had saved us some peanuts. In the end, our team lost, by a lot, but Cricket stood and applauded them anyway.

Twenty-Nine

To Melinda Darley's office, with the entourage. We rolled deep, feeling the occasion required a show of strength.

It had been a week since Miles's team—our team—had been trounced by hers in baseball, and although the conversation with my mother had left me a bit rattled, slipping back into my office and my work had given me a renewed sense of purpose.

As we marched through the tunnels underneath the Capitol, interns jumping out of our path, we discussed strategy and topics for disarming small talk.

"Her kids," Bo offered. "We can always bullshit about them."

"No mention of kids," I said, sharp. "No mention of Blake."

"Her dead husband was a Baptist minister," L.K. said. "Weren't you raised Baptist, Miles?"

"Lord," said Miles, "not her kind of Baptist."

We bypassed the elevators and made for the stairs, Miles's preference when a busy day's schedule prevented a work-out. I was out of breath by the time we reached Melinda Darley's floor. Outside her office, flags, obviously, and a few tourists taking pictures of the wall plaque bearing her name and state. Her receptionist, a young woman fresh out of the sorority house, asked us to *Please wait just a sec* while she made the call.

I wiped my damp palms on my suit pants and tried to gather my wits. I would need them. Melinda Darley was many things, shrewd and ruthless among them. But when we were escorted back to her office a few minutes later, her greetings were cordial. Handshakes. Offers of water, coffee. The *Please do sit down*s. *Your sports team, they're really something. Gosh, this weather.*

Once the pleasantries had been dispatched, Miles began. He was in one of the armchairs—upholstered a jarring shade of chartreuse—in front of her dark wood desk. From the matching love seat in the corner where Bo and I sat, perched, ready for battle, I thought smugly how awful her taste was. "Off the record," he said. "Are you sure you want to get inside this administration? We've seen what it's like over there."

"The reports, I believe, are grossly exaggerated," replied Melinda. Her dress and lips both burgundy, she sat with fingers tented under her chin, framed by a window with aluminum blinds, her loose papers stacked perfectly in three piles by her right elbow.

"Don't think someone won't try to smear you," Miles said. "Whatever bodies you have buried will be exhumed."

"I'm a simple girl from Turbeville, South Carolina." She glanced at her chief of staff, the same guy from the cemetery and the bar in Charleston, who let loose two barks of laughter. She smiled, too, both rows of teeth. "I've got no bodies buried except for my childhood cat. He's under the old sycamore in my parents' backyard. He has a little headstone, too. Made it from some mortar mix my Daddy had leftover at the hardware store."

I had to mindfully resist rolling my eyes. The story was stump-speech quaint. That is to say, bullshit. After a long pause, Miles prepared to strike. "This is what it's come to, then," he said. Ever so briefly, Melinda cast her eyes in my direction, and I did my best to mask my satisfaction with a professional, pensive expression. "All right, since we're not getting any younger. Our office has come to understand that you bribed some staff at your son's university a while back. That's what this meeting is about. I'm not sure what to do with this information. Therefore, we're hoping you can help."

"Huh." She barely blinked. "How interesting."

"Indeed," said Miles.

"What's stopping you from releasing this information?" she asked. "As you said, media would pounce upon it. So would your colleagues. So why don't you just be frank, Senator. What do you want?"

"Firstly," said Miles, "my mental health study is stuck. And it confuses me as to why. My staff has worked tirelessly with HHS to get the logistics in place. The money, once we get it, will be well used."

"Did you try to get it on the omnibus last year?"

This, from the woman who blocked that exact effort. Bo and I exchanged a skeptical look, marveling at her selective amnesia. It was a pretty brazen tactic, even for the Hill.

"Yes," Miles said. "You didn't bring it up for a committee vote."

In a move I was beginning to recognize as a habit, she pursed her lips and hummed. "I don't remember that."

"I do," Miles said. "But since your memory is foggy, let me remind you, getting the funding should be a no-brainer."

"And you want me to get something earmarked for you," she said.

"That would be helpful. And I imagine there'll be some more specific projects we'd like funded, as well," Miles said, "once you're confirmed."

"I see." Her placid smile remained in place. "The *or else* goes unsaid." The room was quiet again. On the wall behind her desk was a framed yellow flag: the words DON'T TREAD ON ME were printed below a coiled rattlesnake, its hissing tongue extended like a bayonet. I tried not to let it make me nervous, but my heart was now beating unevenly at her acknowledgment of the grenade we had just thrown on her desk. "You've done your research," she said. "And—actually—we have, too. It's all a little embarrassing, isn't it? Having to get into the muck like this. But that's the job."

"My job is working for the people of Mary—"

She cut him off, a slice of her hand through the air. "Save it. You know, you bring up the time when Blake was at college. So, I can't help but remind you about your own chief of staff, and how *she* paid for college. Rather, how *her father* paid for it." Melinda stared at me for a moment, daring me to speak. I could not, for I wasn't really there anymore. I was in my mind, tumbling through possibilities, turning over stone after stone, wondering how in the world she knew. Melinda Darley waited, patiently, until I came to. Then she held my eyes, so when she said the next thing, it was right at me. "Your choice to employ the daughter of one of the most corrupt and shameless thieves this body has ever seen speaks volumes about your judgment, Senator, does it not?"

A less adept politician might have let his shock at this revelation show. Miles did not. "It seems that we are at an impasse."

She drummed her fingernails on her desk. "An impasse? No, a compromise, I think. We will both sit on our respective piles of—what did you call it?—information. And the sanctity of the system will be somewhat preserved. I don't expect your vote to advance me out of committee. Nor do I need it. But I would prefer not to be met in committee with a walkout."

Miles, sturdy as can be, pushed back. "You know I don't have the power to decide—"

"Then find some power," she said, all perkiness and pep. "Maybe it is in the same place you found this ludicrous gossip about me." She spun to her chief of staff. "Can you imagine?"

"I think we're done here," Miles said, rising, arms stiff at his sides.

"Just one more thing, Daisy," she added, standing as well and turning to me. "I know you and my son and your sister were quite close, once. And although Blake was *adamant* that we not hold this tuition thing over either of your heads"—she looked convincingly abashed—"I'm afraid I must overrule him. You understand? Whatever my son said to you during the course of his friendship with your sister will remain a distant memory. If someone asks you about him, you say, *who*?" Then she smiled politely and nodded like this was the simplest instruction in the world.

As she walked out, staffers emerged from their offices along the main corridor to observe the mood, spot the trampled. Their mission was an easy one. But before I could blink, Melinda Darley was gone, back into the open arms of her staff, who would surely cheer once she confirmed their victory.

"Is it true?" Bo whispered when we were down the hall and out of earshot.

L.K., who had waited for us outside, was ahead with Miles, handing him a bottle of water, a tissue.

"I don't know," I said, the lie making me feel even worse. Miles sped down the steps, and we all had to hurry more than usual to keep up. We passed into our office building, and the tunnel structure changed, became narrower, the lighting harsher. I felt exposed. The shock of Melinda Darley's knowledge was beginning to wear off; taking its place was scorching regret. Why did I think this would work? Bo had been right—it was blackmail. I'd just tried to *blackmail* a sitting senator. I turned my face away from Bo, but not before I saw the disappointment in his eyes.

We caught up to Miles and L.K. at the elevator. "Daisy." Miles frowned. "Go to that meeting on rural broadband for me, will you? I need to get back to the office."

I questioned whether a dull, overly long basement meeting would be the worst of my punishment. "Miles, can I just say—"

"Please," he said without looking at me. "Don't want to know. Let's go, Bo."

I had always thought that someday Bo would have my job. I'd assumed it would be a peaceful transition, he—brilliant, capable, my chosen successor. It hit me then that the decision would likely be taken out of my hands. I doubted this epic calamity would result in another round of leave; if Miles did anything, he would fire me.

When the car arrived, everyone stepped in but me. "In your opening remarks during the hearing," I said as the doors began to close. I raised my voice, "You can still press her on the temperament issue! Can emphasize her hypoc-risy!"

But Miles, conferring with L.K. and Bo, did not so much as glance in my direction.

Thirty

I'd made it through the week without being fired. Barely. In the hours and first days after meeting with Melinda Darley, Miles was monosyllabic when he spoke to me at all. He continued to send me to the worst assignments, pointless meetings, random panels. He, or maybe Bo, had told L.K. about what happened, and as truly sympathetic people are wont to be, she absorbed this upsetting news by becoming upset herself. *So unfair, Daisy,* she'd said. *Another piece of terrible gossip leveled against you.* She'd promised not to repeat it. It didn't serve Miles for this to spread anyway.

Though L.K. thought I was being treated badly, it was actually the reverse, and then some. I'd put Miles in jeopardy with my brilliant little plan, so desperate to get my job back, I'd wounded the person and the causes I most wanted to support.

When it felt safe, after the worst of Miles's anger had dimmed, I had remorsefully, tentatively brought to him my idea for Literacy Week. It was met with a grunt of approval, and a gradual easing of tensions around the office. Still, my nerves made me feel like I'd never sleep again. Midnight on Saturday found me in my tattered terry bathrobe, one I'd had since college and couldn't bring myself to throw away, watching cable news. Even at this late hour, anchors and pundits were chewing over Melinda's upcoming confirmation hearings; a contentious nominee had practically everyone on air salivating.

The fact that *Melinda Darley*, of all people, was aware my father had stolen for me was especially brutal. Had she known when we ran into her at the graveyard presser? Had others? While I trusted L.K., Bo, and Miles, I didn't have the same confidence that Melinda Darley's office would remain close-lipped. Putting my faith in her and her staff would be like trusting a stool with two legs to hold my weight.

But as much as I resented Melinda Darley, she'd brought something into stark relief: even though she'd never admit it, she and my father were remarkably similar. They both threw money at problems, flouted decency and sometimes laws, all the while thinking they were helping their children, and by extension themselves, burnishing their reputations. At least, that must've been Gregory's motivation.

When Bo had asked me for the truth, all I'd said was *I don't know.* What I meant was, *I don't know what to say.* If I came clean about what my father had done, I would dislocate the lives of my mother and sister further, lose my job, my credibility, everything I'd tried to rebuild in the wake of my father's death.

But the question still nagged: How many more bad choices before I became entirely unrecognizable? I kept dead-ending there, and a trapdoor kept opening under my feet, causing me to fall back to the start.

My phone buzzed: Atlas.

"Did I wake you?" he asked.

"Of course not." I pressed the phone into my ear, willing him closer.

"I figured you'd be watching the news," he said, referring to Melinda. "Turn it off, please, would you?"

"Because I'm about to throw myself off the roof?"

"You're not on the roof," he said. "If you were, I would see you."

"You're outside?" I got up and shuffled to the window. It was dark, but I could make out his figure on the sidewalk below. He raised an arm and saluted. Unsure why he was outside my building after midnight, I waved back slowly. "What in the world are you doing?" I asked into the phone. Our positions made me think of Romeo, or Lloyd Dobler.

"Honesty time," replied Atlas, and I thought I might've seen him sway on his feet. "I'm inebriated."

I wondered if Ari was at his apartment, asleep perhaps, waiting for him to get home. I wondered why he was here, and not with her. But then he hiccuped, and said "Oh, excuse me" in such a cute, polite way, I put Ari aside and told him to come on up. "I have coffee," I said, "or your favorite bourbon."

We ended the call—his slurry *Yay!*—was the last thing I heard, and I buzzed him inside. Turning off the television, I evaluated my outfit. I was wearing soft clothes in large sizes, the bathrobe did nothing for my figure, and my hair was piled on top of my head. I considered whether I should change, put on makeup, but then opted to open my door and wait, just as I was. Even if there'd been time, what did I need to impress him for?

A minute later he rounded the stairs with a broad smile. "Daisy," he sang when he hugged me, lifting me easily off my feet. Had he always been this strong, or was it the booze? "I was grabbing pints with mates from work right around the corner, and when I walked past your window and saw the light I just had to ring."

He was drunk, all right, and it had thickened his accent. I silently gave thanks for my own soberness. God help me if I'd been tipsy like at the wedding. Then I could officially add homewrecker to my résumé.

He followed me inside; it took him two tries to get his jacket hooked onto my coat tree. When he succeeded, he looked at me proudly, and I gave him a little applause. I'd only seen him like this once, on the trail years ago. There was something delightful about witnessing a normally buttoned-up man loosen his collar.

"I have to tell you a story about what happened to me today," he said, flopping on my couch. "It involves my apartment building email LISTSERV, an emotional support peacock, a broken elevator, and Vlad, my maintenance man, whose side hustle involves selling energy crystals and men's jewelry."

"Perfect." I made the executive decision that water was the best choice for him, so I grabbed us two glasses from the kitchen and joined him on the couch. His hair was disheveled on top, his dress shirt, which seemed like it was once crisp, was untucked from his jeans.

He took the glass and chugged most of it in a few gulps. "But first," he said when he surfaced, "tell me about your day. Where did you go, who did you see, what was everything about everything?"

I dropped my head back into the cushions and laughed. "What was everything?" I repeated.

"It's a simple question." His shoulders began to heave with laughter. "What is everything regarding everything?"

With his *inebriation*, as he'd called it, my week felt less devastatingly serious. "Help me with something," I said, comforted by his presence, thinking I might as well bring up the subject that had been eating at me before he'd waltzed in. He was the only one in the world, at this point, with whom I felt secure enough to talk to about it. Not wanting to ruin the mood, I kept my voice casual. "How do you think Melinda Darley—soon to be Secretary Darley—found out about my father and the tuition money?"

"*She* knows?" He ran his hand over his end-of-day stubble. "Shit. Her camp must've gotten to Andrea Pell, too. That's the way I found out. Your father, apparently, had said something to her, and I followed the clues to his office's expenditure statements…"

"Andrea. His…lover," I muttered, tripping over the last word. Here was yet *another* person in the world who knew, or at least suspected, that I was the reason for my father's entrée into financial dishonesty. "What more," I asked, "did she tell you? I'm just wondering what else Darley's people know."

Atlas finished his water; he appeared more sober now, his eyes less squiggly. He faced me, serious. "If it gives you any peace," he said, "she did say that your father had every intention in the world of paying the money back. But—"

"But he never did."

"One bad decision becomes another, and then another."
He winced. "If Melinda Darley knows—"

"We have intel on her. And we've made an arrangement,"
I interrupted. "Thanks to Ari, actually." Her name seemed
to have an effect on him. He blinked, shifted, breaking our
eye contact. "Your turn," I prompted, trying to reclaim the
light mood of moments ago. "Tell me about Vlad?"

"Oh, yes," he laughed, and reclined, settling in. And just
like that we were back, just us, Ari's name like the smoke
from an extinguished flame. And for the next hour, I let
his voice silence all others.

Thirty-One

In the back of a second-grade classroom, below a cork-board with posters of Harriet Tubman and Cal Ripken—both famous Marylanders, to be sure, yet one *slightly* more accomplished than the other—Bo and I had contorted ourselves on plastic chairs built for much smaller bodies. This was the final event we had planned for Literacy Week. Over the course of the seven days, we'd met with community organizers and teachers, school counselors and adult day-care workers, and I'd come away with a notebook full of appropriation ideas and tasks to complete. Yes, I found myself saying thankfully, gladly. We can help get your arts center a new HVAC system. Yes, absolutely the women and children's shelter should have a library. Yes, Miles can certainly help you with a letter of recommendation for the Naval Academy. Here's my email address. Here, take my card.

In the front of the room, the children sat crisscross-applesauce on the reading rug, with only minor interruptions shushed out from Miss Brown behind her teacher's desk. As the students listened to Miles finish a story about a bunny who started a book club, Bo showed me headlines emailed from the press office. One of the programs we were promoting—1000 Books Before Kindergarten—was trending. And Miles's reaction to meeting Charlie, the rescued pit bull who let children read to him at the Elliott City Library, had even gone viral. "Miles is a meme," whispered Bo. We pounded fists, proud that Literacy Week seemed to have legs.

When Miles was done, the children applauded and Miss Brown asked if they had any questions for their senator.

Bo and I observed a young scholar rise to her knees, begging Miles to call on her. "If you weren't you, who would you be?" the girl asked. Her school-mandated polo was royal purple and only partially tucked. Her sneakers were new and her pants just a bit short.

Miles said that he would be himself, an answer that was both perfectly him and perfectly appropriate for a classroom full of seven-year-olds. "What's your name, and what do you want to be when you grow up?" he asked her.

"Well, sir," she started, bouncing her bottom on her heels, sounding very much like she'd given this a lot of thought. "My name is Fiona. I want to be a doctor and a ballerina and a mommy and a senator."

Bo and I shared a discreet laugh. Miles, though, slid from his chair to join the children on the rug, and nodded. "Those are noble professions," he said. "I want to ask the children here, what do all those jobs have in common?"

"Money!" several yelled.

"Helping!" said others.

"Yes," said Miles, calming the chatter that had bubbled up in the group. "But I mean what do you *need* to do those jobs?" The children were stumped. Miles looked to the back of the classroom, to Bo and me. "Maybe my chief of staff can answer my question. Daisy?"

The children, each one of them, along with Miss Brown, focused their attention on me. I tried not to fidget. Oh, this was the part of school I hated the most. The dreaded cold call. "Character?" I proposed.

"And education," said Bo helpfully.

"Indeed," said Miles, glad to finally hear the answer he was waiting for. "An education is important, not just because Miss Brown is teaching you all how to read and write well and do difficult math problems, but because an education teaches us how to be good people, strong people. Everyone, show me your muscles." In a flash, the children flexed their tiny biceps. "Impressive." He gave a few skinny arms around the circle a squeeze. "Now, strength is there, but it's also here." He pointed to his chest.

Fiona, who was fast becoming my favorite, raised her hand again. "Mama says if I want to be a doctor, I have to be smart in my brain and brave in my soul."

"If you want to do any job well, Fiona, you have to be smart and brave." Miss Brown tapped her knuckles on her desk, as though to say *this is important*.

"And nice, right, Miss Brown?" said a little boy with a gap in his front teeth. When she confirmed he was correct, the class erupted again, each volunteering the characteristics they believed important to success. Good painter was one. Funny was another.

"And telling the truth," said Fiona, waving both hands in the air with an impish grin. "Can't be a dirty liar!"

The children loved this one, falling over each other with giggles. Miles, charmed, chuckled too. But they all faded away to the background, and suddenly it was just me, alone, unable to join in. Because when Fiona had proclaimed that one should not be a dirty liar, the face that popped into my mind was not my father's. It was my own.

"Language," said Miss Brown, clapping her hands sharply. "Fiona, you try again."

It took Fiona a few seconds, but she got there. "Honest," she said. "A person has got to be honest."

~

Miles set off for a short tour of the school's library, and I, requiring space to think, wandered the building's hallways. Memorial Day was a big thing to celebrate here, it seemed, as the main corridor was lined with stars and stripes, rendered in the familiar chunky, brutalist paint strokes of children. Several versions I actually liked, and made a mental note to inquire with the school if Miles could have one for his office. Maybe I would ask for one, as well, to remind myself what this was all for.

I pushed open a set of doors at the end of one hallway and walked out the school's main entrance and into the humid weight of early summer, which had blazed in this last week of May and clapped over us like a lid. I thought I might sit in one of the benches nearby—one, a gift from the class of 2009 seemed clean enough—but down the stairs leading into the parking lot, I spotted the back of Bo's head.

I descended a dozen stairs to where he was perched in a patch of shade and sat beside him. "Hi," I said, feeling the heat of concrete through the thin fabric of my work pants regardless.

"I had to make for the exit," Bo said, passing his phone

from one hand to the other, his gaze focused into the distance beyond the school buses in the parking lot.

"Me, too," I admitted. "Too many precocious children trying to teach me lessons."

"Yeah?" Bo asked. "What are they teaching us jaded old cynics today?"

Not feeling equipped quite yet to answer his question, I posed one instead. "Why are you out here? You disappeared. I thought you were going to take up that teacher's offer to see the coding studio. I thought you'd heed the call of the nerds."

He laughed softly, then took a ragged breath as he stored his phone in his jacket pocket. "No, I—needed air. It's something about this school. I swear I had a teacher exactly like Miss Brown. Just got me thinking about the past."

My phone rang; Wallis's name lit up the screen. "Blake Darley won his primary last night," I said. It had been close, but winning is winning, whether it's by one vote or one million. He'd be facing his opponent the third Tuesday of July. "I'm sure that's why she's calling." But one look at Bo's face had me silencing it. "I'll get back to her later."

"That fucking guy." Bo dragged his hands down his cheeks. "He wasn't nice to my sister and he wasn't nice to Wallis. And once he wins, we are going to start seeing him at work. Perfect." Off to our right, a smaller side door opened, and a class of squealing children streamed onto a big mulched playground fenced in by chain-link. "I'm sorry. It's been an odd day."

"Tell me," I said. A person prone to worry and melancholy such as I can usually spy another. "Because this isn't about bunny's book club or Blake Darley."

We watched a group on the playground tussle over the

single working swing. "My sister has decided to go for her PhD. My mother is thrilled. All of them are in Italy, you know. My parents and my sister and her fiancé. Some monastery outside Florence. There isn't supposed to be Wi-Fi, but somehow the Judge got an email out to the whole family. She couldn't be prouder of Jessica." He said this last line with the grand sweep of an arm.

"And you're still waiting for your affirmation?"

"Affirmation? Hell, I'm still waiting for her to say, 'I love you, Robert.'"

"She loves you," I assured him, recalling the way she had spoken about her son that night in the glow of her kitchen, the pain in her voice when she'd acknowledged their estrangement.

"I know that," Bo conceded. "Just would be nice to hear it from time to time. I have this chronic fear that I'll never make her proud." He rubbed his knees and sighed. "What am I doing, Daisy? I passed up a vacation with my family to help Miles become a meme?"

I scratched the back of my damp neck. When Bo put it like that, it made me realize the frivolousness of our so-called accomplishment. Still, I couldn't trivialize this event we'd worked so hard on. Because then where would that leave the list I'd made after Charleston? Where would that leave me? "We're hopefully doing some good. We're getting the message out, in whatever way people will receive it. Even if that is solely through GIFs." When this didn't seem to have an effect, I nudged him with an elbow. "You're really going through something here. Is this crisis early midlife, or simply existential?"

He smiled, but it quickly slid off his face. "I just—do you ever think, what if I'm wasting my life? What if I accomplish a whole lot of nothing? The fear lives here"—he patted his heart—"and it is *constant*. I can't get rid of it. How do we shake it, Daisy? Please tell me you know."

I laughed cynically and looked to the sky. Bo had just put into words the same anxiety that incessantly nipped at my heels, informing my every move. "I have no idea, Bo. I can't hide from that fear, either." Maybe it was Bo's vulnerability, or little Fiona's insistence that one should not be a *dirty liar*, but right then, I couldn't avoid meeting my regrets honestly. I looked them in the face, and, as Grandduff used to say, they were as ugly as homemade sin. "I've made some bad choices recently," I said. I'd been meaning to say something to Bo since the Darley fiasco, and now I had the words. "My plan, basically, of blackmailing Melinda Darley was a stupid idea, and it was wrong, and I'm really sorry I put you and Miles in that position."

"You were playing the game," replied Bo. He wasn't sympathetic, just stating a fact.

"Yes," I agreed, picturing the classroom, the children with their muscles and the word that had come to me: *character*. "But maybe I'm done playing it."

Bo nodded. "I think that's right," he said. "I think that might be part of what gets this knot out of my chest. We have to live on our own terms, not disappearing into someone else's expectations for us." He was serious for a moment, then let his head fall back and yelled, startling into flight some birds settled under the school's cornice, drawing some very confused stares from the playground's occupants, each word its own exclamation: "I'm. Never. Going. To. Be. A. Lawyer!"

It was so wildly out of character that we both burst out laughing.

"I'd recommend some screaming," said Bo after I had wiped my eyes with a napkin he'd found in a pocket. "Very therapeutic. Get your voice out there. Make it loud. Do you want to try it?"

"Yes!" I smiled. "What should I say?"

"It's your last day on earth," said Bo. "What do you want people to know?"

Before I could think too hard about the kindergartners and their teachers less than fifty feet away, I cupped my hands around my mouth and, somewhere between a yell and a holler, declared to the world, "My. Father. Stole. For. Me!"

Bo widened his eyes. "Damn," he croaked. "That was a little more—*truthful* than I expected."

"Melinda Darley wasn't wrong," I said, strangely peaceful, a lightness in my body that hadn't been there before. "My tuition, my father stole it. I don't want to be dishonest to you anymore."

"You do know what would happen if—" said Bo.

He didn't have to finish his sentence. "I know," I said.

We were quiet for a time, listening to the drone of bugs and chattering of children. My announcement had made only a minor ripple in the summer air; people were now back to their regularly scheduled playground business, not sparing us another glance. There was reassurance in the reminder that I was just another random person in the world. I could do something silly in public and it wouldn't really matter, in the end.

June

Thirty-Two

Ari marched into my office in a coral body-hugging dress and navy blazer, her hair in a no-nonsense bun. She had emailed late the night before, saying it was urgent.

"Coffee?" I asked after we did the required hug.

"I don't suppose you have an espresso machine?" she said as she placed herself in one of the chairs across from my desk.

I almost laughed but then realized she was serious. "This is the government. We have a tub of Maxwell House."

"In that case, I'll decline."

I closed the door, though it was seven thirty in the morning and we were the only two there. Since the meeting with Melinda Darley and Co. last month, I'd always made sure I was in first. Sara would come in next, followed by Bo, but hopefully this was early enough to squirrel Ari out before anyone discovered she'd been there. I didn't know the reason for her request, but the terseness of her email led to me to believe this wouldn't be another friendly chat. Was she upset about Atlas showing up drunk at my apartment? He'd told me a funny story, went home to his bed, and I went back to mine. A couple of weeks passed. Roll credits.

"I appreciate you coming so early," I said. "I have to go to the Bowie office today." It was a torturous assignment—the Bowie office was full of well-intentioned yet notorious time-wasters and slackers-off—but at least Miles wasn't sending me to basement meetings anymore, thanks in no small measure to the success of Literacy Week. If I could keep making myself useful, delivering respectable victories, both legislative and otherwise, I just might be able to scrape and claw my way back. Which is to say, I could leave what happened in the past there, and focus on improvements for the future.

"Bowie?" Ari made a face: *ew.*

She didn't take her eyes off me as I fell into my seat and folded my hands on my desk, near my phone. I doubted anyone would call me at this hour, but I wanted to be quick on the draw in case someone might rescue me and allow me to excuse myself. "You were rather cryptic in your email," I said. "What did you need to talk to me about?"

"I watched the Darley hearings," Ari said, rolling her neck like she was ready to box. "And was underwhelmed. I kept waiting for Miles's big moment, to reveal our ace in the hole."

"Right," I said deliberately, needing to pivot from thoughts of Atlas to Miles. "Turns out it wasn't such an ace. More like a three of clubs."

This stunned her. "You've got to be kidding. Daisy, you were supposed to use that intel. Otherwise, I would've leaked to our guy at the *Post* a week ago. We needed Darley weakened."

Not wanting to divulge the particulars of why we hadn't, I considered my next move carefully. "It was my total intention to use it. Miles thinks we are best served by keeping it quiet for now. Using it as leverage after she gets confirmed."

"Get your story straight, Daisy." She got up from her chair and placed both palms on my desk. "Either you didn't use it because it's nothing, or it's something, and you're going to wield it later. I did you a favor, bringing you this. Daisy." She said my name again, this time stretching out the last syllable. In her mouth, my name sounded like a rebuke. "Were you too afraid of using it, or what?"

This I did not like. I'd presumed she'd be disappointed, perplexed, maybe even angry. But calling me a chicken? Too far. "Don't confuse patient strategy with panic, Ari. You gave me the intel. You told me I could do with it what I wanted. Well, we want to wait."

"All right." She shrugged, sat again, recrossed her legs. "The confirmation vote is tomorrow. I guess I can leak it today and we might get somewhere."

I lounged back, tried to look disinterested. If she leaked this, Melinda Darley would surely assume it was us, and my and Wallis's secret would be out. I would have to call Ari's bluff; it was the only way to protect our agreement with Melinda Darley. "Come on, Ari. You don't want to do that. The confirmation vote will steamroll the coverage, and media will move on before it can gain any traction. Releasing it now would barely cause a ripple. Wait, though, until later, and see where we can use it. She might screw up, and we can bundle it on top of other gaffes or missteps." I paused, unbreathing, hoping she would buy it.

She pouted, but didn't object. "God, okay, but this isn't a good look for me. I'm going to have to sell this to people."

I turned to my computer, clicked randomly on a few browser tabs, just so she wouldn't catch the relief on my face. "It seems like you could sell a screen door to a submarine," I said and meant it. "I don't imagine you'll—"

My office phone beeped. Sara, on the intercom. "Good morning," she said. "Your next meeting is here."

"My next meeting?" I flipped through my day planner. Had I forgotten one?

"Daisy." Atlas's voice filled the office from the intercom. "I'm due to be on the Hill soon, but I thought I'd take a chance and drop in on you."

"Um," I said, as Ari cocked her head. My hand hovered over the receiver; I contemplated whether I should take him off speaker. But would that look more suspicious? "Well—" I stalled.

"I brought you that latte you like, from that place. Went six blocks out of my way. I stole a sip, and you're right, it is truly fantastic."

I waited for Ari to broadcast her presence. But she didn't. Her lips were pressed tight, her smile painted and insincere. Here was her boyfriend, I saw, bringing me gourmet coffee. But he was my friend, and we, the three of us, would have to make it work. "Come on back," I said. When I hung up, I raised my hands to Ari, as if to prove my innocence.

"Is this a habit of his?" she asked, gesturing around my office, her enamel bangles rattling on her wrist. "Dropping in unannounced?"

I didn't dislike Ari, but bearing witness to her jealousy was a small luxury I couldn't help but welcome. Later that night, she might post a photo of herself and Atlas, together, smiling lovingly, but today, this morning, I could have this.

We both heard his footsteps in the hall. I got up to open

my office door and met him with a smile. Atlas gave me a friendly hug and handed me a very tall to-go cup. "There," he said. "An offering. Forgive me, for dropping in on you so abominably early." Out of the corner of my eye, I watched Ari, sitting, observing.

"You better come in," I said before he could say anything truly incriminating, "and see who's here."

"Hi, babe!" She rose and embraced him with a tenderness that seemed overly theatrical.

I retreated behind my desk as they sorted where to sit.

"This is a happy coincidence," Atlas said after an uncomfortable silence. Then, to his girlfriend: "I didn't know you were seeing Daisy today. I could've tagged along."

"That's what you get for spending the night at your apartment instead of mine." Ari spun her finger in the air. "You fall out of the loop."

"Yeah," he said, although it didn't seem like he knew what he was agreeing with. He chewed his bottom lip. "Yeah," he repeated, to his own nervous beat. "Yeah, yeah."

"Thank you for the coffee," I jumped in. "It's much needed."

"Isn't he the sweetest man on the planet?" Ari asked me. "He does these kinds of things for his friends. He's so thoughtful. But you know this, of course."

"I do." I sipped from my cup, though the drink had gone cold, to hide my smile.

"So," Atlas said. "How is everyone?" Then he laughed, sounding strained.

"We were just catching up," Ari said. "On the latest gossip. Girl stuff."

Atlas looked at me. "Daisy, discussing girl stuff?"

I shrugged. "I am a girl, Atlas."

"Like he needs the reminder," Ari said. "What are you doing here, babe? Besides being a coffee lackey."

I studied Atlas, the way he ran his fingertips over his temple, considering, always considering. If only I could know what he was thinking now. "I was," he said, "just— I mean—" He started patting the pockets of his jeans as though looking for his wallet or keys.

"Jesus!" exclaimed Ari. "It's not an algebra problem."

I hated to see him unsettled. "He's making perfect sense to me," I said. He, grateful, was finally able to meet my eyes. And for a moment, it was just Atlas and me in the room, our history between us, a rope pulled taut.

There was a brief knock on the door, and Wallis shot in like a comet, arms outstretched, going on about how happy she had been to hear from Sara that Atlas was here, how much she'd missed him. Atlas stood, and when they hugged, she kicked up both her feet from the floor.

"This," I said, as they finished greeting each other, "is quite the party at eight in the morning. What are you doing here, Wallis?" And what were the chances of her leaving without a formal introduction to Ari? Next to impossible? No. Intertwined with impossible.

"I'm meeting with a deputy LA down the hall later," Wallis said, attention still on Atlas, who was back in his chair, crossing and recrossing his legs restlessly, "and thought I'd pop in to say hello."

"How was Charleston?" he asked her. "I haven't seen you in what, over a month?"

"Awful," Wallis said, coming to sit on the edge of my desk. "Both the trip and the fact that it's been that long since we've hung out. I mean, Charleston is a gorgeous city, but it ended up being a disaster. Daisy can fill you in. At least Daisy came back looking positively sun-kissed."

Three sets of eyes focused on me, and I resisted the urge to squirm in my chair. "It's faded by now," I said.

"We're working on Daisy's ability to take a compliment," Wallis said, turning back to Atlas. "Aren't we?"

"We are." On Atlas's face was a measure of amusement and something else I couldn't place.

"It's likely our poor Daisy doesn't like being the center of attention," Ari said, and Wallis's head swiveled toward her. "I wonder if we should just let her be. Look how she's blushing! I don't think *that* is the sun."

"Wallis," I said, submitting myself to the inevitable and gesturing toward Ari. "I'd like to introduce you to Ari. She's on K Street."

Ari stood and stretched out her hand. "So good," she said, "to meet you. Atlas talks about how fabulous you are."

Wallis was the picture of confusion. "You know Atlas?" she asked.

"They're together," I answered for the room.

"Happily," Ari said, with a tilt of the head. "I have the very good fortune of being this tall drink of water's girlfriend."

Wallis stared at me, speechless, though I felt nothing except a calm hollowness in my core, as though I were the eye of a storm.

Atlas continued to look at his shoes. It didn't seem he'd prepared himself for the day the three of us would be together. Which, I had to be honest, was strange. What did he expect? Ari and I had hung out. She was on K Street and I on the Hill. He had to predict that our worlds would collide. I'd go to my grave loving him, but, God, sometimes he was so dense. If Ari thought I placed her relationship in any kind of jeopardy, she had severely overestimated me. And Atlas was not a cheater. When he made a commitment, he did not betray it. "Ari's been living in London," I said. "She's back now." In the silence that followed, I drank from the latte Atlas had delivered.

As for Ari, she reached over the arm of her chair and wrapped her hand around Atlas's forearm, her fingertips digging into his shirt. "We should all get dinner," she declared, and I almost choked on my coffee. That was exactly what we all needed, more weird tension, next time with appetizers! "You should come over to my apartment. I'll cook. What about this Saturday?"

"I'm not sure," said Wallis, collecting herself. "Maybe Daisy and I should check our calendars before committing."

"Of course," said Ari. "You both are no doubt in high demand, you single girls in the city. Unlike us old homebody types." With this she smiled at Atlas, saccharine.

"Thanks for coming by," I announced, thoroughly done with the show.

"No trouble at all," Ari said. "Now, I've got a meeting with the Speaker. That man is useless at keeping staff." She rolled her eyes, as though to say, *men.* "At least there's always good chocolate at his reception desk."

"And I'm off, too," Atlas said.

"No," Wallis said, "I've only just gotten here. We have so much to catch up on. You can't leave yet."

Her pleas, as enthusiastic as they were, did nothing to sway him. As I followed them out, I noticed Miles's door was still closed. He'd scheduled a breakfast meeting this morning, and he wouldn't be in for another hour or so. This was good; I suspected when I returned to my office,

Wallis would have some words for me, and I'd rather not my boss overhear.

Once my door was shut again, Wallis wheeled on me. "Why didn't you tell me?"

"There's been a lot going on, Wallis. I only found out a few weeks ago." The emptiness I'd just felt upon seeing Atlas and Ari together, for the first time in the flesh, was now filling with a burning, aching heat. I was tempted to fan myself with printer paper.

"What's a few?" she asked. "Two? More?"

"I'm not sure." Why did I still feel the need to obfuscate? Wallis had seen Ari with her own two eyes, heard the word *girlfriend*, seen her clutch Atlas in front of me.

"That's a lie," she said, arms crossed over her chest.

I collapsed into my office chair and leaned my head against the back of it. "Ari came back in April. I ran into her at your boss's book party. And here we are."

"In *April*? Before we went to Charleston? Dodo, why on *earth* didn't you tell me? I'm your *sister*. If we don't share each other's burdens then what is the *point*?"

I removed my eyes from my office ceiling and trained them across the desk on Wallis. "Don't be angry," I said, stretching my arms out, gesturing that she should sit in the chair Atlas had occupied only minutes ago. "Please."

"I'm not angry!" Her tone, and the fact that she remained in her current stance, undercut these words to some extent. "I love you. I just wish you could be as vulnerable with me as I am with you. It's so easy for me to open up to you. I don't even give it a second thought. Sometimes it hurts when I see you holding things back. God, Daisy." She sighed. "All this time. All this time you've been carrying this by yourself. How have you managed it?"

"I've managed just fine." She didn't want to sit? All right. I stood and walked to my window. I had a view of the squat police station below, an armed officer keeping watch from behind concrete barricades. The image was reflective of how I'd been feeling these past months: defensive, on guard. The unintended by-product had been missing my mother's grief, isolating myself from my sister's honest gaze that always held me to account. But I'd done it for all of us. "There were other things that took precedence."

"Like what?"

At her question, a wave of exhaustion overtook me. Concealing had taken an enormous amount of emotional energy, and I had tapped out of my reserves. Had Gregory felt the same, near the end? I forced myself to face her. "Like the fact that our father paid for our tuition with money that wasn't his, Wallis. Is that important enough for you?"

Her jaw hit the floor, her hands slowly rose and landed on the top of her head. My chest tightened as I waited to see how she'd handle this news. I prepared myself to console, to act as a sounding board, perhaps even to absorb her anger. But, to my surprise, after she blinked a few times, her arms fell to her sides and she went back to firing. "You love Atlas. All these years, you've loved him. I know you have—"

Wallis was obviously deflecting. Wearily, I crossed the half dozen steps that separated us and joined her on the other side of my desk. "Did you hear me? Gregory stole to pay for our colleges."

"I understood you the first time," she said, quiet but firm. "Deep down, I think…we all suspected something like this might be around the corner."

"*Suspected*, not expected. Now I'm doing gymnastics to keep it secret."

"Why?" When I didn't answer, she continued. "Seriously, Daisy, why bother?"

"Do. You. Remember," I said, purposefully spacing out the words, wondering how she could be so calm, "the sound the brick made as it crashed through Cricket's window?"

"There are other things," she said, affecting my slower cadence, "that take precedence."

I stifled a groan; I didn't know how much more I could handle of my sister's fearless, defiant optimism regarding me and Atlas. "The love I have for him is my problem, not yours."

"Really? This is how you've been thinking about love all this time? As something to be endured? As something that can be replaced by other things? Dodo, I can't think of anything sadder."

"All my happiness," I insisted, tapping the back of one hand on the palm of the other, "cannot rely on one person. Think of what happened to you when Blake left. What you went through. Extrapolate, then, what might happen to me if I was to rest every single one of my hopes with Atlas. I kissed him, Wallis." I said it before I knew I was going to. "At the wedding months ago. I kissed him, and he didn't kiss me back."

This astounded her. "He didn't kiss you back? That can't be right." She shook her head until she saw how perfectly serious I was. "God! He's such an idiot. Sorry, sorry, I know you love him." She stepped closer now, rubbed my arms. "You've been so steady," she said, more tender. "You've been like a rock, and I've just been crashing against you, battering you with every bit of my broken heart, and you didn't say one word."

"Yes! Exactly!" I moved away from her and began to

pace my already worry-warn carpet. "I have pushed this down. I have done this because I had to. What good would it have done if we *both* suffered like you did? Do you think it wasn't hard for me? You pity me because I've *endured* this? You can't think of anything *sadder* than the way I choose to cope with this? I have soldiered on, despite the fact that the one man I love most in this world is with another woman. But do not—do *not*—feel sad for me, Wallis. I don't want your pity. You needed my strength, and I gave it to you, day after day, week after week."

"I never asked for that," Wallis said, urgent, attempting to reach me through my pacing. "You think strength means pushing everything you felt down so far it was hidden from me? God, Dodo, I'm sorry, I love you, I adore you more than anyone in this world, but you're *so* wrong."

"No." I pivoted at the corner, resisting her words. I didn't want to be wrong. If I'd been mistaken, how many days had I wasted?

"Yes." She pressed on. "Daisy, you asked what good it would have done if we both suffered. Telling me the truth about Atlas would not have compounded our pain. That's not how pain works, and that's not how love works. We would've leaned on each other and shared the load." I stopped and blinked up at the ceiling, willing the tears not to fall. "I'm so sorry, Dodo," she said. "If you felt like I was demanding something from you, I'm sorry. I wasn't asking you to carry all my burdens. I was just asking for *you*. To be with me. To be my sister."

She was right—she'd never explicitly asked. No one had asked me to build the guardhouse. I recalled my father's books and photographs that I'd thrown away, everything I'd asked Atlas to bury, all that I'd withheld from the people I'd loved the most. I had believed I was protecting my family, but hoarding secrets, stashing away all the discomforting aspects of my past and present, had also made me feel safe.

How devastatingly unfair I'd been, to all of us and especially to myself. A few tears escaped, and she handed me a tissue from the box on my desk. We each folded and touched them to the skin below our bottom eyelashes, a trick passed down from Cricket. We saw this and laughed, rueful.

Wallis wrapped her arms around me. Into my shoulder, she whispered, "I know you were doing your best. So why do I get the feeling like you are disappointed in yourself?"

"Because I am. I'm not particularly strong, or brilliant, or even good."

"Don't talk about my sister that way." Wallis released me, dabbed her eyes once more, then entwined our fingers. "She's my best friend, and I won't let you disparage her like that."

I smiled, buoyed by my sister, who, I saw now, was incredibly brave. Her vulnerability and loyalty to those she loved, her ability to remain staunchly by my side in spite of everything I'd hidden from her was an act of grace, really. One I wasn't sure I deserved.

"Now, the tuition. Tell me more." Wallis led me to my chair, had me sit.

I needed a few deep breaths. Then: "Atlas did some sleuthing," I said softly. "But he's not the only one who knows. Melinda Darley does, and at least a few of her staff. They're not doing anything with it for now. But I don't know how long the détente will hold, and others might find out themselves."

Wallis stood before me, sure-footed, full of conviction. "Okay, so, like I said earlier. Why bother holding it, if it's going to come out? You're still looking at me like I'm out of my mind. Listen, Daisy. All this time you've been dealing with Mom and me, Dad, and now Atlas, I think you've been picturing yourself as the broken glass, lying in shards on the floor of our old house. But you're not." My office phone rang, but I ignored it. "You have another option, Daisy."

"I do?" It was an honest question.

Her smile, before she made her big pronouncement, was broad and easy. "Be the brick."

Thirty-Three

After Wallis left my office, I sat for a long time, thinking.

By a long time, I mean a full workday. Imagine a movie montage. The sun rises high then sets. The shadows shift across my face. The flurry of activity around my desk, people coming and going, dropping papers, picking them up. Miles, pacing. The fluorescent lights go on, the janitorial staff vacuums around me. Everyone in double time, except me, so still I might've been confused for a statue.

It was a news alert on my phone that woke me up around dinnertime. Another man—prominent, respected, you can surmise the rest—had been caught cheating. The details didn't really matter; I knew them by heart anyway.

I placed my phone back on my desk.

~

That night, I found Cricket at her computer. "My journal," she said. "Be right with you." She fussed over a single sentence, deleting, rewriting. Finally satisfied, she pressed save and swiveled her chair around to face me in the doorway.

"I have to tell you something," I said.

She pushed her glasses to the top of her head and pointed to her bed. "Sit."

She was smiling, curious. Perhaps she assumed this was about Atlas. I drew a frilly pillow into my lap. "It's bad, Cricket." Her smile faded. I confided about the tuition, just as I'd practiced. I watched her expression fall into the routine, by now, we Richardson women knew as muscle memory. Confusion. Shock. Denial. Sadness.

"Why would he do this?" She stood, then dropped next to me on the bed.

"In typical fashion," I said, "he abandoned us to figure that out on our own."

Cricket, ignoring my cynicism, began to answer her own question. "He loved you more than you realized, Daisy. He just saw so much of himself in you. That's why I think he was so hard on you, and, I suspect, that's the reason he went to those lengths even if it put you in such jeopardy. Not to excuse him, but he must've wanted to help you, to remove an obstacle from your path. He thought he was doing this for good reasons."

"If he thought his reasons were honorable, then why didn't he tell you?"

"Because he knew he was wrong."

My gaze drifted to the painting hanging over Cricket's tufted headboard. One of Gregory's favorites, it had once hung in his Senate office—a pure abstraction in oil, a red circle on the right, a shimmering white one on the left, both layered on a luminous yellow sky. Often I'd catch him staring at it, deep in thought. What had he seen? The red devil on one shoulder, the white angel on the other, both anxious to speak? I knew which had proven more persuasive. "I think the power got to him," I said, turning back to Cricket.

"People aren't corrupted by power, Daisy. Power just amplifies who they already are. As Gregory's power grew, it made him that much more obstinate and difficult."

"It was all about him, all the time." I'd heard parents refer to their children as a reflection of themselves. But I was not a mirror to my father. Instead, I was one of his limbs, an extension of him and his public persona. He moved me through life as he wished.

Cricket played absentmindedly with her reading glasses. "When I married him, my greatest fear was failing him, not keeping up my end of the bargain to do, to say the right things. It never crossed my mind that he might fail me. Or you." She touched her fingertips to my cheek. "I'm sorry you had to keep this burden. I just—had no idea. And I never would've asked..." She looked down to her hands, to the gold-and-diamond wedding band she still wore. She twirled it around her finger. "But this is his doing, isn't it? Not just what he did at the end, but everything he did to us for years. Remember how each of us *knew* that he was having an affair, but kept it quiet?"

I straightened, knowing she was right. "Our loyalty to him was greater than our loyalty to each other. That's not good enough anymore. So, no more apologies, full stop. At least when it comes to Gregory. We won't give him that power anymore." I cleared my throat, because there was more to my story, in particular how *I* had wielded my power. "After Atlas discovered that Gregory was funneling money back to the family, he asked me if I wanted to make the entire article go away." Cricket raised her eyebrows. "I said yes. I wanted everything to go away. The article first, then, later, the tuition."

"Ah," said Cricket, as though she'd just stumbled upon a lost trinket. "There it is. I knew something was up with Atlas at that dinner. With you both, actually."

I rose and went to Cricket's dresser, started fiddling with her perfume bottles, perfectly arranged on a silver tray. "And I used our friendship as leverage against him, because I was scared of what the article might do to us, to our family."

"Are you still scared now?" she asked.

I pried my eyes away from the perfume. "Are you?"

She thought about it for a moment. "Our loyalty to Gregory was greater than our loyalty to each other," Cricket repeated. "I'm loyal to you. Let Atlas publish the article. Or don't. Either way, I trust you."

I caught a glimpse of myself in her dresser mirror. There had been days when I woke up unsure of everything about me, down to my own last name. But today was no longer one of those days. The truth was that I'd spent too much time hiding behind rationalizations and excuses and smoke screens. Which is to say, instead of wielding my power differently from my father, I'd come dangerously close to mimicking him. I'd taken the easy way out, and what would follow would be hard, but necessary. But I would do it, even if no one noticed. Or if everyone noticed and condemned me anyway. Because that's what it meant to have character, and I wouldn't lose sight of that the way my father had.

"I've talked a big game about how I'm trying to do some good in the world. I think it's about time I actually start doing it. I'm going to talk to Atlas."

"Good," Cricket declared. Then, because my mother was still my mother: "Wear something nice when you do."

Thirty-Four

I arrived at Ari's apartment building on Saturday night; the doorman had to call up to verify my visit, then accompanied me to the elevator, swiping a card to make it move. It was a lot of procedure for a building that looked mostly to be occupied by people aged thirty and under. When I thanked him, he shrugged.

Twelve floors up, I knocked on the door. Atlas answered. Hellos. One-armed hugs. He drew me inside, commenting on the rain, the London-like dreariness of the summer. He took my jacket and hung it up with care, as though it were a mink. My dripping umbrella I placed next to the door.

"I'm sorry to miss Wallis," Atlas said. "Ari told me she couldn't make it."

"She's with Bo, actually," I said. "There's a bookstore opening in Anacostia. Bo wanted to go. So did she." That was true. Also, when I'd explained to her my reasons for going to the dinner, and why I wanted to go alone, she'd understood.

I trailed Atlas farther into the apartment, which was just as these new things are—one great room with a kitchen island, quartz topped, the size of a rowboat. Tall windows overlooked H Street, thick enough to hear nothing below.

Atlas, in a striped apron, resumed his place back at the island. "Ari has just dashed out for a missing ingredient," he said. "She'll be back soon. She's given me some tasks with the assumption that I can manage a charcuterie board. Stuffed grape leaf?"

"Please." I slid next to him and helped myself. "How are you?"

"Well," he said, slicing into a wheel of Gouda. "I'm not bad. Had to deal today with my latest fan." He made air quotes around this last word with his free hand. "Why write a letter to the editor when one can compose a series of sadistic tweets? Do you think Ari will like how I've sliced this? Probably not. I've left the rind on. Perhaps I was supposed to take it off."

"I'm sorry you're having to deal with trolls." I smoothed my skirt—Wallis's actually. I'd raided her closet, for a change, and found something—forest green, rather stretchy, flattering tulip shape—that fit me. It hit higher above the knee than anything I owned, and was, you know, a *color*, but I'd had the urge to be daring. "I know what that's like."

"Ari wants me to take a job that doesn't involve violent threats," he said, running the back of his hand across his forehead. He was sweating mildly, and I wondered if he was nervous, or stressed, or a combination of both. I wanted to put him at ease. I certainly hoped this dinner would not be a redo of the awkwardness we encountered in my office the other day and, continuing with my efforts to live with integrity, I had committed myself to being cordial and friendly to his girlfriend.

"Ari told me," I said. "She has other ideas for you that don't involve long hours and lots of travel."

He went back to slicing. "Funny she said that," he said to the cheese board. "I have a suspicion she likes me better when I'm not around so much."

"Really?" My shock made this question louder than intended. "What gives you that idea?"

"For one," Atlas said, "she said so." He glanced up. "She told me last week that I was annoying her, and that she likes me better when I'm on the road. In her defense, I was being annoying."

"She was joking?" I used a toothpick to spear an olive. "Or did she mean it?" My eyes fluttered back to his.

"Yes," he said. "I mean, both. Both? No, she was joking. Probably. But the truth is, we do get along better when we're apart. Is that the way it's supposed to be?" He concentrated again on slicing, this time a hunk of orange cheddar. "I suppose we've got that backwards."

I was in the woman's apartment, eating her appetizers. *Run*, I wanted to say, and pull him out of there. "Wine?" I asked, remembering I'd brought a bottle of sauv blanc. I pushed it forward on the island.

He laughed and put down his knife. "My God, I'm an awful host. Let me just find the opener. I can never remember which drawer—ah, here! I'll pour you some. I'm abstaining. Too much left to read tonight."

"Before Ari gets here," I said, watching him cut the foil of the wine's seal. "I have to talk to you about something that will add to your workload." In the day or so since I'd set the course, I'd been oddly calm. But now my pulse hammered. Maybe he heard the nerves in my voice, for he retrieved a glass from the cabinet and filled it almost to the rim. "I want to do the article, Atlas. About my father. About everything."

He did this thing, sometimes, when he was startled— he liked to call it pudding arms—where his body kind of flopped dramatically. Thank goodness, in this case, he'd already put down the wine. "Daisy," he said.

"I know."

"About everything?"

"Everything, everything," I said, steadfast.

"Why now?" A fair question. "I thought you said you'd signed a treaty with Darley's office? I thought there was a truce?"

"There was." I shrugged. "I'll break it."

"You'll break it." He paused, seemingly taking this in. Then, with sudden haste, he rounded the island and swooped me into his arms.

I returned his hug, smelling him, feeling his heart under his T-shirt, feeling safe.

When he released me, he asked if I was sure.

"Yes," I said, combing my fingers through my hair, checking to make sure it wasn't standing on end. "It's the right thing to do. It feels necessary. But, Atlas, listen. I don't want you to take it easy on me. I don't want you to write this to encourage people to feel sorry for me. Because they shouldn't. You shouldn't."

"I don't," he said. "I won't."

"I will talk about everything my father did. I will acknowledge and try to reckon with it, out, in fresh air. Done with hiding."

His next question: "When?"

"Tomorrow?" In the old romantic comedies, those of our childhoods, there was always the running scene, was there not? Through the crowd. Dashing, not a moment to spare. To the choice that should've been clear as day. To destiny. When you know how the rest of your life should be lived, you want to start the rest of your life as soon as possible.

My destination, though—not a man, but *my* true and best self.

"All right, tomorrow." He lay his elbows on the island. I saw his mind beginning to plan, to map out routes.

"Thank you," I said. "I continue to ask things from you. And you keep saying yes, no matter how difficult I'm being."

"You may ask things that are difficult, Daisy," he said softly. "But that's not the same as *being* difficult. You know?" I did now, and smiled with relief. "That's why, when I think about you, I—"

Whatever he was about to say was cut off; the sound of a key in the door made us both jolt. "I'm here!" Ari said, joining us in the kitchen, a small carton in her hand. She hugged me. "I had to walk ten blocks up," she said, "to find organic cream." She wiggled out of her jacket, surveyed the half-assembled charcuterie board. "You left the rind on the Gouda." She pointed to the cheese, then to Atlas, before sailing off and disappearing behind a door.

He looked at me. "Told you."

⁓

Dinner was fettuccine with homemade Alfredo, an odd choice for June, but rather good nonetheless. As soon as we sat at her square glass dining table, Ari brought up Melinda Darley. "Seems like the minute she got confirmed, she's set her mind to make my migraines flare up," Ari said, piqued. "She's too fit to expect something like a heart attack. If only she didn't eat so many salads. I bet she's one of those women who goes to the gym at four in the morning."

"*You* go to the gym at four in the morning," Atlas said.

"I'm doing good in this town," responded Ari. "You want to keep *me* around. Melinda Darley I need gone."

"Do we really wish for the death," Atlas said, using his knife to scoot salad onto the back of his fork, "of people who antagonize us?"

"She never said anything about death," I said. Ari had lit tea lights and asked her home assistant to play classical music. We were bantering in a friendly way, the tension of our previous meeting a distant memory. Maybe, in someone else's story, the girlfriend of the love interest would be a heinous monster. In mine, I was realizing, she was just a woman with both redeemable qualities and obvious flaws.

"Thank you, Daisy." She swirled her wine in her glass. "Not death. Just unconsciousness. Or career-wrecking scandal."

"I know a little something about those," I said. "I'm about to wreck my own career shortly." I looked to Atlas. As he did the work of explaining to Ari what I meant, I scrutinized her face for signs of disgust. Out of all the reactions I predicted people might feel once reading Atlas's article, this would be the one I'd have the most trouble accepting.

Once Atlas was done, though, Ari's only words were of consolation. She had her own story, it seemed, a familiar one—her father, money, a younger woman, divorce, scandal. There had been secret credit cards, a club named Whipped and Cream. This had happened in Atlanta, when she was in high school. She rarely discussed it, she said. Last time she talked to her father was New Year's Eve 2008.

"That must've been truly awful," I said. There must be many more stories like ours out there.

"It was." She gazed over my shoulder. "Then—I just didn't let it be awful anymore. I stopped letting it affect me."

"How?" I asked, genuinely curious. I would need to work on this in the upcoming weeks.

"You just don't think about it. Pass the salad?"

"I get that part," I said, handing over the bowl of arugula and shaved parm. "But *how* do you stop?"

"I know it sounds, like, mysterious. But I promise you, it works. Every time you start thinking about the pain, and the unfairness of it all, just—don't."

"Easy enough," said Atlas, smiling. "I'm familiar with the stiff upper lip."

"This is going to be the best advice anyone has ever given you," she told me. "When you start thinking about your dad, or when someone calls you a name, or you begin to dip a toe into the self-pity pool, just pinch yourself, or scream a little bit. Go for runs, organize closets and drawers, buy fresh flowers."

"That's why your clothes are so perfectly folded," said Atlas. "Now I see."

"You're going to be fine, Daisy," Ari went on, ignoring him. "It's clear to me you're brilliant and smart and sweet and everyone loves you. People like us don't suffer forever. We just don't."

Imagine, this whole time, that all I had to do was not *think*. It was no accident Ari lobbied for the likes of Big Pharma. That was practically their slogan. Bless her heart, as Bo would say. Still, she was so earnest in her attempt to be helpful, I managed not to laugh at how overly simple she made it all sound. I could only hope there was some truth in it. "Thank you for sharing this secret." I raised my glass. "A toast, to the end of suffering."

We touched the rims of our delicate glasses together and drank.

—

After a dessert of strawberries and ice cream, which was unfussy and—I had to admit—pretty chic, Atlas, ever the gentleman, escorted me out. "You know," he said when we were on the elevator, descending, "once I found out the extent of it, part of me was relieved you'd told me to kill the article."

"How big a part?" I asked, surprised. I'd thought my choice had disappointed him and he'd just done a great job at hiding it.

"A big part," he confessed. The doors opened to the lobby. We crossed toward the front exit, but stopped halfway below the massive light fixture, which resembled a galactic spiral. "That part of me is still resistant to the idea of making this information public, knowing how it might affect you. You realize what will happen once I publish this?"

"Exactly what happened before," I said. I appreciated his protective instincts, but nothing he'd say would change my mind. "Maybe worse."

"Pitchforks," he said, miming it.

"Literal." The doorman, from the lobby's control center, gave us nonresidents the once-over. "And metaphorical."

"You sound like you've made up your mind, done and dusted."

"I have." I focused on Atlas, ignoring, for the moment, the vigilante at his desk. "I can't go on like everything is normal, like what he did was okay. It's not right or fair. Think about Ari, and her dad. How many more of us are out there, going through similar situations?" I paused. "You're right about how the article will affect me. It will act as a sledgehammer to my life as I know it. I'll have to resign—"

His hand went to his forehead. "Miles. Jesus, Daisy, of course. I hadn't considered—"

I stilled him. "It's okay. Like I said, things are going to get broken. And that's the way it should be."

"This is wild, Daisy," Atlas said. Then he lowered his head and smiled. "Courageous, reckless—maybe both. It's certainly not something I imagine the Daisy of last year would do."

I felt myself blushing. His was the only attention I didn't mind in the least. "Ari," I said, "is a great cook and a gracious host. Please thank her again for me."

He rocked back on his heels. "You know, she asked me to move in with her."

I had to accept that I'd be ever the friend, the confidante. Which is to say, I'd just have to make do, because I loved him too much to say goodbye. "And?" I prompted.

"I know she wants me to marry her, too."

"And?" I gestured with my hand, scrolling him forward.

"And, I don't know. It's hard to know. I am *consistently* unsure. I wonder if that is me lacking confidence generally, or if it has something to do with the relationship."

My breath caught. I became aware of the other people strolling through the lobby, checking their mailboxes, and the surly doorman, who'd definitely overheard. I wished Atlas and I were in private. I wanted to get us both into sweatpants, pour a nightcap, put music on, and chat for hours more. "Wallis used to think that when you know, you know."

"Used to?" He tucked a winged lock of hair behind his ear.

"With what's happened with Blake, I can't say she believes like she did, before." When she'd met Blake, there had been a small bit of me that had judged her for falling so hard, so fast, thinking she'd misplaced her trust in love, rather than in caution and good sense. But I didn't like the possibility that it might be gone, or that Blake had taken it from her. The world would be much grimmer without Wallis truly as herself.

"Do you—do you ever find yourself wishing that there were aspects of your life you could just coast through? That there was just *one* thing you could put on autopilot?"

"Yes, of course. It means something, though," I added, hesitant, not wanting him to feel like I was pressing him one way or the other, "that you wish your autopilot could control this." I motioned to the elevator and up, toward Ari's apartment, with the nice view and hand-hewn dinner plates, the bed and its linen sheets, the bathroom with the lavender candle. A bad relationship was bad for both of them. I looked him straight in the eye. "I think that she wants to love you very much, Atlas. But I could be wrong. Or not. In any event, I wish you nothing but happiness."

"You're no help at all," he said, laughing, though his heart wasn't in it. "Everything is an honest-to-God wreck right now, Daisy. My father is declining. I think he may have to sell the London house. Can't work the stairs anymore. Last week he was stuck in the bathtub all night."

"I'm so sorry," I said, giving his side a squeeze. Atlas and his father weren't always on the same page—there had been trouble, after his mother had left for the States, and hurt on both sides—but they loved each other, in spite of it. Yet illness has a way of magnifying fissures in even the strongest relationships, and I sensed the pain in Atlas's face, in the slight twist of his mouth. "Nothing happens for a very long time, then everything comes at once. That's the law."

Under the constellation of lights in the lobby, we talked growing up and getting old, living and dying. Ari—not mentioned again. Just us, old friends who knew each other well, who loved each other despite the centrifugal forces of adult life continually trying to rip us apart. Not the kind of love I'd hoped for, but love nonetheless. And there was beauty and meaning in that, just being there for each other, laughing at the pain of it all.

Thirty-Five

Wallis was making gazpacho. I disliked cold soup, but hadn't the inclination to remind her; I was glad she was feeling like cooking again. She'd also mixed sangria, which we were drinking out of mismatched wineglasses. Cricket was puttering around the kitchen, seeming to stand in front of whatever drawer Wallis needed to get into. I, nervous, having promised myself one glass, was silently rehearsing some of what I wanted to say on the record.

I was picking at an orange slice in my drink, wondering if using the word *puissant* to describe my father would be overdoing it, when Atlas knocked a tune on the door. We called for him to *Come on in*. Wearing trim jeans and a relaxed polo, he arrived in the kitchen with a bottle of pinot gris for Cricket and a hug and a kind word for Wallis. For me, the same. I stepped away, gave him space, wishing that it wasn't necessary to do so. It did, however, give me some distance to watch him. I hadn't wanted him to wake up this morning uncomfortable with what he'd shared with me the night previous. But there were no signs in his body language and smile that he felt anything but ease in our company. Cricket poured him sangria from the pitcher, mostly ice and sliced stone fruit, but he didn't complain.

"Thank you for coming," I said, leaning against the countertop. Did he see it on my face—my worry about the interview? He placed himself next to me, drink in hand.

"You've been hunting down Gregory's crimes," Cricket said, ignoring my protestations and topping up my drink. "Daisy has told me."

"I have," Atlas said, swirling the ice in his glass.

"But this is the right thing to do," said Cricket, "telling the story."

"All of it," agreed Wallis, transferring her vegetable concoction into a blender. "And Daisy is the right person to do it." I began to quibble this point, for surely there were more intelligent women out there, braver ones, women who hadn't screwed up so badly or obfuscated the truth, who could share their stories instead, but Wallis insisted, tapping the counter with her wooden spoon. "You are a human being; you're not perfect. And, sure, you're risking criticism, but that's the only way to get things to change."

I noticed her looking over my shoulder, perhaps imagining storms in the distance. The night before, we'd discussed, as a family, my choice to do the interview and, as Wallis referenced, the risks inherent therein. We all knew it would restart the clock on the scandal. Whatever friendships we'd been able to rebuild, scant in number as they were, would be jeopardized. The hate mail might multiply; our financial liability, too. The bricks. Very possible.

We'd weathered it once. We could do it again.

It didn't mean we couldn't still be scared.

———

"State your name for the record." Atlas, recorder on, pulling my leg.

Dinner was done, bowls had been cleared. The soup hadn't been terrible. Cricket had bought a baguette, of which I ate most, slathered in butter. Good bread can soothe the nerves. And I didn't want my voice to shake. I'd been thinking so much about the sentences, the individual words I would use. I didn't want a single one to tremble. The people reading wouldn't hear my voice, but Atlas would. I would.

Wallis and Cricket had gone out to a movie—animated, family, they wanted something light—and now I sat on Cricket's couch, Atlas in the chair across from me. He'd drawn it forward, moving the coffee table aside, and our knees almost touched.

"Daisy Catherine Richardson," I said.

"Catherine?" He tilted his head. Had I really never told him?

"Cricket," I said.

"Of course. Duh."

I laughed. I'd never heard him use that word. "You even managed the valley girl accent. A true Renaissance man."

"And your astrological sign, please?" He continued to scrawl in his spiral notebook, acting the proper reporter.

"Cancer." I gestured to my body—the hard, external shell of the crab. "Obviously."

"That's right. June 25. Coming up in a couple weeks. We'll have to celebrate," he said. "Next. If heaven existed, who would you want to meet first and what question would you ask them?"

I bit back a grin. He was disarming me, making me comfortable, and I loved him for it. "So much for the easy questions."

"An answer, please." He flipped some notebook pages back and forth industriously. "We're all business here."

I considered. "Eleanor Roosevelt. I'd ask, well, I'd ask if I could be her friend."

Then Atlas was himself again, kind and studious, and I knew the game was over. "And your father? What would you say to him in heaven?"

"If it existed." This was a throwback to one of the early conversations we'd had, more than a decade ago, about religion and God and our separate dabblings with Buddhism in college, in a shabby hotel bar—somewhere outside Norfolk, after a visit to a peanut farm—drinking bad cabernet until the bartender started mopping under our stools.

"Purely hypothetical," Atlas agreed. His gaze drifted from his notebook to me, his eyes seeming to melt, and I knew he was also remembering.

"How much time do we have?" I asked.

~

When we were done, it was almost midnight. Cricket and Wallis had returned, yawning and droopy-eyed, to wish us a brief good-night. I'd gone through two bottles of sparkling water; we'd had to pause midway for snacks—more bread, honey-roasted peanuts, rosemary-flecked crackers, dredged out from the back of Cricket's pantry, saved from some holiday gift basket of yesteryear. Atlas had filled up one notebook, and most of a second. Although I'd emptied myself of the story I'd prepared, I felt as full as I'd ever been. I was tired but content, my voice scratchy from hours of talking.

"I'll call you tomorrow," he said as he swung his bag onto his shoulder. He didn't seem sleepy at all; I had the sense he was going to write for the rest of the night. "But, you're going to be—I mean, I think we have something here, Daisy. I really do."

Then he was gone. And I, back to my own apartment and to my bed, Atlas and his article never far from my mind.

Thirty-Six

Monday, Miles's office; L.K. and I were on one couch, Bo and our boss on the opposite, talking headlines, administrative chores, tasks for the week. A rural police department needed three new vehicles. Maryland needed a dam, flood prevention studies, protection for crabs and oysters. Miles took notes in a college-ruled composition book, which he brought everywhere. It was old-fashioned; people either found it charming or excessive. I knew it was utilitarian—recess was over. Class was in session. There was work to be done.

I was sorry I wouldn't be there to see it completed.

When we made it through the list, Bo had some gossip: there were rumors, he said, that Melinda Darley had chartered a jet, naturally at taxpayer expense, to fly to Columbia to meet her son at a campaign event.

Miles was about to respond to this when we were interrupted by a knock; we all turned and Sara peeked her head in. "Is this still morning meeting?" she asked. "Or have you all transitioned to shooting the shit?"

"We're done." Miles leaned back, rested his brown penny loafers on the coffee table between the couches, seemingly glad to be off the topic of the Darleys.

"There's a photographer here to see Daisy," Sara said.

I'd forgotten about that. Sometime last night between the peanuts and the crackers, Atlas had scheduled a time for me to have my portrait taken. He'd thought my office would make a good backdrop—the law books, the papers, the dry-erase board with plans and agenda items. Now I realized this had been a bad decision, made when my attention was consumed by the interview. Of course I couldn't be in my office for the picture. My employment here would only last about five more minutes.

Miles looked at me, seeking an explanation. L.K., too, all curiosity. Bo, though, was nodding, as though to say, *On with it*. In my head, I'd imagined explaining the article to Miles alone, at the end of the day, when I'd had a chance to reply to required emails, clean my office, prepare. I'd gone through scripts, role-playing both sides. This wasn't the way I'd planned it, but—spoiler alert!—sometimes plans don't work out.

"Thanks, Sara," I said, and she withdrew, closing the door behind her. I shuffled my papers and my binders to form a neat stack on my lap. My phone I silenced, then lay it facedown on the top. "There will be an article coming out next week," I said, halting at first, then gradually with more confidence. "It will be about my father, our family, and how he stole from his office to help support us as well as another woman who was not his wife. I am one of the sources, and not an anonymous one."

"What Melinda Darley said that day, about your tuition," said L.K., tapping her pen, in a slow rhythm, against her knee, "was true, then?"

"Yes," I said, meeting her eyes, then Miles's.

But Miles and L.K. seemed about as shocked as the average DC insider when it came to public scandal. Which is to say, not very.

Instead, Miles articulated what I suspected was on everyone's mind. "So, you're throwing yourself to the wolves." His feet were on the ground again, his arms crossed. "Why?"

"Because I'm done hiding from them," I said.

"Bo," Miles said, rising, beginning to pace, "talk her out of this, my God."

"Don't do that," I said to Miles. "That's not his job. And I won't be persuaded."

"You may have to resign." L.K. scooted closer to me on the couch, her hand pressed to her stomach. "If this goes south."

"I *will* have to resign," I said. "Atlas will write in his article that I am a former staffer of yours. Not a current one. It will sound better."

Miles and L.K. began to voice their objections. They talked over me and around me. Their verbal battle, if I could understand it, was about who disagreed with my choice to resign more.

"I'm sorry to ambush you!" I raised my voice, intent on making it heard. "This all happened quickly. But I don't want you to think I take it lightly." I had the sensation that people were quieting, drawing breaths. Or maybe it was just them drawing back the arrows in their bows. I resumed at normal volume. "This was, in so many ways, my home.

You were—are—still my people. I can't have the fallout from this, whatever it ends up being, land on this office. That's why you're going to let me go."

"How much time do we have?" Miles, pausing to ask for a prognosis.

"My official employment with you will end today. But I'll be in for the next two weeks or so, unofficially, to help Bo transition into his new role. Though everyone in this room knows he won't need my help." It wasn't presumptuous, I bet, to state the obvious; it went unsaid that Bo would be Miles's next chief of staff, and I assumed we could just do away with formalities. I was grateful for Bo, my friend, and whatever millions of tiny life decisions had bent our roads toward each other. We'd been a team for years, partners in work and buddies outside of it, and an era was coming to an end. But the world, and this office, would keep spinning. "It will be hard, but only for me. You all will be fine."

Bo looked up and met my gaze from across the coffee table. He'd been silent so far, and when he spoke his tone was unemotional, but in his eyes I saw more. "'Nothing forces us to know what we don't want to know,'" quoted Bo, "'except pain.'"

"Which of your favorite dead Irishmen said that one?" asked L.K. From somewhere on her person she had procured mousse, a comb, and started on my hair, prepping me for the photographer. She adjusted my part, smoothed my flyaways and the collar on my jacket.

"Aeschylus, actually," said Bo, ever our resident scholar, "coming in hot with the wisdom."

"So, what do you know now, Daisy, that you didn't know before?" Miles asked, taking his seat again next to Bo.

"You'll be able to read the answer to that question," I said, playful, "in next week's *Post*."

"Well, fuck." Miles rolled his shoulders; I sensed he was adjusting, resetting. "I hope this works for you, Daisy."

"I'm optimistic," I said. And I was, mostly. My hair already felt fuller, thanks to L.K., so that didn't hurt.

"Well, optimism is contagious," Miles said, smiling slowly. "So, let's raise our coffee mugs. L.K., put the lint roller down and raise your cup of tea, Bo, your can of toxic energy slurry. There. Now, let's cheers to Daisy. The swamp will miss you."

Hear, hear, they said. *Cheers*.

———

Shortly after the meeting ended, and we all dispersed to our separate offices, the photographer Atlas had sent—a petite girl with straw-yellow hair and a mammoth camera bag—appeared at my door. She asked where she should set up her gear. "Not here," I said. "This isn't where I work." Not anymore.

I led her out, to the elevators, across Constitution Avenue, to the Grounds. I knew the Hill's best side, and wanted to make sure she got it. We marched through the gardens, past my father's favorite bench under a canopy of wisteria, down the cascade of marble steps, heading west toward the monuments of improbable victories and higher loyalties. *"Perfect,"* she said when we arrived on the great expanse of lawn in front of the Capitol. With the cupola rising grand behind me, she turned me this way and that, straight on, profile, standing, sitting, into the light. Outside of it.

Thirty-Seven

The Good Daughter No More: The Older Child of Late
Senator Gregory Richardson Grapples with His Legacy—
and Her Own
By Atlas Braidy-Lowes
June 21 at 3:01 p.m.

A few weeks after Daisy Richardson found out her father had written checks to the University of Virginia with money that wasn't his, she tells the story of how, after the most recent and particularly brutal reelection season, her father decided that he wanted a quiet Christmas with his family in their Georgetown row house.

This was a surprise. If you remember anything about Senator Gregory Richardson, besides the fact that he died in bed with his lover and saddled his widow with leaden bags of debt and detritus, it is probably his reputation for being an indefatigable good-timer, who never refused a cocktail or a free steak dinner. People said that he'd survive a nuclear fallout, him and the cockroaches, and they meant it as a compliment. He was unbeatable, which is not to say he was unassailable; it turns out Gregory Richardson made just as many enemies as friends in this town. But we can say that the heart attack, to kill him, had to have been powerful. Anything less than massive and Gregory Richardson would have fought back, tooth to gum, nail to quick.

That Christmas, Daisy Richardson recalls, he had it in his head to make Peking duck. Neither she nor her mother was in the habit of questioning these sorts of whims. So Gregory took to the kitchen, dealing with baking soda, boiling water, and, at one point in the process, a bicycle pump. But the duck skin would not dehydrate. Daisy found her father, the last Christmas he was alive, softly weeping at his kitchen table. He looked small, and wounded, and—this was important—worried.

"It wasn't about the duck skin," she says now. "I knew it wasn't. But I backed away, left him in peace, because I was scared to know what it was that had him in tears." She sits on her mother's couch, casually dressed, a senator's former chief of staff, as of this week. For the first time since her father's death, she is ready to discuss the depth and breadth of his deception to the American people and his own family, and what she's learned in the aftermath.

"I worked for my father for many years." Richardson speaks softly, with precise, thoughtful phrasing. "All my life I'd thought he was an honest public servant. I even accepted his erratic, harmful behavior as a parent because he was, as far as I knew, doing good in the world. That's what he had trained me to believe. So when I found out that he'd stolen public funds, for *me*, it was such an incredible betrayal.

Even if he thought it was for the right reasons, he had taken control of my life in this awful way that was harmful to other people. I had no say in the matter. I couldn't go back in time and change it."

On the table before her, she's placed three framed photographs, all with her mother, Catherine, and younger sister, Wallis. "The only way I could think of dealing with it was to be silent. Speaking out, seeing the words written on the page or aired across television screens, would have confirmed just how wrong I'd been about my father, and how so much of my life had been lived based on a lie.

"And, honestly, I thought there had been power in silence. I felt that by even being able to make this choice not to speak, I'd regained some control of my own life, at a time when control was in short supply. I realize now that was me just taking the easy way out. Because I did have power. But instead of using it to be open, accountable, I used it to bury truths that were inconvenient to me—painful, yes, but also inconvenient. In staying silent, I had become like my father...

"We are in the process of paying back all we can of the money Gregory owes this country, but I can't give back the time I spent trying to conceal his mess so no one would find it. And that's what I regret most. I hope by speaking out I can begin to reckon with my father's actions and, in whatever small way, make it easier for those who find themselves in similar positions. Because nothing good in this world was made so by a woman keeping her mouth shut..."

Thirty-Eight

I got ahold of Atlas on the phone that afternoon. He'd had to fly to London last week, only a day after our interview. His father had needed him. I was on Cricket's couch, a copy of the *Post* scattered around me. We'd read the article first online, Cricket, Wallis, and I, shortly after dawn. Immersed in Atlas's words about me, I had the sensation of standing in a waterfall. There was pressure on my shoulders, but it was a welcome force. I felt the power of the world, but also freedom and wholeness. Cricket had remained mostly silent, neither compliments nor scolding, and then had gone off on an "errand." That was five hours ago.

"How are you holding up?" Atlas asked after I'd heaped praise on his prose.

"I have so many voice mails that I need to listen to. Wallis is in the next room watching my name trend." Through my sister's open door, I saw her stretched out on her stomach on her bed, her eyes scanning her computer. She'd turned on music, orchestral, dramatic. "I'm girding myself to open my email."

"The noise is going to get louder," Atlas said. "But—hey—did you see that picture of you that was printed? You look regal. One day someone will paint you in oil."

"Now you're lying." L.K. had worked magic on my hair, but I'd been far from regal. My outfit was nothing special, but my legs looked—I won't say shapely—not unattractive, at least. And the photographer had managed to capture my eyes, clear, thoughtful, contemplating the future. I removed the phone from my ear; another call was trying to get through: unknown number. And look, sixteen new texts. I ignored them all, for now, and savored the few remaining minutes before Atlas had to run and help his father in the bath.

After we hung up, Wallis emerged from her room in an oversize sweater and what appeared to be a pair of Cricket's old jeans, so out of fashion they were in again. She tugged at her cuffs so they covered most of her hands and walked to the living room window, lifted the edge of the curtain. "The cop car is outside," she observed.

"Cricket called them before she left." I sipped from my mug of tea. I'd fixed it, thinking it would relax me, but I had let it steep too long and had to dump in volumes of sugar to compensate. I'd be up on my feet and doing laps around the apartment in a minute. "I think she wanted us to be protected. Where is she, anyway? Have you heard from her?"

"She went to Uncle Rob's in McLean," Wallis said. "It's funny. All these months she told us that he cut off communication with her because of our father, but—" Wallis shrugged, turned to rest against the windowsill. "Actually, she had stopped talking to *him*. Was embarrassed. Anyway, I'm glad they're talking again."

"Me, too." I pulled my computer onto my lap and patted the seat beside me. "Will you come sit with me? Might as well get this over with."

As we snuggled into each other's sides and went through my email and then my phone messages, I discovered that while I was on the receiving end of some vitriol (*fat ugly skank*), the vast majority were positive. Television producers had been trying to get in touch, each more enthused than the previous. Wallis and I weighed my options, did some research, watched clips, and returned the call of an especially persistent one, a young woman. Her show, too, was anchored by a woman. There were women on staff, and not just in hair and makeup.

The thought of facing a stranger, live, on-air, was already giving me heart palpitations, and I was still in my apartment building. Even being photographed, having just *one* woman and her camera focused on me, had been entirely discomfiting. But growth never came out of comfort. One interview, enough to face my fear and, if I didn't screw up massively, articulate my message. And that would be it. There were too many more important issues, and women, who needed airtime.

Thirty-Nine

My sister, as usual, entered my apartment without knocking. Her hair was down, waves loose, dress flouncy and pink. "You ready?" she asked, plunking the gold hoop earrings I'd asked to borrow on the coffee table beside me.

I was sitting on the floor of my living room, still in my stage hair and makeup, painting my nails royal purple. We were celebrating, which is to say we were putting on nicer clothes and shoes that were not sneakers and going down the block for dinner, before my interview aired.

"Just about," I told her as I put the finishing touches on my left pinky.

"Before we go, you need to come up and help Cricket choose which outfit to wear to dinner," said Wallis.

I twisted the cap back on the polish, glancing at the clock on my cable box. "Isn't the reservation at seven? We're supposed to be leaving in three minutes."

Wallis rolled her eyes. "You know Cricket."

I did. Not wanting to be late, I stood and hustled into my room to grab my flat sandals and clutch, trying not to mess up my nails in the process.

"Excited for the show?" she asked once we were in the hall.

The answer to this question wasn't as complicated as I might've predicted. I'd done the taping earlier that day, and although I'd been in news studios before with Miles, it had always been behind the cameras, never underneath the impossibly bright lights myself. So yes, I had nerves regarding seeing myself on television. But they weren't leaden. The anchor, Monica, imposing and confident, had begun the segment by saying she'd been fascinated by my story. I must've said a few passingly intelligent things, because when we had stopped rolling, and a production assistant unraveled the mic and its wire from my blazer, Monica had told me I'd done well. I had left the studio thinking about what Miles said recently, about how people can be infected by optimism.

There were things to look forward to: I had a job interview scheduled for Monday—my birthday, it turned out—in Alexandria. A nonprofit advocacy group for open and honest government needed a new deputy director of operations, and I'd be meeting with the HR rep, the president, the chairman of the board. They seemed excited; so was I.

And Atlas was coming back from London next Sunday, almost exactly nine and a half days away, but who was counting? He'd been in England for almost two weeks already, moving his father, resistant and incontinent, into a smaller place. Although there had been some moments of reconnection and grace, the experience was, as he explained it to me, mostly torturous. I was anxious to wrap my arms around him. There was only so much encouragement that could be doled out over FaceTime.

"Yes, I'm actually really excited," I told Wallis as we began our walk up the hallway stairs. An earlier version of me might've been inclined to downplay my expectations, but I was going to try to follow my sister's example and rip up those tendencies by their poisoned roots.

"Me, too," she said. "I'm just over the moon for you. I just wish I were as brave. And…well, you see the world for what it is, Daisy. You're not floating around believing if we just *loved* harder things will get better. I wish I could be more like you."

Her contrite tone, and the fact that she was comparing herself to me unfavorably, gave me pause. "You are as brave as I am," I said, stopping her on the third-floor landing with a hand to her arm. How could she not see? "Wallis, you were the one who encouraged me."

"I just don't feel—" She cut herself off and began to fidget with her delicate silver necklace. "Ugh, sorry." She smiled bracingly, stuck out her tongue. "I'm all out of sorts. I'm going to get it together. But full truth, I'm kind of floundering." We continued down the hall toward Cricket's, but our pace was slow, our strides tiny, both of us stalling to make sure what needed to be said was said. "I didn't used to care so much about what people thought of me. But now I do, and, wow, it's not a great time to have changed. People online are debating whether I'm worthy of contempt or sympathy." She pressed her hand to her heart. "I just feel very different in some ways. It's sort of a delayed reaction to everything, I guess. The more time passes, the more I feel like I should be cautious. Especially in relationships, and even at work. But in other ways I feel absolutely the same.

I still want to fall in love and agitate for causes I believe in and not care if people call me all the names."

"And why shouldn't you do all those things?" I asked as we arrived at Cricket's door. I thought of the segment I'd taped that afternoon, and the conversation I'd had with Monica. We'd talked about this exact feeling my sister was describing. How unfair it was that women have to make the choice to be nice or to be powerful. "Don't let what other people say, good or bad, pressure you into feeling small. The world does that enough to women. I won't let it happen to my own sister." I hugged Wallis, who hugged back. "We're going to live the way we want, and try to do some good in the process. And that will be too much for some people and too little for others. But, you know, this is our story and if they don't like it, they can go read another one."

Wallis grinned. "That's good, Daisy. I'm going to borrow that one."

I remembered those moments many months ago, when we'd held each other in the pew at our father's memorial, thinking the hardest parts were behind us, thinking the goodbye to Gregory was the end. And it had been terrifying, in the aftermath, when I couldn't control the story, or the past, or anyone else around me, for that matter. I couldn't even control my own feelings. I should've just opened my eyes and looked at Wallis; she would've told me, if I'd only asked, that it was all right to be scared.

Cricket's knob was tricky with my nails. I ended up using two hands and my hip to get the door open—I really didn't want to ruin my paint—but then everyone yelled *surprise!* and I stumbled into the wall and had to grab someone's coat to steady myself, and my dreams of a perfect manicure were dashed.

Shocked out of my wits, I noticed Wallis, jubilant, now beside me. "Happy birthday!" She joined the chorus, throwing up her hands.

"But it's not till Monday," I blubbered.

Cricket, resplendent in red, emerged from the crowd, took my purse and handed me champagne. "What's a few days when you're thirty-five?" she said, kissing me on the cheek. I still was frozen; she had to take me by the arm and pull me into the party.

Wallis and Cricket had filled the apartment with my friends and yellow and white balloons. Bo, L.K., Miles, Sara, and a few others from the office. Uncle Robert was there, and his wife. My two college roommates—they'd flown from Atlanta. Some of Cricket's old pals who called me *Lovie*.

It wasn't until my second glass of champagne that I could catch my breath. Wallis turned on music and made sure no one's drink was empty. They'd been planning this for weeks, she said, immensely proud of herself, and now it was a birthday slash watch party. What could be better? I ate Brie and crackers and crudités and babbled *Oh, my gosh* repetitively as people enveloped me in hugs.

Miles had brought a date, his contractor, actually, who'd completed his master bathroom renovation on time and under budget. *You don't see that much in DC,* laughed Miles, *so I knew he was a keeper.* Carl, this handy, tall redhead, was a dream, considerate and funny and a lover of all my favorite shows. Uncle Rob said *Good to see you, kiddo.* Sara updated me on all the latest office gossip. I located L.K., who looked very cute in a stylish black jumpsuit, by Wallis's makeshift sound system—a phone plugged into a portable speaker. L.K. scrolled until she found her favorite, an

'80s classic rock station; satisfied with the direction of the playlist, she affectionately pinched my arm and leaned close. "Happy birthday, babe. What a great party. I can't wait to watch your interview, among other things."

Her mischievous tone had me asking, "What other things?"

L.K. wiggled her eyebrows. "I'm here to see if Bo finally makes a move on Wallis. I know July Fourth is still, like, two weeks away, but maybe we'll see some fireworks tonight. Am I right, or am I right?"

I could've sworn I heard the sound of a latch clicking open. I looked at Cricket's door, expecting a new guest to stride in. But, no, the click was just inside my head: Charleston, their companionship, his nickname for her, his obvious distaste for Blake—I had thought it had been simple fondness. Wrong. "That tracks," I said softly, still processing.

"You truly didn't know?" L.K. asked. We both glanced at Bo, who, I realized now, had never been far from Wallis's side at this party. He was dressed rather chic tonight, or at least more put-together than usual, in those sustainable wool sneakers with colorful laces, a tailored pair of jeans, a shirt that wasn't one size too big. And he was currently beholding her as one totally smitten; I guessed that if I watched for long enough, I might catch his heart thump right out of his chest and land at her feet.

I was, for the next handful of seconds, positively afloat with possibility. My sister! My friend! And Bo was *such* a catch. But then: "I don't think she likes him that way."

I'd expected this admission to spear the heart-shaped balloons floating around L.K.'s head. But she was unmoved. "No offense, Daisy, but I don't trust you when it comes to this." Then, giddy, she practically squealed, "They're coming over here!"

"Just try not to make it weird," I begged, still spinning.

"I make no promises. Hi, Wallis!" They embraced, kissed on the cheek. "Amazing party. You look stunning. Right, Bo?"

"Yes," said Bo, "to both."

Wallis took both compliments gracefully, smiling warmly, and giving me a good squeeze. "Anything for my famous and brilliant Daisy."

"I'm famous now, am I?" I asked, laughing at the idea.

But L.K. agreed with Wallis. "Your story is resonating with people. I know it did with me. Word is you're going to make it onto The List next month."

We all pretended to faint or swoon or fan ourselves exaggeratedly. The List was the silliest thing in DC everyone took seriously, and measured nothing except how germane one was to the current conversation.

There was a knock on the door, and a familiar face poked through the crack. Miles's press sec had arrived, and Wallis scampered off to welcome him.

"Thanks for coming," I said to Bo and L.K. for probably the fifth time that night. "This is outrageous."

Bo was curious. "That someone should throw you a party? You're an easy person to celebrate, my friend."

I smiled. "It's just unexpected, I guess."

"Then Wallis succeeded," he said. "She was sure you were onto her."

Wallis had already found the new arrival a glass of champagne, and now was holding forth near the couch, cracking people up. I watched Bo watch my sister, formulating a plan for how to acknowledge it when Bo asked, "How is Wallis?" He cleared his throat. "I mean, she tells me she's fine, but, according to the polls, it looks like Darley will win. Is she…prepared for when he descends on DC?"

L.K.'s elbow briefly dug into my side, as if to say *See?* I did, I saw it, and all that was unspoken in his question. I didn't want to trick Bo into believing something was there between him and my sister if there wasn't, but I didn't want to flatten his hopes, either. So I tried to remember the last time I heard Blake Darley's name from Wallis. It had been a while. Immediately following his primary win, maybe. "I think she's on her way to finishing that chapter of her life," I hedged.

He nodded, and I saw a hint of pleasure in the curve of his lips. "That's good."

From across the room, Wallis held out her hand to beckon him over. "Help me get people arranged for the viewing, Bo? I think it's time to turn it on."

Bo looked at me, apologetic, and I gave him a shove forward. "By all means," I said, grinning. "Go."

As he walked away, L.K. did a little shimmy of excitement.

—

I stood in the back of the room with Wallis and Cricket as my interview played, and tried not to dwell too much on how weird my voice sounded, or how my blazer was higher on one shoulder than the other. Guests piled on the sofa and the arms of the chair and cross-legged on the floor where the coffee table normally would go.

"As a wise friend once put it, women feel the need to either apologize for or deny the behavior of men we love," I was saying to Monica, recalling my late-night chat with the Judge and Aunt Jane in Charleston.

"That's my daughter!" whispered Cricket, proud.

"That's the game many women have to play, though," said Monica. "To get ahead, or to get approval, or to just stay alive."

I remembered this next part. I'd been so taken by the

conversation that I'd briefly forgotten the lights, the stage makeup, the video and the tape. "Exactly. I'm guilty of playing that game myself." I thought here of Cricket and Wallis, the pain we'd been through. "I felt my only option was to cover up my father's behavior. I didn't think there was another way that would allow me to keep my family afloat. I know other women, too, have been convinced that they have no good options in the wake of a man's bad behavior. Because, if we draw attention to it, history tells us what will happen—we'll be blamed for being complicit, for being permissive, for being too dumb to see him for what he was, or for somehow encouraging him to act that way in the first place."

"So, how do we escape this cycle?" Monica asked. "How can we change the future?"

"Sharing our lived experiences is one option, though I *know* how challenging this can be. It absolutely was for me." Here I paused. "It was my sister, actually, who helped me evolve. She demonstrated, time and again, that being vulnerable and opening up *isn't* a sign of weakness. It's a sign of strength, of trust in oneself and empathy for others. I want to embrace this new approach now, for myself and for my family. And, maybe, for women who've been persuaded that it's best to stay quiet. Because I have to ask this question—best for whom?"

I glanced at Wallis, hoping she'd be pleased to hear this, but she had gotten a notification on her phone, and was now absorbed with something on Instagram. *Shit*, I saw her mouth.

I scooted closer to her. "What is it?"

"Daisy," Wallis whispered, moving her phone to her chest to hide her screen. "Have you seen it?"

"Seen what?" Cricket asked, leaning in.

"Why don't you just tell me, Wallis?" I said, beginning to fear. "What do I need to see?"

Wallis motioned for us to follow her into the kitchen, then reluctantly held out her phone. I stared down at a black-and-white picture of a diamond solitaire on a ring finger.

"Who is that?" Cricket asked, peering over my shoulder at the social media post. "Is that? Oh. Oh, no, is that someone who Blake...?"

"No," I said, finally able to process what I was seeing. I gripped the counter. "No, it's Ari. It's Atlas's girlfriend." She'd tagged her location as London. Under the photo, this caption: WHIRLWIND! Then heart emojis. So many hearts.

"She's in London." Wallis, stating the obvious. "Did he really propose to her?"

"He texted me this morning," I managed. "He told me that he wanted to talk when he got back."

"Oh, Atlas," Wallis murmured.

A few minutes earlier, I'd been drinking champagne, feeling like I maybe had it together, feeling grand about it all. Now, all I could do was croak the first thing that came to mind. "Wonderful," I said.

"You have to say something," said Wallis. "He loves you, I know he does."

"I agree," said Cricket. "Stand up and yell *I object*!"

"I won't," I said. "If he loved me, that ring wouldn't be on her finger."

"If he knew how you felt—" said my mother.

"Daisy is right," said Wallis. "No, Mom, stop making that face and listen. Daisy is right. Atlas has made his choice. Why is it up to Daisy to tell him he's wrong?"

We heard applause from the other room, and the sound of a commercial. My segment had concluded. I pushed my sister's phone away, left the kitchen. My heart was ruined, but it wouldn't do to abandon our guests, who were rising from their seats, patting me on the back, high-fiving, telling me *bravo.*

Thank you, was my mantra, and I said it again and again. *Aw, thanks.*

Wallis and Cricket trailed me out of the kitchen; someone found the remote and turned off the television. Wallis clinked her glass, inviting everyone's attention, and made a lovely toast in my honor. Afterward, L.K. said she'd send me the video of it. More surprises—party hats with daisies on them, a sheet cake with my face on it. It was the picture that had appeared with Atlas's article.

Cricket sliced me a corner, and while everyone else waited to be served, I ate my part of my forehead in my mother's dark bedroom, where I'd slunk off to check my phone. There had been a text from Atlas waiting for me:

I'm so sorry I couldn't be at your party. Were you surprised? Hope you're having a ball. You deserve all the champagne and cake in the world. Save me a piece, will you?

Alone with the coats and purses, I cried tears that were both happy and sad because I felt both whole and empty. Eventually, someone called my name from the living room. I left my phone on the dresser, used the side of my plastic fork to savor the last bit of blue icing, then went back to my party.

Forty

Though I was no longer officially employed by Miles, there
were some loose ends to tie up before I walked away for
good. A few days after my birthday, I commuted to the
Hill one last time to turn in my credentials and pick up
my last box of pictures and trinkets. Though L.K. wanted
to throw me a goodbye party, I'd politely refused, done for
now with parties, but I delivered cards to those who I was
closest with, gave hugs to all the rest, and my newest contact information to everyone. Beginning next week, they
could find me at The Daylight Project in Arlington.

"I'm going to be keeping you and Miles accountable,"
I said to Bo, before he and Miles dashed off to a full day
of events in Maryland. As expected, Bo became chief of
staff as easily as one stepping off an escalator. This was his
floor. He strode confidently, knowing exactly in which
direction to head.

When I was at the front desk, exchanging final bits of

gossip with Sara at lunchtime, a few high school interns tentatively approached. Would I mind, they wondered, giving them a tour of the Capitol? These interns, all young women, had seen my name in the press. Of course, I said. With the Senate now adjourned for recess, they wouldn't be missed around the office. And it would be a farewell, of sorts, to a place that I knew well and loved—and a good distraction from Atlas.

The truth was I'd thought about him almost constantly since the news of his engagement Friday. Now that he was getting married, I was not only bidding goodbye to the last, loitering hope we might be something more, but also to our friendship as it had been. Marriage can reconfigure a life; I might as well predict that Atlas's priorities would necessarily change once he had a wife.

A *wife*.

The day following the party, Wallis and Cricket had checked on me only to discover me lying atop my covers, bent like a bug in death. Wallis had knelt before me, just as I'd done for her all those months ago, the space between us crumpled, and then I was crying on her shoulder, unable to hold it in anymore, hating the sounds I was making, but forgiving myself for my tears. *There*, she had said to me, so quiet I barely heard. *Better.*

After a while—I don't know how long—Cricket took a book from my shelf and placed herself in the small chair reserved for clothes not quite dirty enough for laundry, and began to read aloud about Matthew and Marilla and Anne. Wallis curled around me on the bed.

At different times, they went upstairs, retrieved snacks, more pillows, an additional blanket, the heating pad. I was never alone. I was fed caramel popcorn, orange juice. Wallis brought me my contact case, my solution. On Cricket read, for hours; eventually her voice became white noise, and I was able to rest.

Their efforts had not been in vain. Though I still wasn't myself, I did feel fortified enough to put on makeup and tackle my to-do list. And this tour I could also manage.

On the tram over to the Capitol Visitor Center, it felt as though I was walking through a storm. Not a particularly violent one, but that of an insistent, cleansing rain. Everyone I knew, and many people I didn't, greeted me like we were already midconversation. *What a wild story*, they said. I sensed some of them wanted me to exhibit shame. Others, it seemed, were expecting me to chat as candidly as I had to Atlas and to Monica, deconstructing, reviewing, retelling, even joking. I was aware I was still a spectacle, but the trauma I might have felt months ago never surfaced. Whatever they thought about me, finally, was not the same as what I thought about myself.

I walked the interns through the Old Senate and Supreme Court Chambers, then the Senate gallery, where the majority leader was getting ready to make a unanimous consent request to recess. The interns, savvy and prepared for their school credit, didn't need me to explain what that was. "You give me hope," I told them.

I ended their tour in the Rotunda, at the foot of suffragettes Mott, Anthony, Stanton, carved in towering white marble. "They unveiled this statue six months after the ratification of the nineteenth amendment," I said. "Then, the *very* next day, it was moved to the basement, where it lived in storage with brooms and mops." This fact, when delivered, produced horrified expressions from my new friends. "It wasn't until 1997 that it was finally brought back here, to its rightful place. An original inscription," I continued, "reads, 'Woman first denied a soul, then called mindless, now arisen, declaring herself an entity to be reckoned.'"

"Where is this inscription?" one asked. "Where are you looking?"

"It was taken off," I said. "The same day the statue was moved to the basement. And never replaced."

For many minutes, I let them discuss how they could organize—perhaps with other interns—to get the inscription reinstated. "You give me hope," I said yet again. Our conversation carried on, we talked about glass ceilings, men who constantly interrupted, icons Fannie Lou Hamer and Shirley Chisholm, who refused to be silent, who battled while dancing backward in heels.

Their lunch break over, they departed, chatting about their favorite anecdote from the tour: the one about the senator who beat his colleague to unconsciousness on the floor of the chamber with his metal-topped cane.

As I descended the steps to Emancipation Hall, I considered having a leisurely lunch in the Visitor Center café. I'd be working again soon, and I might as well imagine this week as a kind of budget vacation. But my thoughts were interrupted when I heard my name. Turning my head, I saw none other than Blake Darley, in an orange polo shirt the color of a Creamsicle and sunglasses on his head, striding determinately down the stairs behind me. He looked like he was coming from the golf course, or the tennis club, but his expression was the opposite of casual. I took the last few steps at a hurry, fleeing as fast as I could, but I didn't get far. It was summertime high season, and too many people with backpacks and guidebooks blocked my path.

Blake caught my elbow. "Daisy," he said, supplicating, "please. Ten minutes. That's all I need."

I drew my arm free, not wanting to be seen with him. Or have anything else to do with him, for that matter. I started to move, maneuvering my way through the crowd.

"Five minutes," he said, following me. "Two."

"What are you doing?" I stopped by the feet of the Statue of Freedom, spun to face him. "How did you know I was here?"

"I called your office," he said. "The guy at the desk told me you were here."

Another intern, probably, sitting in while Sara was at lunch, not knowing any better. What rotten luck, I thought, for me.

"I've been trying to contact you for the past few days, since your segment on Monica's show." His hand was out-stretched—on his palm I saw those fine, thin scars, and re-membered angrily the apocryphal story that he had told us about their origins. When I sank back, he closed his fist, then let it fall. "I'm really sorry to sneak up on you."

"I don't like this." He'd cornered me, and I wasn't even near a wall. If only I could reach up, grab the laurel wreath from the statue's plaster hand! I might smack him with it.

"We just need to speak, then I'll leave you alone forever."

The shock of seeing him had worn off. "You can't talk to me here," I whispered. "Jesus, look where we are." I couldn't help it; I still worried about Miles, about appearances.

I led us as quickly as possible out of the great hall and toward the House appointment desk. It was more secluded there, less risk that we might be overheard. I took him all the way down to the emergency exit doors. There was my ground; I would stand it. "You have two minutes," I said. I waited, barely breathing.

He stared down at the floor, his hands in his pockets. He appeared small but not tender, and pensive, but maybe only in the DC way. That is to say, I couldn't tell if he was truly reflecting or just wearing a mask. "Do you think I'm a bad guy?" he eventually asked.

At this, I was able to exhale. I waited until he met my eyes, and then I rolled them. "That question is a waste of time. You can't possibly care what I think of you."

"I don't care? I do." His accent had gotten thicker; I wondered if this was the unintended result of being in South Carolina more, or if it was an affect aimed at wooing his electorate.

"Men only ask questions like that for one reason—absolution. I'm not your priest. I'm not your girlfriend or wife. You have no business asking me that, because you don't want my honesty." I spoke quickly. After so long, I was saying what I needed. "You want me to feel bad for you, and to lie, and to collapse on your shoulder and cry about how the world has misunderstood you."

"I'm not—" he stuttered. "I'm not asking the right question. I'm dancing around it because I'm so fucking nervous I'm not thinking straight."

As he stood before me, shifting, agitated, I saw him for who he was: a guy who was clearly confused and in pain. But no matter what he said, I couldn't forget that his own choices were responsible for getting him in this position in the first place. "After everything that has happened these past months, why are you tracking me down now?"

"The way I left things," he said. "Wallis must hate me."

"Of all the things Wallis feels," I said honestly, "hate is not one."

"Listen," he said, and the command irked me. "I think if I explained things from my perspective—"

"God," I said, shaking my head, "please, don't."

"At first," he continued anyway, "I didn't think Wallis and I were headed anywhere serious. It was fun. I loved how excited she was when I was around. Can you understand?"

"How you toyed with her?"

"No," he said, the ache in his voice becoming more pronounced. "It wasn't a game. You can't be *astonished* by cards, by cornhole. She was—is—astonishing. And as the days went on. Then weeks. That was the closest I've ever come to falling in love."

"The closest you came?" I asked.

"To avoid falling out with my family, I gave up the only thing that could've made the estrangement easier. My mother, she was perhaps willing to overlook Wallis and me when things were quiet. But then the pictures of us started to surface."

Blake and I stepped apart to let a group of teenagers wearing matching neon T-shirts and lost expressions ramble through. "Oh, I remember," I said once they were out of earshot.

"The pressure to leave Wallis became intense."

"You should've pushed back, with equal pressure," I said.

"I did," Blake said, and it was awfully close to a whine. "Me leaving DC—that was pushing back! That was the only thing I could think of to keep both my family happy and Wallis in my life. I just needed time to figure something out. I thought my mother would come around."

His eyes silently begged me to take it easy on him. I could not. "You strung her behind you for weeks, Blake.

You gave her hope. You tossed her crumbs. For weeks this went on, until Charleston, when you acted—"

"I know! I know. Seeing her in Charleston was devastating for me. I know it seemed like I was a sociopath, but I was overwhelmed. I didn't know what to say or how to act. My mother had sent her chief of staff down to spy on me, and I knew he was going to report back."

"Do you hear yourself?" I asked him, truly astounded at how easily he deflected blame, and onto a woman, no less. Onto his own mother.

"Daisy!" he said. "Of all people, how do you not understand? This family is my life. Their work is my life. There's no separating it. There are no professional and personal compartments for me. How could Wallis coexist with my mother? What would family meals look like? Wallis can't just sit and nod politely. When she disagrees, people hear about it. Maybe if there had been a way for her to be a little more accommodating—"

"Accommodating? Of your family? The corrosive nonsense you all spout makes my hair stand on end!" My voice was raised, and I feared soon I would be shouting. All he was explaining to me was that he was playing the same old game of linear ambition and domination at all costs, and I was tired of it. "You think you're something special, don't you? You think you're unique. But you're just one of the millions in this town who will regularly choose power above all."

"Do you despise all those millions forever?" he asked. "Or just me?"

A dawning—yes, finally, I understood. "You're worried," I said slowly, and my anger of a moment ago morphed into something more manageable, something that felt a lot like smugness. "You think Wallis and I have dirt on you?"

"You do." He glanced around, worried, seemingly for the first time, that someone would hear us. "My mother told me."

"And now that I've aired my dirty laundry, you think I would air yours? What kind of person do you take me for?"

"Daisy." He sighed my name, as though to say, *come on*. "This is ridiculous. I want to call a truce. So, can we? Just—can you not speak about me or my mother? I see you're going on shows, speaking to media. Can we move on with our lives and leave each other be?"

"No," I said. I had no plans to speak on the Darleys, but he didn't need to know that.

"If you come forward with something about me, something I maybe said to you, or to Wallis, I'll have to discredit you. I'll have to say you lied."

"Yes," I said. "I suppose you would."

"I'm a good person, Daisy," he said. "I'm always trying to be a good man, and to do the best for the people I love."

"So you did love my sister," I said. "I think maybe you still do."

"She'll *always* be that person for me," he said. He admitted this like he was admitting to a crime. "There will always be something there. But I can't be the person who fell in love with her, and also be a senator from South Carolina." He looked irate now, as though the way of the world was *my* fault, as though *I* had built our current reality from scratch. "I had to choose."

Before I made my way back through the hall, threaded through the crowds around the statues of humans far better than I'd been, I drew myself to my full height and mustered one last line:

"You chose wrong."

July

Forty-One

We were enjoying morning coffee and soft Sunday light on Cricket's couch. I was borrowing her reading glasses to scour the front page of the real estate section of the *Post*. "Bo told me it's here," I said.

"There you go," Wallis said, pointing to a thumbnail picture at the bottom of the paper. "Oh, God, it looks like they painted it."

"And they changed the windows," Cricket said, squinting, lips pursed.

"We're going," Wallis said. "We have to see it."

"Open house begins in an hour," I said.

"I just need to brush my hair," Cricket said.

"Atlas landed earlier this morning," I said, folding up the paper and tossing it aside. "He wants to come see me." When I'd gotten his text, my reaction had been decidedly muted. I recognized the necessity of the meeting, but I dreaded it just the same. I knew what he was going to tell me. Regardless, tomorrow was my first day at the new job, and I was determined not to spend the rest of my minivacation a wreck.

"You're done waiting for him," Wallis said. "If he wants to see you so badly, tell him to meet you at the house."

We're going to the house on P. I'll be there in an hour. Then I'm booked for the rest of the day.

———

When the taxi arrived at the address that used to be ours, Cricket was the first to exit. We stood on the sidewalk and inspected. "Look at that," Cricket lamented, pointing to the clapboard siding that was once yellow. "Are people supposed to like this color? I've never seen an uglier gray. And they took off the shutters!"

"This is what you get when all people care about is cashing in," Wallis said. "A generic disappointment. A dearth of style. God, I hate it."

"I like the windows," I said, and almost immediately I was wheeled on. They were aghast. "The bay window," I said, ready to defend myself, gesturing to the one that had been shattered by a brick earlier this year. Only January? It seemed longer. "The way they replaced it with—what is that? Looks like black wood, I guess. It's like a shop window, or something you'd find in an old English Tudor. I don't mind it."

"This used to be our house," Wallis told a young couple who were standing near, clearly admiring the curb appeal. The husband—boyfriend?—gave us a polite smile before being pulled up the steps and inside by his companion, a woman with a straight spine and a no-nonsense expression who clearly called the shots.

"All right, let's see what else they've done to it," Cricket said. "I wonder if Daisy will like the interior as much as she likes the windows."

In short: no, I did not like the interior. The renovators had made choices that clearly were intended to dazzle, but had no such effect on me. There was marble, quartz, cheetah-print wallpaper in the powder room, a light fixture that looked like a crown of barbed wire hanging over the dining room table. *The kitchen drawers*, the agent, short, slicked, blue-loafered, told me, *are soft close*. They did not keep Cricket's butcher-block counters.

Cricket and Wallis stood by the fireplace, which had been converted to gas, muttering. I left them to it and ventured upstairs. I ached to hear the staircase creak in the same spots.

My old bedroom was similar and also different. Much like me, I supposed. I had the sensation of looking both backward and forward in time, into my past, but also the future, altered, unexpected, in both good and bad ways. What would my father think of this house now? Easy. He would've hated it. Not because of what the flippers had done, but because *he* hadn't been a part of the transformation.

This had been his biggest flaw: he'd clung so tightly to the displays he presumed would make him relevant, and needed, and powerful, he forgot about where power truly lay. With us, his family, his wife and daughters, and the happiness and peace we'd found with each other and ourselves.

We didn't have the house, or the money, but this knowledge was my inheritance. His mistakes, ironically, had become my saving graces. In this way, I could never cast him as worthless, I could never say *good riddance*, because that would be writing off myself, too. And I wasn't going to be doing that anymore. I couldn't erase my past, but I could try and reconcile it with who I wanted to be.

And Gregory, for his part, *had* helped set me on this path. It was Gregory, years ago, who had caught me one day in the office watching a clip of Miles early in his Senate run. I'd felt energized then, as I listened to him rally for systemic change, and also reason, decency, the wisdom of an evolving majority.

Gregory had seen it. *Go work for him*, my father had said. *Go on. You're fired.*

At the time, I'd taken this as an act of selflessness. Gregory was letting me go, not because he wanted to, but because he could see I needed it.

Now, looking back, I questioned whether he had also been trying to protect me from the scandal; he *had* to have known it would eventually be exposed. He'd certainly started stepping out on Cricket by that point. And the stealing had already started. I wondered if he'd wanted me not to see. I would never get answers to these questions, but I could use them to help me forgive, and to nurture gratitude for all that had transpired. Because even though I wasn't working for Miles anymore, I was still undeniably grateful to be one of his many true believers.

That's where Atlas found me as I sat on the staged twin bed and studied the new closet doors—nice quality, heavy, paneled on the outside with mercury glass. He said hello, and I turned. He looked rumpled, a bit rough around the edges, but otherwise himself. "What do you make of it?" he asked me. He was nervous; he had both hands in his pockets, one jiggling spare change.

I smiled, determined to keep it, no matter how much this conversation would pain me. "I'm a little jarred," I said.

"This room also looks smaller than it did before. Which doesn't make any sense at all."

"You're coming into it with fresh eyes," he replied. He removed the strap of his computer bag from his shoulder, lowered it to the foot of the bed. "I've been meaning to talk to you for weeks. I kept putting it off because I've been out of town. I also convinced myself I needed to see you in person to say what needs to be said. I'm not sure if that's totally fair, though. The truth is, I've been putting this off because I'm absolutely chicken."

"You're here now," I said. My heart thudded so loudly I wondered if he heard. Of course he would be worried about telling me of his engagement. I think he suspected— he knew—that it would hurt me. But I would not retreat from him, or deny my love, or fall back into the patterns I pledged to leave behind.

"Indeed." He cleared his throat and sat carefully beside me. I'd finally gotten him in bed, I thought, and such *perfect* timing.

Steps in the hallway, and Wallis and Cricket made their entrance before he could say another word. They greeted Atlas without their usual warmth, courteous but stiff. They stood, awkwardly looking at their feet and at the strange, beige carpet newly slapped over the original heart pine. Wallis broke the silence. "Congratulations," she told him.

"For what?" he asked, without the slightest hint of insincerity. I had the urge to scream.

"Your engagement," Wallis said. "Obviously." Her little laugh was skeptical. "We saw Ari's post. You did a nice job picking the ring. It's huge. It suits her." Wallis was needling him, and I wasn't sure I minded.

"Oh," he said. His eyes flicked back and forth between all of us. "Oh, no—I mean—yes, Ari's engaged, but not to me."

"Not to you!" Cricket said, drawing back in disbelief.

"No," Atlas said. "No, we've been broken up for about a month now. She went traveling for a bit, back to London, actually. She reconnected with a former boyfriend there, and he proposed. When you know, you know, it seems. She called me last week to inform me."

That young couple from before, holding hands, came to the door, peeked in. Wallis rounded on them. "Move along," she snapped.

"Are you serious?" the woman asked her.

"Deadly," Wallis said.

They grumbled, but did as they were told. Perhaps they saw that I was failing to hold back tears. Perhaps that scared them off.

"Don't cry," Atlas murmured, rubbing my shoulder. "I'm so sorry to have upset you."

"She thought you were going to marry another woman," Wallis said. "Let her be upset for a minute."

"Of course," Atlas said, repentant, hand back at his side.

From me, this question, as soon as my tears allowed: "Why did you break up?"

Atlas waited a moment, chewing his bottom lip, as Wallis and Cricket backed out of the room. Then: "A few weeks ago, I was staring at my lease renewal, and Ari demanded my answer about living together. I'd postponed it long enough, she said. She was right, of course. So, I opened my mouth, thinking I was going to say yes because it was so clearly the next step for us, but what came out was very different. It was borderline incoherent, but as I was giving her the longest possible answer about why we couldn't move in with each other, I stumbled into the truth I'd been trying to resist for ages. The thing I'd been doing, I just couldn't do anymore."

I knew *exactly* how he felt, and I couldn't hold back, not for another second. "I'm in love with you," I said, because that's all there was. "I'm glad you stumbled into your truth, but there's mine. I love you. So, I hope you'll understand when I say, unless all of this is about how you love me, too, I'll have to go. And you'll have to talk about your breakup with your buddies, or someone else. Because I just can't nod and pretend. I can't. I love you, but I can't." I pressed my fingers into my wet eyes, then released them, snuck a peek at the man beside me.

"Thank God," he said. He lifted his face to my old ceiling, the one that looked down upon all of my teenage imaginings, the dark dreams of my early adulthood, and shivered as though he'd been caught in the rain. "Here's the truth, and it doesn't make me look good, and I blame myself over and over again for not seeing it sooner. But for so many years, I believed that if I couldn't have you, I guess I should have *someone*. I was able to spend many months thinking I could trick myself into loving Ari like I love you."

I'd waited so long to hear those words that I had trouble staying upright. I leaned sideways, let my flushed face slip onto his shoulder. "Atlas," I said. "That's awful." I wiped my nose with my sleeve.

"I was stupid," he said, his fingers, tentative, on the nape of my neck. "I treated her incredibly unfairly. When I told her I was in love with you, she was furious, as she had every right to be. I'm just hoping—like I've never hoped before—that you'll forgive me for taking so long to get this right."

"I kissed you." I tugged his hair to draw his head down

toward mine, searched his eyes. "And you didn't think you could have me?"

"After," he said softly, his warm breath on my jaw, just below my ear, "you told me it was a mistake. I believed you. God, that word followed me around for months."

"But I was lying," I said, sniffling.

"Well," he said gently, smiling, "I guess I can see that now."

"I just need you to know," I said, my voice now steady, "that if we do this, if we get together, you will be forbidden from changing your mind. No takebacks. No undos. You won't be able to get rid of me. Do you understand?"

"Completely. Why are you trying to scare me?"

"Because this is it for me. It is. And if that doesn't scare you, then I don't know if this can be."

I barely blinked, and I was on his lap. I think he'd lifted me there. His arms were around my waist, his hands underneath the bottom of my shirt, and he was clinging so hard I thought he might leave prints on my skin. Someone, Wallis or Cricket, had shut the bedroom door. "This room is off-limits," I heard Cricket say to a passerby in the hall. "Doing some construction in there."

"I love you," he said, his voice thick, "and I've never been so scared in my life."

In my childhood bedroom, surrounded by syrupy brown walls that used to be a hopeful shade of pink, he kissed me. My past, all around me, paved over; inside I felt a shift. I wrapped my arms around his neck, wondering if something this good could be sustained. Eventually we came up for breath. He touched the cold tip of his nose to mine, and I thought, *yes, lovely world, it can.*

Epilogue

Wallis has packed us a picnic: soft cheese and salami, wheat crackers and spinach dip, lots and lots of rosé. Cricket brought the good, thick knit blanket from the back of her couch; Bo had one from his place, too, and we pick a viewing spot in the grass near the edge of the Mall, just north of the Reflecting Pool, facing the Lincoln Memorial. Atlas, wanting to be helpful, arrives with his rain jacket and a poncho still in its wrapper, thinking the ground might still be wet from the thunderstorm yesterday, thinking of our bottoms. We laugh when he unveils this, and applaud once it is revealed he's also brought champagne, which is much better received.

The sky becomes peach sherbet, and we eat strawberries and dark chocolate caramels that Wallis has somehow kept from melting most of the day. On the main stage back at the Capitol, the drummers and the fifers and the military chorus get going; we hear wisps of their cadences, but mostly the classic Springsteen mix from the portable radio of the group immediately to our right. Evening arrives, and the frieze of Lincoln's temple is lit, and the columns, and the worn, resolute face of the man himself.

We take turns telling stories, walking through memories, filling each other in on parts of our lives the others have missed. Wallis has her legs flung over Bo's lap, and on her ankle he is tracing intricate designs with his thumb.

I snuggle further into Atlas, grateful for where this world has spun us. He is dressed, as is his patriotic duty, in a plain white polo and navy blue shorts; he's even brought his red Nationals cap. I know what's under that hat, a mind that is thoughtful and generous and inquisitive and reliable.

Who are we kidding? I should also add—

I know exactly what is under those shorts.

Because he and I both agreed that we'd wasted too much time apart, and threw ourselves into making up for it. Considering those first hours and nights together, I've felt myself wanting to call the thing between us easy. But that is the wrong word. Because, yes, waking up tangled, laughing, sharing a slice of toast and a bathroom mirror, his breath on my neck and his hands in my hair, all that is as comfortable as a dance to a familiar song. But there is also something so stupefyingly rare and fragile about finding your person and *choosing* them for forever.

The night is finally dark enough for fireworks, and the hundreds of people around us on the Mall start to straighten, expectant. Any second now.

Cricket takes this opportunity to clear her throat, then, once she has our attention, she says, as matter-of-fact as one can be, "This is going to make a good last scene in my book."

Wallis and I don't closely resemble each other, but catch us at the right moment, and you'll see our expressions are often identical. Cricket looks between us and simply shrugs a shoulder. "I've been approached by a few agents, one of whom I actually like. She thinks I might have a book proposal in me somewhere. I've been journaling, as you know. And with Daisy off telling her story, I thought it's high time I tell mine."

"A book, Mom." Each word of Wallis's might've been its own sentence.

"Don't look so dumbfounded. I wrote for the Vassar *Miscellany*," Cricket reminds us. "I read *The Elements of Style*."

"Amazing achievement," says Atlas, beginning to clap.

"Bravo," says Bo, reaching over Wallis to give Cricket a high five.

"We underestimated you," I say to our mother, grinning.

"When can we read it?" Wallis is still bewildered but smiling.

"When it's done," Cricket says. We groan and begin to complain but she clucks her tongue. "Respect the artistic process, please."

"Just give me nicer hair," I request. "And soften my most strident edges, please."

"And I'd like to be less of a sad sack," says Wallis. She cozies further into Bo, and I hear him whisper something into her ear. Whatever he's said makes her smile.

"If you're taking entreaties," says Atlas, "and if I end up appearing at all, could you make me less of a bumbling fool?"

"No promises," says Cricket. "Now Atlas, where's that champagne?"

We fill our plastic glasses with bubbly and get a toast

in, just before the first firework shoots up over the river, with a pop and a bang and *ooh*s and *aah*s from the crowd, and explodes into the sky in a perfect patriot's red dahlia. Right on its tail, a shining white pom-pom flashes forth, then gracefully falls, like branches of a willow tree, glittering tendrils reaching down to marvel those below.

———

If that ending wasn't happy enough, I'll offer a new one.

Women begin to see that our fates are linked more with each other than with the fates of men. As such, we begin to act less in our own self-interest, and more in the interest of *all* women.

Good guys win. So, naturally, Blake Darley loses his race. Bad guys—exiled to the trash heap of history, their statues taken down, their names taken off buildings. How easy it becomes to differentiate between the two!

The world changes, and so does DC, is what I'm saying.

But you've made it this far, so it's safe to say that you know: this way of the world is not to be, at least not yet.

What will Atlas and I do, then, once the fireworks have ended, once we allow our shoes back on our feet, once we let each other out of arm's reach? What of Wallis? Of Bo and Cricket? Like my father, someday we'll all be gone. We'll have lived and died within an era, within a chapter— a paragraph?—of a history book. We might not know what the pages will say. Or who will write them.

For now, though, we will not worry about what will become of us.

We will ask instead: What will the world become because of us?

★ ★ ★ ★ ★

Acknowledgments

Melanie Fried took scraps of a story and knitted them into something real. Her enthusiasm and dedication were undiminishing. I'm in awe of her editor's mind.

Sarah Phair championed this book, and believed in the Richardsons and me from the start. Thanks for letting me hitch my wagon to your star.

Thank you to the team at Harlequin/HarperCollins for their advocacy: Pamela Osti, Justine Sha, and Samantha McVeigh. Quinn Banting designed the beautiful cover, which captures Georgetown and the novel so perfectly.

Thank you to those who graciously provided help, insight, and inspiration at various stages of the novel: Blake Albohm, Tricia Chambers Batchelor, Broderick Dunn, Meghan Faughnan, Daniel Meyer, and Amanda Whiting.

Jim and Jane Edmondson, to whom this book is dedicated, were also first readers. Thank you for always flagging when I incorrectly use *I* instead of *me*.

Bellamy Meghan Carstens cannot read yet, but for when she does: I love you.

And to Christopher Vollmond–Carstens, who continues to give me such support on this journey, I can't thank you enough for your patience, good humor, and unconditional love.

Author's Note

Sense and Sensibility has long been my favorite Jane Austen novel; the concept of a modern retelling was floating around in my head for many years before I actually had any idea of what that would, in practice, look like on the page. It seems many readers don't find *Sense* as hilarious as *Emma* or romantic as *Pride and Prejudice*, but I've always been drawn to the novel's pointed depictions of womanhood. Unlike in Austen's other works, fathers are mostly absent from *Sense*, and the Dashwood sisters' love interests almost entirely disappear from large sections of the novel. This absence of men focuses our gaze on the female characters, but the patriarchal systems of power still drive the story, allowing Austen room to explore what it means for women to demonstrate "proper" conduct.

Long fascinated by how women have approached such societal expectations across history, I thought adapting Austen's framework to a contemporary setting would provide an enlightening contrast and benchmark for how women's lives have and have not changed. Like *Sense and Sensibility*, my novel, *Ladies of the House*, also features two sisters, Daisy and Wallis Richardson, who must rebuild their lives following the passing of the family patriarch. But, as they live two centuries later, they have tools the Dashwood sisters would *envy*: they can vote, their educational and employment opportunities are greater, there is less stigma around premarital sex and cohabitation. They don't *have* to marry men and give birth to sons in order to have security and protection.

Still, while the Richardsons have far more legal rights and agency than women in Austen's era, they too find themselves constrained by that question of *how a woman should be*. When older sister Daisy Richardson is faced with the dilemma to speak out or stay quiet regarding her late father's corrupt behavior, at first she chooses the latter. Her silence, she rationalizes, is the safest, most practical choice because women are often excoriated when they publicly speak truth about powerful men. I wanted my novel to be hopeful, though, and so while at first Daisy obeys the demands of the patriarchy, she and Wallis ultimately triumph by writing and following *their own* set of rules, learning how to use their power in a way that reflects who they are and not who society says they should be.

While some may read Marianne and Elinor Dashwood as each representing two contrasting types of impulses—sense and sensibility—in my view, Austen's novel, and my own, are not so much about the *differences* between the sisters, but the unbreakable bond between them—how the women's support and love for each other is the real, transformative power.

LADIES
OF THE
HOUSE

LAUREN EDMONDSON

Reader's Guide

GRAYDON
HOUSE

QUESTIONS FOR DISCUSSION

1. Discuss the plot differences between *Ladies of the House* and Jane Austen's *Sense and Sensibility*. How does Lauren Edmondson's novel update Jane Austen's?

2. What do you think Jane Austen might say about the society in which Daisy and Wallis operate? What has or has not changed for women since the Austen era?

3. Did you understand Daisy's justifications for not initially going public about her father's behavior?

4. Did you think Daisy's ultimate decision to speak out was the right move? Why or why not? What might you have done in her situation?

5. How did you feel about Wallis at the beginning of the novel versus the end? Do you think she grew as a character? In what way?

6. Daisy at first has trouble accepting Blake because of his family's actions. Is this something you have ever faced

in your own life? Can you separate a person from their beliefs?

7. Toward the end of the novel, Daisy tells Blake Darley: "You think you're something special, don't you? You think you're unique. But you're just one of the millions in this town who will regularly choose power above all." Is this a fair assessment of him? Or did you have more sympathy for Blake?

8. As parents, how are Gregory Richardson, Cricket Richardson, Melinda Darley, and Judge Collette Reed similar and/or different?

9. Which character(s) did you most identify with in the novel? Why?

10. How can society better support women and raise up their voices?